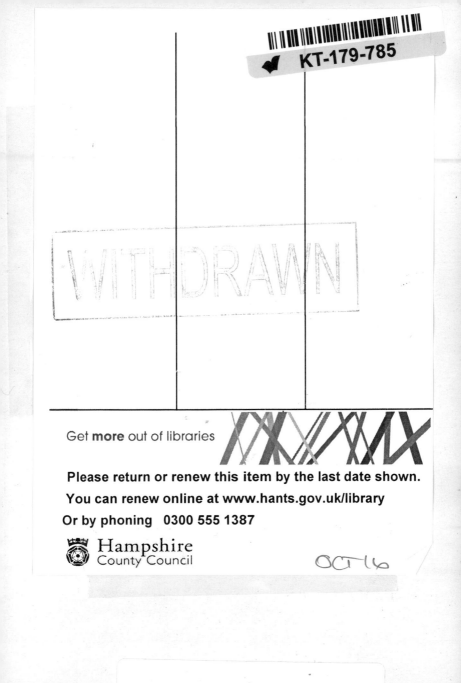

Get **more** out of libraries

Please return or renew this item by the last date shown.

You can renew online at www.hants.gov.uk/library

Or by phoning   0300 555 1387

Hampshire
County Council

OCT 16

Also by Quentin Letts

50 People Who Buggered Up Britain

Bog-Standard Britain

Letts Rip!

The Speaker's Wife

By Quentin Letts

CONSTABLE • LONDON

CONSTABLE

First published in Great Britain in 2015 by Constable

This paperback edition published in 2016

Copyright © Quentin Letts, 2015

1 3 5 7 9 10 8 6 4 2

The moral right of the author has been asserted.

A CIP catalogue record for this book is available from the British Library.

ISBN: 978-1-47212-201-8

Typeset in Bembo by SX Composing DTP, Rayleigh, Essex
Printed and bound by CPI Group (UK) Ltd, Croydon, CR0 4YY

Papers used by Constable are from well-managed forests and
other responsible sources.

MIX
Paper from
responsible sources
FSC® C104740

Constable
is an imprint of
Little, Brown Book Group
Carmelite House
50 Victoria Embankment
London EC4Y 0DZ

An Hachette UK Company
www.hachette.co.uk

www.littlebrown.co.uk

To Melinda, Penny, Alexander and the
brother we never knew, Stephen

That we shew forth thy praise, not only with
our lips, but in our lives – *A General Thanksgiving,
The Book of Common Prayer*

Dramatis personae

Ecclesiastical London

Matt – a young hothead
Bashirah – his girlfriend, exiled in Pakistan
Petroc Stone – newly-arrived pastor of the church of Alleluia, Jesus!
Mark – church organist
Georgina Brack – warden of the church of Alleluia, Jesus!
'Beetle' – real name Antonia, a sceptic and friend of Mrs Brack
Derrick Banks – muscular volunteer at the church of Alleluia, Jesus!
The Rev Tony Calvert – Dean of Communications, Church House

The shires

Tom Ross – Herefordshire parson and chaplain to the Speaker of the
    House of Commons
Theresa Ross – his wife, keen on gardening
Andrew Ross – son of Tom and Theresa, runs children's adventure
    courses in Wales
Morwen Ross – wife of Andrew
Barney – Tom and Theresa Ross's Sealyham terrier, likes to explore
    Bluebell Wood

Palace of Westminster

Speaker Aldred – ailing Speaker of the House of Commons
Mike Branton-Day MP – MP for a rich seat in Sussex
Bryce – Government Deputy Chief Whip and member of the All
    Party Group on Russia
Hamid Butt MP – Government backbencher, worships Sir Tudor
    Matthews
Adrian Calvert – slim-hipped intern employed by Bryce; nephew of
    Tony Calvert
George Chance MP – chairman of the Home Affairs select
    committee
Elfyn Davies MP – Welsh Nationalist and deputy chairman of the
    Housing select committee

Miss Harris – day nurse to Speaker Aldred
Hilda Hawke MP – a member of the Housing select committee
Eleanor Haye MP – Leader of the House of Commons
Jean – secretary in the office of Leslie Mears
Tristan Kendrick MP – a Welshman of fervent principles
George Leakey MP – Second Church Estates Commissioner
Mackie – Independent socialist MP for a Luton seat, ardent fighter of
   Islamophobia
Phyllis Mates – wife of…
Walter Mates – doorkeeper and former Guardsman
Sir Tudor Matthews MP – 'Father' of the House of Commons
Leslie Mears MP – former Shadow Minister for Local Government,
   ambitious
Lionel Moss MP – chairman of the All-Party Group on
   Housebuilding
Natascha 'Netty' Peake – Opposition MP, unofficial convener of the
   feminist sisterhood
Sir Roger Richards – whiskered Clerk of the Commons
George Tewk – Deputy Speaker

Non-ecclesiastical London

Magnus Bacton – one of London's best-known lawyers and a
   television presenter
Charlie – she is a chauffeur employed by the Thought Foundation
Gabriel 'Chundy' Chundrigar – son of Indian hoteliers; betrothed to
   Nettle Greenhill
Denzil – a Buddhist
Augustus Dymock – the 'Don of Doubt'; celebrity atheist, leads the
   Thought Foundation
Zac Dymock – teenage son of Augustus
Sheila Henderson – trade unionist
Jo – manager at the Thought Foundation
Gordon Greenhill – property developer
Mrs Greenhill – wife of Gordon
Nettle Greenhill – ripe daughter of the above
Phoebe – a junior associate at the Thought Foundation
Paul Pike – gossip columnist on The Dispatch newspaper
Olga Zolnerova – Russian assistant to Dymock and new flatmate of
   Leslie Mears

1

Sunday

EMERGENCY services logged the incident shortly before nine that October Sunday morning. 'Disturbance, Victoria Street,' typed a duty clerk.

A white youth wearing hoodie, jeans and trainers had driven his Ford Ka into, more accurately through, the windows of a Pakistani airline office. Those windows had advertised immodest fares to the subcontinent. 'Fly your dreams,' purred a logo. 'Brushed by magic.' Smash.

The little car plopped through the shopfront neatly enough. As in other things there was a moment of delay before the bang blew down the street scattering litter, leaves, sparrow-song. This was followed by the trill of burglar alarms from adjacent premises. The explosion had set their clappers going, yackadacka, whoop-doop, clang-clang.

The youth emerged from the wreckage unhurt save for minor damage to his left leg. Having pushed open the Ford's dented door, he alighted, closed-circuit television pictures suggested, with hip-hoppity excitement. He sprayed pink graffiti over the walls – 'airline slave trade' and 'stop Muslim rape of young British girls'. A libel lawyer might prefer 'alleged rape' but our perpetrator was no student of defamation law. To the airline's image of a pretty woman partly veiled he added a handlebar moustache not unlike that of the Pakistani president. His message concluded with a graffiti tagline of an elaborate M, the tail ending in a cross.

The incident may have occurred near New Scotland Yard but the boys in blue were slow to arrive. Come, come. The croissants served in the Yard canteen of a Sunday morning bear comparison with those found in the most chichi arrondissement of Paris. No Yard officer was immediately available to attend the emergency. That task fell to a patrol car from south of the Thames, which welcomed the chance to activate its siren and have a burn through central London at this quiet hour.

The patrol car arrived to a scene of disarray and fire. This sort of thing was common enough. The national crisis had seen riots in most cities. Flames danced round the Ford. The police saw the youth run from the scene. One of the officers gave pursuit on foot while the other spoke into her collar microphone and summoned the fire brigade. We leave her to her duties and follow the sprint between the driver of the Ford and the first constable.

Athletics fans would have enjoyed this contest – scampering underdog versus long-legged officer of the law. The latter ran well, confident in his police-issue shoes. The driver of the Ford was limping and seemed lost. First he turned right, then left, runty nostrils lifting as though to scent the breeze. His feet struck an uneven beat, one splaying in moderate pain. The distance between hare and hound shortened. In the ears of the prey there rang panic. Under his breath he cursed the Christian God from whom his generation had drifted.

The policeman was closing on his quarry when the youth spotted a crowd leaving the Church of Alleluia Jesus! (previously St Michael and All Angels, Westminster). He saw hugging. A few children held orange balloons with the slogan 'Rise to God'. A man carried a guitar. The service had been taken by a stout, bearded curate in his early thirties. An old woman was taking her leave. The youth, hurtling onwards, nearly managed to bypass the little gathering but his shoulder clipped the man of the cloth, who was pushed into the old woman. She clattered to the ground.

Our tearaway could have kept running. He could have shouted obscenities. Instead he stopped and said 'sorry, sorry'. The priest checked an instinct to respond with anger. The youngster was holding out his hands. Take my troubles, Lord.

One of the church organisers muscled over – a big guy. Tattoos. 'I need help,' blurted the youth. 'I've done something. Please.' He cast over his shoulder towards the policeman. 'My girl's been taken by the Muslims. Please.' He now spoke to the old skittle on the ground. 'You OK, darling?' The boy took one of the old woman's purple-veined hands and gave it a squeeze of concern.

The policeman was thirty yards away and the hunted youngster had no other hole. He darted left. 'Just a minute,' cried the priest. But the lad was gone. Up a flight of steps he scuttled, under the arch.

The Church of Alleluia Jesus! may from outside have been a forbidding prospect but its Victorian interior was admired even by secularists. It had a musical reputation, though the organist resented liturgical changes and still referred to it as St Michael's. The brown floor tiles were spotless. The chairs, which had recently replaced pews, were numbered. New hymnals – *Worship Songs for Here and Now!* – were stacked under the exhortation 'Jive for Jesus!' Tambourines, triangles and wrist bells were in a box marked 'Help Yourself!' Tins had been stacked for the food bank. The leaflets on display in a rack contained yet more exclamation marks and photographs of families with white teeth and clean fingernails. A poster listed charity helplines. Rape counselling, debt, sexual infidelity, Aids: these and other horrors were addressed in words of no more than three syllables. Never let it be said that the world's ills did not darken the doors of Alleluia Jesus! and its banjo-billy outreach programme.

Blue and purple light shone through a stained-glass window depicting St Michael with th' angelic host. A hint of communion wine flavoured the air. In this noiseless pod our joyrider screeched to a halt.

Outside, the policeman shouted: 'Where did the little sod go?' His language caused a frisson of displeasure among the church-goers. The policeman whacked his walkie-talkie, which was proving uncooperative. 'Bugger,' he said. On the throng a froideur fell.

'Now look here,' began the tattooed church organiser, quite the Alpha Course male.

'That kid I was chasing,' snarled the policeman. 'Where'd he go?' Quislings at the back of the crowd pointed to the church door. The policeman had made his walkie-talkie work and was shouting to his station that the suspect had been located to a church and that he was going in to effect an arrest. Had he been on his own he might have said 'nick the bastard', but not under the gaze of these buzzards.

'Out the way,' said the policeman.

'Wait!' said the stout young priest. 'Let us say a prayer. Let us link hands and ask God to guide us. Speak to us, Lord!' The police station chose that moment to respond via the walkie-talkie. The churchgoers closed eyes and jibbered, as though saying their three times table.

Inside the church, our hare pondered its options. There were three exits. One was the south door, through which he had entered. The others were the big west doors, which looked as though they were never used, and near them a small northern door. He noticed the used communion chalice standing on an altar whose candles were still burning. As he glanced right and left, two eyes watched silently from the organ loft's mirror.

The policeman barged past his onlookers. The northern door was ajar and his sleuth's eye spotted that the bell ropes were swaying. He hastened to the door and saw that it gave on to a small garden which led to an alley. At the end of the alley he looked left and right, ran to a junction with the road and thought he saw a form slip round a distant bend. 'Sod it.' He grabbed his walkie-talkie and reported that the suspect had escaped towards Pimlico. As the policeman left he stated loudly to the curious parishioners that he expected a patrol car to be round in case the slippery suspect returned.

The church organist descended the spiral staircase under his loft. He scuttled away, head down, without speaking to the congregants. Organists were like that.

Later a television crew arrived and interviewed the priest – the camera focusing on his hairy hands, fingers yellowed by nicotine. The item went out that evening on the local news. Pakistan's High Commission had expressed concern at the attack on the airline office. Muslim leaders said arranged marriages were their cultural right, beyond question. Viewers heard the priest say that the suspect 'ran into the church and found the back door'. Technically, this was not a lie. The young man had found the back door and opened it a fraction. To have claimed that he had left the church would have been a different matter. Had he been asked if the driver of the Ford Ka had indeed disappeared in the direction of Pimlico, what would the answer have been? Would he have told the truth?

Pastor Petroc Stone, evangelical minister, was not entirely sure.

MORE than a hundred miles to the west, key turned in ancient lock. Evensong was done for another week. The *Nunc dimittis* had been sung by a congregation of four. Two votive candles flickered near the end of their wax.

Sunday's rhythms near complete, a cassocked figure pocketed the key and trudged through the graveyard, whistling at a dog. Tombs were tumbledown, molehills here, grassy tufts there. A whirl of twigs and dust danced in the dying day. Was that a chorus line of elves doing a country jig? Did sprites skip, kicking crackly leaves? Ash boughs creaked like bones.

Father Tom Ross had preached on acceptance. He had kept it to five minutes. Sadness was God's tithe and we must succumb to it as wood to the Almighty's lathe. Ross had struggled to persuade himself. He often did. There was just enough light in the grey-streaked sky to see the graveyard's familiars: a seventeenth-century squire 'buried with his belov'd wyfe, dyed nexte day from greefe'; a miller, suffocated in flour after being mangled in his wheel; infant twins from the time of Waterloo, martyrs to fever; and an RAF pilot, veteran of Bomber Command. His grieving widow – Ross's mother – had stood by that grave, shivering in her maternity coat as the coffin ropes lowered her man to eternal rest. The airman's grave was speckled by lichen and had lifted at one corner.

Ross was stooped, balding, in his mid-sixties. His mouth had a slight overbite and his grey eyebrows straggled behind some pale spectacle frames. He cut a crumpled figure, scuffed by disappointments. The last hymn had been *The Day Thou Gavest* and the final verse hung in his mind: *So be it, Lord; thy throne shall never, Like earth's proud empires, pass away*. Humming, Ross lowered his chin and gave it a bit of trombone. To the graveyard's occupants he said 'soft night, beloved', pausing at his father's grave. He pulled in his robes against the cold and was comforted by the whiff of mothball. Moonlight would soon silhouette the trees, owls would hoot, foxes yowl. Nobody else was out. In the approaching season of souls, the quick shuddered for the dead. Terrier Barney yapped and Ross clutched the prayer book. This was the longest graveyard in England – the most haunted hundred yards in the kingdom, the pub landlord told tourists.

Behind Ross, as darkness claimed its dominion, a hinge squeaked. Without sign of any hand, the locked church door opened. A draught made the flames on the two candles bend hard. Then – was that with an audible 'pouff'? – the flames died and the door closed with a slam. In the lych-gate yew an owl stood sentinel, spooking only those who believed.

Ross ambled homeward. He never liked Sunday nights after Evensong. The prospect of another week at Westminster wearied him. The political world, all those stressy strivers, was so untrusting and restless. Ross was chaplain to the Speaker of the House of Commons and he knew some Members regarded him as a carefree non-combatant, unburdened by their insecurity. They did not know about Calvert and his latest demand. They did not know the acid juices of the doubting parson.

His ancestral house was just beyond the next dip, half hidden by round-shouldered hills. Mobile telephones never worked here. That suited Ross for it helped him to escape. Prayer book in pocket, he loved to take Barney for walks through Bluebell Wood, past the disused cottage whose roof had been destroyed by ivy and sycamore saplings. Once a roof went, structures soon collapsed. From Bluebell Wood it was a short distance to the church where he could inhale the ageless air and feel free. Barney would sniff round the graveyard and lie at the airman's grave, chin to the grass. Like any terrier, Barney loved to dig and would vanish down holes; yet he never dug in the graveyard. Inside the church Ross would make sure everything was orderly for crowds that never came. He would brush bat droppings off the hymnals and check the donations box, usually empty. Bringing his key chain out of his corduroys, he would think of a statue he saw in a Tuscan church of a strong-necked, bearded St Peter holding the remarkably simple key to Heaven. Perhaps its very simplicity was indeed the key to Heaven: lack of complications, the detritus of other lives.

In the darkness Ross could smell the chimney's woodsmoke. It hung above the house, as it must have done over the huts of primitive ancestors before Roman days. The same scent snaked up the nostrils of Norman serfs and left its tang on Tudor tunics.

It stung the eyes of medieval martyrs as they writhed at the stake. The cremation smoke of unborn men would smell the same.

Barney skittered ahead and was waiting when Ross pushed on the boot-room door. Theresa called from her study: 'I did boiled eggs ten minutes ago.'

'I'm not hungry.'

'Oh well, don't bother.' Her tone was terse. Lunch had not gone well.

'No, I will,' said Ross. 'You went to the trouble.' Still robed, he sat at the age-blackened table. Theresa had laid a place for him with salt cellar and a slice of margarined bread. The eggs stood under felt cosies designed like mitres. Andrew had made them when he was a child, back when there was hope Daddy might make it to bishop. Ross lit a candle in a silver stick and bowed his head, the light bouncing off his knobbled pate. He muttered a grace, removed the cosies, poured a mound of salt and decapitated the eggs with one vicious swipe. He drank two schooners of burgundy and one generous scotch.

In bed he failed to complete many crossword clues. Theresa had switched off her light and was staring at the ceiling. 'Calvert rang,' she said, her tone dull.

'On a Sunday?'

'He wanted to know how you were. I said it was time you retired.'

'Not you as well.'

'He said he knew this debate was an imposition but they're worried about Dymock.'

'They're right to be.'

'He was all over my radio this morning, that man, talking about his favourite records. They might have spared us Dymock on a Sunday.'

'The Left is entranced by him, even though he's a brutal egomaniac who preaches the law of the jungle.'

'Calvert said they need to raise the profile of the Commons chaplaincy. This debate will do that.'

'Well he can sod off.'

'Tom!'

'They can all sod off. Get someone else to do it – one of those ambitious women, one of the soundbite gang. That's what they need to fight the secularists. It's not my sort of thing. I'm not modern enough.' A moth flew down from the light and landed on the sheet beside him. Ross whacked it with his right hand. What had one second been a living creature with wings, antennae and head was reduced in the next to a smudge of dust.

The burgundy and scotch gave him a bad night; nothing new in that. The long-case clock on the landing woke him when it struck midnight. Theresa was snoring and he resented her oblivion. His mind raced – to Calvert, this debate, the row at lunch, the imminent arrival of his housemate in London, some young evangelical priest from what had once been St Michael and All Angels. Good days were becoming rare. He feared the driven secularists with their glib certainties, their litany about reason, as if human logic was a match for celestial force. They stoked public anxiety and had all the easy, ironic tunes.

His legs felt so heavy they must soon drop through the mattress and dangle below the springs, useless, flaccid. He glowered at the blackness until, shortly before three, he found some sleep.

THE altar cloth's side flap was pushed aside and a pale, youthful face checked for trouble. Coast clear. The interior of the London church of Alleulia Jesus! was not entirely dark. An orange glow of street lights penetrated its higher windows.

The young man straightened his spine. His foot hurt. He limped down the nave and bumped into a flower-stand, which clattered to the floor. Next he collided with a drum kit and cymbals. Christ! A bloody drum kit in church? His third collision was with a pyramid of food bank tins. He felt an urge to laugh but that only made him want to pee. He blipped the mobile and used its light to reach the vestry and its lavatory.

Through the window he could see that a police patrol car was parked under a street lamp.

2

Monday Morning

CLUNK went the door, sealing Ross into Theresa's Rover for the start of his hateful weekly journey to London. Herefordshire never looked clearer than on Monday mornings, gossamer pearling the grass. A spider had strung a web from the top of an apple tree to the handle of Theresa's wheelbarrow. It had made a leap and trusted the breeze – an act of instinct or faith.

Theresa drove. She was faster than Ross, quicker at junctions. He sat in the front passenger seat, hands flat on knees. Thorns littered the verges, for this was the season when farmers trimmed the hedges. The fields had been levelled and the countryside was starting to smell of death. On the car radio the headlines reported the police investigation of a suspected racist attack on the Pakistani airline office in London. Soon a wheezing rabbi was offering a bland homily laced with Americanisms.

'So you'll say no to this debate, then?' Theresa asked her husband, turning down the radio. Ross sighed. 'Tell Calvert to get lost,' she persisted. 'It'll make you feel happier.'

'I don't know,' said Ross, sucking his front teeth. He removed his glasses and gave his eyes a hard rub.

'Ambition is pointless at our age, darling.' Theresa, who at sixty was in fact five years younger and a good deal more sprightly than Ross, yanked down on the gearstick when she said 'pointless'.

She was never much good at silences. 'I mean it's not as if we make pots of money from London. You hate town. You're near retirement age. Why not just tell the Speaker you've had enough?'

'I don't just do it for the money. Or from ambition.'

'Andrew is pretty much launched now. This new venture of his sounds promising.' Andrew, their son, had started running adventure-training courses for youngsters. 'We don't need much money.'

'Aldred is a friend of the Dean and he asked me to do the Commons job. It's an honour for the county. They wanted to give me something.' The chaplaincy to the Speaker had fallen vacant five years ago and Speaker Aldred, the local MP, recruited from his city's cathedral. The Dean had been glad to suggest Ross. He had blocked Ross from being made Precentor for he lacked tact and sobriety. Ross was just not political enough; so he had been sent to Westminster.

Theresa indicated right at a crossroads. 'You're stressed about this debate,' she said, looking beyond Ross to check for traffic.

'There's more to life than happy,' snapped Ross. 'Parliament matters. Anyway, I'd forgotten about that ruddy debate. Thanks.' The red soil of the fields flitted past the Rover's windows. 'The atheists are on the rampage and now our son has joined them. He used to love church.'

'He was a boy, darling. Now he's a man and he has to work these things out for himself. He'll come back to it.'

They ate away at civilisation, these people. Worship songs, pauses for thought: Ross turned off the radio, no longer able to tolerate such rubbish. Centuries of devotion boiled into a sixty-second platitude by a wheezing rabbi with a transatlantic accent and mother complex. Anglicanism was being expelled from the courts and hospitals. No one queried the Muslims. Yet the risibly moist Church of England was attacked for being dogmatic and misogynistic – even while Islam forced women behind the veil. Ross felt besieged.

'You can't take all the world's troubles on your shoulders, darling,' said Theresa.

'What am I meant to do? Let some trashing moderniser be Speaker's chaplain? What would our fathers have thought of that? But I'm no good on a stage. It feels like a trap. Such a bloody awful title. Big Faith Debate. A big debate? Or a big faith?'

'Forget I mentioned it.'

'Why can't we have small faith? Why must everything be big and garish? Doubt belongs as much to us as to the atheists. Without doubt there would be nothing noble about belief.'

'If it's a trap, tell Calvert to get lost.'

'I can't.'

'Last night you said you would. Look, we're almost there now.'

'Bloody Calvert.'

'You keep saying he's only a marketing man,' said Theresa.

'National Dean of Communications, whatever that means. But he knows everyone. He's modern. He's trouble.'

They arrived at the station. Ross extracted his bag from the Rover's boot, closing it with a 'bye then'. She offered an unreturned 'love you' and in her mirror watched him trudge to the ticket office. Later, tidying his clothes, she found he had forgotten his Westminster security pass.

When Ross reached Paddington, he and the other passengers were greeted in the concourse by pretty girls in tight t-shirts, eyes popping. 'Reason Week,' they cooed. 'Wanna badge?' They looked half frozen in shorts and high heels.

'Reason Week?' said Ross. Was it reasonable to wear so few clothes on a cold day? He himself wore a scarf over his clerical collar.

Magnetism, animal allure, smell: Nature contained more mysteries than the Book of Revelation. Reason dictated that a parson his age should not waste time talking to advertising-agency hotties promoting an Augustus Dymock stunt. Yet Ross was still

13

drawn to them. The girls soon moved on, repeating the sales patter to the next wave of wan commuters coming through the ticket barriers. They swooped like gulls. 'Hi there. Wanna badge? Reason Week! Hi, girlfriend. Wanna leaflet? Have a great day.'

The leaflet advertised a secularist gig, singles nights, a rally, a world record attempt atheist get-together. Ross read the small print. 'Reason Week is a trademark of the Thought Foundation Ltd.' Perhaps the Church should register God as a trademark.

Already these commuters had to remember train times, passwords, meetings, office protocols, lists, rules: who wanted more reason? They were assailed by factual hassle. Yet atheism's termites gnawed at ancient, unspoken certainties which remained now but as struts on a burnt pier. Was more Reason wanted? Beauty Week might come as a relief. Reassurance through Tradition Week. Love Week. Someone with energy might mount such a defence but Tom Ross's bones hung loose in his skin. Confrontation exhausted him.

PETROC Stone bought his usual cigarettes but also toothpaste, shaving cream and cheap razors. The old Afghan who ran Ruby Street's corner shop invariably complimented him on his beard.

'It got blacker when you were in Kashmir, Pastor Petroc.'

'Maybe, Mohammed.'

'All that curry.'

'Yeah.'

The newspaper front pages carried a blurred photograph of the Ford Ka driver under headlines 'Do You Know This Man?' Mohammed rambled on about how the holy men back home wore beards to make them look ancient and wise. Maybe Pastor Petroc too was wise? This morning, Petroc thought not.

Mohammed examined the shaving foam with sorrow. 'It's not for me,' said Petroc. The old man was relieved. A man of Pastor Petroc's girth would not be improved by going clean-shaven.

'Ma'salaam.'

'See ya, Mohammed.'

Many market stallholders already knew Petroc, though he had been vicar of Alleluia Jesus! just a few months. 'Fancy an apple, vicar?'

'Thanks, mate.'

'Hello there, Petroc.'

'Gloria! Have you been taking care?'

'Course not.' Dirty laugh.

'You find a new flat, Pastor?' asked a hairdresser, stepping out of his shop to ask the question. Petroc's old place had been condemned.

'Yes. The Church has found a place near Vincent Square. I'm going to be sharing with the chaplain to the Speaker of the Commons, no less.'

'Oooh.'

On Petroc pressed, past the chippie, the mobile-telephone shop, the bookie, the halal butcher – he knew them all. But he did not know this youth with the clipboard and tabard.

'Hi there, I'm Zac, can I grab two minutes?' It was a boy, big teeth and yellowy curls, a street charity seller. He had a slight squint, which did not entirely mar his beauty.

'What are you selling, Zac?'

'We're letting people know – oh, hang on, you're a vicar.'

'Yes.' Petroc kept his tone informal. Despite his bulk and the thick beard, he was still young enough to be able to pull off the youth routine. He asked the boy again: 'What are you selling?'

'It's not exactly selling.'

Petroc took a leaflet from his hand. 'Reason Week. Ah, the Thought Foundation.'

'See? It's not really for you.'

'No,' said Petroc. 'Nor should it be for you, Zac. If I wasn't in a hurry I'd tell you about God's love and what that can do for you. But I can tell you're not fully committed to this negative stuff.'

'You can?'

'Your eyes. They are kind eyes.' He looked into the boy's imperfect eyes. The boy looked away. Petroc said: 'God loves you, if you would only let him. You're better than this atheist sales stuff, Zac. Does your mum know you're doing this?'

'My mum? I don't see her much.'

'Your dad?'

The boy shuffled his feet. 'Yeah, he knows. He's . . .'

'Such a male thing, atheism.'

'Priests always used to be men.'

'Good point! But we have changed and it has improved us. Look, I wish I didn't, but I have to go. Open your heart, Zac. Let your eyes see the possibilities of the unknown. Maybe we'll meet again.'

A passing van tooted and Petroc waved. Yes, they all knew Pastor Petroc with his donkey jacket and sucked-to-the-filter fags. Even the pimps. He was direct with them – told them straight that they were wrong. It was the same with his services, which were smiling, modern, blunt. He served up Biblical sermons laced with social action and moral renewal. He spoke of global warming alongside the fires of Hell. He attacked sloth and City excess. He endorsed Christian love, railed against loose sex. Depravity and faithlessness would get you in the end. It was surprising how much denunciation you could get away with if you delivered it with glottal stops and the odd nod to Wittgenstein or some philosopher whose name was familiar but work unknown. If you made it sound modern – if you said 'yeah?' every few breaths – you could bludgeon your way into the Twitter generation. Atheists thought this was the age of Reason but it was the age of Assertion. Reason demanded too much time.

Services at Alleluia Jesus! were upbeat – even when talking about death. The teenage band would bash away on the drums and former Army corporal Derrick, all muscles and tattoos, would play electric guitar. Derrick would point to Heaven during hits such as *Search the Tomb* and *Bethl'em Callin'* and the syncopated *Tarsus Taxman Saul Saw the Light*. Congregants would sway their arms in the air and close their eyes. In his loft, organist Mark would stare bleakly at his shelf of sacred music and wonder how much longer he could tolerate Petroc's modernity.

At Alleluia Jesus! services, blessings were dispensed like toffees. At the sign of the peace, Petroc would kiss the women at least three times, especially those with false teeth and whiskers. He shook the men – gripped them – by the hand. Younger lads were given a playful punch on the shoulder. To lead an evangelical church was not so different from being a politician. You had to suspend inner reserve, forget you were English, vibrate – tingle! – with the zeal of the Lord. Dem bones dem bones, why, alleluia Jesus.

The new regulars were loudly enthusiastic and told themselves that they were restoring vitality to the Church. It did not occur to young Petroc that others would be deterred by such insistent whooper-doopery, would find the gleaming certitude unpersuasive because it exceeded their own fumbling faith. Totalism was the default setting for the new Church. Petroc was no pioneer – there were many more zealous than he – and he would not question this new Establishment. He considered himself a Christian, not an Anglican. He was a member of a team, not a lone Protestant.

At a market stall he bought nylon pyjamas for five pounds. The money would only have ended up in his gut otherwise or in some collecting tin. Petroc and cash were never long wed. He bowled along, forward to fate. A police incident van was parked near the church and officers were handing out notices seeking information about the airline office attack. The airline had offered a reward. 'Had one of these, Reverend?' said a policewoman.

'I have.'

'We don't want him coming back.'

'Second comings? That's my line of business!'

Inside the church, it took a moment for Petroc's eyes to adjust from the outdoor glare. Mark was just finishing a practice session. After dribbling through the next service's happy-clappy hymns he ended with a defiant few verses of *My Song is Love Unknown* and some top-volume Buxtehude before descending the spiral staircase from the organ loft. Mark played at various churches. Not all of them were as yippety-yea as this one had become. With a scuttle and grunt, he left. Only when Petroc was sure the organist was not returning did he approach the altar saying: 'It's just me. I've brought some stuff so you can wash.'

THERESA Ross's trug was full. This young tree at the top of the garden was always last to surrender its tart, rough-skinned apples. October wasps ignored them but once these russets dropped, worms fell to work. Theresa brushed tiny, pink maggots off one of the apples. Fruit went the way of all flesh.

'I'll have to stake you before next year, little tree,' said Theresa. 'You are stooped, like your owner.' She straightened her back and felt a pang at the sight of swallows on the telephone wire above the lane. Soon they, too, would be gone and the dead season would set in for months. She ran a hand through the branches. Satisfied that every last apple was picked, she wandered down to the house and whistled for Barney. The terrier skittered down from the log pile where he had been ratting.

Barney did not notice, as he passed the tree, that two large apples had grown on the very branches his mistress had just checked.

THE fugitive under the altar was called Matt. He accepted the shaving gear and toothpaste and said: 'Thanks, Father. Here's your phone.'

'Keep it longer if you want. And don't call me "Father". I'm not that sort of priest.'

'What sort of priest is that?'

'High. Well, not high in the sense you'd understand. Did you call your family? They'll be worrying.'

'I texted my sister,' said Matt.

'You need to tell your parents.'

'They're not talking to me.'

'They're angry about the car?' asked Petroc.

'Nah, they haven't been talking to me since I took up with Bashirah.'

'Bashirah?'

'My girl. The one who was sent to Pakistan.'

The previous night the boy had spoken about his girlfriend. Officialdom normally asked incessant questions; social workers, teachers, benefits officers, cops, they were all the same. This pastor just smiled and listened. Matt had talked about how Bashirah hadn't wanted to go. They forced her, screaming, kicking. Said he wasn't good enough for her. 'She had to find a Muslim boy. But I'm not Muslim. I'm English.'

'Muslims can be English,' said Petroc.

'Infidel, they called me. Non-believer.'

'There are plenty of those, Matt.' The story of Bashirah's fundamentalist father reminded Petroc of his recent time in Kashmir as a missionary. Matt was impressed that the vicar knew something about the sub-continent. He wanted to know if it was hot there. What would Bashirah be eating?

Matt himself was bolting some breakfast, suppressing indigestion. 'My sister's found some lawyer,' he said. 'What are these things?'

'Pilchards. The ladies of the congregation always donate them to the food bank. Pilchards and, look, tinned custard. Not to be combined.'

Matt sucked his fingers. The apostles would not have had dainty manners. St Peter would have wolfed down broiled fish and honeycomb and burped afterwards. Table etiquette at the Last

Supper – now there was a sermon. They had arrived hungry, for a feast. Jesus told them he was leaving. The food must have dried in their mouths, the wine still wet on their beards.

'Something I want to ask,' said the boy. He looked at Petroc. One of his eyebrows had a stripe shaved into it. 'You think I can, like, stay here a bit? This lawyer my sister has found. He says I could ask for "sanctuary".'

'Does he now?'

'Reckon I can doss here a day or so?'

'You might want to reconsider that after the All Stars have had a rehearsal.'

'What are they like?'

'Noisy. Drums, ukuleles, triangles, electric guitar. I may be singing. *Jailhouse Rock*. Probably the last song you want to hear right now.' Petroc grabbed hold of a candle-stand and impersonated Elvis with a microphone. Matt laughed. Petroc threw him the shopping bag containing the pyjamas. 'Here. You might find these useful. I'll need to talk to the church but so far as I'm concerned, you can stay.'

AUBURN Olga, haloed by sunlight, distributed a list round the penthouse board table. London sparkled below, the Thames a silvery flatworm. She had not been in England long – not yet long enough to find this view boring.

A hedge-fund guy, two lawyers, a pension-fund man plus trade unionist Sheila Henderson sat at a coffin-shaped table with a dazzling top. Olga stood near the door. She knew she would not learn all their names. Prominent at the table was a figure with hair as white as Elijah. Augustus Dymock's hair had long been that colour and it was no indicator of his age – he was a mere fifty-four, and fit at that. He sat serene in his stereotype. Newspapers had labelled him the 'Don of Doubt' and this, pleasingly, had stuck. He watched with rehearsed amusement, tapping his fingertips against one another. It was a look he had perfected during countless magazine photo sessions. Emperor Augustus, Ayatollah of Atheism, Dr Reason: each interview brought some new epithet. Olga knew Dymock all right. She was his frisky lover.

The meeting's participants started to read the list. The hush was broken by the occasional chink of coffee cup on saucer and the gut-rumbles from a man in a Jermyn Street shirt and chunky cufflinks. Gordon Greenhill, bullish, over-cologned, sat directly opposite Sheila Henderson, the better to admire the trade unionist's front. His eyes were slightly hooded and one had a flaw on the upper lid, a worm cast of skin.

The penthouse was on the nineteenth storey. Up here one might have felt close to Heaven had Dymock's Thought Foundation not cancelled Heaven. As Dymock had told Olga, Heaven was a myth for primitives, childishly superstitious. How could a place exist without title deeds and a report from a chartered surveyor? Rational proof: that was Dymock's demand. At the Thought Foundation, truth was only that which could be boxed and measured. Truth was something you could enter in a game of animal, vegetable or mineral and thus show to exist. Such a solid concept could also, therefore, be destroyed. It could be burnt. Truth could never inhabit some higher plane, for that might demand faith, and faith, come on, was away with the fairies.

Grey-eyed, with pale lipstick and a few freckles on her pert, twenty-something nose, Olga held her head at an angle conveying sullen allure. The auburn hair cascaded over one shoulder and she gave it occasional shakes, each time with a lick. She was a sporty proposition and knew it.

Sheila Henderson said: 'This is a list of churches.'

'Today's churches, tomorrow's luxury homes,' said Gordon Greenhill, he of the gut. 'It's the Jesus Jackpot, love. Invest now in Greenhill Developments and your union of moaning public-sector workers makes a packet.'

The occasional gull rose on the building's swirling thermals, trusting in its ability to remain aloft. What cold eyes birds had, as soulless as those of the fish they gobbled. Gordon Greenhill's hooded gaze glistened at Sheila.

'I'm not your "love", thank you,' said Sheila. The unions were full of apes like Greenhill.

The windows reached from floor to ceiling. Olga edged round the table, her hourglass figure brushing against Dymock's back. Were she a seagull, she would never wish to look down, for that would make her feel dizzy. She would keep this irrational fear to herself, though. Logic. Reason. The Thought Foundation demanded it every moment. She would not dare to cross Dymock, not yet. She had a sick father in Moscow to support and this position was lucrative.

'Gentlemen, lady,' began Dymock. Just the one lady? Did Olga not count as one? Dymock addressed the meeting: 'Now that you have had a chance to skim the list, let's walk through the highlights. Gordon.'

Greenhill stood. 'It's an impressive portfolio, some of the finest sites in town,' he said. 'The Church of England is a power when it comes to property assets. Lights down, please.' Olga twisted the dimmer nipple to lower the blinds and lights. Dymock took no notice of her.

'From Paternoster Square,' said Greenhill, 'to Marble Arch, Sloane Square to Regent Street.' Images flashed on a screen – photographs of St Peter's Church in Sloane Square, All Souls', Langham Place. 'That last one, imagine. Loft spaces for BBC executives? But I'm not going to start with the obvious ones. Look at these.' He clicked on another image: a broad, colonnaded church. 'Hoxton, St Jude's, tiny congregation, big potential. Mature trees line the communal garden.'

'The graveyard,' explained Dymock.

'Graves and their contents will be reassigned. Imagine residents' gardens, a barbecue area, a grass tennis court. See this artist's impression.' The room's occupants murmured approval. Dymock took a sip of herbal tea.

'I'd need turn-around times, how fast from acquisition to sales revenue,' said the hedge-fund man, looking only at his mobile. 'Presumably we have to bung a few grand in sweeteners to Church leaders.'

'Not at a local level,' said Greenhill. 'A little persuasion money may be required for Church suits at national level but I don't envisage much. Already I have surveyors at some of the sites. Their arrival helps create local unease, an expectation of change, and they give us feedback on local attitudes to planning. Next slide: St Teddy's, Acton, described as a community church because they have tried to share their building with the community. It hasn't worked. Never does. The church committee is dying to be euthanased. The inner suburbs carry almost no political dangers – no marginal seats, so ministers seldom intervene on planning.

'Next picture: Holy Trinity Church near Shepherd's Bush. A church hall big enough to make an arthouse cinema. Public-benefit test will be a cinch. St Anselm's, Hampstead, spacious, solid Victorian job. Empty. There's no one now to use it. Not in Hampstead.'

'Some of our best supporters live in Hampstead,' said Dymock. 'All those direct-debit Fabians keen to salve souls they don't believe in. Hampstead *surges* with Doubt.'

'Most of them with second houses in Tuscany,' muttered Sheila Henderson.

'Here's a map of London,' continued Greenhill. 'Each red cross is a church. Not all are deadbeat causes. The evangelicals have an irritating habit of starting satellite churches but they are fighting on too many fronts. Let me filter out the churches which are still doing OK.' He pressed a button. Thirty per cent of the red crosses disappeared. 'And let me give you a snatch of the rural beauties. Here's one in Kent, two minutes from a high-speed rail connection to St Pancras. Worth zilch as a church but an easy five mill' as residential units. West Oxfordshire: a wool church, could make several weekend homes. The congregation fits into one pew. And just in today, this one near the Welsh border. They say the graveyard is haunted – 'the most haunted hundred yards in the kingdom'. I already have informal interest from a London club looking for a rural retreat.'

Dymock, from his throne, said: 'Property is a public obsession and the moral case is unanswerable. Henry the Eighth dissolved the monasteries.'

'The inner suburbs are where we start,' said Greenhill. 'National media couldn't care about them. The only people who live in inner suburbia are office cleaners and their mugger children.' Sheila Henderson bit her scarlet lip.

Dymock added: 'And in the shires, planning officials tend to hate their posh residents. We will play the social justice card.' Greenhill laughed.

'There's nothing comical about social justice,' said Sheila.

'Is it moral for a Church to waste so much precious land?' said Dymock. 'They are in a position, here, to aid economic growth.'

'Nationalise the churches!' said Greenhill.

'Now you're talking,' said Sheila.

'No,' said Dymock. 'Establishment is already a form of nationalisation. We will privatise the churches. We will realise their assets to create public good. We need the financial strength of venture capitalism and the campaigning power of the unions. Without you both, we will not defeat centuries of superstition. We will create jobs and new homes. Private profit and social benefit in tandem. Commercial gain can be shared by the unions if they invest. Any questions? No? Olga – the fruit sorbets.'

3

That Afternoon

TWO hours later Dymock left a wriggling Olga in his bedroom and strode across Westminster Bridge with two bodyguards, cutting through the crowd. Few of these people deserved a glance. Modern medicine saved too many losers.

The morning's meeting had been satisfactory. Greenhill had a brute determination. The money men would be discreet. Sheila was needed for her union links but would fret about principles. A private bung to Sheila might be needed. Dymock trusted in the Darwinian principle of greed. Adapt to survive. Refine. Winnow out weaknesses, as he told Olga. She sometimes said she loved him but love held back a species. Look at these dawdlers on the bridge, pathetically holding hands and buying snacks for their kids. They were no more competitive than suet puddings. That's what love did to you.

Wind ruffled Dymock's white hair as it might an angora rug. He patted his fringe. Each little detail must be checked to maintain momentum. He listened to his breathing and kept to a rhythm – inhale, exhale – like a scuba diver. Efficient utilisation of time, energy, oxygen. That was what winners did, every day. Win they would with this church–land project. Win they must. It was too good an opportunity to undermine the hierarchy, shelter for so many inadequates. It would make a bundle of money. It would destroy and provide, all in one.

One of his minders snowploughed a dawdler out of the way. If Dymock had to break step he became itchy. He overtook meandering tourists and bent crones with shopping baskets. Look at this moron in the baseball cap, tracksuit bottoms low on his backside. Take this overweight mother, stuffing chips into her toddler. She would die early and the world would not notice. That tramp there, swigging beer. His early demise, a certainty, would save the welfare state thousands of pounds. Let them smoke and drink. Let them kill themselves. State intervention was an obstacle to natural selection. All these dragging anchors – the country had a death wish. Christian tolerance would be England's undoing.

As he passed Westminster Tube station he saw a newspaper hoarding which read 'Airline attack – Muslim fury'. When were the Muslims NOT furious?

Today it was nine hundred and seventy three paces to the St Stephen's entrance of the Commons. Dymock disliked it when the number varied by more than twenty. That was a fair margin of error – he was, above all, a reasonable man. The destination was reached with three minutes to spare. Satisfactory. One of the gate police vaguely recognised this white-haired bloke in the poncey trench coat. Wasn't he on telly? He watched Dymock peel away from his bodyguards and enter the parliamentary building. Which cog in the works was he off to oil?

Inside, a slim intern asked: 'You here for Mr Bryce?'

'Yes.'

'I'm Adrian.' The youth flicked his tongue and led Dymock down carpeted passages, waggling his rump. 'Here we are,' he mewed. The door said 'Deputy Chief Whip'.

Two sets of long fingers clapped in delight. 'The Don of Doubt,' said Deputy Chief Whip Bryce.

'This is for you,' said Dymock. He handed him a grip.

'How good of you to come,' said Bryce. The grip was secreted in a locking cupboard. 'A cup of gunpowder tea in the Pugin

Room, I thought. Then we will watch the Speaker's procession. Adrian, my dear, I have a meeting here in an hour with the Usual Channels. Give them a glug of white if I am late. There's a reasonable Pouilly-Fuissé in the fridge.'

As they made their way to the Pugin Room, Dymock said: 'The Usual Channels?'

'The Opposition Whips,' said Bryce. 'Our opponents and friends. If you don't talk to the other side, how can you ever fix anything? Adrian knows the form. He's my work-experience slave. Adrian Calvert. An uncle is big at Church House. These people often have youngsters who want internships. Favours. Such a useful scheme.'

BIG Ben's chimes began for the half-hour. Deep in the gubbins of the Palace of Westminster, a clerk with a mouse's snout nodded to an official in tails.

Doorkeeper Mates flicked his cigarette towards the Thames, straightened his tails and re-entered the Robing Room from the terrace. His fag landed on the old ferryman's seat before extinguishing.

As the eighth chime faded, the official pushed on the Robing Room door and signalled to a constable who passed the word. Two thirty: time for the procession. Pomp, toot, tan-tara. Being chaplain to the Speaker, Ross had been through this routine many times, yet he tensed. He gripped his father's prayer book and gave a not entirely watery smile.

From the distant lobby came the sing-song of another policeman's 'Spee-kah!', the second syllable five notes higher. The Serjeant at Arms, having given her hair a last squirt of lacquer, moved off, mace held aloft. In her wake walked Mates, a retired Guardsman with a lived-in face. Click, click, click went their heels. The procession took only half-steps to allow for the Speaker's geriatric progress. 'Hats off, strangers!' came another burly command. Hats off, pride on, play up, play up, for tomorrow we die. And so, among the throng, spread word of their coming and all in the citadel did marvel at the mighty panoply. Or something like that.

Spectators fell silent. Ross forced himself forward, the rhythm of steps soothing his nerves, lines of the hymn *Blessed City Heavenly Salem* strengthening him as they ran through his head. *In their places now compacted, by the heavenly Architect.* Why had he ever thought he could flourish here among these swish poltroons? Theresa's words that morning came back at him. 'Ambition is pointless at our age, darling.' Robes swayed to the march. Ross could just about do it when there were other souls to join. It was acts of lone courage that floored him. Speaker Aldred shuffled over the flagstones. Ross concentrated on the old man's full-bottomed wig.

The spectators in the Central Lobby included Bryce and Dymock. They saw the little convoy take twenty half-strides, right turn, click, clack, tick, tock, the march of time. Each day the procession moved more slowly. The Speaker could no longer lift his heels yet he stared ahead, two watery eyes in gummy sockets, his tongue protruding to lick the air. He and his entourage were castled in a vol-au-vent of ceremonial esteem. As for Ross, he concentrated on his hymn: *Consubstantial, co-eternal, while unending ages run.*

In the Commons Chamber, he uttered the usual words. A prayer for the oft-mocked Monarch, for Parliament and its members. *May they never lead the Nation wrongly through love of power, desire to please, or unworthy ideals but laying aside all private interests and prejudice.* Lay aside prejudice against soapsters and charlatans and foreign gods? Was this sensible?

Psalm 142 was appointed for Latimer, Ridley and Cranmer's day. *Listen to my cry for help, for I have been brought very low; save me from those who pursue me, for they are too strong for me.* Ross's fingers tightened on the prayer book. Those martyrs had burned, flames blistering their skin while they screamed. Yet while they screamed they remained true. How could he ever walk in their wake?

'Amen,' grunted the Second Church Estates Commissioner, a rotund fellow called Leakey. The Father of the House, Sir Tudor Matthews, was also present. Sir Tudor had been in the House since the 1950s and placed unswerving trust in the institutions of Church, Parliament and Lunch, not necessarily in that order. Beside him sat Hamid Butt, a British Iranian Muslim with a rural English seat. Butt worshipped Sir Tudor as an emblem of all that was great in his adopted country. His ambition was one day to wear a three-piece Savile Row suit and cracked black brogues with Sir Tudor's aplomb.

The Chamber was pretty full. Questions to the Home Secretary were to follow and always attracted a crowd. The chairman of the Home Affairs Select Committee was besieged by some alleged corruption scandal. MPs would also want to discuss the previous day's suspected racial attack on the Pakistani airline office in London. Members from Glasgow, Birmingham and Bradford planned to ask if the response to the airline-office attack so far showed that authorities were 'going soft on Islamophobia'. Mackie, a socialist from Luton, intended to ask if the incident was the work of white supremacists. The Home Secretary would jump through hoops of Concern and Sympathy, imparting nothing. The Islamophobia gambit was for the benefit of Members with significant numbers of Muslim voters. They did not necessarily believe that the Government was going soft on Islamophobia, but politicians who believed everything they said would soon run out of words.

During prayers, MPs stood facing the rear wall. Ross spoke to their backs. It was easier this way. There was no chance of a flash of doubting eye while the chaplain spoke his lines. In this bullring of bravado, prayer seemed pointless. The true creed of this jeering conventicle? 'I believe in myself, I manoeuvre so that I may prevail over rivals.' Even at the start of the Commons day, competitiveness lingered like sweat in a squash court.

Speaker Aldred's Order Paper shook in his hands. His deputy, Tewk, stood to the right in tails. Ross could hear doorkeeper Mates recite the Lord's Prayer in his deep voice with childlike precision, a beat behind everyone else. Ross was finishing the session even further from his Maker than when he had begun. When the last 'Amen' had been done, Speaker Aldred husked out a 'Well done, Timothy.' He called everyone Timothy and said 'Well done' to everyone, too. He was consistent in his insincerity.

The Speaker maintained a chaplain because it cost little – a stipend paid from an obscure budget – and added maybe an ounce of dignity to the Speakership. Did Aldred believe? Like most politicians he was a time-starved sceptic who paid heed to complainants and figures who could do him a favour. God did not write difficult letters to his constituency office. Nor did God have direct control over Government funds. God did not edit a local newspaper. God was unlikely to cause much trouble, at least this side of Doomsday. What was there to fear from the modern God of quavering songs and baby-talk prayers? But if there was a budget provided for a chaplain, let it be used. Never let a budget go to waste.

Ross gathered his sleeves and retreated from the Chamber, walking backwards, bowing to the Chair. He caught the eye of the Commons Clerk, Sir Roger Richards, a devotee of fob watches, quill pens and the latest tablet computers. Sir Roger wore spectacular whiskers. He shot Ross a twinkle as though to say 'Lucky you – I have to stay and listen'. Later the House would go into committee to continue consideration of the wide-ranging Civic Regulations Bill, seventh day. As Ross departed through the double swing doors a couple of Members passed him on their way to their seats. They offered no greeting. All he heard was 'missed prayers again – hell!' and laughter. The last words Ross heard as the doors swung shut were a trembling 'order, order'.

★

BIG Ben's half-past two had also been audible in the offices of Leslie Mears MP, though amid the bustle it went unnoticed. Work was afoot. There were endorsements to be won. Mears's moustache twitched, a rusty caterpillar arching its spine.

Middle-aged Mears, MP for Oakford, a safe Midlands seat, was standing for a select committee chairmanship. Such prizes did not happen by themselves. In the outer room three researchers stared at screens. An older figure, hair in a bun, rootled through a filing cabinet. This was Jean. A kettle was coming to the boil on a fridge top soiled by spilt sugar and splodges of instant coffee. A landline rang. Bun-haired Jean dropped her weak chin into the receiver. 'Oh, hello, Mr Bryce. Yes, he's here. Do drop round.' She wrote a brisk, legible note and took it next door. As she left the room the younger researchers smirked. Jean was so old-fashioned. Filing cabinets!

Above the fridge was a large picture of a politician making a speech. The margins of his face, running to fat, were accentuated by spotlighting. The photographer had caught him pointing – with fingertips that had been chewed – at some horizon, a word frozen on his lips so that it looked as though he was about to say 'sausage'. This snapshot of Mears had been taken at a party conference and was perhaps the most flattering image ever taken of him. It was in black and white, so the orange moustache did not leap out so much.

When the kettle boiled, one of the researchers made tea. A splosh of semi-skimmed milk. Three sugars. The packet of custard creams was already empty. Greedy bugger, Mears. Why couldn't he leave a few biccies for the staff? Unlike Jean, the researchers did not adore their employer. He was not a man automatically to instil affection. The interns knew him as 'Smears' or 'Mouldy Mears', for there was something furred and rancid about him.

From the inner sanctum came a gabble of salesmanship as Mears jabbered down the line to his latest best friend. 'So pleased you're on board, Gary,' he said, tapping an impatient rhythm on his knee with a ballpoint pen. The office smelled of dead mouse and socks. Mears's shoeless feet barely touched the ground and he swivelled in his executive chair, pausing to check his texts while talking on the landline. One swivel brought him face to face with a photograph of a young woman. She had an hourglass figure, a head of cascading auburn hair, the nose of a questing doe. Mears stared at the photograph.

He sucked the front of his teeth as men do when seeking some stubborn pip. Every second of the day had to be filled with some fresh gesture or twitch. This restlessness afflicted not just Mears but all of them in this office except Jean. There were buttons to be pressed, screens to be consulted, teaspoons to tap on desktops. Eyes darted, elastic bands were wound round fingers, feeds and sites and blogs and trends were monitored and rebutted and forwarded and liked. Typing pools of old were never so frenzied.

A moment later the call was done and Mears ticked the list in front of him, muttering that the man he had been talking to was a 'prick'. His right hand darted into a bag of chocolate violet creams. He extracted one, subjected it to an expert examination, then popped it into his small mouth, his moustache hairs ridging and rippling as he ate it.

He shouted through the door, 'For chrissake, where's that tea?' but corrected his curt manner when his next call picked up. 'Miiiiike! Long time no speak, my friend. It's Les. What? No, Les *Mears*. That's right. 'Little Les Mis'! Ha ha. Now, sir, I wonder if I can steal a minute of your precious time? What? Oh, sorry. I'll try later. Of course. Wouldn't want you to miss your tee-off time. Bye!' He said the last word more like 'bah!' – mighty casual – and made another mark on his list before lifting one buttock from his chair and expressing a tuba fart. The man he had just called was Mike Branton-Day from Long Valley, a Sussex constituency. Another prick, rich and handsome at that, with a sleek wife. Mears hated him, envied him. Never mind. Mears would make his mark. He would regain his lost ground and beat the bastards. Chairman of the Commons Select Committee on Housing might not look the world's greatest job but it would do. As Bryce said, housing is land, housing is votes, housing is power.

Until a few months earlier, Mears would not have thought of the committee job. Back then he had retained the 'full confidence' of his party leader and rejoiced in the style, title and appurtenances of Shadow Minister for Local Government. That had been when his name still appeared on the website under 'our Government in waiting' and when he had been mentioned by ill-informed pundits as a member of his party's inner clique. He was 'Les Mears – one to watch.' Since those heady endorsements the life of Leslie Mears had encountered a spot of turbulence. At an evening reception a day after some local elections he had described his party leader as 'not much more than a schmoozing bimbo'. The words had been uttered with quixotic bravado to the political editor of one of the broadcasters. The political editor repeated the verdict on radio the next morning to illustrate 'concern' in the Opposition at 'the direction' of its leadership.

Colleagues of the Leader often called the fellow a public relations spiv. However, they spoke on an unattributable basis. Mears had forgotten to say that his words were off the record. 'Not much more than a schmoozing bimbo' was an attributable attack by a Shadow Minister. So it was that listeners to the radio programme, who included the schmoozing bimbo himself, had been treated to Leslie Mears's verdict. 'Was he in his cups at one of those Westminster booze-ups?' ventured the show's co-presenter. 'Remarkably not,' laughed the political editor. 'Mr Mears is a man many feel could benefit from an injection of fizz; he was, I almost regret to say, stone cold sober.' Five minutes later Her Majesty's Opposition announced that the Hon Leslie Mears had been sacked as Shadow Minister for Local Government.

The Housing Committee chairmanship fell vacant a month later, when the incumbent had been caught in bed with an Algerian spy. One politician's ruin is another's opportunity, as his Government Whip friend Bryce said. Mears bashed out another telephone number with his bitten fingertips. Damn. Some of the melted chocolate from the violet cream made his finger slip. He re-entered the number. 'Netty! Les Mears here. Hi, hi, hi.' Natascha 'Netty' Peake, Opposition backbencher, was unofficial convener of the party's feminist sisterhood. 'Look, Netty, as you may know, I have decided not to do any overt campaigning for the Housing select committee chair. I thought I'd treat Members like grown-ups.' Mears twiddled with his moustache and cast an eye down the tyres of his gut. 'I mean, that sales routine really isn't my style. So look, I'm ringing one or two serious figures to see if there are any thoughts on the direction the committee should take, issues we should grapple. I'd appreciate your input. You're the first I have phoned.'

The tea-boy wandered in with a mug. Mears accepted it and motioned that the researcher should skedaddle. Mears was nodding his head, saying 'quite' and 'exactly, Netty', while flicking through a red-top newspaper, briefly ogling page three. God, these campaign calls were a bore. Yet the select committee chairmanship would offer a platform. It would also bring extra cash – more than a thousand quid more a month. Maybe he could take his new flatmate Olga out for a splashy dinner. She'd like that. So would he.

Another body shimmered into the room. Mears was about to scowl when he realised that it was Bryce and he remembered Jean's note. Bryce made himself comfortable in the armchair while Mears finished his call.

'That was Natascha Peake.' His hand shot into the bag of chocolates to grab another violet cream.

'Netty the Yeti.'

'She is going to talk to the sisters.'

'Very Macbeth.'

'And may come up with ideas for my chairship.'

'Your chairship, eh?'

'One hesitates to use the term with regard to Netty but I think I may have scored.'

Bryce, though in a different party, was the closest Mears had to a friend. As youngsters they had been on a debating tour of the Scottish universities and Bryce donated Mears one of his unsought female admirers, a stodgy Borders girl with teeth and a Hitchcock chin. They had fumblingly relieved each other of their virginity and for a few days were inseparable. Spotty young Leslie had never enjoyed much success in the love department.

'It will help that Netty is no friend of your Leader,' said Bryce. He flexed fingertips slender as haricot beans, scented by a thyme embrocation from a Bond Street fragrance shop. It fought the stink of dead mouse and Mears's socks. 'Any enemy of your Leader is now prepared to break bread with you.'

'You really think this select committee can get me back in the chase?'

'You were sacked. Colleagues look at you afresh. A quick, clean sacking is never as bad as a drawn-out struggle for survival. You are now seen as a player who had to be taken out.' Bryce churched his fingers. 'Opportunities, Leslie. Plot your comeback. Baroness Luck has given you a chance. A select committee chairmanship bestows a title, broadcasting slots, a chance to make ministers angry. Atkinson hasn't a hope.' Atkinson, another Opposition backbencher, was Mears's rival for the job.

'I could do with the chairman's money, certainly.'

'This office is pretty bloody awful,' said Bryce. 'I can see why you spend so much time in the Smoking Room.'

'Only place I can escape the smell of dead mouse.'

'Is that what it is? I thought it must be Jean's after-shave. Poor Jean. Are relations any better?'

'Tricky,' said Mears. 'She doesn't approve of Olga.'

'Ah, your new flatmate. Decorative, isn't she?'

'You bet.' Mears gave a greasy smirk. He held the photograph up off his desk and waved it at Bryce. The snapshot had been sent to him when he had asked Olga for landlord references.

'Use her,' said Bryce. 'Squire her round town. She could help your select committee campaign.'

'She's a bit young for me. I'm fifty.'

'And you look older,' said Bryce.

'The internet geeks running my party all seem to be in their thirties. They cycle to work, use shower gel and chew gum, wear manbags and trainers. Their wives go to Ibiza rave clubs on holiday. I have nothing in common with them.' Mears, for his relaxation, preferred to read back issues of *Hansard* and the occasional Dennis Wheatley novel. The goats' skulls on the front covers reminded him of Jean.

Bryce said: 'That is where your little Russian could help you. Image, Les. It affects how people see you. Why not invite her to something? There's the charity ball next month after the State Opening. Tickets are still for sale.' He looked at a text message on his telephone. 'The old boy has made it into his Chair for another day.'

'What do you mean?'

'I watched the Speaker's procession and he is embarrassingly frail. Dymock was with me. Must give you an update on that later. Now, must go, I have a vote to rig.'

'And I must ring Olga.'

'My felicitations to Comrade Zolnerova. Get her along to that charity ball.' Bryce swept out of the room to attend to his misdoings.

Mears rang a number. 'Olga?' Mears's receiver communicated what sounded like grunts of struggle. 'You all right, Olga?'

'I jus' a bit tied up,' came the reply. 'Will see you later, Les–uh–lee.'

The line died. Mears's puzzlement abated as he took another violet cream and allowed himself to linger over it, slicing off its sugar floret with his sharp top teeth and tonguing the scented, fondant filling from its chocolate shell. The ball next month: it was not a bad idea.

In a penthouse bedroom on the other side of the Thames, the Palace of Westminster visible through its window, a lithe young woman with an hourglass figure and the nose of a questing doe was indeed tied up, crossly awaiting her boss's return from his rendezvous with Bryce.

ROSS did possess a mobile telephone but seldom carried it and had certainly not mastered its voice mail. Commons Clerk Sir Roger Richards occasionally tried to give him lessons. 'You've got to get with it, Tom,' Sir Roger would say in his spongebag trousers and horsehair wig. Ross was with it in one sense. Andrew had given him an iPod and, knowing his father was useless with technology, had downloaded it with hymns. Ross had learned to press the on button. When he had his earphones in and *Lord, enthroned in heavenly splendour* blasting at top volume, he was even more lost to modern London.

His telephonic shortcomings were one of the things that drove Calvert mad about Ross. Theresa was always getting at her husband about it, too. She would tell him he needed to 'forge a treaty with the twenty-first century, dear'. Ross would pull a face – and continue to ignore his mobile. As Ross wandered down the cold-stoned parliamentary corridors the following message therefore went unheard: 'Hi, Tom, Tony Calvert from Church House here, Monday afternoon. I know you're, like, really busy but I'd appreciate a call back. It's about this Big Faith Debate.' Calvert. Lean, rimless spectacles, an Adam's apple big as a knot on a walking stick. Calvert was a proselytiser for outreach and modern hymns and diocesan organograms.

He was rushing his words – could have been an air steward hastening through a pre-flight announcement. There was the same blasé torpor, the thin observance of formula. Telephone speech had become a secular liturgy. Voices would lift, even when not questioning, to assure the listener that they were consensual, modern. People said that this came from Californian beach babes but it also followed the rhythm of medieval plainsong. 'The bishop wants us to nail down a strategy,' said Calvert, pausing with a tiny lift in tone. 'I need to run a few things by you.' Another lift. 'We've just heard that Dymock is going to take part. Augustus Dymock.' Again a lift. 'We need an executive-level voice at this event and Bishop Tony agrees your face fits. You can get me at the Church House Comm's Hub. Ta, Tom. God bless.'

Another clergyman might have prayed for Calvert, might have asked God to help him see value in every diocesan busybody. Not Ross. Did Calvert ever pray for Ross? What efficient prayers they would be, each ticked off the must-do list as it was uttered in that tangy Mancunian accent, formulaic in its politeness. Did he give his voice an uplift when it came to the Gloria? Did his Amens rise like the corners of a Melba toast?

QUESTIONS to the Home Secretary lasted an hour. The Secretary of State for once enjoyed herself at the expense of George Chance, chairman of the Home Affairs Select Committee. There had been an 'unfortunate matter', a term Westminster uses to describe delectable scandal. Chance had been caught lobbying for British passports for the family of a Kenyan hotelier who had given thousands of pounds to his constituency party. For this to happen to any MP would be bad, but for it to happen to the chairman of the Home Affairs Select Committee – well! The story was helping to distract public attention from anti-fascist riots in Bristol, the murder of a Romanian thief in Ipswich and the airline office ram-raid.

The Home Secretary defended the Government's 'robust and impartial approach to immigration'. Despite 'pressures, sometimes from surprising quarters, we continue to defend our borders and our waters'. Our waters? Was she a urologist? 'We must never sell the soul of this country for a potage of foreign coins.' MPs behind her cried 'hear hear!'

The Home Secretary looked up from her script and said: 'The sanctity of our borders cannot be left to Chance.' Ho ho!

George Chance did not flinch. To have done so would have betrayed weakness. A Sphinx's calm colonised his plump face. When he later contributed to the debate it was to express the desire that immigration authorities 'accept that the global market moves faster than the pettifogging secretariats of far-flung diplomatic outposts'.

The Home Secretary said she was 'sorry to have read of the Rt Hon Gentleman's current difficulties but I am sure that he will deal with them with his customary honesty'. This amused the Shadow Home Secretary, who found Chance's self-grandeur no less irksome than did the Secretary of State.

As for the incident at the airline office in Victoria Street, the Home Secretary allowed the police minister to play a dead bat. 'Forensic specialists have been siftin' through the wreckage,' he said. 'All leads are bein' followed.' The police minister had spent so much time with officers of the law that he now spoke like a desk sergeant.

Mackie, the Luton independent, suggested that racism was behind the attack. Mackie liked to tint his utterances with a prophet's foreboding. He flourished a forefinger and wondered if the authorities, 'by dint of sloth or something more sinister', were being 'dilatory in their prosecution of an unsavoury cabal, simply because the target here was foreign and Muslim. Will he give my constituents the reassurance they seek, from an all-too white Whitehall, that this is not the case?' Government backbenchers flapped their hands to show they thought him a hyperventilating loon.

'My, my,' said the Minister, 'it seems to be blame-public-servants day. If he has evidence of racism, let him hand it to the police.' At which point Speaker Aldred's small voice summoned the next question on the Order Paper, and, in due course, the latest committee stages of the long-running Civic Regulations Bill.

PETROC, in donkey jacket, was waiting in the Commons' Robing Room to collect keys to Base Camp, as Ross called his grace-and-favour residence. Ross had only just bothered to get spare keys cut – the prospect of sharing the house was as unwelcome to him as any change. Through the Robing Room's windows could be seen the Thames in her pomp. Pleasure craft pootled past.

'You found me,' said Ross, detaching his ears from *On Jordan's Bank the Baptist's Cry*.

'They directed me from central lobby. The dog collar convinced them I was not a terrorist.'

'Wrong sort of cleric for that.' One of the boats sounded its horn. 'I had to go through security checks myself today. Managed to leave my blasted pass in Herefordshire. Anyway, Base Camp. You won't like your room.'

'I'm sure it will be fine.'

'It's a parliamentary house. They say it's too big for me and they want some rent.'

'I'm sorry to impose . . .'

'I can't bear talk at breakfast.'

'Fine.'

'Gaiety before eight o'clock is indecent. Can't say I much like it at any hour. There's no cleaner any more.'

'We can take turns to clean,' said Petroc.

'You don't whistle, do you?'

'No,' said Petroc.

'Well that's something. Fancy a drop?' Ross had retrieved a hip flask from his inner folds.

'Bit early for me,' said Petroc. He had been warned about Ross's drinking by Calvert – keen-eyed, snippety Calvert, admonition made flesh. 'I don't, on the whole.'

'Don't drink? Good God.' Was this why they had sent him to Base Camp? A teetotal spy? He had expected Petroc to be leaner and older. He can't have been much more than thirty.

'But I do like these.' Petroc produced a packet of Silk Cut. 'You?'

'Nope,' said Ross. 'But I like the smell of them. Anything that irritates the health police. You can smoke on the terrace. Come outside.' Children were laughing on the pleasure boats. Petroc's cigarette competed with a stench of algae and bird droppings. Ross said: 'Did you get one of these?' He pulled from his pocket a Calvert memo that urged the clergy to avoid militaristic hymns on Remembrance Sunday. *I Vow to Thee My Country* was held to be particularly troublesome as it glorified nationhood. 'They have sent it to all "worship leaders". I didn't think they approved of anyone being a leader.'

'I think of myself as an enabler,' said Petroc.

'Oh bollocks. They look up to you, man. Even if you make it hard for them by wearing that coat. Next you'll be telling me you agree that *I Vow to Thee My Country* is jingoistic.'

'I might.'

'People love that hymn. Salutes in church, lowered flags. This is the Church of England – our country. I intend to ignore this bloody memo.'

'Then why get angry about it?' asked Petroc.

'Because it's so bloody wet. Spastic political correctness.'

'Unlike your language.'

'Well they drive me to it.' Ross took another, bitter swig. 'They could at least have sent me someone I could get pissed with. Here, house keys.' They were attached with baler twine. Ross lobbed them at Petroc. 'Good catch. Not much to tell you, really, except the burglar alarm has never worked. Thieves don't target vicarages. We're poorer than they are.'

'Money doesn't interest me.'

'I can tell that from your attire. The central heating is iffy but there's a two-bar electric job in your room. The drawing room has a real fire. The cats were there before me. They caught a pigeon the other day. Scoffed most of it but the beak is still there.' A police launch surged down the river. 'Sometimes I flick them a V sign and they think I'm waving.'

'Where do those steps lead?' asked Petroc. Smoke blew across his eyes.

'Down to the ferryman's platform. It was a small landing stage once. I like the idea of a ferryman. Silent Charon rowing the dead. Silence. That's what I miss most at your sort of services.'

'My sort?'

'Happy clappy. Bet they are, aren't they? Electric guitars and weirdos in t-shirts organising discos.'

'You can't say that!'

'At least the black churches have spiritual authenticity. I don't mind an enormous negress singing *Amazing Grace*. They're built for it. But you evangelicals. It's like going to a barbecue. Dress-down Sunday. Jiggly worship songs, twangy prayers. Might as well serve Diet Coke in the chalice. And they're always so bloody noisy. Handshakes and hugs. Freestyle worship led by wannabe groovers with rings through their eyelids.'

'At least people turn up.'

'There's nothing inherently wrong with an empty church. It's easier to find God there. Boasting about belief is not the point. The private quest, the sketching of possibilities, a sacred aesthetic – that should be our business. The more certain people are, the less they will have pondered. Shall we go back in? I'm cold.'

'What's the book?'

'My father's prayer book. He was in the RAF. Took it with him on his flights. The war fried his mind. Dresden. That, he said, was Hell. So many died in one fell furnace.'

'You're lucky to have known him.'

'I didn't. He died three months before I was born. They were on the way home from a peacetime flight in Germany not long after the Berlin airlift. Crashed into a forest. The cause was never known. It was the one time he didn't take this prayer book.'

'May I look?' Ross allowed Petroc to examine the prayer book. Petroc, as though by exchange, disclosed that he had never known who his father was and his mother had been a Cornish wastrel. Petroc was first-generation Church. An evangelical minister had met him on the streets in Truro when he was a shoplifting teenager. That had been his salvation.

'I've never really looked at this old stuff,' he said. 'They didn't tell us about it when we were training.' He turned the book's slender pages with care while Ross hung his cassock on his hook. He almost stroked the book as he handed it back to Ross.

A message had been delivered. Ross read it, dropped it in the bin, and continued: 'My son Andrew was originally going to come to London but he met a woman and changed his mind. My wife is hardly ever here. Can't say I blame her. I hate this city more and more.' They exchanged numbers. Ross continued: 'I can't stand the traffic and the cyclists crouched over their handlebars. Concrete and right angles and sweat-stained go-go-go men yelling at you for crossing the road too slowly. I grieve for the morning mists – Our Lord in a brume. That's how I picture the scene at the tomb. Mary Magdalene, sad and cold, suddenly sees Him through a mist, His feet not touching the ground. It would have been silent, that dawn, the night's fires still smouldering. You wouldn't get that in London.'

'I love this city.'

'Well you must be mad.' Ross stared wildly. The grey hair needed brushing at the side, though he was bald on his crown. At the corner of his eyes was a filmy residue. He had not shaved well. The storm passing, he said: 'I hear some criminal ran into your church.'

'Yes,' said Petroc. 'Quite exciting. Calvert has already asked for a report.'

'They love reports.'

'The lad's name is Matt. He's a boy.'

'You know him?'

Petroc paused. 'He's still there. You're the first I've told. I've lent him my mobile. That number I gave you may not be any good for a couple of days.'

'The papers said he ran out of your church.'

'He never left. Just hid from the cops. Bit like you flicking them a V sign. He lost his own telephone when he crashed his car. I can do without one for a while.'

'You can have mine if you want,' shrugged Ross.

The flask was returned to its discreet pocket. One thing about being a clergyman was that you could legitimately smell of drink. Sorry, officer, but we have to knock back the last of the com-munion vino at the daily Eucharist. Orders. Drink ye all of this.

'He wants sanctuary,' said Petroc.

'Don't we all?' Ross consulted his wristwatch.

'You're busy.'

'Sanctuary. That could cause a few grumbles round here. The secularists won't like it. Talking of which, I'm supposed to be writing something for the *Spectator* – a book review of Augustus Dymock's latest atheist screed. Not that the mean sods pay much.'

'I mustn't keep you.'

'Are you going to give him sanctuary? This youngster.'

'Depends.'

'See what Calvert says, eh? He's away on some fancy retreat in the Lake District at the moment.'

'Sod Calvert,' said Petroc.

'Ha! Good for you!' barked Ross. There might be something in the man after all. 'Look, I have a Mrs Greenhill coming to Base Camp later today. It's about a wedding in the Undercroft. Her daughter's. It's our first meeting so I'll need the drawing room.'

'Is she an MP's wife?'

'Worse.' Ross rubbed the tips of his right thumb and forefinger. 'A donor. Find your own way out.'

Petroc was left alone. He retrieved the note Ross had scrunched. It bore the crest of the Clerk of the Commons. '*Tom, thanks for lunch. Warning: Dymock is on the premises. Mates saw him with one of the Whips. Time for exorcism rites? R.*' Petroc left the room to find a commotion. Police were frogmarching some smartly suited man down the corridor. Petroc asked what had happened. 'That's the Arts Minister,' said an officer. 'Been arrested for shoplifting women's underwear. Apparently he takes a D cup.'

IN her Herefordshire kitchen Theresa Ross sucked on a self-rolled cig and checked her letter. From the brisk uprights to the corrugation of her r's, her blue-black handwriting spoke of floral-patterned drawing rooms, gin-scented in the speckled sunlight. It spoke of wet boot rooms, curling copies of *The Field* by a thunderbox, Bakelite fuseboxes: all were found in this house. The Rayburn's innards grumbled. Balls of bluish dust gathered in the corners of the floor. On the fridge was a photograph of a young couple in outdoors gear.

Ross's family had lived here more than two centuries. One reason they gave him the benefice all those years ago was that he would not need a vicarage. The house's stones altered colour, pink in summer, grey as the year aged. Beside it stood a spinney of ash trees, home to a rookery. Attempts to eradicate the rooks always failed. Theresa's fountain pen was steered by fingernails muddy from the potato patch. She wore an Army jumper, Oxfam skirt, thermal smalls. Soignée was not the word. Soignée could have been a ski resort in the Alps.

Darling, Here is the stupid security pass you left in your jacket. Easy mistake. All your suits look the same. Of course your work is important. I was being selfish. Always loathe it when the house empties. London is a priority while you are needed there. We made our vows and you're stuck with me so bad luck.

She pulled on the cigarette but it gave her little satisfaction. She stubbed it out on a side plate which still had crumbs from breakfast. Why were men so unhappy? Why could Tom not rejoice that their son had found a girl he loved and, after an upsetting split, had now quietly married? Her gaze lingered on the photograph on the fridge. The operation had been over a year ago, when they were apart.

Will do Andrew and Morwen's room once this is in the post. I know you were upset about their news. Try to melt a little, darling. Andrew was nervous. We need to keep a relationship with Morwen, though I dread to think what she makes of us. Try not to let London destroy your capacity for love. All I can hear is the grandfather clock and Barney letting off. Andrew has half-term courses starting in the Lake District soon. See you on Friday. T.

She jammed the letter into a used envelope whose stamps the franking machine had missed. The sticky tape shrieked as she gave it a yank and sealed the envelope. 'Come on Barney.' The Sealyham was in his basket by the Rayburn, wagging and whimpering through some doggy dream. He opened an eye and gauged his mistress's seriousness. Not a false alarm. Good. Afternoon walk. He stretched his neck and skipped to the door. Theresa stuffed her baccy tin in her coat pocket and was about to leave when she remembered something. On the back of the envelope she scribbled: *PS. A. needs safety equipt for advtre training. Can you transfer £5k to his a/c?* Ross always needed persuading to lend money. He regarded his savings as proof of accomplishment. Yet he and Theresa never took holidays. They had no expensive hobby.

She headed down the drive for the postbox, Barney scampering ahead. There was still time to catch the post. Barney put up a couple of pheasant in the hedge. A flash of streaking blue caught Theresa's eye. The kingfisher was back. There must be trout in the stream.

AFTER dealing with Mrs Greenhill, Ross sensed, he would need a drink. She had come to discuss the wedding of her daughter Nettle. Mrs Greenhill was determined to make it the greatest day of her life. Her own life, that was.

Often Ross intended not to drink yet there arose some matter to wreck his intentions. A tiny triumph or trial might allow him to deserve a few lovely glugs. Then a few more. Lent was the only time he managed to resist. In Lent the soul asserted landlord's rights over the body. Mrs Greenhill, in fuchsia suit with ten talons to match, had driven many men to the bottle. Women, too. She arrived at Base Camp bearing a gift – a book by a fashionable Eastern mystic. 'His name is Gyumpi,' said Mrs Greenhill, pronouncing it with acrobatic zeal. 'I just had to give it to you. They interviewed him on breakfast television. You'll love it. It helped me find myself.'

'Oh good.' Ross bowed his thanks. Namaste.

'It's so,' she paused, 'spiritual!' Four sets of lacquered eyelashes popped wide.

'Spiritual,' said Ross. 'We can all do with a bit of that.'

'This is Nettle.'

'Hello, Nettle.'

'Hi.' The greeting came from under a broad, floppy hat. Blonde hair fell to Nettle's shoulders. Her lips glistened candy-pink and Ross thought he detected a smell of talcum powder. She was not far into her twenties and she had a cleavage.

Ross led mother and cleavage into Base Camp's drawing room, kicking a cat out of the way and palming the book by Gyumpi on to the crowded table next to his armchair. It was already piled high with books – a Tower of Babel of titles with more on the floor between the table and the fireplace. Mrs Greenhill caught brief sight of the cats' litter tray on some crumpled pages of the *Dispatch*. Out of the French windows, framed by reddening creeper, a squirrel scampered up a sycamore. The garden was large by central London standards. Raindrops plopped through the canopy.

'Do take a seat.' He removed a pile of books from the sofa and dropped them on the floor. They sent up a cloud of dust. Mrs Greenhill coughed.

'Over there, Nettle. Let me sit near Vicar. We won't have tea.' Ross had not in fact offered.

'Now then!' Ross clapped his hands and the cat, which had been spraying into the wood basket, squealed out of the room, hair on end. 'When do you hope to have this wedding? The Speaker's Office mentioned six weeks' time. Sounds tight.'

'Just before Christmas,' said Mrs Greenhill. 'If you have any room at the inn.' She pocketed his small laugh. 'That,' she said, 'gives me just long enough to organise but should not allow Nettle and her – husband – time to change their minds. How *is* Mr Speaker?' Her face twisted with concern. 'He was *so* helpful when I went to see Speaker's House. The reception is to be held there.'

'Speaker Aldred is as well as can be hoped,' said Ross. Bugger, he would have to stay in town for that Saturday but the Greenhills were big money. Ross was trapped. 'What is the young man's name?' There were forms to be filled.

'Gabriel Chundrigar. They shorten it to Chundy, I'm sorry to say. Not exactly young. His family are Gujuratis. They have beach hotels. At Mandvi. Know it?' She spoke in woodpecker bursts. Nettle sat in silence, fiddling with a large ring on her engagement finger. When she noticed Ross glancing at her, she responded with sad, long-lashed smiles. Her cheeks were Demerara brown.

'No.'

'Five-star resort. Well, it will be five next season. Terribly good. Now then, I will complete these forms and send them with the reservation fee. It will have to be a cheque as you don't take cards.' Ross waved his hand feebly in acknowledgement of this archaic inconvenience. Mrs Greenhill placed the forms in a crocodile-skin briefcase that clipped shut with a 'splack!' The noise made Ross jump.

'What else do we need to tell you?' said Mrs Greenhill. She turned to Nettle, a radar dish seeking a signal. Nettle was neither receiving nor transmitting. Ross suspected she was more one for tactile communication than the written or spoken word.

Calvert had only that month sent out a team memo saying the Church must do more to welcome bookings from non-traditional churchgoers for 'life events'. By this he meant christenings, weddings, funerals. Nothing else counted as life, perhaps. Mrs Greenhill, to use Calvert-ese, was a new prospect, in that she was not a regular worshipper. 'We don't tend to go to church. It's finding the time.'

'Never mind,' said Ross. 'Welcome aboard and all that.' The squirrel stared at him from its tree. He had read a newspaper article recently about a man who shot squirrels with an air rifle and cooked them in casseroles. Skinned by Mrs Greenhill, he felt a bond.

'Big garden,' said Mrs Greenhill professionally.

'Yes,' said Ross.

'I mean I admire the Church,' continued Mrs Greenhill. 'But . . .' She shrugged.

'Yes.'

'It has all become so multicultural. When Nettle was at school they kept making her celebrate Diwali. Are you a multicultural?'

'Not entirely.'

'Can we have proper hymns? My husband won't like anything with butterflies or rainbows. We once went to a wedding where they played a banjo. We won't have banjo.'

'Banjo no-go.'

'Nor an ukulele.' She pronounced it as though it could be a Nigerian province.

'No.'

'My husband would have been here today,' she said, 'but he is clinching some deal. It never stops.'

'We'll manage,' said Ross.

'Manage we will for manage we must, Vicar. It's the survival instinct. My husband has no idea – no idea – how much work is involved.'

Experience teaches generals to retreat from unwinnable battles. Gordon Greenhill had learned that although he could cut millions off building project budgets, he would never prevent his fuchsia martinet from spending vast sums at home. To Ross, she now spoke in sharp sentences about flower arrangements, seating capacities and mounting a camera above the altar ('Perhaps my wedding director could contact your people about it?'). Ross let it wash over him. Would there be a parking bay for the bridal chariot? Mr Greenhill's associates had security needs and it would be convenient if there were a VIP entrance. Mrs Greenhill persevered, a rollerball pen gripped in her fingernails. What did Ross think of semi-mature trees lining the nave? 'The royals had something similar at the Abbey. Confetti. Any rules?'

'We're adaptable, I'm sure,' said Ross. Music for the signing of the register. Vases for flowers. Spare chairs. Questions ricocheted round the room. To most of them Ross replied 'as you wish' and 'we can probably live with that'. The quicker he agreed, the quicker she would leave. The new prospect was always right. He had no wish to give Calvert an excuse to interfere. Speaker Aldred might once have been his protector but Aldred's strength was ebbing.

'We thought one of the readings could come from the Book of Kama Sutra,' said Mrs Greenhill. She explained that it was a favourite since her days on an ashram in the early Seventies. Did Vicar have any objection? Actually, he did – not because the Book was without philosophical merit but because it would provoke slatternish titters and rob the service of dignity. Did something inside Ross snap? Not quite. But there was an unexpected hardening of resolve. He got like this sometimes when the tank was running dry. 'Problem?' said Mrs Greenhill. Ross grimaced. Mrs Greenhill's rollerball pen halted. 'Okaaaay,' she said, lending the word gummy elasticity. 'Would your line manager have a view?' She probably meant the bishop. Or Calvert. Did any priest have a line manager? Was God a manager? Did He have a self-billing operation? Did He subscribe to recent employment laws and place an 'Investor in People' certificate on Heaven's office wall?

The longer Mrs Greenhill spoke, the more Ross ached for a glass of Gascony at the Green Man. 'Actually, I'm sure we can get round any problem if the order of service just says "Indian fourteenth-century meditation". Would that do?' Few people actually listened to the readings at a wedding.

'Deal,' said Mrs Greenhill, placing her pen in her briefcase, which again closed so noisily that Ross winced. Nettle, who had earlier been having trouble with a contact lens, was playing a game on her mobile. She was a Greenhill far away.

Calvert's office had devised a welcome package for new prospects. It gave them a reference number, a 'biog' of Jesus and a mission statement which stressed that the Church believed in the living wage and climate change. The welcome package, available in minority languages, had been funded by the Equalities Department and an agency of the European Union. 'You may find this useful,' said Ross, who had crossed the room to collect the welcome package from a shelf. The little journey allowed him an aviator's view of Nettle's bombs.

Mrs Greenhill had but one tongue – not forked, as it happens – and this was poised between her teeth as she inspected the clergyman. She had expected more from a chaplain to the Speaker. She had expected to be sold to, to have options laid before her like silks in the souk. She expected to be *thanked* for choosing a church wedding. Instead he had merely given her a welcome pack showing smiley black faces. His hands seemed shaky and this dusty room stank of cat. She wafted away the welcome pack.

'Come, Nettle. We will leave Vicar to his busy life. And his big garden.'

ALL of this Ross did his best to forget over a snifter or two at the Green Man. He sat at his usual perch in the back, under the sloping ceiling. He often did his paperwork here before attempting the crossword. He wrote a couple of cheques – bills for electricity, water. There was another cheque he needed to write. What was it?

In his pocket a red light blinked on his mobile telephone, indicating a message. If Ross had only known how to listen to it he would have heard a nasal, managerial voice with Australian-surfer uplift. 'Oh, Tom, Tony Calvert from Church House. We're running out of time regarding this debate. Can you ring me? God bless.'

The barmaid said: 'Top up?'

'Thank you, dear.'

As she poured his drink she bade goodbye to another customer. 'See you, Mark, thanks.'

'Good luck with the playschool dirges,' shouted Ross. The departing drinker – organist Mark – mimed a pair of hands round his throat and gave a mocking cry of strangulation. Ross had known Mark since he had started using this boozer five years ago. Mark had been a useful source of intelligence on Petroc; not that they told Petroc they knew each other.

'Penny for your thoughts,' said the barmaid.

'They're not worth that,' said Ross. 'But you can help me with five down if you want.'

'Let's have a look.' She glanced at his newspaper, reached for his pen and filled in the clue. 'See? We have our uses.' It was a pity she couldn't remind him of that payment he had forgotten. He flicked through the newspaper. The attack on the airline office was reported at length. The Commissioner for Equality had made a speech about race-hate incidents. Augustus Dymock, in his comment, had deplored 'medieval religious oppression of women'. Would Dymock say that if he knew Mrs Greenhill?

Ross switched on his iPod and sank into *O Praise ye the Lord!*, Parry's organ working double-time in the final verse of *Laudate Dominum*. Ross pressed the repeat button three times. He envied organists their expertise and their pummelling abandon and the way music unleashed emotions beyond reason's earthly reach. The Prayer Book offered him that, too, with its rhythms and beauty. The Church let him use the old prayers in the Commons. MPs were considered bright enough to cope with it and the church's modern puritans would not patronise MPs as they did the unwashed. But Calvert and Co did not want the little people to drink poetry in their prayers. So the Church poured them liturgical Kool-Aid, all the sugary assertions of simplistic belief without any of the mystery; and the numbers dwindled.

4

They Shall Go To The Ball

CLAP of hands, clap of hands, clap of hands – 'Jesus!' Clap of hands, clap of hands, clap of hands – 'Christ!' This was repeated before the next verse. Tuesday mid-morning service at the Church of Alleluia Jesus! was under way with a zingy worship song.

> Yeah we adore you, Lord
> You are our bread, our sword
> You help us cross the ford
> In life's big river
> You sent mankind your Son
> To save us every one
> Now let us praise – have fun!
> Cheers to the Giver.

Derrick was playing air guitar at the front. His All Stars band, three of whom had turned up, compensated for imprecision with volume. A congregation of sorts had gathered, drawn more by the advertised free coffee and cakes than by any thought of spiritual sustenance. They had been issued with whistles, tambourines, rattles. Fugitive Matt had retreated to the organ loft.

The churchwarden, Georgina Brack, was on the visitor information table and was sitting out this particular masterpiece. Her friend Antonia – known as Beetle – had been jiggling her bottom and bouncing from foot to foot.

'You do look a fool, Beetle,' said Mrs Brack.

'At least I'm trying,' said Beetle. The nickname was a variation on Ant, short for Antonia.

'You're holding that tambourine as if it were a poppadum.'

Beetle gave it a shake. 'Better?'

'Not much.'

Another chorus of clapping and 'Jesus Christ!' ended. Petroc stepped to his microphone and said 'Wow!' He added: 'Now, folks, if we can just offer a moment of prayer before I say a few words. Then a last song. Then coffee.' Congregants were instructed to hold hands with their neighbours. They were urged to pray – for commuters, for Christians in a flyblown corner of Indonesia and, last, for anyone fleeing injustice. This was followed by a 'pulpit point' talk of less than a minute. Petroc, in a creased clerical shirt, told them: 'We all overdo it sometimes. I happen to smoke. I know I shouldn't. But I do it well away from others, so they are not hurt by passive smoking. The same can't be said for casual sex. Sorry, didn't mean to make you jump this early in the day. But sleeping around is harmful – you or the other person is likely to be upset. It's selfish. Cruel. And hey, if the other person is married or going steady. Come on. You'll be causing social damage. That's not cool. It's not Christian. End of sermon! Now, how about a song before breakfast? Derrick and his All Stars here have a number for us. What is it, Del?'

'*He's Got the Whole World in His Hands*, Petroc.'

'Indeed He has, Derrick. Indeed He has.'

MEARS bought two tickets for the charity ball. It had become an annual knees-up on the night of the State Opening of Parliament. MPs and peers would doll themselves up and have a jolly in Westminster Hall with a live band, proceeds going to a good cause.

Tickets were a hundred pounds a pop and Mears had always left that sort of thing to the Bryces and Mike Branton-Days of this world – Branton-Day, the Sussex smoothie with the perfect life. This year would be different. This year he had felt a tingle in his fingers, a sensation that would be recognised by Lotharios but was alien to Leslie Mears. It was the inclination, the readiness, the *desire* to spend money. He would have a beauty at his side and pearled wine in his belly. He would be a player, a personality!

Mears touched the tickets, running a chewed forefinger over their raised, italic lettering. 'The House of Commons Commission invites Mr Leslie Mears and Miss Olga Zolnerova' – the names had been added in exquisite handwriting – 'to the Annual Charity Ball, Westminster Hall; Black Tie, Ballgowns, Decorations; Champagne Seven O'Clock; Dancing to The Palpitations; Carriages Midnight.'

The Palpitations? They would surely have gleaming cornets and offer slinky rhythms. Mears's moustache twitched as he contemplated the hot dinner that would be laid before him and Olga. Would it be guinea fowl? He did not mind saying he was partial to the breast and succulent thighs of guinea fowl, particularly if served with gravy and Parmentier potatoes. Thinking about it made his juices run.

He left the tickets on the narrow table in his Pimlico kitchenette. Olga would see them when she eventually rose and made herself coffee. Mears saw little of his new flatmate and wished it could be more, though of course she was busy at the Thought Foundation. It had been Bryce who had fixed it all up. Bryce's acquaintance Dymock had said there was this Russian secretary who needed digs and would pay cash. Bryce knew Mears had a spare room and was always looking for a little extra money – if it was cash, even better. Olga kept irregular hours but she was self-contained. Nor did she seem to mind that Mears watched her closely when they were in the flat. His attentiveness balanced Dymock's post-coital coldness.

Before bustling off to the Commons, Mears left a short note beside the tickets. It expressed the hope that the ball would be fun and that Olga would permit him to buy her a dress. The prime minister always made a short speech at the ball so Olga would meet important people. The food would be tasty and the band lively. He thought about signing the note with a small kiss but desisted. He settled for imagining Olga in a lovely gown, twirling in the moonlight in the shadow of Big Ben, rewarding him with a smile.

Olga rose two hours later. Dishevelled, cupping a black coffee in her hands, she was still sore where Dymock's straps had bit into her. She knew better than to complain – in her world, that was men for you. Dymock was her master, but she hoped he might eventually care for her, for then he might stop hurting her.

She read Mears's note while sitting on the kitchenette stool. A black-tie dance? She had known such things in stories. She decided it would be – was the word 'fun'? No, the word was 'wonderful'! She would enjoy finding a pretty dress, if Les-uh-lee was sure he was happy to pay. He had a terrible moustache, smelly feet and did keep looking at her like a dog gazing at raw liver, but he was easy to control. And the ball invitation might irk Augustus.

MEARS waddled along the pavement, pushing himself to cover a paving stone with each step. Good for the avoirdupois, he had been told. His briefcase bulged with paperwork and bashed his right leg in the wind. Autumn leaves squelched under his not entirely leather shoes. With his left hand he held on to the trilby he had recently affected in the hope it would lend him panache. Bryce wanted him to become more of a 'character'. It did not matter if one was criticised, said Bryce. It mattered simply to be noticed. A backbencher helped his chance of winning committee elections if he was a figure of chit-chat. Hence the hat.

Turning into Smith Square and passing the former church of St John's, Mears bit on his moustache and pondered recent events.

Dismissal from the frontbench is brutal but Westminster has ways to alleviate the pain. The victim will be treated with initial sympathy and can expect to catch the Speaker's eye easily for a few weeks. Gracious words are bestowed by opponents. They write notes of commiseration, signed 'best', or some such untruth. Mears had received several such messages. The Leader of the House, Eleanor Haye, had been among the first, lifelessly calling his return to the backbenches 'welcome news for those of us who value a lively Chamber'. There had been a card from Lionel Moss, one of the House's greedier bees. 'Can you come and speak to my builders?' he asked. Moss, an inveterate greaser with a ridiculous hair weave, ran the all-party group on housebuilding and organised annual fact-finding trips to the Algarve and Costa del Sol. 'I am sure they'd be interested to hear your views about what a future Government might do about land release. I can promise you a good lunch and a reasonably interesting crowd.' Lies. Both would be interminably dreary but they might help Mears's campaign for the select committee chairmanship.

On his first appearance in the House after his downfall, Mears had been greeted by 'hear hears' and pats on the back. He blushed as he should. Humility after a ghastly comeuppance: this was required. There had even been a tribute from the Local Administration Minister whom Mears had often attacked. Though she thought Mears verminous, she praised the fallen warrior as 'a conviction politician who was always courteous in our private dealings'.

He scuttled past Millbank and entered the palace by the House of Lords entrance, offering a 'How do' to the policeman and receiving a 'Good morning, my lord' for his troubles. My lord! One day, maybe. Even so, it was good to be grovelled to by coppers. Yes! He was still in the swim, still in with a nibble of a chance. Mears felt emboldened, perkier than for days.

Westminster's compliments to political demotees were

58

liturgical proprieties, the varnish of old. He had received a letter of thanks from the very party leader he had besmirched. It thanked Mears for his 'contribution towards making us again an essential force in British politics' and for his 'continuing commitment to our movement whose constituency party will, I know, value his loyalty'. These ostensibly warm words were sent to Mears's constituency newspaper. Its readers would see that there existed between the two statesmen a state of harmony. Privately it would be understood that the words 'value his loyalty' carried a hint. If he caused trouble for the party leadership he would be deselected as the party's candidate at the next general election.

He had been offered various little jobs. The point of this exercise was to keep a sackee out of the bars of Westminster, where he or she might fall into bad company and start plotting. So it was that he found himself invited by the chairman of the all-party group on climate change (an ally of the Leader) to join a delegation to the Maldives in early January. A letter said that 'the workload should be pretty light, allowing us at least four days on the beach'. He had also been asked to lend his 'celebrated expertise' to a panel restocking the House's wine cellars. 'Celebrated expertise', indeed! The cheeky sods.

'Your life could be a round of wine tastings and foreign freebies,' said Bryce later that morning. Bryce had been doing his rounds and they included a courtesy call on Mears, just to see how the old sausage was frying.

'Blatant bribes,' snorted Mears.

'Of course,' said Bryce. 'But we must use these approaches to help your committee chairmanship campaign. I bet they're still buzzing up to you in the tea room, aren't they? Still wanting to see how you're coping.'

'Yes.'

'They know it may happen to them one day and they hope that if they show kindness, it will be remembered.'

'The frauds.'

'Of course,' said Bryce. 'Everything done here has a motive. Cultivate these new acquaintances. You do realise that if you win this select committee job, it puts you in the running?'

'The running for what?'

'Oh,' said Bryce, looking out of the window, 'things.'

After a pause, Mears said: 'Mr Speaker can't last much longer, I suppose.'

'My boy, you are a mind reader.'

'What do you mean?' said Mears.

'Well why not?'

'What do you mean?' persisted Mears.

'Don't repeat yourself.'

'What do you mean?'

'Leslie, have you never thought of seeking the Chair?'

Of course he had. Every MP, at some point, has a little fantasy, a degustation, rolling round the mouth the imagined flavour of Speakerly power. It was the same with the premiership. Even the feeblest backbencher has a distant fancy he or she could do the job. 'There are others better qualified,' said Mears.

'A select committee chairmanship will give you position.'

'Other people have been positioning.'

'No doubt they have. That nonentity Tewk, for instance.' Deputy Speaker Tewk was one of life's number twos, as the saying went. 'But why should we want them?'

'We?'

'The Government. Dear heart, Speaker Aldred has perhaps a few months left before he croaks. He can barely remember anyone's name. He's even more shaky than the Foreign Secretary.' The Foreign Secretary had just been photographed at the American ambassador's Thanksgiving drinks, one eye closed, the better to focus. Bryce continued: 'Aldred is becoming a joke. When that happens, Parliament becomes a joke.'

'Which should suit you lot.'

'The Commons is a nuisance at present but we are unlikely to win the next election. It will suit us to have a strong Parliament to make life itchy for a new Government. A vigorous Speaker is in our interest, particularly one who thinks the Leader of the Opposition, likely to become prime minister, is a schmoozing tosspot. First we land this select committee chairmanship. Then we eye the Speakership. A Speaker is freed of his party ties. You could never be deselected by your revolting local party sweats if you were Speaker.'

After a pause Mears said: 'It was "schmoozing bimbo", actually.' But he was speaking to an empty hovel. Bryce had left the room. There was only so much a man could take of the smell of dead mouse.

SPECULATION about the airline-office attack would once have been limited to newspapers and the broadcasters, with all their caution. Social media had no such filters. Some commentators were convinced the attack was racist. Others were delighted by that thought, saying 'the Muslims deserved it' – and worse. A small crowd took up camp in Whitehall opposite Downing Street to tell the Prime Minister to catch the 'hate criminal' responsible for the attack. Further up Whitehall, a more restrained group protested against forced marriages. Reporters interviewed angry supporters of Pakistan but balanced this with reports about the practice of involuntary arranged marriages, which was understood to have provoked Sunday's dramatic events in Victoria Street. The more everyone talked, the more tempers frayed.

ONCE a week, late-afternoon communion was held in the Undercroft chapel at Westminster. It began with a silence – mourning the truths that perish in politics, Ross told himself. He stood over the kneeling faithful. Here was God's stream, trickling below his fingers. To dispense the wafers and wine, even after all these years, stilled him. All the communicants saw were his toecaps and his fingertips pinching either side of the wafer. All he saw of them was a nape of neck, palms turned upwards, beggars before God.

'The body of Christ.' Ross saw the older ones shuffle forward, slow to kneel. He saw dandruff and worn patches on jacket shoulders. He saw humans needy, perplexed, struggling to hold the line. Some names he knew. 'The body of Christ.' This one, for instance. Jean. Scottish. A genteel bun. She had once come to him and sought confession, rare in the C of E. She had given herself to a man who had not loved her. She wanted help to forgive him.

Here was a surgical dressing on the back of a hand. Though we are many, though we teeter towards death, we are one in the swell of hymn and prayer, preparing to join the regiment of the dead. In the beginning was the Word and after that came decay. Though we will die, others will live. The end will come only when all witness withers.

When Andrew was small and would come up for a blessing, Ross sometimes realised only halfway through the words who the boy was. 'Bless this thy child, O Lord.' Whose child? His own? Hardly. Parents were fellow recruits, as much children of God as the rest in the ranks of souls. As we age we learn how frightened our parents must have been.

After the service, Mates, at the entrance to the crypt, said: 'Thank you, sir.'

'Mates.' Mates with his Guardsman's face. Mates the doorkeeper. Mates the worried husband. His Christian name was Walter.

'My wife, sir. Phyllis.' The old soldier gestured proudly to a frail woman with the purest, pale skin. She was the one with the surgical dressing on the back of her hand.

'Hello, vicar. He's told me all about you.'

'Mrs Mates. You have not been well.'

'I had to come up today for tests at St Thomas's so I came and found Walter afterwards. We thought we'd come to the service. We don't go as often as I'd like. Our local church has gone all clappy.'

'I am glad you came. I hope the tests bring good news.'

'They won't. But you have to let the doctors try. They're so young and keen.'

'We all were once, Mrs Mates.'

'Thank you again, sir.' Mates's tobaccoey voice gave the hint of a crack. He took Phyllis's arm. In *O Jesus I Have Promised*, the melody moves down a gear – a small car meeting a hill. It lasts a couple of lines:'I shall not fear the battle, if thou art by my side' in the first verse, and in the final one, 'O guide me, call me, draw me, uphold me to the end.' Ross saw Mates help his dying wife up the Undercroft steps, upholding her to the end.

PETROC had asked his parochial church council to attend an emergency meeting that evening. The message naturally ignited gossip among the regulars. They speculated that the new vicar had a money problem, maybe something to do with the accounts. The diminutive Beetle, who at once rang churchwarden Georgina Brack, said:'Maybe he's going to tell us he's gay.'

The widow Brack told her not to be so silly. It was more likely to be about that intruder on Sunday. She firmly told her friend Beetle:'I felt sorry for the young man. The police have not been the same since they started to carry machine guns.'

By the time the ladies arrived at the church of Alleluia Jesus!, Petroc had arranged chairs in a horseshoe pattern. On a table in the middle he had placed a lemon drizzle cake and a jumbo bottle of cola. 'Thank you for coming,' he said, walking into the horseshoe. Muscular Derrick Banks was in situ, as were a few others, among them Jean. She had been glad to have an excuse to leave her bedsit for a while.

'We will start with a prayer,' said Petroc. Derrick, seizing the nearest limb, almost pulled Mrs Brack's arm out of its socket. Jean longed for someone to hold her hand. Prayers completed, Petroc said: 'I have called this meeting because you are the custodians of this church. You are its parliament, its mini synod.'

'Puh!' snorted Derrick. He mistrusted hierarchies.

'Has something happened?' asked Mrs Brack.

'Yes, something has happened. Something unnerving but potentially exciting. A moment of discovery.'

'Told you,' hissed Beetle, mouthing the word 'poof'.

Petroc continued: 'We are a community bound more by faith than rules. In its earliest days the Church took in refugees. The first Christians met in secret. They feared that knock on the door by a Roman fist. They were, in the narrow sense, illegal.'

'Are we about to be raided?' said Derrick. His t-shirt showed off tattoos – a blue anchor on each forearm – and a pair of pumped nipples. He chewed spearmint gum.

'Though we render to Caesar what is Caesar's, there is a role in faith for dissent,' said Petroc. 'I have been reading the old Book of Common Prayer. Not my usual, OK, but it has some good lines. It tells us to respect the laws of the land but also to obey the "king of kings, Lord of lords"…'

'"The only ruler of princes",' said Georgina Brack, from memory. It brought a glow to her face. 'Have we broken the law, Petroc?'

'I don't think so, but I may not have helped it exactly. Will you all please once more close your eyes?' Petroc urged them to pray for prisoners of conscience and for wisdom for those in authority. God was, in the old words, our 'Advocate and Mediator', our stay in times of need. While speaking, Petroc beckoned at the vestry.

When they opened their eyes, Matt was beside Petroc. How skinny and hairless he looked, a runty mongrel. 'It's that boy,' hissed Beetle.

'What's he doing here?' asked Derrick. 'The police are looking for you, young man.'

'Funny eyebrow,' said Beetle.

'If we can just hear him speak,' said Petroc.

Derrick said: 'They're even offering a reward. I said I didn't know anything.'

'And you didn't,' said Petroc.

'OK, so my name is Matt,' said the youngster. 'I am sorry to be a trouble to you.' He fiddled with the cuffs of his hoodie. 'I hid here so the police wouldn't catch me. They thought I ran out the back but I just hid.'

'I thought so,' said Beetle.

'The police can be pretty heavy these days. And the Muslims. Thank you for not giving me away,' said Matt. He spoke these last words directly to Derrick. 'Appreciate it.'

'I didn't know you were here!' said Derrick.

'Matt has a question,' said Petroc.

'What is it?' said Mrs Brack.

'Shout it out,' said Derrick. 'Most of us are a bit deaf.'

Matt said: 'Can I stay in your church? Can I stay here for a couple of days while I sort myself out? Please. I forgot to say that. Please.' Petroc nodded approval.

'A couple of days?' said Derrick.

Petroc intervened. 'Young Matt fears he will be mistreated by the police. He fears others in the community. This young man is asking us for the ancient gifts of sanctuary and forgiveness.'

Georgina Brack asked Petroc: 'How long have you known?'

'I called this meeting as early as I felt it was safe to do so. I could have telephoned the police but I thought I should consult you first. Protecting this young man will not make us popular, but does that make it wrong? I need to talk to the diocese but it is up to you, as a body, to decide. Matt, tell them about Bashirah.'

Matt spoke briefly about his girlfriend and how her father was forcing her to find a Muslim husband. Derrick became indignant, saying: 'I don't blame you, lad. Disgraceful behaviour by that father.' Beetle remained a bundle of fidgets.

'We defend the vulnerable,' said Petroc.

The sermons he would give! He would preach on the threat at Christendom's gates. He would attack the values that enslaved girls. The brawny boys from the local estate, lads who until now had thought the Church limp: did they want their future daughters muzzled? Were their sisters to be bartered, veiled, strapped into airliners as cargo for foreign husbands? How was it manly to buy a wife? A real guy won his woman by love and respect. These estate lads were the ones whose streets could soon echo to the muezzin. Church bells. Let that be the English way. Be proud: our Church taking the lead, speaking up for our way of life. Christian freedoms needed defending. Enough inertia! Let young British Christians look to their faith foundations, to their culture's crumbling battlements.

'You all right, vicar?' said Derrick.

'Sorry. Daydreaming. Matt, you must promise you will behave. No drugs. No disrespect.'

'OK, Father.'

'And if you go on calling me that, the police will think I really am your dad.'

'You might as well be,' said the boy.

'Do we have a decision?' asked Petroc. They did. Matt was staying.

Petroc poured the cola into cups and distributed it with offers of cake. It was, said Petroc, as the early Christians would have done it – a supper swallowed in trepidation. Almost everyone was excited, if wary. Petroc's whole being tingled.

'Quite a day,' said Georgina Brack on the walk away from the church.

'He looks like a mugger,' grumbled Beetle. 'I'm only surprised the eyebrow wasn't pierced.'

'It's the modern world, dear, and I suppose that is where we need our Church to be.'

They passed a police incident board. It restated, Beetle noticed, the reward for information about the airline-office attack. There was an easily remembered telephone number.

BY the time Ross got home (after an agreeably liquid reception given by a substance-abuse charity) he found Petroc had made a fire in the drawing room. He had bought a bag of anthracite cheaply from a market stallholder. The draw on the chimney was unexpectedly good and the fire blazed.

A thick package awaited Ross. It had been pushed through the Base Camp letterbox by a courier and contained a dossier marked 'Greenhill–Chundrigar Ceremony Planning'. A cover note, handwritten with a flourish by Mrs Greenhill on vellum paper, explained that this folder would 'prove helpful to the Working Party'. Ross appeared in the index as 'Religion Provider'. A swirling turquoise postscript read: 'Don't seem to have email address for you. Mobile number/Facebook page/Twitter? Perhaps your secretary could assist.'

Ross made the call himself, hardly expecting it to be answered at this supper hour. Mrs Greenhill's personal assistant swiftly connected him to the fuchsia one. 'I don't have a computer here,' he told her.

'No computer? Good God. Goodness me, I should say.'

Her oath had put him at a small advantage. Ross said: 'I wonder if it might be possible for me to see Nettle and her young man.' Ross continued: 'I will be saying a few words at the service before we send Nettle and her husband into the world. I always like to spend a small amount of time with the couple beforehand.'

'He's still in India. There is a delay on the visa. But you could see Nettle on her own, I suppose.'

'Next Monday afternoon,' said Ross. 'Might that work for Nettle?'

'I'll tell her,' said Mrs Greenhill. 'She won't be doing anything except eating too many chocolates. Shall we say 15.30?'

'Er, yes, OK. Toodle pip.'

Toodle pip? Mrs Greenhill shuddered.

Ross put down the telephone with relief and extracted the whisky bottle while humming *Gracious Spirit, Holy Ghost*. A scotch in front of a real fire. Bliss. Petroc was dozing in the opposite chair and Ross himself soon drifted off while reading the Greenhill dossier. His father's prayer book was on the table beside his chair.

It was almost nine o'clock when the silence was shattered by the telephone. Ross awoke with such a start that he knocked the side table and the prayer book fell. He stumped over to the phone and his mood was not helped when he heard that the caller was a cold-call salesman from an insurance company, based by the sound of it in Calcutta. Petroc, stirring, laughed at Ross's indignation at the uninvited call.

'What's that smell?' asked Petroc.

'Smell?'

'Oh no, Tom, it's a book in the fire.'

'My prayer book!' The little, leather-bound book had indeed fallen from the table into the edge of Petroc's fire. Both men stared at it for a second, helpless.

'Have we any tongs?' asked Petroc.

'No.'

'I'll get some water.' Petroc was about to rush to the kitchen when Ross told him there was no time. The book's precious pages were about to catch. Ross plunged his right hand into the fire, retrieving the book and dropping it on the floor where he could smother it and stop it burning.

'Well done, Tom! Are you all right?'

Ross inspected his hand. It barely hurt at first. Soon it started to sting and throb. 'Water,' said Petroc. 'We must plunge it in water.' He led Ross to the kitchen and ran a sinkful. Ross winced as his hand touched the water. The burn was not too grave – the flesh had barely blistered yet the pain was increasing. His sleeve was smoking.

'Is the book OK?'

'You saved it, Tom. Well done, mate! Man of action!'

Ross refused to go to the hospital – the emergency department at this time of night was 'full of drunks'. Petroc smeared butter on the wound and gave Ross painkillers. With his intake of hooch they should soon knock him out.

'Thank you,' said Ross. 'Decent of you. And I never asked. How did your meeting go?'

Petroc reported that the sanctuary plan had been approved. 'Are you sure this is entirely wise?' asked Ross.

To which the answer was no. It was a punt, a leap. Petroc pulled on a cigarette. He smoked like a gambler throwing banknotes under a bookie's grille. 'What will Calvert say?' said Ross. 'There'll be the most fearful stink.'

Petroc exhaled. A shaft of smoke shot horizontally from his lips. 'Yeah.' He grinned.

5

Wednesday

PETROC rose at dawn. Through the night he had been wormed by doubt. Should he ring the police anonymously and tell them the boy was in the church? Tell Matt to get lost? Or stand firm and accept the consequences, which might mean loss of incumbency? Things were clearer once he had washed his face and dressed and settled himself with a coffee and a dawn smoke. One of Base Camp's cats jumped on his lap. Its purring settled him. An hour later he set out for the church and let himself in using the key.

'Matt! Where are you?'

A voice answered but it did not belong to the boy. A woman had walked through the unlocked door. 'My name's Lin, actually, and I'm a reporter from the *Standard*,' she said, 'but it is Matt I have come about. We had a call from one of our readers. Any chance of an interview? Are you the vicar? Mr Stone, isn't it? Mind if I grab a picture?' And she took one just as Petroc was saying 'no', he didn't mind. The photograph made him look baffled and furtive, his mouth drawn into an O.

HIGH above the Herefordshire church, a vole wriggled in the beak of a buzzard. Only instinct made the tiny rodent resist. Had it possessed greater powers of reason it might have ceased its struggle and accepted a mundane death this Wednesday morning. There its story might have ceased had a sparrowhawk at that point not attacked the buzzard. In the mêlée the buzzard dropped its lunch and the vole plunged from a great height, legs splaying as it fell. It landed on the airman's grave. That should have been an end to the matter. Gravity should have completed the buzzard's neglected business but the vole landed as though on a mattress of feathers. It accepted its reprieve with casual ingratitude, shaking an ear and scuttling off the tombstone – straight into the jaws of a Sealyham terrier.

Having devoured his elevenses, a happy Barney returned to his chores. Happenstance, or whatever it had been, had rewarded him again.

MEARS'S own mid-morning coffee and slice of Battenberg arrived on a tray. 'Stick it over there,' he told Jean. She was lowering the tray when a kerfuffle began in the outer office.

'Les-uh-lee!' halloed a woman. One of the researchers could be heard telling the woman she could not see Mr Mears without an appointment. 'Les-uh-lee!' Olga, ignoring the researcher, bounced into Mears's office, shopping bags on both arms. Her cheeks burned with that triumphant colour women develop when they have been shopping and have made a kill.

'Olga, how did you get in?'

'Bryce was in a taxi on Oxford Street and saw me. He gave me a ride and we just swooshed – is that the right word, yes? – we swooshed past the policeman on the gates and he did not stop us. I got a dress!' She saw Jean. 'Oh, hello.' Jean clutched the empty tray to her front and left in silence. Olga continued: 'I got such a dress! It is very pretty and not so expensive. Shall I show you?'

'What, here?' said Mears. He had rather been looking forward to his Battenberg cake.

'Maybe I keep for surprise,' said Olga.

'Bit tricky here, really,' said Mears. 'The staff.'

'OK,' said Olga. Sweetly earnest, she looked at him intently and asked: 'How is it going? Your campaign, Les-uh-lee, will you win? You will be very famous soon, yes?'

'Well . . .' said Mears.

'Tha's great, tha's great!' cried Olga. 'Omigod, Oxford Street? So busy! The crowds were crazy.' She spotted the Battenberg and examined it as an antiques collector might inspect a trinket, looking for hallmarks. She took a bite, liked it, and devoured the entire slice. Mears hoped he did not betray his sense of loss, though he feared that his moustache had possibly sagged.

'Did my pass arrive?' asked Olga.

'Yes,' said Mears. 'This morning. You now have the run of the Palace of Westminster so there will be no need for Bryce to smuggle you past the checkpoint. I had to pull a bit of a fast one to get it, mind.'

'Pull fast one?'

'A white lie. Harmless untruth. My quota for staff passes is at its limit, you see. So I had to tell them that we were partners.'

'Partners?'

'Husband, wife. Lovers. That sort of thing.' Olga licked Battenberg crumbs off her fingertips. She shrugged. 'You don't mind?' said Mears. He looked at her keenly.

'I get a pass.' She yawned and stretched her arms, thus arching her back, accentuating her breasts. Dymock had been hassling her to get a parliamentary pass. He said it was one of the reasons he had set up the flat-share through Bryce in the first place. Every day he would ask how her quest for a pass was going. Now she would have something to show him. Perhaps he would tell her she had been a good girl and would be kinder to her. She looked at Mears matter-of-factly and said: 'I need taxi to get these bags home. Do you have ten pounds, please, Les-uh-lee?'

★

'YOU'VE got some text messages, Father.'

'Oh yes.' Petroc's mobile was thick with them, mostly from journalists. They must have seen his mobile number on the church's website. The *Standard* had gone big with the story, complete with a picture of Petroc saying 'oh'.

Matt's sister had been busy on the internet once she heard that his cover was blown. She started a Facebook page which reported that Matt had taken shelter at the Church of Alleluia Jesus! (map provided) and that he was 'holding out for justice, thanks to local vicar Petroc Stone who is really cool'. There were photographs of Petroc from Sunday night's television interview. A #SanctuaryMatt Twitter account directed readers to the Facebook page and similar sites that were soon supporting Matt. Photographs of Bashirah were prominent and an emotive account of forced-marriage kidnapping had been written by a Muslim girl. 'We don't want to upset our families but they leave us no alternative,' she wrote. 'New-generation British Muslims demand respect from our Asian brothers and fathers. No more domestic rape. Airlines should not agree to fly us to these enslaving marriage ceremonies without first checking that we go willingly.' People left messages of support for 'this brave English boy Matt whose only crime was to fall in love with a beautiful British–Asian girl'. The website was adorned with photographs of Gandhi, Martin Luther King and stills from a recent Hollywood version of *Romeo and Juliet*. The story was soon trending. Prominent comedians promoted it, as did an England football player who was an ambassador for the Government campaign against human trafficking. It also attracted Twitter follows from the English Patriotic League, better known for skinhead violence than any Wildean repartee.

A BRISK fist bashed on the church's side door near the vestry. Three officers, two of them male: 'Police!' Georgina Brack answered it. She had been doing some cleaning and was wearing her Marigolds.

'We've had a report you are sheltering a suspected terrorist.'

'Would you like to talk to our pastor?'

'I'm here,' said Petroc, appearing behind her.

'You in charge?'

'You can talk to me.'

'We've had a report . . .'

'It's true,' said Petroc.

' . . . from a member of the public.'

'Yes,' said Petroc.

'What's true?' asked the police.

Petroc said: 'We are sheltering a vulnerable young man who drove his car into the airline office on Victoria Street. He himself is a victim of aggression.'

'Hand him over.'

'That I cannot do. But you are welcome to enter our church and talk to him.'

'Provided you leave those weapons outside,' said Georgina Brack, pointing at them with her yellow gloves.

'Yes,' said Petroc. 'I'm afraid we cannot have guns on sacred ground.'

'Is the suspect armed?'

'Certainly not!' snorted the widow Brack. 'We wouldn't have admitted him if he had been, would we?'

One of the police officers pointed a machine gun at Petroc but the priest took no obvious notice. He had been threatened in the past by druggies waving needles, by pimps, by crazies. The modern curate sees a lot of life. The police agreed that two of them would enter the church, unarmed, while the third remained outside with the firepower.

Petroc said: 'Please remember this is a church and it will be respected as such. It is not a police interrogation room.'

'We can see it's a church, sir.'

'The young man is called Matt and he is our guest. I will advise him to listen to what you say. He is frightened but he has been open with us and I see no reason he should not be equally open with you, provided you conduct yourselves properly.' Petroc noticed that one of the officers was holding up a mobile telephone and was filming the moment.

'Has he admitted the crime?' asked the policewoman. She never liked men with beards and this one smelled of tobacco.

'He has told us what he has done and he understands there may be consequences,' said Petroc. 'He has asked us for the holy tradition of sanctuary. We believe it is our right to insist that our consecrated ground be respected. I give you a solemn undertaking we will not deceive you. But we seek your equally solemn undertaking that you will not use force to remove Matt from this church against his will. We demand the same respect you would show a synagogue or mosque.'

The police hesitated.

'Do I have that undertaking?' repeated Petroc. 'I must have it before I can honestly welcome you. Will you respect our faith identity? As you are filming this, perhaps you can also film your response to my question.'

'Deal,' said one of the policemen. The paperwork with any infringement of cultural rights was horrendous.

'Good,' said Petroc. 'Welcome to Alleluia Jesus!'

'Would you like a cup of tea while you wait with your guns?' Mrs Brack asked the policewoman. 'And a custard cream? Always a good idea, don't you think? What was your name again, dear?'

The first protestors arrived a couple of hours later. They were peaceful, taking up position in the road outside the church.

CALVERT was back, full of snap. Ross, middayish, bumped into him outside the Commons. Sunlight glinted off a single earring.

'Just the man I wanted!' said Calvert. He moved to shake Ross's right hand but Ross resisted. The burns on his hand were still sore.

'Oh, hello. How was the Lake District?'

'Great! Clears the head. You should try it.'

Ross ignored the dig. He said: 'Sorry to be elusive.'

'Rapid communications, Tom – *Certa Cito*.'

'You what?'

'Swift and sure. Motto of the Royal Corps of Signals. You'd never find them ignoring a message.'

'No.'

'Now, meeting! Let me knock a hole into my schedule.' He produced an electronic diary. 'One o'clock?'

'Today?' Ross, appalled, was unable to think of an excuse. He could hardly admit he was hoping to be sinking a schooner of something sherryish in the Strangers' Bar at that hour.

'Great!' said Calvert. With that he had yomped off to his next triumph.

Calvert's office in Comms Hub, as Church House's old press office had been renamed, had mushroom carpet, magnolia blinds, a modernist daub on the walls. The painting was almost entirely white except for a rip of episcopal purple. He was at a glass-topped desk when Ross was shown in by a casually dressed curate called Paul. Paul had called him 'Tom', had asked him if he 'wanted anything'. Ross was tempted to say 'a glass of chilled white, how kind' but resisted. Paul smelled of TCP.

Calvert guided Ross to two chairs in the corner. They were heinously uncomfortable, quite the latest thing. 'This debate,' he said in his Mancunian sales-manager voice. 'I've prepared you an idiot's guide. Not that I'm calling you an idiot, ha ha.' He handed Ross a plastic folder. Paul re-entered the room to bring Calvert a mug of tea. 'Cheers,' said Calvert. Cheers? Did he mean to twist the knife?

Ross started to fantasise about inserting a corkscrew into a wine bottle, better still into Calvert's tongue and plucking it from its moorings. One good wrench and there would be silence. Calvert said: 'We had confirmation today that the debate will be chaired by Magnus Bacton. Media celebrity. Lawyer. As you'll know.' Ross didn't. 'And it's big news that Dymock is taking part. He had a choice between us or a seminar in New York and decided he couldn't face another flight across the pond so soon after his triumph at the Lincoln Center. You heard about that, I guess.'

Again, no, but Ross said: 'The man's an egomaniac.'

'When they think they only have one life, they get like that. Don't I always say that, Paul?'

'Yeah,' said Paul. 'By the way, Tony, Professor Dymock has asked you to some event at the National Portrait Gallery. Invitation arrived today.'

'Really?' said Calvert. He looked at Ross and tweaked his neck with a 'now there's a thing' gesture and double-clicked his tongue.

Ross started to leaf through Calvert's folder. The pages had headlines such as *OUR AIM* and *AUDIENCE PROFILE* and *PREPARE YOUR SOUNDBITES*. How much more effective St Luke could have been had he only prepared his soundbites. The Acts of the Apostles could have given the media suggested news lines, complete with a social media link and a number for his press officer. Missed opportunities. Foolish Luke.

'Do you Tweet?' asked Calvert.

'Not that I'm aware of,' said Ross.

'Might be useful, particularly at the moment.'

'What do you mean?'

'We can sometimes arrange covering fire through the evangelical network. It's likely the debate will be podcast. Instant opinion can guide reaction and neutralise early attacks. I sometimes think the Twitter network is very much what the early Church was.'

'Do you?'

'Jesus would have been brilliant at it. Hashtag Saviour.'

'It's a wonder He coped without it.'

Calvert was wearing a small collar and a short-sleeved shirt, not unlike those favoured by male nurses. The backs of his hands were unnaturally hairless. 'Unfortunately Bishop Derek won't be able to attend the debate because he'll be on a mission in the Maldives,' said Calvert, 'but he has asked me to talk you through this assignment and impress on you its importance to our mission.'

'The Maldives?'

'I knooooow,' said Calvert. 'Great for the Airmiles! But back to the debate.'

'I'm not much good at debates. I haven't said I'll do it.'

'Modesty does you credit, Tom, but look, you went to a great university. An Oxford man. That's what they always say, isn't it? "Tom Ross? He's an Oxford man." And you're chaplain to the Speaker of the Commons and they spend all day debating. We need someone with your brain, Tom. I'd do it myself but I'm already involved as an online moderator.'

'So you'll be there on the platform.'

'I'll be on the web table. But I will need to maintain my objectivity. Perhaps you should check the lie of the land first. Have a look at the venue.'

'I don't think that'll help much.'

'Up to you, Tom. You're the boss. By the way, before you go, what do you make of Petroc Stone? Is he entirely stable?'

WHILE Ross was being monstered by Calvert, his mobile took another voicemail message, doomed never to be heard. 'Dad, it's Andrew. Look, I didn't handle that too well at Sunday lunch. Guess I should have put myself in your position a bit more. Give me a call sometime, though I know you're busy. Oh, and did Mum mention this equipment I have to buy? She said you were sending a cheque. That would be great. Thanks.'

★

DYMOCK liked to do one chat show a month. A television turn generated Thought Foundation membership applications and lecture bookings. His interviewer today was Maddy Fancy, a peroxide blonde whose jaunty show was brand leader in the teatime slot. Four days a week Maddy and her tongue stud and Goth nail varnish were paraded for the edification of the nation's microwaving classes. Dymock's bodyguards sat in the wings.

The studio clock reached ten minutes past the hour. 'Right, everyone,' whooped Maddy, with her generic butch-lass voice, 'time for our Ten at Ten interview!' Cheers from the studio crew. 'Our celebrity today is the Don of Doubt, top atheist Augustus Dymock! Great to have you here, Augustus. How's business?'

'Maddy, doubt is booming.'

'So I believe.'

'Not that word, please.'

'You never did, yourself? Believe?'

'What? In Father Christmas?'

Maddy Fancy received a blast in her ear from the show's editor. It would not do to upset the nation's youngsters.

'Religion,' she said. 'You know, God an' all that.'

'The idea that we are ruled by some extraterrestrial being – it's the stuff of *Star Wars*, Maddy. Fairytales.'

'Hey, I love Luke Skywalker. May the force be wiv ya! Okey-doke. You've kindly agreed to do Ten at Ten. Let's rock.'

'Shoot,' said Dymock.

The programme was being watched by Jean in her bedsit in Battersea. She had left the office early, pleading a headache. On her lap was a tray with two boiled eggs and some soldiers but she had little appetite. She had undone her bun. Her hair looked greyer when it was down, yet more girlish.

Olga's supper was a packet of cheese crisps, which she ate while waxing her legs. She, too, watched Dymock, half hoping he would make a fool of himself.

'OK, what was your first home?' said Maddy Fancy.

'A farm in Northern Ireland. We lived there until I was eight.'

'Your first memory?'

'I was going to say pigs having their throats cut by the local slaughter-man who was the church warden. But that will upset your viewers. I have an early memory of the wallpaper in my nanny's bedroom. I used to slip into her bed for a cuddle.'

'Ah,' said Maddy. 'You were close to your Nan?'

'My nanny, yes. Not my grandmother.'

'Nanny. Very la-di-dah. What makes you angry?'

'The religious authorities. Their lies infantilise the poor, robbing them of ambition.'

'Infantilise. Big word. Take it down, boys and girls. Next question: where did you last go on holiday?'

'Cuba.'

'Nice one. Favourite food?'

'Sushi.'

'Me too. Love it. Favourite joke?'

'The Church of England.'

'Ooh! Question seven: are you in a relationship and will you marry that person?'

'Well, I am indeed dating a beautiful young lady at present but it's complicated.'

'We understand,' said Maddy. 'Well, we don't actually. But we'd better not be too nosey.' She gave the camera a heavy wink and touched her biceps in a 'phwoarr' gesture. 'Three more questions. Favourite book?'

'Anything by me.'

'Worst thing about living in England?'

'The taxes.'

'Final question: what would be your ideal date?'

'My ideal date would be sitting on a mountain top, having ambrosia spooned into my mouth by a new lover, views stretching hundreds of miles while cherubs poured chilled lemon vodka into crystal goblets and a eunuch strummed a harp.'

'Sounds heaven.'

'Heaven does not exist, Maddy.'

'Folks, give him a hand. Augustus Dymock! And now over to Josh at the News Pod.'

Olga turned off the television. Lemon vodka had been what she and Dymock drank when they first made love. Yet why did he want a 'new lover'. Was he already bored of her? She continued waxing her legs, but the more she did so, the more she missed Moscow and a few tears fell.

TEATIME snorts at the Green Man had been necessary post-Calvert but Ross was back at Base Camp and sitting in the drawing room with his whisky decanter. Stainer's *Crucifixion* was blasting at high volume, Ross conducting it from his deep armchair. The throbbing in his right hand had abated a little.

In one of those 'ping' moments that can arise during sottishness, he remembered the other cheque he should have written: the five thousand pounds for Andrew. That boy must think money grew on compost. Ross scrawled a cheque in large letters and stuffed it into an envelope with a note saying: 'Here is your money for the so-called safety equipment. Don't drink it all at once!' Now where was Andrew's address? Somewhere upstairs. What an effort. It could wait until morning. He left the cheque on the drawing-room table.

'I'm back,' shouted Petroc. 'Want a cup of tea?' Ross was lost in *God So Loved the World*. Petroc repeated the question.

'Nah,' replied Ross over the din. 'I'll stick with this medicine.'

'You drink too much,' said Petroc, turning down the music. He threw his donkey jacket on the table.

'Oi, why did you do that?' said Ross.

'To talk some sense into you. Stop drinking so much.'

'You smoke.'

'It doesn't fuddle the brain.'

'Don't preach. We're off-duty.'

'I'm never off-duty, Tom. And what's this rubbish?' Petroc held up the Gyumpi meditations left by Mrs Greenhill.

'It was given to me by the mother of the bride.'

'This book has no place here.'

'All right, all right,' said Ross.

'No, it is not all right. Look at the price. I don't see how you can love the Book of Common Prayer yet tolerate this dross. Fifteen quid for a hundred pages of lies. We weaken ourselves by our tolerance. Fifteen quid for a hundred pages!' He threw the Gyumpi in the bin.

'You'd be happier if the book were longer?'

He sat down and groaned. 'Sorry, bad day.' He explained that Matt was all over the news. Ross did recall hearing something to that effect at the Green Man. He did not say that the source of the gossip was organist Mark. When Petroc had calmed a little, Ross mentioned Mrs Greenhill's demand for the Kama Sutra. 'You should have refused firmly to have anything to do with it,' snapped Petroc.

'These people have given a small fortune to the Speaker's charitable fund. They're having the reception in Speaker's House. I did the Anglican thing: compromise.'

'Interesting word, compromise. As a noun it means a meeting of two reasonable minds. As a verb it means to squander principles. As in "the minister was compromised". As in, Western culture was compromised by its overweening desire to be polite.'

'Don't be so molten.'

'Have some pride, Tom. Be jealous of our dignity. This couple will be marrying before God. The words chosen mean something.'

'Dignity in worship? You lot are always telling us that liturgy is an aesthetic falsehood, a block to true faith.'

'You can't let this shallow woman have the run of your church.'

'I agree with you! The trouble is I'm a hire, a locum, a by-the-hour man.' Ross fought against a whisky burp. 'The politicians run Westminster. The Church's authority is a dwindled brook.'

'So it will remain until we defend our beliefs. That's enough of that soul-rot for you tonight.' Petroc removed the decanter. 'I'm going to make you a cup of sweet tea. Then you are going to your bed.'

'Oh piss off.'

'No I will not. I am well used to dealing with drunks, usually with a great deal more to be sorry about than you.' Stainer was on to the Litany of the Passion, describing the denials before Calvary. Ross allowed himself to be shepherded to his pit. As Petroc steered him out of the room he retrieved his donkey jacket from the table. The coat caught the envelope containing Ross's cheque for Andrew. It fell to the floor under the table, out of sight.

BEFORE climbing between the sheets of his single bed, Mears liked to brush his hair. It was something he had been taught by his mother. His hairbrushes were now on the window ledge in the lavatory, Olga having commandeered most of the bathroom – and so much else of the flat. Postcards of Moscow, of Red Square and Izmailovsky Park cluttered the shelves. There was even one of Putin, idealised like a Soviet waxwork of old.

Mears could have complained, but a man of his age and dullness was in no position to negotiate with a pretty face. He stood at the mirror over the lavatory sink, an L motif sewn into the top pocket of his striped pyjamas, their top button fastened. Ten strokes of the hairbrush on the right, ten strokes on the left, a couple of dabs to his moustache. He angled his head to make sure that everything was in place and, finding that it was, headed for his bedroom. As he passed through the living room, Vladimir Putin seemed to pull a face.

At the same hour, in a well-appointed flat near Berkeley Square, Bryce poured himself a glass of chilled Chablis and sat by his green-shaded desk lamp. His silk kimono, jade with dancing dragons, matched a light application of avocado face-mask moisturiser. He had the number on auto-dial. One haricot fingertip touched the button. The call was answered at first ring. 'This is your political consultant,' said Bryce. 'I hear you were on the electric television earlier. Can't say I watched it, though I am sure you were masterly. I have mulled on your question and may have a solution. There is something called the Civic Regulations Bill, a dreary little vessel chugging through the Commons. It is mainly to do with the provision of lay-bys, the purchase of land for power substations and mandatory eviction procedures for strategic construction projects. Dreary but wide-ranging.'

'Go on,' said Augustus Dymock, who had himself retired to his bed, alone, with a signed copy of his autobiography.

'The parliamentary draughtsmen see no reason our proposal could not be amended to this Bill,' said Bryce. 'We could use a manoeuvre called a manuscript amendment. Good for ambushes. But we need a Speaker who would call the amendment.'

'It can't be long, from what I saw at his procession on Monday.'

'The Grim Reaper works at his own rate,' said Bryce. 'Aldred will go but we cannot be sure when. We can use the time, though. We can soften the ground.'

'How do you mean?'

Bryce said: 'We can mould opinion. Arrange seminars for the usual sheep. Plant a couple of prominent newspaper articles. Produce an opinion poll − fixed in the usual way. This church giving sanctuary to the airline-office lunatic is not helping their cause. Protests have started. Church ownership is becoming a legitimate debate. Let me arrange the parliamentary end. You do some presentational landscaping.'

6

A Church Under Siege

GEORGINA Brack came steaming into the vestry at the church of Alleluia Jesus!, Beetle in her wake. 'Some *frightful* little man tried to stop us coming in here,' said the widow. She blinked with corvid indignation.

'Oh?' said Petroc.

Beetle was hopping about, a sparrow beside the crow. 'He is wearing a day-glo jacket,' she said.

Mrs Brack continued: 'He says he is a policeman though he looks more like a car-park attendant. They are "expecting trouble" today. He has been told to stop people entering the church. I told him that he was not just expecting trouble – he had got it with me, there and then, unless he let me through.'

Beetle grinned. 'She gave it to him, all right.'

Mrs Brack continued: 'I told him the Commissioner of the Metropolitan police would be hearing from me and that I had recently played bridge with his mother.'

'Oh?' enquired Petroc.

'She was not a natural card player but she did make a very acceptable cheese straw. Now, where's the stowaway?'

'In the organ loft,' said Petroc. 'He is helping Mark tidy his music shelves.'

'Mark is talking to someone? Miracle,' said Beetle.

'We have flowers to arrange, Antonia,' said Mrs Brack. 'Make yourself useful and brew a pot of tea. I'm dry as a lizard.'

Jean, en route to the Commons, arrived with some floral displays. She was wearing a smart new bonnet which, with her bun, gave her a touch of Jemima Puddleduck. She had rather been hoping to catch Petroc on his own.

'You got past Checkpoint Charlie,' said Beetle.

'Well,' said Jean, 'a man did try to stop me but his heart did not seem in it.'

'Mrs B gave him a bollocking earlier.'

'Language, Antonia,' said Mrs Brack.

'Oh well done, Georgina,' said Jean. 'You are *good* at telling people off. It's a pity you aren't prime minister.'

Petroc stepped outside for a cigarette. Mrs Brack's car-park attendant was a community support officer, cap pushed to the back of his head. Protestors were arriving, middle-aged, sandaled men with dhoti trousers and hats that resembled Eccles cakes. They were soon augmented by a second, younger group in trainers, jeans, t-shirts and a mixture of baseball caps and prayer caps. These younger men carried placards saying 'Christian insult to ISLAM'.

'What's going on?' Petroc asked the community support officer.

'You from the church?'

'Yes.'

'I had some of your crowd on at me earlier.'

'Our ladies.'

'Right couple of woodpeckers. More frightening than this lot.' As he gestured at the crowd, one of its members started a slow, muezzin-style moan about the racist West insulting his religion, his lone voice occasionally joined by mutterings from various beards around him.

FOR twenty minutes every month, the Attorney-General and the Solicitor-General eased themselves on to the green leather of the

Treasury bench and responded to questions from the Commons. The Attorney was one of the pre-eminent egalitarians of her day, a daughter of the nobility who had been in the House since her flower-power youth. There had once been talk of her attaining the highest office but she lacked the charm and naked vulgarity required. The Solicitor was a demon for small print, punctilious in three-piece suits. There is a caste of lawyer who finds the partisanship of the House undignified. Such creatures find the Law, with its turrets and filigrees and penumbral alleys, more satisfying than the illogical emotions of popular politics. Such was the Solicitor.

Talk in the Chamber had been about amendments to the Magistrates Courts Bill, evidence in rape cases, perjury concerns at public inquiries. The Attorney coped with the more political matters. The Solicitor handled questions that required legalese.

'Topical Questions,' said Speaker Aldred, his voice no more than the swish of poplar branches in a summer breeze. There was little expectation of trouble. The duty Whip thought about resting his eyes. Members on the Order Paper were Plodders or Dignified Old Men. A Government supporter called Kendrick caught the Speaker's eye. Short, wiry, salted, he gripped the bench in front of him with two firm hands. Speaking without notes, he rocked the upper part of his body lightly to and fro.

'Thank you, Mr Speaker.' Was there a hint of the Valleys to his voice? It radiated an unsentimental impatience. 'Ministers will have heard of the attack on a Pakistani airline office in London. Is it true that the culprit has been granted sanctuary in an Anglican church not far from this Parliament? Are the authorities happy that a suspect may be hiding on consecrated premises? What is truly sacred here? A Victorian temple or the higher principle of the laws of the land?'

The Solicitor-General, hearing mention of legal principle, made a little move, his buttocks hovering above the bench, before the Attorney-General held out her hand. She rose slowly. 'This is a live operational matter for the police. We must avoid a running commentary, but the Hon Gentleman would not expect me to do anything other than defend the might and majesty of the Law.'

When the session ended, this Kendrick, who had asked the question, scurried to the terrace cafeteria to buy a tea. He did not like to eat at the cafeteria, finding its prices too high. In a modest, two-up-two-down beside a butcher's shop in some drenched village in Glamorgan there huddled a Mrs Kendrick and two wet-nosed infant Kendricks. It was not his intention that they should remain there forever. His parliamentary salary, along with the sums earned by his spouse from her supply teaching, would one day buy them an end-of-terrace house in Treherbert or even Ogmore-by-Sea. A tea would do him fine and he would return to his office to consume the egg sandwiches and two Conference pears he had placed in his lunchbox that morning at his lodgings in Croydon.

'Allow me,' said a honeyed voice.

'Sorry?'

'Please allow me to stand you that cup of tea, Tristan.'

'Oh. Thank you.' Kendrick knew who Bryce was, but they had not previously spoken.

'No,' said Bryce. 'Thank *you*.'

'For what?'

'For that excellent question to the Attorney.'

'I didn't see you in there.'

'I was watching the monitor. A good point. Not that you received a proper answer.'

'Does one ever?'

'As a Whip, I do hope not. But you are right, dear boy. This idea of sanctuary – outrageous.'

'Church sovereignty is something we need to look at,' said Kendrick, who had never been called 'dear boy' before – not even by that pederast of a Sunday-school teacher near Ebbw Vale.

'I wrote a Centre for Land Rights pamphlet last year. Didn't gain much attention.' They had made their way to the sugar and milk station. Kendrick was opening four sachets for his tea. 'I can send you a copy of it if you like. Sugar?'

'I won't, thank you. It rather overpowers a herbal infusion.'

'I might put in for a Westminster Hall debate, or maybe try a Ten-Minute Rule Bill.'

'About . . .'

'About land rights,' said Kendrick urgently. 'Land control, political command, the power of Parliament over the Church.' The words crunched in his mouth.

'Charming idea,' said Bryce.

'Well, thank you for the tea.'

'Pleasure.'

'I must away to my work.'

'You must. Your important work.'

ACROSS the limed ceiling of the country church porch loomed an angel's wings. Two broad shapes were joined by a head and two limbs. The shadow flapped erratically.

Even this late in the season, moths were drawn to the electric light bulb, which burst into action on a motion switch. With the uplighter shade, the insect's wings were magnified, creating the angelic effect. A vixen is not to understand such things. Having activated the light when she loped past the porch, the vixen shied away. A dead pheasant hung, floppy, in her jaw. She saw the dancing shadows and ran warily from this uncomprehended presence.

Inside, Theresa Ross did not notice. She came here to pray for her son, to placate her fears. The walls were filled with memorial slabs. What English country church was not a jumble of monuments? In the side chapel was a plaque acknowledging a squire's boy who died in Calcutta while serving the East India Company.

Another commemorated a farmer who distributed alms, a merchant lost at sea, a mother who died giving birth. Here were children of the village, offspring all. The village dead of the two world wars were marked, high and low alike, equal in memory. Death was here in the living Church. In the midst of life we are in death. Autumn's rot was infectious. Here was the border of a dank domain, decorated by hassocks and a dried-out geranium.

NUMBERS outside Petroc's church swelled slowly. There is not much point holding a protest if no one takes any notice – and the easiest way to create attention is to resort to bad behaviour. Parents long ago learned to ignore such tactics but western civilisation is a sucker for them. Agents of change are seldom obedient. The organiser of the protest outside the church understood this and his stooges resorted, first, to blocking the road outside the church. This caused traffic jams and a low level of police interference. Next there was an announcement of a hunger strike, the burning of an effigy of the Bishop of London, a street sermon by a rabble-rousing mullah, and a confected scuffle between two groups of young men.

Although the London nights were closing in, the crowd outside the church grew steadily, particularly in the evenings, most of all on Fridays when the mosques had finished their main worship for the week and sent busloads of men to the protest site to join the demonstration.

Petroc watched with concern. Derrick had taken to carrying a clipboard and his gait acquired a roll. He had recruited a couple of Armed Forces veterans and given them t-shirts saying 'Pew Patrol'. They included an almost toothless ex-Welsh Guardsman and a taciturn ex-submariner whose only sign of life had been the occasional twitch of his neck (discreet enough to evade detection by a minesweeper). Jean volunteered for an hour of pew-patrol duties. Derrick was wary with Jean. In services, at the sign of the peace, he did not embrace her as he did others. There was a tension to her that made him hesitate. Yet at least she did her stint. Beetle declined the chance of door rota, saying she had to take a niece to the zoo. 'At this time of year?' asked the widow Brack.

The late-duty officer outside the church was almost grateful when Mark arrived. Organist Mark, fresh from the Green Man, often practised late at night.

There were the usual simplistic hymns to prepare for Sunday. Once they were out of the way, he could let his fancy run: Bach's pedal-rooted *Passacaglia* and some Warlock. He was nearing the end of a Rawsthorne arrangement of *Pieds en l'Air* from *Capriol Suite* when he heard Matt climbing the organ-loft ladder. The Suite's discordant, accelerating chords filled the church with turmoil.

'Come to listen to some proper music, then? Warlock. Peter Warlock. An odd man but a musical genius.'

'Noisy, man, more like. What else did he write?'

'A few things. Sit down. I'll play you some more.'

'Why did they ever swap that sort of music for the modern stuff? Didn't the regulars complain? Didn't they say they preferred the old tunes?'

'Quite a few did but they were ignored. They complained that their culture was being abandoned. They were told they did not understand the young.'

'But I'm young and I like this old stuff.'

7

'Next Monday Afternoon'

CLICK went two pale fingers, clean as hospital tongs. 'Olga!' One of the digits summoned her. It was an impatient finger, a finger that knew its mind.

Dymock's personal quarters were on the same floor as the Thought Foundation's penthouse boardroom. The view made decoration superfluous. The area by the lifts was floor-to-ceiling mirrors, save two chairs where his bodyguards sat, examining their knuckles. This vestibule led to a hall vacant save for an orchid in a vase on a glass stand. The flower was changed every three days to ensure that it appeared never to age. Passing a rowing machine and parallel bars you reached the main living pod. Dymock permitted himself a leather armchair and a flock rug, so white it might almost have been assembled from his barber's trimmings. At a steel-and-rubber table were two hard chairs of latticed titanium. Halogen lights were set into both ceiling and floor. There were no paintings or clocks on the walls. The one concession to sentiment was a large photograph of a child with yellow curls and a squint. The room's lights were operated by vocal command, having been set to obey the timbre of Dymock himself and, at present, that of Olga too. The security engineer, when giving Olga vocal-access rights, had to programme a certain elasticity for her accent. Blinds would rise, fall, open and shut according to climatic conditions. Dymock need never be subjected to wrinkling rays.

'Olga!' The carpet was the same throughout, a taupey affair that betrayed few stains and was shampooed once a month using scent-free solution. Suede, wool and cotton were the dominant textiles. One of Dymock's fetishes – and it had to remain private, for was he not a man of logic and modernity? – was his aversion to synthetic fabrics.

Dymock was different from anything Olga had known. Back in Moscow there glowered, to this day, the thirsty knuckler who had ruled their drab family flat, dominating his women. She had accepted it until the week her mother died after a long illness.

Olga still sent money back to her father, for blood was thicker than vodka. The foreign ministry, where she worked, had fixed her a student-exchange visa in Britain and she had travelled light. Bryce – her contact – had introduced her first to Dymock, then had helped to arrange the room with Mears. Bryce belonged to the All Party Group on Russia and his interest in an exchange scheme was not entirely implausible.

'Olga!' Again the finger waggled. Dymock was in the lavatory area. He saw no logic in the bourgeois horror of seeing other people at their ablutions. The little throne was in the corner of the bedroom area. She rose from her desk and stretched her neck so that granules of sand could have dropped through her hourglass figure. The Thames lay below, its glint having faded to an afternoon sheen.

'Da?'

'When is Zac coming up?'

'About an hour. During his break.'

The lavatory flushed. Olga looked away. 'I want to check progress on the gallery party for my portrait unveiling,' said Dymock, 'and there are some other bits and bobs. Make sure Bryce is on the guest list.'

'Bits, bobs?'

'Small matters. Little things.' He came over to her, cleaning his hands on a bio-wipe, which he disposed of with care. 'Little things.' He placed his clean hands on the top part of the hour glass. 'And not so little things. Hmmmn.' Olga's doe-shaped nose twitched and she robotically went about the usual preparations.

HALF past three. Petroc had only dropped into Base Camp to collect some paperwork when the doorbell rang. 'Tom, can you get that?' he shouted. Another ring. 'Tom? Tom!' But Ross was out. Probably at the Green Man. 'Blast.' A drumroll of feet down the stairs. He could see the caller's shape on the other side. A yank on the door to open it was followed by 'Oh, hello.'

'Hello,' purred Nettle. 'I'm . . .'

'You're . . .'

'Nettle.'

'Of course you are.'

' . . . Greenhill.'

'Ah yes . . .'

'I was looking for . . .'

'Tom Ross?'

'Vicar.'

'He's not here,' said Petroc.

There came a husky 'oh'. A perfectly white tooth rested on a gorgeously plump lower lip. Her toes pigeoned and she twisted her hands together. 'It is Monday, isn't it?'

'Er, yeah. Was it something I can help with?' said Petroc.

'I don't know.' The broad hat accentuated her shyness. She was now digging her fingers into the sleeve end of her pale pink jumper. That movement betrayed an inch or two of suntanned shoulder to the elements – and to Petroc's flaring eye. 'I was told to drop round with my fiancé. My mother set a time with Vicar.'

'Your fiancé?'

'But he's not here.'

'He must have forgotten about your appointment.'

'No, I mean my fiancé. My fiancé's not here. He – he couldn't make it.'

'Great. I mean, well, that's good, isn't it. Because Tom is not here. And that would have meant a wasted journey for your fiancé.'

'He's in India.'

'Hey, I was there recently.'

'You were?'

'Look, do you want to come in? Tom isn't here but I can at least offer you some tea. Maybe I can answer any questions you have.'

'Oh. OK. Thanks. Are you a vicar, too? I thought you must be his son.'

'Ha!'

EVIDENCE of intimacy was cleared away before Zac appeared. The seventeen-year old telephoned from downstairs to gain admittance to his father's lair. Dymock, who never looked at Olga after their couplings, put on his Dad face. 'Zac!'

'Hello, Dad.'

'You want a cola?' said Olga. The boy nodded. He was grateful she had not tried to kiss him. The temple maidens did sometimes insist.

'How has the work gone today, matey? You've been downstairs with Jo and the cold-calling team, yeah? Have you signed up some unbelievers? Been a knock-out?' Dymock made a play-punch move at his son's stomach.

'I was doing street promotions the other day.'

'Great!'

'Don't think I was much good at it.'

'Nonsense. You're a Dymock! I must get Jo to give me your performance figures. If they're good, we're looking at a bonus. Pay by results. It's how our people improve, how they EVOLVE! Get Jo to come up here, Olga.' Olga made a quiet call to the Thought Foundation's trading floor with its booths of telesales operators.

Dymock was still talking to Zac. 'Speaking to strangers about their beliefs isn't easy but it's essential work, Zac. Probing at the soft undergut of doubt. But are they more open to the strength of our ideas when they are at home or at the shopping centre?' Zac's curls were not as yellow as in the photograph, which had been taken years earlier. He wore retro trainers and a Thought Foundation sweatshirt. The motif showed a bishop's crook that had been turned into a question mark.

'At home they can be cowed by family belief systems,' Dymock was saying. 'They catch a glimpse of Uncle Jim's urn in the corner or a snapshot of their wedding day and they become more defensive of tradition. In the street they are truer to the society about them.'

'Most just told me to get lost. The only person who chatted to me was a vicar.'

'What else is your news, kiddo? Got a girlfriend? Plenty of babes on the trading floor.'

Zac's embarrassment was saved by the arrival of Jo: dark, a fringe cut like theatre curtains under a proscenium arch. She had a drainpipe physique, a drainpipe voice. When Jo had come to work for Dymock she had been miserable and underpaid. Now she was just miserable. She was holding a thin file.

'Looking stressed, Jo,' said Dymock.

'Long days, I guess.' Head of Operations Jo had been Dymock's favourite before Olga.

'It's a compliment. Response to pressure is essential to progress. If you don't increase your productivity when you need to, you will be eaten by the next lion. Happens on the veldt. Happens here. Stress makes us succeed and that makes us attractive.'

Jo was loyal. That depressed Dymock, for loyalty was born

of groupthink, conforming to pack values, tribal blindness. He could not admire it, just as he could not admire homosexuality or patience or generosity – unless it had a goal. The Etruscans had no doubt been served by loyal retainers who had told them they were great men who need not worry about the uppity Romans. Loyalty: next stop oblivion.

'Come on, Zac. I fix you sandwich.' Olga took Zac towards the kitchen.

'How are last week's figures?' Dymock asked Jo, once the others were out of earshot.

'OK in places.' She paused. 'Continued growth on social media. Radio phone-ins with our people posing as members of the public. We have submitted the usual levels of complaints to official bodies about religious imperialism. We've been pushing the atheism app quite hard. Railway terminus glamour gangs. But chugging is now creating more resentment than support. One of our sellers was thumped the other day. By a Jehovah's Witness.'

'Anything pressing?'

'Two things.' Jo opened her slender file.

The first message was from his accountant about his tax returns. 'So silly, the way they set these end-of-month deadlines,' said Dymock. 'It means everyone returns their information at the same time.'

'Tell me about it,' said Jo. This expression meant 'don't tell me about it'.

The accountant wanted to know the date of some Greenhill Land donations. Were these officially loans or taxable income? Were they personal/corporate? Dymock's pale brow wrinkled. He resented paying tax. Why should he have to support the broken-winged? Man was programmed to procreate and raise his own. Why should he pay for other families?

The second letter was from the Diocese of London, Com- munications Dean Tony Calvert. Dymock felt he had heard the name, then remembered the boy who had shown him to Bryce's office. Gays. They were everywhere. What was the genetic point? Anyway. Calvert. The letter was studiously polite. It gave the arrangements for the coming debate at the Royal Political Society. Dean Calvert assured Professor Dymock – ah, yes, Professor – that the evening was sizing up to be a memorable occasion. A modest fee was offered. Would he be needing a car? Would he be accompanied by aides? Were there any dietary requirements for the refreshments beforehand?

'This guy is apparently a player. I think we invited him to the gallery party. But I won't talk to him myself.'

'Of course not, Augustus.'

'The aura, Jo. We must maintain the aura. Can you get Events to talk to him? On the fee I'll need cash.'

'Events is off. She's on holiday.'

'Events is a non-Event.'

'And publicity is on paternity leave.'

'Pathetic. Can we sack publicity?'

'Publicity might plant a nasty story about us if we did, although given how useless he is, I doubt he would get it published. But he could sue us. Employment laws.'

'Ugh. Protection of the indolent and infirm. No wonder this country is on the junk heap. Who else can handle it?'

'There's Zac.'

Dymock thought for a moment. 'How's he getting on?'

'Not bad,' Jo lied.

Zac's work experience at the Foundation had seen him amble through various departments. Dymock was keen to establish 'which suits him best', but the comparative was misleading. None suited him. At the moment he was in Outreach, that part of the Trading Floor which cold-called people with Anglo-Saxon surnames. Those with Islamic or Sikh or Jewish names were not rung for fear of causing offence. There was no knowing how a Khan or

Singh might kick off if told that religion was a fairy tale. There might be no soothing a Cohen who was blithely told that the God of Abraham did not exist. And so Outreach concentrated on the Smiths and Joneses and trouble was avoided. Outreach also joined online chats and developed multiple identities that gave apparently objective plugs to Dymock and his foundation's ideas. Zac had not enjoyed this, arguing that it was deceit. The boy seemed to have uncommon difficulty telling lies. His colleagues treated him with tact. They did not complain when he arrived late and left early, or spent long half-hours on the telephone to his boyfriend. If he was absent, he could not screw up their projects. Zac spent the time fingering his blond curls and staring at his nails, wondering if he dared to paint them.

'I could walk him though the contacts with this Calvert,' said Jo.

'Could you?'

'Sure. We're dealing with Christians. They're forgiving.'

'Forgiving? Does Zac need that?'

'I didn't mean that. Augustus, Zac is fine.'

'I'm glad you say that. Now, we need to get some support data to an MP called Kendrick. He's going to push the church-decommissioning idea.'

'OK.'

Jo returned to the Trading Floor in the lift, pondering her burdens. Dymock pushed a button on the wall. The window blinds lowered. The lights dimmed. The sound-system started to play the noise of bubbles rising through a fish tank. He switched the telephones to mute, pulled a lever and his armchair reclined almost to horizontal. He closed his eyes and within a minute – efficiently – was asleep.

THEIR talk had lasted longer than either of them expected. 'You know where I am. Where we are.'

'Thank you for listening. I've never really done that before.'

'Well you should have done. You needed it!'

She laughed, sniffled. 'I feel better.'

Nettle checked herself in the mirror at the door, straightening her hat. The eyes were a little red but that made her look all the more gorgeous. She pulled the hem of her top, to remove the creases. It would have taken Saint Augustine not to cop her twenty-three-year-old curves.

'Will you tell Vicar?'

'Tell him what?'

'That I came round to see him as arranged?'

'He's always forgetting things.'

'I'm glad he did, in a way.' She reached out delicate fingertips to shake his hand. She was conscious of the ring on one of the fingers. She tried an air-kiss but her hat got in the way.

'Oops.' They laughed. 'Goodbye. See you soon.'

'Hope so,' said Petroc. And a few minutes later he himself was out of the door, almost with a skip, heading back to his increasingly beleaguered church. The crowd had again grown and the chants were becoming louder, yet Petroc found his head light and his heart thumping with sunnier thoughts.

THE first mouthfuls of the Green Man's white Gascony were the best – that initial lemony burst, a tingle as it touched the tongue. When the sensation hit the chest it was almost as if Ross was inhaling the drink.

The Gyumpi, which he had retrieved from the bin, was not so bad as Petroc supposed. Ross flicked through its pages. Odd that the Greenhill girl had not turned up. He was sure they had agreed half past five. Oh well, perhaps the mother had confined her to barracks. He had waited half an hour at Base Camp before coming to the pub.

Writer Gyumpi spoke the language of the aromatherapy parlour – peace, spiritual oases, pools of quiet – and in that it was little different from many modern sermons. Ross liked the word 'pool'. The plosive was satisfying, though a p could pop at pulpit microphones. Pooool. Pooool. He sometimes fantasised about diving into a pooool of white Gascony without any clothes, kicking, wriggling as the liquid surrounded his parts. He said 'pool' to himself a few times before the barmaid shot him a look. To fill the awkward moment he emptied his pockets of some of their clutter – pens, handkerchief, prayer book, old receipts – and settled on using his handkerchief to clean his spectacles.

The Gyumpi was at least more substantial than Nettle's intended, this Chundy. Ross had now mentioned him a few times to Mrs Greenhill and each time she became vague and offered some excuse for his absence.

A second glass of wine stood before him on the bar, its flank beaded by condensation. What a pity they could never serve a chilled Gascony in the chalice. On a hot summer's morning it would go down so much better than watered port – a thrill of something cold and chalkily citrus, the cool shower of God's love before they stepped back into the hot scents of a country Sunday in July. Such days were the best, when the smell of summer and the drone of a single bee could remind us that the Prayer Book had been written for generations gone and for generations yet to come. *Rank on rank the host of heaven spreads its vanguard on the way* – Ancient & Modern 390, sung to an old French melody, Picardy. The English did not have all the best tunes, see? Age gave it a grandeur, a nobility. There might be some who heard its cresting chords and briefly forgot today's hassles and allowed their souls to soar.

Why were the English so blind to these comforts? Gyumpi was allowed to revere his people's ancient texts and chants. Gyumpi-ites would sit round a glowing brazier on a Goan beach, palms clasped, foreheads dotted, saying 'ohmmm' to a single note until it was time for another suck on a bong. Why could mouldering Anglicans not have their Prayer Book and their old hymns? Rhythm and repetition were not rational. They had an animal force reaching below reason, into our very guts where this wine would soon glow.

'Your telephone's ringing,' said the barmaid.

'What?'

'Your mobile. Look.' Ross lifted the device, which was still on top of the bar.

'Oh crumbs.'

'You going to answer it?'

'I can never make the button work.'

'Here. Give it to me.' She pressed the green button. 'There you are. You'd better speak into it now!'

'Oh yes,' said Ross. 'Hello? Hello?'

The voice at the other end was that of the Clerk of the Commons, Sir Roger Richards. 'Tom, I need you here. The Speaker has had a bit of a turn and I can't shift him.'

'Where are you?'

'I'm in the Robing Room. Thank God I got you. Are you nearby?'

'Not too far.'

'How fast can you get here?'

Ross was there in less than ten minutes. By that point Speaker Aldred was, by his own assertion, 'much better' and was sitting on a chair, talking lucidly. The Commons sitting day had finished early and Sir Roger and Ross managed to get the old boy into a lift and over to Speaker's House without too much difficulty, Ross discreetly holding one arm, leaning into Aldred as though simply listening to some story he was telling. Sir Roger related how the Speaker had briefly blacked out in the Robing Room a few minutes after the end of the Adjournment debate. He had been sitting at the time so there was no fall, no great drama. Yet it would not be helpful if the incident leaked. Sir Roger had called Ross because he knew that he had, as he put it, 'the discretion of the confessional'.

'Not that he has ever let me hear his confession,' said Ross as they walked away from Speaker's House. 'He demonstrates no interest in religion. I don't know what drives him. It can't be ambition at his age.'

'Not exactly ambition,' said Sir Roger. 'It's more bloody-minded than that. He just doesn't want anyone else taking his role. That's what drives most of them. Sorry to have disturbed you. I'm sure you were busy. Goodnight, Tom.'

THE concept of a church being open to everyone is fine, so far as it goes. When entrance to that church is blocked by a barricade and the adjacent street is a late-night stand-off between police horses and protestors, the principle starts to shrivel.

Petroc was returning from parish visiting. He knew something was up when he saw three vans full of anti-riot police parked in Ruby Street. He could hear chanting – 'We wan' JUS-tice! We wan' JUS-tice!' Close to the church he was stopped by the policeman who had originally chased Matt on the morning of the airline-office incident.

'Hello again,' said Petroc.

'I wouldn't recommend going further, sir. Hey, I recognise you. All this has happened because you wouldn't let me nab that kid.'

'Can I get through?'

'They haven't been throwing anything yet. But I wouldn't recommend it.' One of the protestors spotted Petroc and put up a new, fiercer shout about the 'racist Church of England'. Petroc told the policeman he would return in the morning.

Inside the church Matt was playing cards with Derrick Banks. He was taking Derrick to the cleaners but they were only betting with matchsticks. Mark was practising: violent, tormented chords from Karg-Elert, and some proper hymns including *The King of Love My Shepherd Is* and *Holy, Holy, Holy*. He had never reconciled himself to the drift to low-church worship songs. The congregants had been so feebly tolerant, so wetly polite about modernisers' demands. The aesthetic had been flattened by a literalism that in another faith would be called fundamentalism. Mark almost punched the stops as he played.

Outside, the organ was audible between the protest shouts. It was going to be a long night.

AT Mears's Commons office, everyone but Jean had gone home. Call it habit, call it Peeblesshire intransigence, Jean kept to the old ways. When a new constituency case came in, she checked the filing cabinet for any past correspondence. Look at today's new queries: a Mrs Bartlett whose mother had died of a superbug at Oakford hospital, a Miss Sheerman displeased by litter in her local park and a Mr Hewer pompously vexed that he had not been treated with respect by a dustman. She began cross-checking in the filing cabinet to see if these complainants had form. It took longer than on a computer but it suited her better.

There was one more name to check: Chapel, a routine letter about noise levels outside a chippie. No. Nothing under Chapel. Yet Jean thought she recognised the name and address. She spotted a file marked 'Churches'. Perhaps it had been placed there – an easy confusion to make. She pulled the file from the cabinet and flicked through it. No, there was nothing on Mrs Chapel, the constituent who was upset about noise. But Jean did find something else – something that filled her with rising anger as she read.

Jean photocopied the documents and replaced them in the filing cabinet. At this time of night she was entitled to take a taxi home but she would go by bus. She did not want Leslie to ask why she was working late. No one on the bus spoke to her. A young couple sat near the doors, their toddler's pushchair in the wheelchair space. The husband played sweetly with the child, though it was well past the little one's bedtime. The mother, in full veil, glanced at Jean but there was little joy in her eyes. Why not? She was a mother. Jean would never have that.

8

A Conversation Overheard

PETROC eventually got round to telling Ross he had missed the appointment with Nettle.

'It was in my diary,' said Ross. 'Maybe the mother made a mistake.'

'The mother was not in attendance.'

'No doubt I'm in trouble.'

'Nettle won't have given you away.'

'What do you mean?'

'I filled in for you. Talked her through things.'

'Oh, thanks. Phew.'

'The boyfriend wasn't there.'

'Mr Elusive. Thanks for looking after little Nettle. Not so little Nettle, actually. Did you manage to get any sense out of her?'

'We got on fine.'

'Half past five, see? In my diary.'

'She got here at half past three. Fifteen thirty was how she put it. Stayed an hour.'

'Sorry. Must have buggered your day.'

'Far from it. It was a relief from the siege.'

'Oh, fifteen thirty. That's half past three, isn't it?'

'Yes.'

'Bloody twenty-four-hour clock. Sorry.'

*

THE 'landscaping' campaign suggested by Bryce had begun. Dymock told Jo to give a bonus to the Thought Foundation team involved. He admired the subtlety, the slyness, with which the proposal was being floated. You waited until one of the political websites was having a brainstorming event – a 'where next for progressive politics?' – and you presented it in a tone of call-me-mad-but-hear-me-out-guys. Throw in a mention of demographics, cite 'young people' and the latest hot political book from America – and close with a nonchalant remark that no politician here was yet ready to think so far ahead.

You did some planting in the online comments. The team had found a clergyman in Liverpool to shoot a video diary about homelessness and compare crowded hostels to the empty pews in churches. This video had been given to one of the rough-sleeping charities and was shown repeatedly in the foyer at the Opposition party's headquarters. A nudge here, a tickle there. Create a sense of crisis. Accentuate a problem. Slip in your preferred solution.

'Shall we action press release with your quotes?' came a text from Jo.

'Quotations,' wrote Dymock.

'Yeah yeah,' replied Jo. 'OK to release?'

'OK,' replied Dymock.

Within half an hour, every parliamentarian, every journalist at Westminster, all the property magazines, homelessness charities and housing authorities had been sent a social action paper called 'Ten Commandments?' It juxtaposed photographs of youngsters sleeping on pavements with photographs of ten underused, inner-city churches. Under the churches were details of their average congregation numbers and estimates of their property value. The press release concluded: *'This is not about bashing religion,' says Thought Foundation director Augustus Dymock. 'If anything, we are doing the Church's work – seeking to help the poor. Let's put aside differences and address the housing crisis. The Church owns buildings it is unable to fill. Bishops should not hoard land.'*

Radio bulletins picked up a Thought Foundation poll saying eighty-five per cent of youngsters cited housing in their 'top five life hassles'. Other questions – Should the Church do more to combat homelessness? Should bishops live in palaces? How many churches does a town need? – were asked. The responses duly found that the Church's property portfolio was too big. The Thought Foundation press release noted that backbench MP Tristan Kendrick had been granted a parliamentary debate about Church land assets and 'he might be worth talking to if you want a lively voice'.

A National Rough Sleeping Day was created, as if it had always existed. A press event at a dingy hostel near London's Waterloo station was arranged. Speakers included house-building advocate Lionel Moss MP, trade unionist Sheila Henderson, and superstar atheist Augustus Dymock. The event publicised the Church's unused land assets and pressed the Government to include a Housing Bill in the Queen's Speech at the State Opening of Parliament later in the week. The platform was chaired by Leslie Mears MP, would-be chairman of the Commons Select Committee on Housing.

ONCE a priest has begun preparing someone for matrimony, he might as well continue. Petroc told himself this, yet he was not untroubled by guilt. Nettle had come to him in a position of trust and he was ten years older than her. To fall in love with her – if this was love – might be an abuse of position, might it not? She was promised to another yet that promise was not made willingly. Did a priest not have a duty to ensure that engaged couples loved each other? If they did not love one another, the marriage might be bogus – arranged to get round visa restrictions. In such a case would it not be Petroc's *duty* to explore his love for her, if, again, this truly was love. Petroc felt both excitement and shame, though the shame was the slighter of the two. Temptation, or love, or lust, would find their levels. He trusted God to sort that out for him.

'Well, if you're happy to do it,' said Ross when Petroc airily suggested that he could continue to counsel Nettle.

'I'll keep you briefed.'

'She seems to think well of you,' said Ross. 'We still haven't seen the groom, I suppose.'

'It's not a problem,' said Petroc.

'You'd better have her telephone number.'

'I have it already.'

'Oh. If the mother asks, we'd better say I'm still in charge of the sessions.'

Petroc asked Nettle to visit Base Camp in the early evening. 'We don't have to stay here discussing marriage the whole time,' he said. 'We'll go for a coffee or maybe do a film.'

'That,' said a husky voice, 'sounds lovely.'

Petroc smelt his armpits and took a shower. He even shampooed his thick, raven beard.

BY the time Mears got home – sober, sooted by public transport – it was past nine. He would have taken a taxi but buying the dress for Olga had left him short of funds.

He had been guest speaker at a constituency party meeting in the East End. One had to do this sort of thing to win round MPs before the Housing Committee chairmanship election. The Member for this run-down seat barely thanked Mears for coming. Westminster people only visited grotty areas when they wanted something. She and Mears knew this. Even so, she might have made more of an effort to be civil. Mears took mental note of the slight. To be avenged: this was a tremendous galvaniser.

The evening, which attracted a small congregation of zealots and bores, had not been pointless. It had given him a live audience and he had road-tested his speech. He delivered it badly – a dull audience receives a dull speech – but practice was useful.

'Friends, land should not be an inheritance. Land is a right – the right to sleep under a roof we can call our own. Housing is not a castle of dreams. Housing must not be the preserve of lottery winners. Housing is a requirement for civilised society. Tax-avoiding oligarchs own tracts of our British land. Bankers are rolling in it, rolling in rolling acres. Billionaires buy blocks in Belgravia and leave them empty. Supermarket giants squat on suburban land banks. And the Church is custodian of many underused buildings.

'How is this sensible? In times of famine, are fields left empty? If children were dying from thirst, would we condemn parents for seizing table water which had been bottled for fancy restaurants? Rich parasites must relinquish those hoarded property portfolios – thousands of acres which stand idle, apparently unwanted. Unwanted? Not by us, the people of this island. Unwanted? How dare they? They ARE wanted. We want them!

'The Church has served our communities for centuries but let us be honest – it is dying on its feet. Correction. It is dying on its knees! My friends, let us demand a national housing audit. We must not rest until this immoral waste of space has been put right. Thank you!'

It had surely been worth a bit more applause than the couple of claps from these gum-sucking spuds. The sitting Member wearily asked 'Any questions?' – there were none – and the remainder of the meeting was a workshop on claiming benefits.

Mears closed the front door of his flat softly. 'I'm back.' He removed his coat and loosened his tie. A few letters on the hall table consisted chiefly of bills and commercial flyers. He took them through to the main room. Olga, her auburn locks turbaned in a towel, was watching a shopping channel. The lights were off.

Blue light from the television screen bounced off her grey eyes. 'Hello,' tried Mears. 'Had a good day?'

When he touched her shoulder, she jumped. 'That give me fright!'

'Have you eaten?'

She switched off the television and told him there was something for him in the oven. He followed her into the kitchenette and watched as she extracted a dish of sorry-looking pie. It sizzled against the dish in the last of its blackened gravy. Olga peered at it with the innocent puzzlement of a naturally bad cook.

'I got you a present,' said Mears, producing the latest *Vogue*. Olga did not have to know that he had pinched it from the Members' Smoking Room. *Vogue* was one of her favourites. She squeaked and bounced off to her room. Mears spooned some food onto his plate but it did not excite him. Never mind: tomorrow would be the time for feasting. Tomorrow was the ball! Before bed, he opened the post: the only interesting letter was an invitation to the Portrait Gallery, a Thought Foundation unveiling of a portrait entitled 'Don of Doubt'. What with the ball tomorrow, and now the Portrait Gallery, things were going really rather well.

THERE were not many reasons to read *The Dispatch* but Paul Pike was one of them. The newspaper had long lost its reputation. Principles on which it had been founded – lack of proprietorial interference, aversion to hyperbole – had been squandered by careerist jockeying among senior staff. Management putsch had followed executive coup, just as it did in the rackety regimes once reported in the paper's foreign news pages. These days those pages were slim. In the opinion columns, Oxbridge languor had yielded to partisan squalor; but there was still Pike's column, spearing reputations, disclosing the little connections that create an elite. Pike, ill-washed product of private school and the LSE, chewed gum, noisily, even while smoking. He felt it lent him street toughness. Was that also why he sniffed so much? In attire he seldom altered: a lean two-piece suit, worn with a grey shirt and disreputable green tie. In moments of abandon he had been known to clench the bony fist at the end of his mottled arm and sing *The Red Flag*. His vibrato tenor bore no trace of the Cockney projected in his daily speech – a Cockney he was hardly entitled to speak, having sprung from a crescent of detached houses in Reigate. His home life now was also unorthodox for a class warrior. His woman Emma was a scion of one of the old trading families of Empire, a multi-millionaire who devoted herself to community dance projects and tofu. Their house near Regent's Park was filled with mid-twentieth-century art and they kept a lodge on Emma's family estate in Norfolk. These ex-directory possessions were kept confidential.

A telephone text from Bryce said, 'Rendezvous tomorrow?'

'Yep,' replied Pike.

Bryce used his long, antiseptic fingers to confirm time and place while Pike reapplied himself to a hatchet job on an elderly nun who presented a motoring show on television. She had lost her licence for drink-driving. 'She was returning from a meeting of her local Lib Dem association,' wrote Pike. 'Can a woman not be excused hitting the bottle after an evening with Lib Dems?'

9

At The State Opening Ball

GUESTS arriving at the State Opening Ball were dropped at the St Stephen's entrance to the Palace of Westminster, its tower picked out with coloured lighting, a red carpet lining the marqueed entrance. A Commons usher in tails, top hat and white gloves sprang forward to open car doors. Ladies, once they were through the doors, expressed relief as they felt the hot air blasting from large heaters. Couples made their way to the top of the wide staircase above Westminster Hall. There they gave a stiff introduction card to a master of ceremonies before a couple of state trumpeters blew a mini fanfare. The master of ceremonies waited for the echo to fade before he bellowed the latest names to the guests below. Only at the bottom of the stairs were new arrivals handed a flute of champagne.

Bryce arrived on his own. Sussex smoothie Mike Branton–Day was there with his daughter, a tall honker with Aintree-paddock teeth. Sir Tudor Matthews, Father of the House, arrived in a dashing cloak, which he handed to the master of ceremonies. Sir Tudor's wife, swathed in white furs, twinkled and waved as she was escorted down the staircase by her fine old gent. Lady Matthews was Hungarian, with everything that entailed. As a young woman she had been smuggled across the Iron Curtain in a rolled-up Persian carpet and it had given her a lifelong taste for adventure that was seldom sated in Sir Tudor's constituency. Sir Tudor was happy to spoil her on occasional forays to the capital, as a man will sometimes be to pay for his vintage Lagonda to be serviced.

'Good evening, Lady Matthews,' said Bryce, bowing. Sir Tudor's wife was sucking dry her first glass. As she came up for air she vouchsafed a basso burp. Behind her and to all sides, guests were perambulating, complimenting one another, lifting eyebrows of greeting.

'Meester Bryce, how nice!' spluttered Lady Matthews, patting her chest with her hand. She laughed at her little rhyme. Bryce, too, laughed. Whereupon Lady Matthews laughed some more.

'Sir Tudor,' said Bryce. He dropped his chin in salute. Sir Tudor had been given custody of his wife's handbag while she grabbed two new drinks from a passing tray. He raised his wrist and gave the silver-lamé bag a little shake of acknowledgement to Bryce.

'The Deputy Prime Minister!' cried the master of ceremonies, and down the Westminster Hall staircase wandered the inane incompetent whose handful of third-party MPs had given him a say in the formation of the Government. To be brought to that high office by a collection of polytechnic lecturers, failed social workers and frotting oddballs! He had chosen not to dress in black tie, disdaining elitism. His consort had chosen to stay at home with their semi-feral children, so the Deputy Prime Minister had brought his spin doctor, who descended the steps while jabbering into his telephone.

Each arrival was appraised, political eyes glinting like those of bloodstock agents at Weatherby's. Some newcomers received murmurs of surprise, others groans. The Deputy Prime Minister had generated open mirth. Opinion was moulded by the side-mutter, by mockery, spiced by scorn and slander. Had Sir So-and-So not lost weight? Was all well with him? Remind me, what is his majority? Could be an interesting by-election. Had the Hon Member for Somewhere South changed her hairdo? Did that signal an upturn in her romantic fortunes? Did the junior Minister for Bicycles know his flies were undone? That fool Perkins is plainly on the drink again. Since when did Willoughby affect such ponderous steps? And was that really the former Chairman of Facilities in the novelty bow-tie and powder-blue tuxedo? Was he raising money for charity or having a mid-life crisis?

Bryce joined a group of Government and Opposition Whips at the champagne bar. They spotted Deputy Speaker Tewk, arriving with a pudding who could have been twin sister to the late Sir Michael Hordern. Whips regarded one another in silence, processing Tewk's mediocrity. Still they came, Westminster's worker-wasps, striving for their queen, genetically ambitious, fated to fail – for fail will we all, by some measure or other – yet still eager to chew, sting, build, buzz.

Olga had been late to leave Pimlico. Dymock kept her at work longer than normal, ordering her to rearrange furniture in his living quarters. This could have been done another time but he had insisted, his manner becoming sharp. He expected obedience – he was her employer. 'Is that all you are?' Olga asked. Dymock busied himself in calls while she completed the task. He was still on the telephone when she left the Foundation's building and hurried home.

It had been arranged that Mears would meet her at the St Stephen's entrance but it was already nearly seven-thirty when she reached the flat. The Ball had started at seven. She was cursing Dymock so much that she struggled to unlock the door. She leapt out of her work clothes, splashed some water under her arms, brushed her teeth and wriggled into her party frock, hoping it would not rip. Seven-forty. Which shoes? The third pair met with her satisfaction. Another minute was sacrificed to a hunt for her clutch bag. Russian swearwords rang forth. She glanced out of the window and saw that a drizzle was falling. Raincoat: she found it on the back of a door and seized a sou'wester hat, too. Slam went the door and she rushed into the road to find, beg, steal a taxi, almost being run over in the process and pinching a cab from under the nose of a young man who had hailed it from the other side of the road. 'Parliament!' she gasped, mouthing 'sorry' to the young man. He, charmingly, blew her a kiss.

At seven-fifty Mears rang the Pimlico flat on his mobile. He got his own voice on the answering machine. It was cold and increasingly wet outside St Stephen's and he kicked his feet just inside the entrance. Again he checked his watch and made sure the tickets were safe. 'Oh, come on, Olga!' he hissed, fingering his moustache and wishing he had worn a coat, for the cold of the night had numbed his pot belly. Near him one of the Ball organisers was on her walkie-talkie, consulting with control about moving people through to dinner.

By seven-fifty-five the conversation in the Hall had risen to a roar. Parliament's proudest were suited, booted, mated, dated, their ranks augmented by ambassadors, Whitehall Permanent Secretaries, Privy Council grandees and emissaries from Clarence House. Here were some of the more presentable academics, one or two vultures of the judiciary, a theatrical dame. There stood a BBC Controller in discussion with a Culture select committee member, stroking this contact. One of the big party donors was leaning on a Trade minister to give more generous consideration to a certain deal. The Cardinal Archbishop was in jocular conversation with a notoriously avid expenses claimant. Sleekness and grandeur fugged the air, expensive scents combining with the tang of hair oil and self-acclaim. Champagne waiters struggled to squeeze past chortling swells. Laughter spiralled high until the very rafters trilled. The state trumpeters, beholding this din, felt sure they had finished for the night but the arrival of old Netty Peake, in an outfit so lumpen it may have been on back-to-front, gave them another fanfare to perform. Netty escorted her ancient mother down the staircase. The mother had to be steered hard to ensure she went in the correct direction.

'Didn't you say Mouldy Mears was coming?' an Opposition Whip asked Bryce. 'Have I missed him?'

'Yes and no,' said Bryce. 'He is coming and you haven't missed him. At this rate he is going to miss it.'

Outside, a taxi driver yanked on his handbrake and told his passenger: 'Here you are, love. Looks quite a do in there. And I originally thought you must be heading for a night on a trawler.'

'Hmppf,' said Olga from under her sou'wester. She stuffed a banknote in his hand and dashed out of the cab without waiting for change. The driver said to her already distant back: 'You have a fun evening, love. God bless.'

Mears had just sought advice from one of the organisers about refunds when he heard her running. 'Quick!'

'I need to get rid of my raincoat . . .'

'I'll tell them not to call dinner yet. The cloakroom's over there.' He rushed to have a word with the master of ceremonies, who had been about to hit an enormous gavel on a wooden block to announce dinner. The man agreed to wait two minutes.

'Look, there's Mouldy at the top of the stairs!' said Bryce's Opposition Whip companion. The trumpeters raised their instruments and gave one last, long blast. If it was their most impressive fanfare of the evening, there was a reason: they had seen the vision approaching them. Mears followed their gaze and he gasped. For there came Olga. The raincoat and hat had gone. Her auburn hair tumbled towards her bared, slender shoulders. The frock was midnight blue with spaghetti straps, cut on the bias and skimming her hips. It fell deep at the nape of the neck and its silk swayed to her confident step. All the hassle of her last two hours, the dinginess of the taxi and the dampness of the night, evaporated. In the instant before she left the cloakroom, a prayer had come to her from Russian childhood. Discreetly she had crossed her heart and raised her eyes to the ornate ceiling and now she stood at the top of the staircase, right elbow held by Mears. With the poise of a princess she claimed her destiny as the Hall stopped and stared.

'See?' said Bryce. 'Told you he was coming.'

10

Mr Bacton Takes The Case

THE following night Nettle told Petroc: 'Thanks for walking me back. You have so much else to worry about.' She meant the continuing siege at the church of Alleluia Jesus! 'Here, get under the brolly.'

'That Tube line is not always safe,' he said. 'Is that the house?'

'Across the road, yes.' It had been not much more than a ten-minute walk from the Tube. Before crossing the road they had to wait for a fast-moving van. It splashed an arc of puddle water over Petroc.

'Bloody hell!'

'Oh my God,' said Nettle. 'You swore!' They laughed.

It was one of those St John's Wood villas with a flight of front steps and a parking area where the front lawn would once have been. The laurel-lined driveway was dark. 'Do you want to come in and use a towel? You're soaked.'

'Well . . .'

'Mum's out. I don't think Dad's in either.'

'There's a light.'

'We always leave that on. Stops burglars.' She rummaged in her bag, throwing a coy smile. 'There's a key somewhere in here. Mum calls it my "handbag soup". I can't see what I'm doing really. One of my contact lenses has gone wonky.' She gave a triumphant squeak and opened the large front door. The house smelled of flowers and cigars. 'There's a laundry room and loo at the end of the hall. I'll show you.' She grabbed his hand. 'Oh dear, you really were soaked, poor darling.' She was soon dabbing him with a fat, heated towel. His donkey jacket had saved him to some extent but his hair and beard were bedraggled. His trousers were drenched.

'Take them off.'

'What?'

'Your trousers. We'll put them in the tumble dryer.'

'But . . .'

'They'll dry in no time. Come on. Shoes off. I've seen a man's legs before. Get 'em off!' With more laughter, the trousers were placed in the tumble dryer. Petroc saw himself in a mirror.

'I look like a wet dog.'

'I still can't see properly – this silly contact.' She fiddled with her right eye.

'Come here, let me see if I can sort it out,' said Petroc. He tidied her fringe off her brow and told her to keep still. 'There. That better?'

'Yes.' They looked at one another and she took his chin in one hand. It was then, lightly, that she kissed him, then more deeply, rising on tiptoes. Petroc moved backwards and his bottom pressed a button on the machine, which stopped. 'Leave it,' said Nettle through another kiss. She pressed against him with greater force.

They were so involved that they did not at first hear the tread on the stairs above them; men's voices. Petroc froze. 'Someone's there,' he whispered.

'Must be Dad!' she said under her kissed breath. She silently turned off the light in the little room.

'Thank you for coming, Leslie,' boomed Gordon Greenhill. The utility room had thin walls.

'The pleasure was mine,' said a second voice.

'Rare to find a politico talking sense.'

'Rare as a developer with a social conscience.'

'Steady on!' Both men laughed loudly. 'That cab should be here any moment. Did you have a coat? And don't forget this. Most important thing!'

'Ah yes.'

'Your campaign is an inspiration.'

'I am glad you think so. Your donation will certainly help.'

'Great do last night. Who was the beauty on your arm?'

'She is my flatmate. Well, maybe a bit more than that. Russian. She works at the Thought Foundation.'

'Dymock's outfit – I knew I'd seen her before. You're a lucky guy. Now, do you need the bathroom before you go? There's one under the stairs here.' The doorbell rang. Petroc and Nettle held tight to one another. They heard the front door open and a third voice – a taxi driver.

'He'll be out in a moment,' said Greenhill. 'Sorry, Leslie, did you say yes to the loo?'

'I'm fine.'

'Thanks again for coming. Goodnight.'

'Goodnight.'

The door closed and footsteps receded. Gordon Greenhill started to climb the stairs. He paused halfway and they heard him talk, this time with less bonhomie. He was on his mobile. 'He's gone. Went fine. Greedy bugger wanted five grand. No. Course not. I gave him three. But told him there was plenty more where that came from. Yeah! He's mad about your little Russian connection.' There was a dirty laugh. 'What about this church guy? Ah, right. Keep me posted. G'night.'

They waited a couple of minutes after Greenhill's steps had receded. Nettle turned on the light and let out a long sigh of relief.

Petroc said: 'I'd better put my trousers on – and scarper.'

'Might be a good idea, yes.' She gave a laugh and blushed.

★

AFTER a decent interval Nettle walked into the drawing room. Both her parents were there, Mrs Greenhill having returned soon after Mears's departure. She was shouting down the telephone at a wedding caterer. Her husband was watching a property and gardening programme on the room's vast television. Nettle joined him on the leather sofa. The programme described the efforts of a penniless aristocrat to do up her walled garden. Gordon Greenhill laughed and said 'Just sell it, you stupid Doris.'

Mrs Greenhill, who had finished her telephone call, cast an eye at the television and said: 'It looks almost as big as the vicar's garden.'

'Which vicar?' said Greenhill.

'The one who's going to take Nettle's wedding. Bang in the middle of town – a garden big enough to take at least a block of flats. Just near Vincent Square.'

'Interesting,' said Greenhill. 'Perhaps I ought to buy it.'

'Dad, no!' said Nettle. 'You can't kick vicars out of their homes.'

'Don't see why not.'

'If you have your way, every last blade of grass in London will be removed.'

'Too right. Keeps you in a pretty royal lifestyle, doesn't it?'

'Leave that vicarage alone, that's all I'm telling you,' said Nettle, more sullen than she perhaps intended.

Mrs Greenhill looked sharply at her daughter and said: 'One day you'll realise that money doesn't grow without pain and hard work. Anyway, where were you tonight? I didn't know you were going out.'

'I was at that vicarage, as it happens,' claimed Nettle. 'I was being instructed about the wedding. And I happen to like it there more than I do here. You don't get told off there.'

'Well!' said Mrs Greenhill.

'It's all right, love,' said Gordon Greenhill. 'Let it pass.'

'Her whole attitude from the beginning has been quite wrong.

It's as though we're being punished for finding her a good prospect. Moaning and pouting and now this sort of rudeness. That's all I get from her, Gordon. All the time. It's impossible.'

'No one else would put up with it!' shouted Nettle.

'No other mother would put up with it, certainly!' said Mrs Greenhill. 'No other husband, either – though I often think your father doesn't love me.'

'Oh don't start that,' sighed Greenhill.

'You know what, Gordon. I think you *should* buy that vicarage. Buy it out. Get that vicar evicted. It would serve him right for filling our daughter's head with such rebellion. I didn't take to him from the start.'

'Now look . . .' said Gordon Greenhill.

'Do it!' shrieked the imperatrix. 'Just do it! What's the point in having all this money you're always boasting about? Get on to that old fool of a Speaker. Or Bryce. Isn't he your master fixer? Bribe whoever needs to be bribed. I don't see why I need to be talked to by my daughter as though I'm dirt.'

'Mum, I didn't mean . . .'

'Yes you did!' She lifted a finger to the space just under her nose and adopted a tragic tone. 'I work night and day for you. I spend my life trying to make this wedding perfect. And this is the gratitude I get! God, it makes me angry. And you're as bad as the rest of them, Gordon. See? You won't buy this vicarage. You're refusing. Just sitting there on your backside, even though I've found it for you and told you about its enormous garden. You could make millions out of it but you won't do as I suggest because you want to make me unhappy. I just do not know why I bother.'

She fled the room, furious. Gordon Greenhill shouted 'Oh for God's sake, you bloody women!' and was soon on the telephone to Bryce and Dymock to see what they thought about buying the vicarage. Nettle did not move. The evening had been so wonderful until her parents had ruined it. She wished she could escape this overheated cage. She wished she could be with Petroc and Ross in companionable untidiness. But how could it be done? And how could she stop her father taking Base Camp from her two adorable vicars?

MEARS won the chairmanship of the Housing select committee with ease. Of course he did. After the ball, who could have doubted it? In the House a frail Speaker Aldred announced that the Hon Member for 'Oakham' had been elected. Commons Clerk Sir Roger Richards gently put him right.

'Oakford. Thank you, Timothy.'

There was a small 'hear hear' from MPs. Atkinson, the former Whip who had been Mears's rival, left the Chamber immediately. It was never wise for ex-Whips to stand for select committee chairmanships. Feared when they were in office, they were hated afterwards because they still knew MPs' secrets.

'Well done, Little Les Mis,' said Mike Branton-Day, who entered the Chamber during the announcement. 'Always knew you could do it. Admirable.' Branton-Day sashayed towards his preferred spot at the top of the gangway where he could stretch his long, pinstriped legs. Mears dropped his head in fake gratitude for the equally fake compliment. Branton-Day had lobbied hard for Atkinson.

Netty Peake scooted along the bench. 'I know I'm on the committee but I decided not to vote in the end,' she said. Her breath smelled of onion. 'Our group felt it was improper to support any man for the job. But I am glad that you got it. Better than horrid Atko.' An alcoholic is someone who drinks more than his doctor. A select committee chairman is someone who is loathed less than other candidates for the post. Bryce, from the Government bench, arched a congratulatory eyebrow.

As Mears left the Chamber in the direction of the parliamentary

shop – he felt a box of violet creams coming on – he was stopped
by that fist of sinuous principle, Tristan Kendrick. He, too, was on
the Housing select committee. 'I'm going to send you a memo,'
he said with zeal. 'There's one area of potential housing we can
liberate. It'll take courage, but you might have that.'

OLGA was pleased for him. 'We heard at work,' she said that
evening in the flat. 'Bryce rang to tell Augustus.'
    'Was he interested?'
    'He is a busy man,' she said.
    'We can push this churches plan now.'
    'Yeah?' said Olga.
    'I don't see why not.'
    Olga kissed him. It was a light kiss, a kiss that did not promise
anything, yet a kiss that all the same was enough to make the hairs
of Mears's moustache quiver and stiffen. 'I make some supper,' she
said. And soon the kitchen was filled with the smell of beef and
onion *kotlety* and slightly singed potato cakes.
    A few streets away, the curtain in a department store's fitting
room was drawn back and Jean emerged to inspect herself in the
mirrors. She was wearing a black, rubber mini skirt, a plunging
top and high heels. Another shopper saw her and recoiled. When
Jean left the store a few minutes later she had not made a purchase.

NETTLE placed the stocking over her face, having already
stuffed a hanky in her mouth. There was not much point wearing
the stocking but it made her feel braver. After deep breaths and
a glance at her script, she dialled the number for the Thought
Foundation hotline.
    People wrote off Nettle as a wallflower, catching flies in her
lower lip. It would certainly not have been accurate to call her an
intellectual. But she was her father's daughter.
    'Hotline, hello,' said a singsong voice.

'Can I speak to Augustus Dymock?'

'He is a bit tied up right now. Can I help?'

Through the handkerchief and the stocking, Nettle mumbled: 'Give me your supervisor. This is important.'

She heard the person on the line put a hand over the receiver and say something to a colleague. Another voice came on the line. 'This is Jo. Can I help?'

'Are you Mr Dymock's assistant?'

'Pretty much. Do you want to report a religious hate crime?'

'The vicar knows everything. He knows all about the money. Greenhill, Dymock, the MPs and all that.'

'The vicar?'

'And if you don't back off his London home, he's going to blow it all wide – the whole shebang.' She slammed down the telephone and, after removing the stocking and hanky, found her hands were shaking. There! She wouldn't tell a soul, not even Petroc. But she felt sure he would be proud of her. That mattered to her more than almost anything.

Jo immediately went upstairs to talk to Dymock. 'Problem,' she said, and explained. It did not take them long to work out which London home the caller had been referring to. It was the house near Vincent Square, the one with the big garden, the one Greenhill had insisted on chasing. Dymock had told him not to push it but Greenhill had muttered something about his wife giving him grief. Dymock had expected better of Greenhill. If his wife was a problem he should dump her.

Dymock pondered in silence, gazing out at the expanse of London. Almost to himself he repeated the words, 'The vicar knows everything.'

'It's only an anonymous tip at the moment,' said Jo. 'We could ignore it.'

'My instincts tell me that would be a mistake,' said Dymock. 'The alternative is that we thump him where it hurts.'

'How so?'

'This chaplain lives in the country, I think someone said.'

Jo said: 'That's right. One of those churches Greenhill was looking at, the one with the haunted graveyard – it's this chaplain's. To be honest, we thought that probably ruled it out. We thought he'd be untouchable with those political contacts.'

'He may think that himself,' said Dymock. 'Let's sweat him a bit. Send down a team of surveyors. Let's put the wind up the little shit and see how he likes blackmail himself.'

THERE must by now have been four hundred protestors outside the church of Alleluia Jesus! and their numbers were augmented not only by police but also by foreign television crews, photographers and Mohammed, the proprietor of the nearby Ruby Street corner shop, who walked among them selling samosas and soft drinks.

Each day Petroc fought off media requests, administrative flak from Church House, insults from the crowd and worries from congregants. He had twice been called to a meeting with the police to discuss procedures if the church had to be evacuated. A community-relations superintendent encouraged Petroc to 'open a dialogue with other faith groups'. Petroc said he was always pre-pared to talk to Muslims. If they came to the church door he would explain his motives. The superintendent said he thought non-Christian ground would be wiser. Petroc said he was prepared to meet anywhere in the parish, on the streets, even in a mosque, but he did not see what he could do to absolve himself of his responsibility to give Matt shelter. Word went back to Government that the Rev Stone was smoking a lot and becoming aggressive.

'How long is this going to last?' asked Ross one evening at Base Camp.

'God knows,' said Petroc. 'And I mean that.'

'I had an apparently chance encounter with the police minister this morning,' said Ross. 'He was asking about you.'

'The police minister?'

'He knows that we share this house. He was digging. His question was "Is he a man one can do business with?"'

'And your verdict?'

'I told him you were perfectly ready to talk to people but that you had firm beliefs.'

'So they're spying on me.'

'For what it's worth, I told them that I wished I had your bloody courage.'

Petroc look at Ross for a long while. 'Thank you, Tom.'

Ross's question of 'How long?' had been the same that Petroc himself had put earlier that day to Magnus Bacton. Bacton was one of London's fancier defence lawyers. His wife was a collected potter – she devised giant amphorae covered in protest slogans – and the Bactons' presence at soirées was coveted. Bacton had been contacted by Matt's solicitor. Would he help? When Bacton saw the case reported on television and mentioned in Parliament, when he saw the numbers of protestors and the root arguments, he accepted.

'How long do you think it will go on?' Petroc asked Bacton down a poor telephone connection. 'How long will the police tolerate it?'

'Call me Magnus.'

'We're under siege.'

'Indeed you are. Sieges can be good. They make a point. Just here, driver. Thanks.' He apologised to Petroc. 'We're just on our way to the World Poverty lunch at the Dorchester. What were you saying?'

'We took in Matt because he was vulnerable. He was defending his girlfriend from her overbearing father.'

'You were making a stand against Islam. Is that not your – our – point here?' Petroc could hear Bacton and his companion closing a car door.

'Will you come and visit Matt?'

'Let me check commitments with my television people. My wife has a show of new work for Prisoners of Conscience tonight. It's a big moment for her so a story like this might work for us. And I have contacts in Pakistan.'

'Contacts?'

'The Prime Minister was a chum of mine at Oxford. She should be able to help us find out what has happened to this boy's girlfriend. This case is doing her country no good internationally. Look, I need to go. My clerk will be in touch.'

THE boardroom at Greenhill Developments had a table so long, Ross felt he could see in it the curvature of the Earth. He had been placed down one end. Pads, pens and mineral water had been provided for this nuptials summit.

Mrs Greenhill, in apricot and mint with nude shoes and a lacquered helmet of hair, presided. She sat halfway down one side of the table, her back to an internal wall of one-way glass. This permitted the room's occupants to see what was happening in the corridor on the other side but it denied anyone in the corridor a view of the boardroom.

A wedding coordinator sat beside his client. He wore a yellow tartan jacket and a gelled, chestnut quiff. A caterer, flower arranger, lighting specialist, bespoke stationer, security consultant, fireworks engineer, dress designer, publicity agent, photographer, hairdresser, manicurist, beauty consultant, bridal-services secretary, protocol adviser, guest gifts enabler, transport chief and speechwriter were in the room. Nettle was on her mother's other side.

Formal proceedings opened with roll call. 'Best man?' Silence. 'Best man: do we not have the best man here?' demanded Mrs Greenhill. Her talons tapped on the table's gleaming surface.

'The best man is in Dubai,' said the bridal-services secretary.

'Did he not send a representative? I asked that we have someone from that department here today,' said Mrs Greenhill.

'Indeed,' said the bridal-services secretary. 'It is most disappointing.'

'Hopeless,' said Mrs Greenhill. 'I suppose that means we have no one representing the groom. No one with lines up that side of the operation.' Silence. The chauffeur had parked himself opposite Ross. He was as expressionless as a man in a rush-hour traffic jam.

'Organist?' said Mrs Greenhill.

'No,' said the secretary. 'But we do have the religion provider.'

'Vicar. Huh,' said Mrs Greenhill. 'You and Nettle met all right last week, as scheduled?'

'Last week?' said Ross. Panic flittered in his eyes.

'I had a lovely meeting,' said Nettle instantly.

'Good,' said Mrs Greenhill. In her notebook she placed a tick so violent that it tore the paper. 'Photographer?'

'Yeah,' said a languid woman with rivets in her nostrils.

'This morning I received confirmation from *Yes!* magazine that it will cover the wedding. You are no longer needed because the magazine has its own photographers. You have had a wasted journey. We will pay for your time.'

'So, like, I'm fired?'

'Yes. Goodbye.' Mrs Greenhill pressed a button and the door was opened by an attendant who escorted the muttering photographer from the room. The rest of the meeting watched as the victim was removed, possibly to an abattoir.

'With those nose piercings she would have had to go, anyway,' said the imperatrix. 'Protocol?'

'Yes?' said Protocol, stiffening.

'Your report on dietary diplomacy is late.'

'Sorry.'

'Can we serve meat when there are vegetarian Hindus present? Will offence be taken? It's no good just gulping, man. Gulping and swallowing will not get us anywhere. Find out!'

'Of course.'

'Now!' The buzzer was deployed a second time and Protocol was led away, if not to the scaffold then to ignominy. Two down. Ross wondered who would be next.

'Stationery.'

'Hullo!' Poor Stationery, giving a silly little wave, almost folded there and then.

'We have had indication that the Indian High Commissioner may attend. You will be emailed a list of VIPs. Not until the last minute will we know who is turning up, so your table maps and place names will need to be adjustable in live time. Capeesh?'

'Bless you,' said Ross, thinking Mrs Greenhill had sneezed.

She continued with her admonition of Stationery: 'Mr Green-hill disliked the italic typeface of the proposed invitations. Said it was poncey and illegible.'

'It always is,' said Stationery.

'Improve it or we will find someone more capable.'

The hairdresser was cut down for proposing a bob. There was an ugly moment when the beauty consultant challenged the manicurist. Mrs Greenhill – with her talons – sided brutally with the manicurist. The beauty consultant fled the room in tears. 'Well, that's going to ruin her mascara,' said Mrs Greenhill. The lighting specialist, sitting by Ross, failed to sparkle. The fireworks chap's ideas went phutt.

Ross was so caught up with the melodrama that he nearly failed to notice a cameo in the corridor. A burly, thick-necked man with sun tan and chunky, gold wristwatch emerged from an adjacent room and bade goodbye to a guest. Ross recognised the guest. The man accepted a small bag, shook hands with the gold wristwatch and departed. Ross was still watching Calvert's departure when he felt a nudge at his elbow. The lighting specialist was trying to give him a warning.

'Vicar!' barked Mrs Greenhill.

'Sorry. In another world.'

'I suppose that is to be expected. The Order of Service. We need it approved at least a fortnight ahead so Stationery can get it printed and ribboned, with bespoke watercolouring for VIPs. Do you want to take a note of it on your pad, which appears to be empty at present?'

'Ah yes, righto. Yes, that should be fine.'

'We,' said Mrs Greenhill, 'will be the judge of that.'

SPEAKER Aldred smacked his lips at the end of a Ten-Minute Rule Bill, hoping no one had noticed that he had been dozing.

'Third Reading, Civic Regulations Bill, eighth day,' said the Clerk, Sir Roger Richards.

'Thank you, Timothy. I propose to select an amendment in the name of Mr Kendrick. Is that right?'

'Yes,' said the Clerk.

Kendrick sprang to his feet, hands poised as for the start of a marathon.

'Mr Speaker, I do not intrude lightly on the Civic Regulations Bill, recognising the important matters it covers. But what can touch more on civic values than the provision of land on which we can build homes for our people? We need more housing. We also need to protect our green fields. I therefore propose that redundant and empty churches be re-categorised as 'reserve building stock' and that these neglected edifices could thus qualify for housing grants and fast-track planning.'

The Minister of State did not react. Not having been given instructions what to think, she did not wish to indicate assent or disagreement. Bryce, in a vivid orange tie, happened to be the duty Whip sitting beside her. He leaned across and murmured that 'it won't do any harm to appear open to reason, whatever happens'.

Mears, who had been told by Kendrick that it would be worth attending, saw a chance to lighten the mood. 'Point of Order, Mr Speaker.'

'Point of Order? Very well. Point of Order, Mr Mears, isn't it?'

'I see, sir, that the Minister of State is being spoken to by the deputy Chief Whip. May I urge her that if he is giving her advice of a sartorial nature, she resist it at all lengths? From the tie he is today wearing, he is not a man to be followed in such matters.' Restrained laughter.

'That is not a Point of Order,' said Aldred. 'It is not even a point of debate. It is, at best, a fashion tip. Mr Kendrick, please continue.'

Kendrick's amendment proposed giving the Government rights of property disposal over empty churches. 'The Valleys once echoed to chapel music, Mr Speaker,' he said, his vowels emphatic, rhythmic. 'The villages of England, likewise, once resounded to Sunday evensong. Those days 'ave vanished like vapour. The vaulted apse is void.' He hit each V with a muffled beat. 'Organ bellows are nibbled by vermin. All is vanquished. But communities could act. They could use these buildings before they collapse. This, Mr Speaker, is a radical, practical amendment which could provide new housing and solve problems for the Church.

'Few people actively seek the discontinuation of a working church. I am not a churchgoer. Reared in the Church of Rome, once an altar boy, I am today a 'umanist. But even Christians must see that there is more good in church buildings being used for 'ousing than in standing empty as Christ's tomb. When church gutters rust and their purpose moulders, let communities find fresh strength in the precious 'ousing they desperately need.'

Under Bryce's slender touch the Kendrick amendment had slipped below a sheaf of other papers until almost the end of the Whips' meeting that morning. 'I don't suppose we need worry much about this one – it seems a boutique issue,' Bryce had told colleagues. The Secretary of State was out of the country and the departmental Whip, hearing of the amendment from Bryce, did not make much of it when advising the Minister of State. He may have mentioned that one of the big property developers, Greenhill

— a party donor — was reportedly keen on the amendment, as were the trade unions. Sheila Henderson had an article on it in one of the heavy papers only at the weekend.

'The minister,' Kendrick was telling the House, 'is an ally of working people — there are few Hon Members with a finer record on social housing — and I am confident she will grasp the potential of a minor amendment, sitting as it does with the ideals of our party.' That had her nodding her head. Bryce, at her side, even said 'hear hear' — though of course he was expressing approval for Kendrick's praise of the minister. Mears, from his side of the Chamber, made a second intervention which sought additional information on some statistic about homeless people. Kendrick was able to give Mears the information he desired.

Kendrick resumed his seat and the minister was about to reply when George Leakey stood.

'Mr Leakey, you rise on the amendment?' said Speaker Aldred. He had rather been looking forward to an early cut.

'Mr Speaker, I wish to oppose it most vehemently.'

'Oh,' said Aldred.

Leakey was Second Church Estates Commissioner, the Church of England's man in the elected House. 'What we have just heard,' he began, 'is a silver fish of an amendment. It flitters across the surface and we may be tempted to think it harmless. I say this to the minister, and I know her to be a serious-minded parliamentarian: have nothing to do with this intruder. It is written in mercury. It is a trap. Ride away from it as Lady Godiva from the masked highwayman.'

Hearing 'Lady Godiva', someone shouted 'He's on his high horse.'

Kendrick said: 'Will the Rt Hon gentleman give way?'

'Certainly.'

'Will he admit that the Churches, and he, have a vested interest in the status quo.'

'A vested interest? A robed interest!' shouted Lionel Moss of the house-builders' lobby.

'I hope I do not have to remind the House that I am the Second Church Estates Commissioner and therefore speak for the Church,' said Leakey. 'Is the Hon Gentleman accusing me of hiding that?'

Kendrick waved aside his hand and said 'Of course not.'

'I am glad he accepts I am not operating from false motives. I simply say this to the House. The Church is owner of her lands. The Church is teamed with the State, as two horses before a carriage. But the Church is not, nor must be, the same as the State. The Church must be able to criticise the State. That independence stems from her financial independence. This cunning amendment – sprung on us in the course of a largely mundane Bill – would weaken the Church and relieve her of her lands.'

Mears rose. 'I thank the Second Church Estates Commissioner for giving way,' he said with elaborate courtesy. 'He keeps referring to the Church in the feminine. We also had some stuff just now about Lady Godiva, perhaps because the minister happens to be a woman. Would he accept that this sounds patronising, particularly in the light of the Anglican Church's historic bigotry against women's rights?'

'Hear hear,' went a couple of Members.

Leakey pinkened. 'I am sorry if I appear old-fashioned to the Hon Gentleman. Immediately this debate is done, I must rush to my optician for an urgent eyesight check so that I am better able to recognise him as a born-again feminist. As I was saying, Mr Speaker, this amendment must not slip through on the nod of a trusting – I nearly said naïve – House and a tolerant minister. It would interfere with property rights and well-set procedures for the management of redundant churches. It would create pressures on churches which may briefly be having a hard time. Parishes would feel compelled to close their churches to meet housing needs which should more properly be met by the private sector. New residents, on moving to a parish, might ask 'Where is our church?' only to be told that it had been turned into flats. This is a charter for atheists and property speculators. It is asset-seizing, asset-trashing, damaging one of our nation's greatest strengths, its churches. Ardently I urge the Government to resist.'

Bryce uncrossed his legs and, before leaving the Government bench, leaned into the minister's ear to say, 'I don't think we should proceed just yet with Mr Kendrick's amendment, do you? Thank him for raising an interesting issue but then play a dead bat. OK?' The minister nodded and did as told. Kendrick withdrew his amendment and the House proceeded on its way.

THE recording was poor. The first voice was Pike. 'What yer got?'

The second voice was Bryce: 'Your refined patience is always such a delight.'

'It's bloody cold and I don't have a posh coat like you!'

'It's an astrakhan,' said Bryce.

'Doesn't he play up front for Fulham?'

'Ho ho. Now, did you realise that Speaker's House is caught up in the Muslim siege of that church in Westminster? The vicar involved. He lives with the Speaker's chaplain.'

'Go on.'

'They share a house,' said Bryce.

'I can't do gay vicar stories.'

'Nor do I! God, I thought you might have worked that out.'

'So why are you telling me?'

'He pays rent.'

'Who?'

'This nutjob vicar – the one who is protecting the criminal.'

'Alleged criminal.'

'He pays rent to the Speaker. Well, to the House of Commons Commission. Don't you see? This creates a financial link. The chaplain who says our prayers every day is mates with a vicar who is upsetting the mosques.'

'Yeah,' said Pike, 'conflict of interest. Reasonably interesting.'

'Particularly when you find out how much their little grace-and-favour house is worth.'

Pike detached the recorder's earphones and he read the story a last time, checking the sentences for mistakes. Why the recording? Simple. Libel actions. You had to be able to fend off the lawyers, so often you recorded sources without telling them.

It was not the greatest item, but every day needed its filler paragraphs.

Ticklish clash of interests for creaky Speaker Aldred. The bearded cleric behind the tense stand-off with Muslims at a Westminster church is his rent boy! Let 'Whispers' clarify. The Rev Petroc Stone, self-styled John the Baptist of SW1, is a tenant of the Commons authorities. Nicotine addict Stone rents a room at the grace-and-favour mansion of Speaker's chaplain Thomas Ross. Think Jack Lemon and Walter Matthau in dog collars. Why not flog the house – worth perhaps five million – and house the chaplain in a B&B off the Old Kent Road? 'Mr Creaker' must surely recuse himself from any Commons debates about the church-sanctuary row that is fast becoming a national problem.

THE protest outside the church became semi-permanent, flags and banners being draped over the crash barriers and left for days. Parking bays was suspended, street cleaning stopped and the police presence was round-the-clock. Inside the church Derrick was doing seven days a week as 'security officer' and organised a door rota until dark. His latest late-night email to Petroc reported: 'Chants, a soapbox speech by a street imam, drums banged, sit-down vigil. Do we need reinforcements?'

Petroc texted Magnus Bacton to let him know things were becoming dicey. The lawyer replied: 'Makes story stronger. Hope to be with you lunchtime today.'

News websites remarked on organ music blasting from inside the church until late at night. Some found it 'spooky'. Organist Mark, a gleam in his eye, was treating the protestors to a range of classic Anglican hymns including *Thy Hand, O God, Has Guided, The God of Abraham Praise* and *Come, Ye Thankful People, Come*. One of the community support officers outside started humming to that last one. Hadn't heard it for years.

There was no Mark at the keyboard this morning. Petroc, arriving just after dawn when the protestors were down to a rump of smouldering resentment, told a policeman: 'I'm expecting a visitor later – a Mr Magnus Bacton. Will he be able to get through?'

'Should be.'

'Surrender the criminal!' shouted one of the protestors from a sleeping bag.

'Good morning,' replied Petroc. The protestor uncertainly raised a hand in greeting.

The policeman said: 'There's a major rally planned later today. On the internet they're calling for volunteers from all over the country.'

Petroc went to look for Matt. With Bacton on his way, the boy had to be prepared. Petroc found him at the bottom of the ladder to the organ loft. He was experimenting with a guitar, picking out the notes of *To Be a Pilgrim*.

POLICE officers spilled out of a van at the bottom of Ruby Street, flies from an autumn window frame. The tempo had increased for a couple of hours, tom-toms adding to the tension. At mid-morning Petroc came out of the church to gauge aggression levels. He felt like a householder checking floodwaters.

'Hello there!' hailed a hearty voice different from the others. 'Are you Stone?' Petroc saw a tall, suntanned man in a long raincoat, accompanied by a camera crew, striding up the section of pavement that was kept clear by the police.

'Yes.'

'Magnus Bacton.' He wore charity bands round his wrists, had flawless teeth and a fringe swept high. 'I've brought along Channel Four. Looks like things are starting to simmer.' The protestors yowled. They had seen the television camera. Veiled women in a separate section of the protest squawked and shook their fists. Petroc only just resisted the un-Christian desire to scream at them to shut up.

Bacton's crew filmed this before going inside for a cup of tea. The lawyer met Matt for the first time. Bacton shook Matt's hand and repeated the exercise twice so the cameras could get it from different angles.

The numbers outside were greater than ever. The majority were under the age of thirty. A robed cleric brandished a heavy book, standing on a raised platform. Was this how Moses had been? We may picture him some snowy-eyebrowed sage but might he not have been a pepperpot revolutionary, igniting zealots? The rabble-rouser here used a megaphone, repeating slogans about blasphemy and the 'rape' of a Muslim girl. If the police did not act it would be a slur against Islam and there would be a harvest of woe. The camera zoomed in on the protestors' cross faces which, once edited, would provide a contrast to the hopelessly genteel churchgoers with their custard creams and flower rotas. In the middle of it all sat a young man with a guitar picking out the notes of an old hymn tune.

Derrick arrived. He had to walk past the crowd and his evangelising gait altered to something more prickly. The protestors gave him the bird and he gave it back with knobs on, making to butt one young black guy who insulted him. 'Hey, man, you racist?' shouted the man. The police moved to intervene but by then Derrick was shouting that Matt was a fine young lad who was himself making a stand against bigotry.

'If you want racism, matey, hear how that boy was treated by his girlfriend's father,' said Derrick. 'That's where the racism is.'

'All right, sir,' said a policeman.

'I can look after myself,' growled Derrick. The crowd jeered. Bacton used this aggression to do a piece-to-camera. He did it in one take.

'You lot are the racists,' yelled Derrick as he was steered to the church by the police. 'They don't like it up 'em!' The submariner from Pew Patrol was next to him, tweaking his neck at double speed. The cameras caught veins prominent at Derrick's temples. 'We're Christians and proud of it,' Derrick told Bacton. 'You have to stand up for your rights. Otherwise you get flattened. Been that way for centuries. We're back to the crusades.'

'What a racket,' said churchwarden Georgina Brack. In the church she and her sidekick Beetle had set up a table where the ladies were making a Christmas crib. It featured a dove. Beetle wondered if the dove should be a hawk, or a dead duck.

'I don't know how we will get home,' said Mrs Brack. 'Listen to the mob. We could do with Mark giving them a defiant blast of organ.'

'*Onward, Christian Soldiers*,' said Beetle. 'More use than butterfly hymns.'

'You all right, Derrick dear?' asked Mrs Brack. 'You look hot and bothered.'

'Too bloody right.'

'Derrick!'

'To be honest I could do with something a bit stronger than this cup of tea. Couple of those fanatics have got knives – and they meant me to see them.'

'Knives? Are you sure?'

'I saw a flash of something metal.'

'We should sing something,' said the widow.

'Good idea,' said Derrick. 'I'll text the All Stars and get them round for a Jam for Jesus.'

'Don't you think we've suffered enough?' said Beetle.

'Derrick, you'll never get your band members through that crowd now.'

'Rubbish,' said Derrick. 'Just you see.'

WHEN Petroc made it back to Base Camp that evening, Ross was in the drawing room, talking to a pink-eyed Nettle Greenhill. 'Sorry, I didn't know you were busy,' said Petroc. He was holding a red-blotched handkerchief to his brow. He made to leave the room.

'Good God,' said Ross. 'You're bleeding. Your trousers are torn.'

'Yes, I only realised just now.'

'Petroc, are you OK?' asked Nettle, blowing her nose.

'What happened?' said Ross. 'Sit down, man.'

'There was a battle – well, a skirmish.'

'In the church?'

'Outside the church so far. Police had to break it up. But we got the old ladies out.'

'Nettle, my dear, you stay here with Petroc. Lay him on the sofa and see if you can do anything with that cut. I'll fetch kitchen roll. Petroc, you're shaking. Hip-flask time.'

'Sweet tea.'

'Both.'

The hymn-singing jam session had hardly been a mass gathering. In addition to Beetle and Mrs Brack there were some eight parishioners, including the pew patrolmen. Three of the All Stars indeed made it past the protestors and this gave Bacton and his cameras adequate material. The band's young drummer threw his sticks in the air and caught them and Derrick held a clenched hand aloft while he sang a modern worship song, *Claim Back the Mountain*. As he sang it, his right foot stamped an aggressive beat. Organist Mark wandered in and listened briefly before slinking up to his loft. Matt soon joined him there, glad to escape Derrick's din.

An edited package was squirted through to the TV studio. It was going to be 'upsummed' by live remarks from Bacton outside the church near the end of the bulletin. This would follow a burst of film that showed the church's occupants singing *Heaven Invites You to a Party* with its chanted refrain 'Everybody! Everybody!' – everybody here being this frail collection of souls. Derrick did a little shake of his bottom at each chant and whooped.

There was a presumption that the crowd would behave once Bacton started drawling to camera about 'the Ruby Street siege' and 'Christianity under the cosh'. Petroc and Derrick escorted the ladies down the open passage created by the police. Mission successful. Petroc and Derrick tried to return to the church and were asked by the TV crew to wait while Bacton finished his 'live'. That was when Derrick was hit by a missile. It was a stone or a clod of earth – hard to tell because the camera lights created such a contrast of brightness and dark night. Derrick should have turned the other cheek, but when you have been hit unexpectedly like that, it is only human to retaliate. He punched the nearest protestor. Channel Four's boxing commentator would have approved of his left hook.

The cameras continued to roll as the fight spread, a couple of policemen losing their helmets, one officer having to be carried away with blood flowing down his neck. A police horse was battered on the nose by a placard wielded by a man in a balaclava. He was taken out by one of Derrick's mates. Another ex-squaddie from the Pew Patrol lingered beside Petroc, protecting him. The news pictures showed a youth in a kufi throw a milk bottle at the church. Bacton's live link had been kept open. Speaking to the studio, he cried: 'Jon, we've now got a pitched battle on our hands – this is breaking news on Channel Four. What you are seeing is nothing less than the front line between two faiths, two cultures, maybe the past and the future.' Behind Bacton was that a flash of clerical dog collar – or a glint of something else? A figure rushed into the throng, fists flailing. There came a whoosh as the milk bottle's contents made contact with the burning taper in the bottle's neck. Another couple of fire bombs followed, though they failed to set the church alight. Windows were damaged. Somewhere in the mêlée, Petroc sustained a blow to the brow.

Using a butterfly plaster from Base Camp's First Aid box, Nettle closed the cut and swabbed the surrounding skin. Petroc submitted to her ministrations. 'We'd better see how it's being reported.'

'I'll look,' said Nettle. 'You keep that head still.' She gave Petroc's brow a soft dab.

Ross was aghast. 'What a disaster.'

'Maybe not,' said Petroc. 'Let's see what the early reports are saying. Any sign, Nettle?'

She looked at her smart phone. 'Hmmn, quite a lot.'

'I told you to be careful,' said Ross.

'What was I meant to do?' said Petroc. 'Just hand the kid to these Islamic nutters?'

'The police aren't Islamic nutters.'

'They do their dirty work.'

'You should never have given the boy house-room in the first place,' shouted Ross.

'Well if that's how you feel, I regret taking house-room here!'

'Calvert will go berserk.'

'Sod, sod, sod Calvert,' said Petroc. 'Sorry, Nettle.'

'I'm not an innocent, you know', said Nettle. The landline rang. Ross handed it to Petroc.

'Yes, speaking. What? When did this happen? Oh, dear Lord, that's terrible. Yes, no, I quite understand. Thank you for letting me know.' He replaced the receiver.

'You all right?' asked Ross.

'That was the police,' said Petroc. 'One of the protestors,' he paused. 'Has died.'

'Oh gracious.'

'It was a knife wound.' Petroc was white. His beard never looked blacker.

'Great,' said Ross. 'So now this is a murder case, too.'

PETROC said: 'About that drink. I'll take a nip, if it's still being offered.'

'I'll see Nettle out,' said Ross. As he and Nettle headed for the front door, the telephone again rang. It was Calvert. Petroc took the call.

Ross made sure Nettle got into her taxi. Re-entering Base Camp, he almost tripped on Petroc's rucksack in the hall. When he leaned down to move it, he felt a wetness and a sharp edge. He presumed Petroc's plastic lunchbox must have been broken in the mêlée but when he investigated he found a bloody rag at the top of the bag. Wrapped in this rag was a blade. Its dullness was what struck him most, its drabness. A blade. An evil-looking blade. Ross hurriedly returned the knife to the bag.

The hall telephone clicked as Petroc finished his call in the drawing room. Ross went into the kitchen to wash his hands. When he returned, he asked how the conversation with Calvert had gone. 'Business-like,' said Petroc. 'We agreed a form of words for a Church House announcement. It urged anyone with information to go to the police. I've been told to be at the church tomorrow to help inquiries.' Ross poured Petroc a double from his flask. They sat. The cats, blessed innocents, were asleep by the fire. Ross fought to stop his eyes darting round the room, darting towards Petroc, accusing him. He felt an urge to stare at his housemate, to look at him and search for a sensible answer to what he had just found in the rucksack. Who put the knife there? Why had Petroc brought it to Base Camp? Somehow he found refuge in small talk and in the fires of martyrdom.

'Mulberry gin,' said Ross. 'I make it at home. Here's to Latimer, Ridley and Cranmer. I always toast them when I'm in a stew.

Makes one's own troubles seem less severe.' He drank from the flask. 'Here's to dousing their fires, poor swine.' Petroc tried his gin. The pink liquid was strong, sweet and quite possibly flammable. It would have made any pyre roar.

'Powerful drop.' He coughed.

Ross reached for his prayer book and gave Petroc a long, quizzical look. Eventually he asked: 'You OK?'

'No. And I don't deserve to be. I took a risk.'

'You want to talk about it?'

'Not sure.'

Ross flicked through the book's onion-skin pages and after another pause said: 'Such delicate paper yet the words could be steel. Now lost to most of our people. Calvert mocks it. Ancient history, he says.'

'I can see I have been rash. That's Calvert's main complaint.'

'There's more blood in a page of this prayer book than in the entire vessel of that man's flesh and veins. I think of my father in his RAF bomber. He was frightened all the time, you know, but couldn't show it.'

'Honour thy father and thy mother, that thy days may be long in the land,' said Petroc. 'See? I've been doing some research. We evangelicals aren't all monsters.'

'Aren't you?' It came out blunter than perhaps intended. Thou shalt not kill. Thou shalt not covet thy neighbour's wife. Or girlfriend.

Petroc glanced at Ross, wondering. He said: 'Be proud of your Book. I would be, if it were mine.'

Ross replied: 'It's everyone's.'

'You wouldn't have liked the hymns we were singing in church today. Organist Mark hid.'

'My lot. Your lot. Then there's their lot. They force their women to wear burkas and chop off their noses if they stray.'

'The lot that don't believe anything are worse,' said Petroc.

'Are they?' After a while Ross said: 'Do you think they screamed? As the flames licked the faggots and their fingers burned, did they weep?' He remembered the pain when he had rescued his prayer book from the fire. It still throbbed.

'Who?'

'Latimer. Ridley. Cranmer. Did their tears and eyeballs steam? When does a man stop feeling pain?' Ross screwed up his own eyes, tunnelling inside.

ROSS dreamed he was in a street, talking to Calvert. Big Ben was striking endless times when a child wandered past, head covered by a hood. The youngster was crying.

'Do you think that child's all right?'

An uninterested Calvert: 'None of our business.'

'But what if . . .'

'What if, what if?' sneered Calvert.

They completed some business and Calvert strode away to his office to complete a hostile takeover of the Methodists. The distressed child was still nearby, snivelling. Ross approached.

'Are you all right?'

The child did not seem to hear.

'Hello there. Are you OK?'

The child stopped crying and Ross felt redeemed. He had brought balm. The child – a boy – turned and, head still down, held out his arms. Ross crouched to be at his level. The boy lifted his head.

There was no face. Just a skull, worms wriggling in its eye sockets. Ross's ears filled with the sound of marching boots.

11

Memory Of A Row

WAKING sweat-soaked, Ross gazed at the ceiling; it took a few seconds for his pulse to slow. In slippers he headed downstairs, tiptoeing past Petroc's bedroom. Petroc was a heavy sleeper, even without mulberry gin. Ross had not had a solid night's sleep for years. The door was half open and he could see Petroc on his back, hands folded on his barrel chest, seemingly as dead to the world as an entombed Crusader.

Once Ross had passed the door, Petroc's eyes flicked open, as they had been much of the night. Events raced through his mind; the loudhailer, the chants, Derrick's fist clenched during the worship songs, the splintering of glass. The knifing.

Ross made a coffee and sat at his desk in the drawing room. His hip flask was where he had left it and there was a sour fug in the room. He opened one of the French windows to let out the cat. Fresh air blew away some of the seediness.

Andrew and Morwen had been in Herefordshire that Sunday when Ross preached about forgiveness. They had arrived from Wales late. Andrew, stepping out of his car at the house, had been almost knocked over by Barney. 'Good boy! Down, Barney. Morwen is home team.' Ross had slow-cooked a leg of lamb – roasts were the one thing he could cook. The smell always sent Barney into orbit. Andrew had kissed his mother and handed

Ross a bottle of cheap red, calling him 'old chap'. It embarrassed him to say 'Daddy'.

'Here's a bottle, old chap. Don't suppose it's up to much.'

'We're glad to have you. Rioja? Thank you.'

'Sorry we're late. Pig of a road.'

'Morwen, good to see you again, dear.' Damn, he shouldn't have called her 'dear'.

'Hello, Thomas.' She always called him Thomas.

'How are the children?'

'They're with their father.' They invariably were.

The news was broken just as pudding was ending. Lunch had passed at a languid pace, Theresa doing most of the talking. They would normally have rushed through lunch to give Barney a walk but the clocks had changed and the light would not last. Poor Barney. Still, he could count on some lamb leftovers.

'There's something I have to tell you two,' said Andrew.

'Something *we* have to tell you,' added Morwen. She had a black fringe, a puffin-beak nose, a stillness. She stared at Andrew.

'Yes, something *we* have, well, done,' said Andrew.

'Is it good news, darling?'

'Yes, Mum. We think so. Very good news.'

'Oh good, I like good news.'

'Go on then,' Ross had said. 'Sick it up in mother's hand!' Another family expression. Family life brought its code words, its own liturgy.

'We got married.'

Looking back, Ross knew he had drunk more than was wise. The welcome-home supermarket cava, times two, had been followed by white wine during soup (vichyssoise fortified by amontillado). There had been red with the lamb and they had even opened that rough Rioja Andrew had brought. Ross made great play of what good value it was. There had also been a couple of glasses of some pudding wine he had been given by a parishioner at Christmas. The prodigal son did not come home every weekend, ha ha.

Not that anyone was laughing now.

Theresa had said 'Darlings' and followed it with a few silent kisses. Her eyes filled. Morwen's avian stare remained no more moist than marble. 'Wonderful news,' added Theresa, and she started taking the dishes next door, where she could have a proper cry. 'Wonderful news.' If she said it often enough, she might believe it.

'Any more of that pudding wine, old chap?' Andrew had reached for it himself.

'Who took the service?' asked Ross.

'Oh, we didn't have a service, Thomas!'

Maybe it was the 'oh' that pushed him over the edge. 'Why not?' He said it sharply. Theresa would have tried to intervene and would have said it didn't matter but she was in the kitchen. Anyway, it did matter, to him, it bloody well did.

'We went to a register office.'

'Where?'

'Aberystwyth.'

'Aberystwyth!'

'We went to a register office because, as you know, Morwen doesn't believe.'

'I do, but I do,' snapped Ross. A stupid sentence. I do but I do. 'I bloody well do know. But I do believe. I'm a parson.'

'You weren't getting married, Thomas. We were.'

'Aberystwyth register office.'

'Tom, darling, it's all right,' said Theresa, coming back in with chocolates.

'Aberystwyth!'

'Stop going on about Aber-bloody-ystwyth,' said Andrew. 'It's where Morwen comes from. It's where my job is.'

'It's just we would have liked to have been there with you for the big day,' said Theresa.

'We wanted to keep it private,' said Morwen. 'Intimate. It wasn't really a big day. It was just a bureaucratic formality, so we can pay less tax.'

'And because we love each other,' said Andrew.

'Private!' Ross had roared. 'A marriage, private?'

'Well, isn't it?' said Morwen, flaring.

'No it isn't. It's a public declaration.'

'We didn't have to tell you. I knew this was a mistake, Andy.'

'Dad, we just didn't want a fuss.'

'If you were going to get married, why didn't you keep that poor child?'

'Oh, Tom, no,' said Theresa

'If you were going to get married, why didn't you have that baby? It was only a year ago.' Ross found he was shaking. 'He could have lived.'

Morwen rose slowly. 'How do you know it wasn't a "she"? Don't you dare tell me how to lead my life. Don't you dare tell me what to do with my body. You're not my father. We got married. I married your son, even though you don't like me. Get over it! You freak me out!'

Morwen, having slammed her wine glass down so hard that red wine jumped over the table, left the room. 'Oh balls,' said Andrew, and he went off to look for her, leaving his pudding wine untouched. Ross slowly lifted it and poured it back in the bottle. The chocolates were still in their box.

Theresa went to have a lie-down and Ross had a strong coffee before walking to evensong. When Andrew was a boy it had been his favourite service. Barney happily accepted the invitation. Lucky Barney, not to comprehend.

At Base Camp, rain played against the French windows. Ross stared at the blank sheet of writing paper in front of him. His own flesh and blood had married a dour, divorced atheist who had aborted his grandchild: it was hardly the stuff of the *Magnificat*, Abraham and his seed forever.

The pen stalled in his hands. In the night he had devised so many phrases. *Did you forget that, as a boy, you promised I would officiate at your wedding? We were going to choose the hymns.* Andrew would not remember. Why should he? He was only ten at the time, such a tender, serious child. *Did you think how this would look to my parishioners? Did you think of the gossip? Of the shame of having a daughter-in-law who is so . . .* So what? So independent? Was that what irked him?

He tried again. *Dear Andrew, your mother tells me we need to talk but you know I am bad on a telephone. I understand there is little chance of your coming back home for some time. Perhaps a letter is the way to proceed. My objection is not to Morwen. You love her. I respect that. My reservation about this marriage is selfish yet I hope understandable. We feel left out of a day which could have been one of the happiest of all our lives.*

Ross heard a noise. He jumped. 'Petroc. I thought you were asleep. How are you feeling?'

'Under par. My head hurts, not entirely from your hooch. Are you writing a sermon?'

'A letter. To my son. Not an easy one.'

'Want to talk about it?'

'Not madly. I'll have another coffee if you're making one.'

They did talk – though only about Ross's family problems. Petroc told Ross: 'You could just ring Andrew. Good invention, the telephone. Tell him you love him.'

'I feel more comfortable with a letter.'

They did not talk about the killing at Petroc's church. They did not mention the knife.

12

Nurse Harris Arrives

BREAKFAST at Maximilian's Hotel, SW1, was served by near-silent, expressionless youths in Maoist uniforms. Maximilian's had a scarlet starburst motif and this adorned the left upper chest of the gunmetal-grey outfits. Designer cruets set a minimalist tone. Spiralling racks held blinis and wholemeal toast, trimmed as though by nail clippers.

'I'll have another passion-fruit infusion,' Bryce told the waiter – or was it a waitress? He turned to his breakfast companion, an untidy fellow rather less wholesome than Maximilian's house muesli. 'Sorry, what were you saying?'

Pike had been talking about Chance, the home affairs committee chairman tangled in the visa scandal. 'Class story,' said Pike. Though he was eating a full English (Maximilian's did not list such a device on its menu but Pike had demanded one all the same) the man from the *Dispatch* had not discarded his chewing gum. He accentuated his fake Cockney accent.

'Poor George,' said Bryce with a lean smile.

Pike: 'Reckon he's brown bread then?' Bryce, who was dribbling organic Lebanese honey over some granary toast, looked blank. Pike explained: 'Reckon he's finished?'

'I doubt it.'

'He was bang to rights.'

'That expression means little at Westminster.'

Bryce had seated himself so that he could see new arrivals. While waiting for Pike, ostensibly studying the financial press, he had spotted three lobbyists, two think-tank directors and one television producer. This breakfast with Pike was off the record but it was no bad thing if word seeped out that Bryce spoke to Pike. It increased the value of Pike's column if people realised that it was well sourced; and it made the inner world warier of Bryce if people knew that he talked to *Westminster Whispers*.

'Much goin' on?' said Pike. 'I hear you're chummy with that Dymock bloke.'

'Augustus?'

'He seems to be plotting the downfall of the Church of England. It's almost Soviet.'

'How melodramatic you are.'

'He's ambitious.'

'He is interested in power and would prefer certain people not to have so much.' A waitress appeared. Pike ordered seconds of black pudding. He called her 'mate'.

'Augustus is not an ideologue,' said Bryce.

'Eh?'

'He is right to question the Church's land bank but he is not fuelled by the anger that fuels most of us. He is a scientist. The human side of politics strikes him as illogical.'

'There was me thinking you were mates.'

'Actually I hate him in some ways. He has a sensitive son and is not good with him. But enough of this. Have you heard about "Mr Creaker" Aldred hiring a black masseuse?'

PARLIAMENTARY opinion was divided as to whether or not the Speaker's West Indian nurse helped matters. Nurse Harris was undoubtedly expert at first aid. She was said to be ace with the ping-pong-bat defibrillators. Yet she possessed so striking a physique, uniformed in starched blue and white, that any old man teetering on life's rim might, when she bent over him, find his pulse pushed to the brink; revs needle to red zone, phutt.

The doorkeepers have nicknamed her 'Bombs' Harris, reported Pike's column. The nickname had in fact been invented by Bryce.

When Ross turned up for the half-past-two procession, Nurse Harris stood in the Robing Room. Mates introduced her to Ross. Her hair was collected beneath her cap and her strong arms were bared to the world. She was in her early forties and had never done a day's dieting in her life. Mates's wife had managed to bake a dark, sticky ginger cake which had risen plumply and cascaded over the tin in an eruption of molasses. Mates offered it round before the procession. Nurse Harris took a large slice, crumbs gambolling down her front.

Ross had barely thrown on his cassock when the cry 'Speeeeekah!' pulled them off on their pavane towards the Chamber. They were out of the door, heading to Central Lobby, when he remembered: Prayers. As panic gripped, he saw a hand stretch in front of him. It belonged to Nurse Harris and it held his prayer book. She had seen it on the Robing Room table and realised he had forgotten it. She was accompanying the procession like a police outrider. 'Thank you,' he mouthed silently. She smiled.

Speaker Aldred needed his new nurse to steer him up the steps into his Chair, her hands on his hips. She made sure he did not trip on his robes and squeezed his twig of an arm.

'Thank you, Timothy.'

Nurse Harris bowed. The eyes of the Father of the House, Sir Tudor Matthews, adhered to her as treacle to a spoon. She moved to the corner just behind the Speaker's Chair and remained there until Aldred finished his stint. Mates would have to organise a chair for the nurse. The Speaker's health was unlikely to improve.

Ross was later walking down the cloisters to Portcullis House, where he hoped to find a cup of tea, when Jean stopped him.

'Chaplain, do you have a moment? You may recall I came to you once before. I'm Jean.'

'Yes.' Ross's mind raced. He did vaguely remember talk of a lover. Yes, that was it. An unhappy affair.

'I wonder if I might come and see you again.' Her eyebrows crested.

Ross said: 'I'm going to the atrium for a cup of tea. Join me.'

They found a space, hardly the most private of places, amid the metal tables in the atrium. Words flowed out of her.

'I'm not sure there's much I can do,' said Ross.

'You have a position. These are your churches they are going to steal.' She had been telling him about the documents she had found in Mears's filing cabinet. Well, documents was perhaps a glorified word. They were really just notes to himself, written after meetings with Dymock and Greenhill.

'I am bound to discretion,' said Ross.

'Not if I absolve you.'

'Absolution is my side of the deal.'

Anyone riding down one of the Portcullis House lifts, with their glass sides, could have seen the woman squeeze the chaplain's hands in apparent exhortation. Mears certainly did as he rode down in the lift from his office. So that's where Jean had gone. He had been wondering why no one had brought him a coffee. What could she be talking about with that waffly vicar?

Waffly, the vicar may have been. He was also, to Mears's good fortune, discreet.

FRIDAY mornings in the Commons seldom amounted to much but Speaker Aldred had assented to a request from Mackie, the peppery Member from Luton.

'Urgent Question, Mr Mackie.'

'Thank you Mr Speaker, for giving me leave to ask the Home Secretary if she will make a statement about events outside the

London church where a suspected criminal is being given illegal sanctuary.' The Speaker had been inclined not to grant the debate but had relented when he saw it suggested – in that morning's *Dispatch* – that he had gone gaga.

The police minister rose to the despatch box. 'Mr Speaker, I have been asked to reply.' Opposition MPs complained that the Home Secretary herself was not in attendance.

'Where is she?' shouted George Chance.

Aldred wobbled to his feet. 'Order. The House should listen to the minister.'

Mackie was envious of the way Tristan Kendrick had made recent running with the church siege. There was a danger that joyless little Welshman could make the issue his own. Mackie, whose constituents would expect him to be at the top of the oratorical game, intended to regain the initiative. Kendrick was seldom in Westminster on Fridays as Welsh MPs scarpered en masse most Thursday lunchtimes. Catching an early train meant they could buy a cheap train ticket yet still claim for a full-priced one. A dodge here, the occasional fifty quid gain there: by such chisel marks did MPs prosper.

The police minister, without enthusiasm, said: 'Thank you, Mr Speaker. The Home Secretary is attending a European Council meeting in Brussels.' The small number of Government backbenchers present said 'Hear hear.'

There followed a brief, factual description of what had occurred. Protestors had gathered outside the church of Alleluia Jesus! (formerly St Michael and All Angels) which was under police surveillance since giving sanctuary to a man suspected of attacking the Pakistani airline office. The crowd had swelled over several days. A Channel Four film crew's arrival may have sparked trouble. The protest had erupted into violence and police had still to work out precisely what had occurred. The minister admitted: 'I could actually hear the trouble from my office in

the Department when working late. An initially small force of
community support officers was augmented by reinforcements
with riot shields and batons. A contretemps took place between
protestors and members of the church, some of them ex-members
of the Armed Forces.'

'Vigilantes!' cried Mackie.

'No,' said the minister. He returned to his script to say that
in the mêlée, bricks and petrol bombs were thrown through the
church windows. Arrests had been made.

'Disgraceful!' said Mackie.

'I can report,' said the police minister, 'that four officers
were taken to hospital with cuts and bruises. Three members of
the public have been charged with minor disorder offences. A
member of the parochial church council has been bound over to
keep the peace. One protestor, unfortunately, died. No arrest has
been made in connection with the death.'

Mackie was swift to his feet: 'While thanking the minister for
his response, can I ask why this matter was ever allowed to get
so far? Why is this church being permitted to give sanctuary –
an absurd concept in this age – to a violent youth who caused
serious damage to commercial premises? Will the police stop this
nonsense? British Muslims are astonished – astonished! – at the
special treatment given to a turbulent priest.

'What is known of the political sympathies of the vicar who
has encouraged this sanctuary? Is it true he is an extreme right-
winger? Will the Home Secretary summon the Bishop of London
to a meeting without coffee and remind him of his duty, as a
parliamentarian, to uphold the law?'

Speaker Aldred thought about interrupting this jeremiad but
had not the strength to do so. Nurse Harris watched her patient
with concern.

Mackie kicked on with his speech: 'We have these bishops,
these draped jays, in our legislature. Let us use the leverage that

provides. My Muslim constituents will not allow their religion to be attacked by the state church. When their religious leaders behave in a provocative manner, they are slammed in Belmarsh or stuck on planes to Jordan. When will this House debate the very matter of Establishment? Will the Government get a grip before the streets of London explode?'

Ross watched the debate on the Robing Room's television monitor. Sir Roger Richards put a head round the door. 'Ah, you're following it, good,' said the clerk. He sat down beside Ross, so lightly he could have been a butterfly landing on a leaf.

Debate after an Urgent Question is limited but Mears, never much one for going to his constituency on a Friday, was among those to contribute. He expressed concern for community relations, the police, the family of the dead man – 'Uncle Tom Cobley and all,' murmured Sir Roger. The Member for Oakford ended by asking the minister 'to tell the Lords Spiritual that while principles of free belief must be observed, the Church should not suppose that its bricks, mortar and steeples are anything but taxable and temporal'.

Lionel Moss from the house-building lobby also threw in his groat's worth, asking: 'Will this alleged malefactor who has been given sanctuary now be handed over to the police, yes or no?'

'The clinging Moss,' said Sir Roger, 'never knowingly original. But Mears could be more significant. This is not entirely helpful, Tom. Does your new housemate understand the potential significance of these rumbles?'

'I'm not sure. But he means well. I'll have a word.' Ross did his best to look resolute but he did not mention the blade he had found in Petroc's rucksack.

EACH sweep of the broom brought a tinkling as broken glass was pulled into the dustpan. The smashed vestry window was being boarded up by a glazier. The stained-glass window above the west door had been cracked. The one that grieved Petroc most was a triple-arched window on the south wall that showed three angels guarded by St George on his charger. A brick had removed St George altogether.

'Tom, what are you doing here?' Petroc still had the plaster on his forehead.

'They let me through security,' said Ross. 'It's a bit of a mess here.'

'I know, but the community has been amazing. Workmen have come out for nothing. Hang on.' His mobile was ringing. 'I'd better take this. Hello?' Ross nosed around while Petroc took the call. There might be no sense of peace but with the smell of petrol – from the firebombs – and the glazier's hammering, this was a building very much alive. A cheap love song played on the glazier's radio. Ross heard a woman's voice sing along to it.

'I'm on my way to Paddington but thought I should let you know,' Ross told Petroc when he had finished his call.

'Know what, Tom?'

'There was an Urgent Question in the Commons this morning. The politicians are on the warpath.' Derrick entered.

'It's OK, Derrick,' said Petroc. 'Tom's one of us. Almost.' Petroc added: 'Derrick was a trooper last night.'

'So I heard,' said Ross.

Derrick, who was limping, said: 'There was a bit of an exchange of views, that's all.'

'The police minister was talking about it in the Commons just now.'

'Uh-oh.'

'Indeed,' said Ross. 'The knifing has given the politicians a reason to interfere. What happened? Did you see?'

'Course not,' said Derrick, slowly. 'If I did, I'd have said, wouldn't I? Give me that broom, Petroc, and I'll get on with cleaning up this lot.' He gave Ross a cold stare and said: 'We've got a wedding tomorrow.'

'It can't possibly go ahead,' said Ross.

'Why not?' said Derrick.

'Someone was killed.'

'This wedding's a big event in the lives of one of our new parish families,' said Derrick. 'Two hundred people expected. The show goes on. We mustn't let the enemy beat us.'

'The enemy?' said Ross. 'The police aren't our enemy.'

'The Muslims, that's who I mean,' said Derrick. 'The Muslims and militant atheists. Politicians never know what they're talking about.'

'Tom, it's good of you to have come,' said Petroc.

'Things can run away with themselves at Westminster,' said Ross. 'They're working themselves into a hoo-hah.'

'They always bloody do,' said Derrick. 'Any excuse to attack the Church.'

'Please, guys,' said Petroc. 'I've got Calvert coming round in an hour.' Derrick limped off, muttering that things had to be done. Ross looked at his departing back and wondered.

'Hello, Vicar,' said Nettle, entering from the vestry where she had been cleaning. It must have been her singing earlier. Dressed in an apron, she scratched her nose with a yellow-gloved hand and left behind some soapsuds.

'Hello, Nettle. Does your mother know you're here?' said Ross.

'I hope not.'

'So do I.'

ONCE he was home in Herefordshire, Ross telephoned Petroc. 'Did Calvert stay long?'

'Quarter of an hour.'

'What did he say?'

'I have been given a yellow card.' Ross did not know the expression. Petroc explained: 'I've been given an official warning. He says I'm out of my depth.'

'You're still new in the parish.'

'That makes me more expendable.'

'Did you get the church tidy for the wedding?'

'So long as the bride and groom don't mind having a demo outside when they emerge as man and wife. Knowing this couple, I suspect they will see it as a Christian challenge. They're charismatics. I fully expect them to try to convert the Muslim mob. These are strong people, Tom.'

'Have you seen the way the media are reporting it?'

'No.'

'I was listening to the news in the car.'

'What was the slant?'

'A Church embattled.'

'Well, that's true.'

'But it was the tone.'

'Tell me.'

'They were serious about the death, but it was almost as if they thought Christianity ridiculous.' The presenter of the drive-time radio programme had first given the context of Matt seeking sanctuary and the protestor's death. There was a brief mention of the Commons Urgent Question, a potted history of sanctuary in western civilisation and a bland official comment from Calvert. Before going live to a reporter outside the church, the presenter used a clip of Derrick leading the rendition of *Jesus is my Sunbeam* while the battle raged outside the previous evening. 'And now to our own little sunbeam, reporter Anthony Purves, outside the church. Anthony, bless you, my son. What happened? What's happening? What will happen?' To which the reporter responded with sing-song gaiety: 'Well, Eddie, congregants here tried to ignore the violence last night and sang worship songs – hymns as they used to be called. They sang about the birds and bees and flowers of the field. If they thought that projected Christian pacifism, it did not work. Protestors mocked what they call the 'child-like delusions' of the churchgoers. They say the singing was 'irrelevant' and 'pathetic'. One Muslim man told me, "These Christians are more interested in butterflies than racial harmony. It is time they got real."' The presenter asked the reporter a couple more larky questions about the childish hymns.

Ross told Petroc: 'They were working up quite a contrast. You had Disney-style hymns inside while outside one of the same church's supporters slipped a Muslim three inches of cold blade. Jihad with sunbeams.'

'That's not fair,' said Petroc.

'Since when are the media fair? It's a pity you weren't singing old favourites. Cherished hymns. The sort the public hear in their heads when or if they ever think of the Church of England. They identify with those. The BBC would not have mocked them.'

'Youngsters don't know those hymns, Tom.'

'And whose ruddy, ruddy fault is that?' Ross tried to control his anger. He rarely tried to argue this out loud because he had been browbeaten into feeling out of kilter with the times, yet he knew he was right. It was hard to say because it was wrapped up with class and nationalism, but how could a Church push itself forward as a serious body, as a faith with a grown-up code for life, when its evangelism – its modern branding – was so babyish? He resumed: 'But the media do know the old hymns, Petroc. The non-churchgoing, adult public does, too. This isn't just tradition for tradition's sake. It's about what lies deep in people – deep in their aesthetic guts.'

'We've moved on from the boring old hymns!'

'You may have done, my friend, but boring old Britain hasn't. Boring old Britain, boring mainstream, middle-class, white, conservative, fifty-something Britain, may not go to church every Sunday any more but it still loves *Jerusalem*. It hears it on Classic FM and it tingles to the chords. It hears it at football tournaments and it thinks "Yes, that's our country and our way of life". And if it had heard those sort of hymns at a moment of crisis for our Church, it would have felt its loyalties tugged.' He could hear Petroc trying to dissent and he urged him: 'It would. It would. God, this is so important. This is core. It's what makes people tick. Believe. Talk to Mark.'

'He's impossible.'

'Organists are!'

'And they drink.'

'So do I. But I'm right about this, trust me. The Church has lost thousands of people by being so pig-headed against tradition. They go to church once or twice a year and if they hear old hymns they are reassured and will return. But instead, too often, they are attacked by the unfamiliar, confronted or "challenged" by something that offends their sensibilities, so they feel a sect has occupied their church and they think, "Why should we bother?" And the upshot of that is that Islam has the faith field practically to itself and the whole edifice of Christianity is imperilled.'

'It can't be that bad.'

'It *is*,' said Ross, and he almost shouted the words. There was a moment's silence before he continued: 'Oh, and Petroc . . .'

'Yes?'

'There's something else I was going to say but I'll save it for when I see you.' Ross had heard about tapping telephones. He would ask about the blade but he would do so one-to-one. 'Just think about making your peace with Mark.'

'OK, OK, I'll think about it. I dunno, Tom. You may be right, I guess. Thanks.'

HE did think about it – and rang back half an hour later. 'Can you talk to Mark for me?'

'You're prepared to be persuaded?' said Ross.

'On this narrow matter of music, yes.'

'Good on you. That says a lot about you. I respect you a lot for it. Look, I know you've had a hellish week. I have left a present for you at Base Camp. On your bed. I hope it may interest you.'

'What is it?'

'You'll see. Goodnight. Get some rest.'

Ross soon placed another call, this time to Mark, and asked: 'Can you find it in yourself to be civil to your vicar?'

'Maybe.'

'Alleluia, Jesus.'

'Don't you bloody start,' said Mark.

CALVERT had not lost his temper. It might have been better for Petroc if he had. The Dean of Communications had been trained to restrain emotions. Aggression was channelled into measured intent. The more oily he was, the more truly furious. 'You need to realise,' he had told Petroc, 'that I am not speaking to you as your friend Tony. I am speaking to you as a messenger from the bishop.'

'OK,' said Petroc. He craved a cigarette but knew it would not help his plight.

'Actually, it's not OK. He's disappointed, Petroc. Concerned. He worries that you are out of your depth. Our professionalism is under attack. The Church's brand is being tarnished. Knifing deaths really aren't us. Have you seen the media coverage?'

'Some of it is supportive.'

'Not much. The Church is meant to provide social glue, Petroc. We exist to bond communities. You are achieving the opposite.'

'We are challenging Islam.'

'Challenging Islam! One small urban church. Challenging them for bloodshed, perhaps. You really don't understand how big this is.'

'I didn't know principles came in sizes.'

'I have been instructed to tell you this. Listen, Petroc.'

'I am listening.'

'The bishop will remove you from this church, using probationary powers, if there is one more unfortunate incident.'

'I . . .'

'The bishop will not tolerate further strains on community relations. The bishop will make sure you never get another parish. If there is further trouble. Do I make myself clear?' Calvert had left in a taxi that had been waiting. It was on the central Church account.

The present on Petroc's bed was a Book of Common Prayer, more than a hundred years old. Andrew did not want it so Ross had found it a willing home. A note in Ross's hand said: 'Petroc, let this book spread its word beyond our family. With admiration, T. Ross.'

13

Evensong Takes An Unusual Turn

FLIGHT BA 4750 from Karachi approached Heathrow airport – wheels descending from the belly of the aircraft – as first light touched the Windsor Castle flagpole. The farmland surrounding the airport bore that bruised-brown, sodden look of English flatlands in winter. A squadron of geese flapped west, below the radar. Rabbits frolicked near the airport's perimeter fence, ignorant of the gods of commerce.

Bacton's old connections with the Pakistani prime minister had activated approvals and assurances. Officialdom had bent to the finger of television. Inside the aircraft a production assistant ensured that everything was recorded. She filmed with a palm-held camera, which gave an impression of snatched reportage, the soundtrack catching the constant pitch inside the jetliner's cabin. A date appeared bottom left of screen, as in family-holiday cine footage. Flight 4750 reached the arrivals gate and its engines whined their last. After passport checks and baggage collection, two women, one in the demure fashions of Islam, walked through Customs. They were met by a larger camera crew. 'Welcome home.'

On the airfield a mole broke through the surface soil just beside a runway light. Its powerful pink feet clawed the soil into a mound which almost covered the light. Although a Jumbo jet was at that very moment screaming overhead, the tiny creature did not flinch. Generations of mole had expected nothing less. Silence would have made its whiskers twitch. To know a time before the airport, the little delver would have had to be the mole equivalent of an Old Testament prophet.

JEAN had again been shopping. In her bedsit, bags from Oxford Street department stores covered the floor. She had remembered the names from the day Olga came to the office. Jean stood in front of her long mirror wearing a frock almost identical to one she had seen on Olga's lithe frame – the midnight-blue one shown in numerous newspaper diary columns after the Westminster Hall ball. Jean inspected herself in various poses, humming. Her hair hung untidily. Pink lipstick was smeared on her lips.

She stepped out of the dress and again stood in front of the mirror, prodding the splodges and bumps and inlets of her body. Coldly she took a pair of kitchen scissors and ran a finger along the sharp blades. After a moment's contemplation she ripped at the frock with the scissors, cutting in a frenzy.

Behind her, on the back of the door, hung another dress – of the purest white. It had not been worn for almost thirty years.

MOST of Pike's tips came by email or from telephone calls. The only letters these days came from mad or ancient readers and the occasional public relations supremo. Even they seldom used the cream vellum paper Pike had just pulled from a plain envelope. He looked for a postmark but it was no more than a line of computerised dots that had missed the stamp. His address was in handwritten capitals as was the message on the vellum paper. There was no sender's address, no signature. Well, well, well. Maybe Bryce had been right about that chaplain being interesting. This would take some digging, though.

★

THE Base Camp drawing-room fire was ablaze. Mark had been in earlier to run through arrangements and Ross had been pleased by how the organist and Petroc had got on. Pax! When Mark had left, shouting 'See you tomorrow, Petroc,' he had sounded really quite comradely. Ross felt that for once he might have done some good.

He and Petroc sat in front of the fire in companionable silence. Ross did his newspaper crossword while Petroc jotted notes for a sermon. Stuck on a clue, Ross lifted his pen to his lips and stared at nothing in particular – before finding that he was staring at Petroc.

'What is it?' said Petroc.

'What, the clue?'

'No. You have something on your mind.'

'No.' A pause. 'Well, yes, actually.'

'What?'

'That night of the fight.'

'What about it?'

'I saw the knife in your rucksack.'

'You did? I see.'

'I wondered, how did it get there?'

'I think I picked it up.'

'You think?'

'When I was hit on the head I blacked out for a few seconds. Everything is a little hazy.'

'Petroc, there was blood on it. A man died.'

'I know. But I can't remember everything. Even the bits I do think I remember may be wrong.'

'Petroc!'

'I've burned the rucksack. In the fire. It went up like kindling. Don't worry – I disposed of the ashes. They went in the cat-litter rubbish.'

'And the knife?'

'The Thames.'

'Good grief.'

'You don't think . . .' said Petroc.

'Think what?'

'You do! You think I killed that man!'

CAMERAS had been placed inside the Church of Alleluia Jesus!, almost as for a *Songs of Praise*. A news reporter spoke in staccato sentences about the likelihood of trouble. Mosques from Finsbury Park had sent a large contingent and a busload of men had arrived from Luton. In the throng outside the church it was possible to see banners reading BRADFORD, SLOUGH, GLASGOW. The knifing had doubled the size of the crowd.

A large congregation gathered, too. The service was due to start at four o'clock and from three the worshippers started to arrive from parishes across the capital. Police had cleared a space for them to be searched for knives and missiles.

Churchwarden Georgina Brack was pounced on by one of the TV crews.

'Why are you here today, madam?'

'Evensong is my favourite service.'

'Can I ask: do these protests worry you?'

'Of course you can ask.'

'Do they worry you?'

'Not if I turn down my hearing aid.'

'Should the young crime suspect not be handed over to the police?'

'I'm glad I'm not in your platoon.'

'He is wanted for a suspected crime.'

'I'm going in now. I may be some time.'

'You'll be singing for Jesus?'

'I'll certainly sing but I don't hit many right notes nowadays. We could do with some younger voices. Like yours.' With which she jabbed the reporter in the chest with her brolly.

By ten to four the church was as full as the street outside. The widow went to the vestry and said: 'Everyone's in. Should we start?' Petroc was consulting his mobile telephone.

'No,' said Petroc. 'Channel 4 was insistent we should wait until twenty seconds after the top of the hour. Have you seen Derrick?'

When Derrick was found, Petroc asked: 'You're sure the west door works?' Derrick was sure, the way any foreman is sure, the way a mechanic will be sure. Worry gnawed at Petroc's gut. If this went wrong, Calvert would issue a fatwa.

The opening sequence of the rolling news every 'top of the hour' took ten seconds. It telescoped on a map of London, accompanied by a whooshing as the image zoomed down from space, ever lower, until it gave the view from the 'news chopper' hovering above the scene. 'Our reporter on the spot' was given seven seconds in which to explain that the dramatic Service of Resistance was about to begin.

The Service of Resistance! The title had been Ross's idea.

Three seconds were spent returning to the studio for looks of plastic butchness and a clenched 'Good evening'. Mark the organist played the first chords of *Jerusalem* and Petroc's priestly processional began. In the news-station gallery, the duty editor ordered the picture to chop intermittently from Mark's keyboards to the protestors, faces twisted with anger.

Mark took *Jerusalem* slowly, to allow Petroc to reach the altar steps. 'Welcome!' he boomed, with just a hint of feedback. A technical person in the gallery made an adjustment. 'Everyone is welcome here, welcome to God's loving protection. I have two announcements. One, there will be no sermon.' This drew a laugh. 'Second, we have nothing to hide. Our service tonight will proceed with two more hymns, one reading and one short prayer. At the end the west doors will open. They have not been opened for several years. This is the church of Jesus. He is our fortress. His church is open to all.'

This caused consternation in the television studio galleries and the police incident room. The anchors went immediately to their reporters for an explanation but the reporters knew no more than anyone else. 'We were expecting everyone to leave normally via the smaller, south door. It's possible the vicar has made a mistake.' All this chat filled time during a reading from the top of St John's Gospel, which would no doubt have bored the general viewer.

Abide with Me followed and collection bags were passed down the pews – the money to go to a charity working in Palestine. Mrs Brack, who was in charge of the collection team, even exacted a five-pound note from one of the cameramen. 'The famous *Abide with Me*,' said the commentators, 'as heard at FA Cup finals for many a year.' Three short prayers were spoken: a prayer for peace, the Lord's Prayer (traditional words) and the Grace. With that, Mark played the opening lines of *Thy Hand, O God, Has Guided*. Petroc bowed low to the altar, turned and walked firmly down the nave. As he approached the back of the church, Derrick and one of his Army veterans pulled hard on the handles. After several tugs there was a squeak of unoiled hinges and the big west doors swung open.

The last line of the hymn – 'one Church, one Faith, one Lord' – rang forth as a London taxi drew up outside the west door. A cameraman placed himself in a good position. The taxi door opened and Magnus Bacton alighted, handing the driver a twenty-pound note. He made sure to say 'Keep the change' loudly. Bacton stood to one side and held the taxi door open. Inside the church, all had turned in their pews.

First they saw a lowered head. Its owner was dressed in a long coat that showed only a hint of slender ankles. Her head was almost entirely covered by a dark silk scarf. In the organ loft, Mark watched with the closest attention. Petroc stepped forward to greet the visitor the moment she entered the church. She had to do so by her own volition. On this, Bacton had been insistent. The lawyer had also ordered that the west doors remain open for the rest of the service, no matter how cold this made the church.

Petroc held out his hands and the woman clasped them for a good ten seconds before she removed her scarf. As she did so, uncovering a dark-haired beauty familiar from countless internet photographs, there was a gasp from the congregation – and from the television commentators. 'We are looking at the face of Bashirah, the British–Asian girl whose plight ignited this dispute about sanctuary and freedom to marry. She was taken to Pakistan allegedly against her will by her family. Now, sensationally, she is here in this church.'

Petroc beckoned to a row of chairs near the doors. Five seats in was Matt. He had been there all along but the television cameras had not noticed him. Petroc remembered Bacton's advice and moved to a position just behind Bashirah. The congregants near Matt made way and Matt stepped forward to engulf Bashirah in his arms, hugging her, holding her, almost crushing the breath out of her. 'Oh God, you're here,' he shouted. 'Thank you. Thank you. Oh God.' All this was picked up by the microphones attached to Petroc's robes. Petroc gave a nod to the organ loft. Mark broke into the opening chords of Parry's *I was Glad*. It would have been better with a choir but the solo-organ version would have to do. Petroc led Matt and Bashirah towards seats in the middle of the congregation.

When the Parry ended, Petroc called for a minute's silence for reconciliation. He explained that this was a service of thanks for Christian pride, a celebration of the unity that had offered protection. May God shower blessings on two young people who, with support, might consider taking steps towards a lifetime's commitment. 'And if you do get married,' he added, 'I bet you will have beautiful children.' Laughter. He announced that as the service ended, the congregation would leave by the still-open west doors and, with the young couple, would progress to New Scotland Yard. There, Matt and Bashirah would offer the police any assistance they might be able to give and the collection just taken would help to start paying for the damage to the airline office. If television viewers wished to donate to this fund, they would find details on the church website. This was a great day for justice, said Petroc. God's love had won.

Petroc led the procession to New Scotland Yard, Magnus Bacton at his side, and behind them, surrounded by congregants, the two lovers, arms locked. Bashirah's smile was framed by long, lustrous curls. Matt had scrubbed up pretty well, too. They left the church to blasts of Widor's *Toccata*, Mark throwing his all into the music, his feet skittering across the pedals, hitting the octaves so that it looked as though he was pivoting on his seat. His fingers flew over the manuals, hands leaping, his whole being devoted to the jumble of black notes as he transformed them into a pumping, insistent call to faith. The tune was driven by a march from the feet, the lowest notes so deep that the very air seemed to growl. It built to a fury, badgering the ears, drumming at the mind, until the final rally and the piercing top F, held through several chords. Widor's miracle of noise made neck hairs stand to attention as his harmonic soldiers finally got their dressing. All present and correct, sir. One force for Christ, now and always, generation to generation.

When the last notes faded, the building was entirely empty but the Church had never felt fuller.

14

Mr Pike Goes Fishing

JO handled tricky Press calls. She put down the telephone and left her desk. The lift took her upstairs. Olga was combing Dymock's hair. He was reclining in a chair with his eyes shut and plugs in his ears while she pulled a brush over his scalp, silent in her duties.

'I need to talk to him,' she said. 'Augustus!'

He did not jump. Never did. His eyes were instantly alert, alive to hazards. 'Leave us, Olga.' Olga did as she was told while Dymock slowly removed his earplugs.

Jo said: 'Now I've had slimy Pike on the phone. It's that vicar again. Pike has been told: Greenhill, you, the MPs. Same tip, basically.'

'Whoaa, girl. Take it more slowly. Tell me what Pike said.'

'He said he's had information about corruption, payments being made to certain top figures. He mentioned you and Greenhill as the people involved with these bribes. And he said he has been told a vicar knows about this.'

'How much evidence does he have?'

'Dunno.'

'Remind me what we were doing about this.'

'I thought we should ignore it. I was obviously wrong about that. You said we should send surveyors to this bloke's church in the country.'

'Did we?'

'I told Greenhill to do it, but didn't say why. Didn't want to alarm him.'

'Probably right. But did the surveyors go down there? Did they make some noise locally?'

'Not yet.'

'Damn. We need to get on to it. Pike may not have enough details to run anything. Let's attack. Always attack, Jo. Kill before being killed.'

EQUIP yourself with a yellow tabard and a newish van with a flashing light on its roof, and you can enter the most hallowed places in Britain unchallenged. Clipboard and hard hat are as good as keys. Thus attired, surveyors from Greenhill Developments would arrive at churches in plum sites. They unpacked from their vans the equipment of officialdom's scouts: gum boots, high-vis jackets, theodolites, infrared reflectors, tripods, spirit measures, a confident air. Readings were taken, diagrams drawn, potential calculated. Barely more than a couple of times were they challenged as to what they were doing. 'We're looking at the council's area plan,' they said. 'Do you want to see our ID? Here's a number for our communities liaison office, sir/madam.' To be called sir/madam: that made it all right. No one ever called the number. Just as well. It did not exist.

One of the sites they visited was the little church in Herefordshire. Barney was there when they arrived. He had been undertaking some duty sniffing checks. He barked at them but the surveyors were used to dogs and took no notice. Barney lingered, watching as they attempted to take readings in the graveyard.

'Is your instrument working properly?' asked one.

'Nah, gone on the blink,' said the other.

'Let's come back this afternoon. We can grab lunch at that pub.' They were puzzled to note that by the time they reached the pub, their instruments were working fine. The landlord told them that the churchyard was haunted. He told them about the miller from olden days and the way he had suffocated in a mound of flour and how sometimes a white-faced figure could be seen strolling the churchyard. They laughed and said they would stick to the soft drinks, thanks all the same. After lunch they returned to the church and found their central locking was stuck and they could not initially open the van doors. When they did so, there blew a draught of rare force, smelling of dank soil. It sent various of their documents fluttering skywards. Crows pestered them, pecking at their hard hats. The surveyors noticed that worms had started to emerge from beside gravestones – hundreds of them, big, fat worms so wriggly that they seemed to be rubbing against one another in a dance. Some were pink. Others were white – as white as fresh-milled flour.

Barney, atop the airman's grave, watched this without undue excitement. It was no particular surprise to him when the surveyors fled. Barney trotted home, pausing only to give the lych-gate a proprietorial cock of his leg.

KENDRICK'S email, promised on the day of Mears's election to the chairmanship, was indeed interesting. It was discussed at the first meeting of the – *his* – Housing select committee. Olga had been attentive to him that morning. She had shown him a glimpse of her inner thigh when she walked round the flat in her dressing gown.

'Order, order.' It was a private meeting but Mears did not see why he shouldn't use the words to open the session. Order, order. He had sometimes, in his bath, tried them for size. Now he was using them for real.

'It is a pleasure to be here as your chairman.'

'Hear hear,' said Kendrick.

'I am sure we can do valuable work.'

'Hear hear,' said Kendrick.

'Our remit,' continued Mears, 'covers some of the biggest social problems in this country today. My door is always open, should you feel you have issues you want to discuss.' Discuss them in private – for ease of stitch-up.

'On behalf of the committee, Chair, welcome.' This came from Elfyn Davies, the committee's senior MP in years of service. Davies had not been enthusiastic about Mears – it was hard to enthuse him about any Englishman – but the Welsh fatalist in him had accepted the election result.

A new committee chairman will take a sheet of paper and divide its members into two columns. The first lists the reliable ones who will cooperate and do as told by their Whips. The second column contains the blowhards, soundbite spouters, publicity whores. Mears calculated that among his eight colleagues he had maybe one and a half troublemakers.

Mears felt safe placing Kendrick on the reliable list. Kendrick was a tunnelling machine without reverse gear. Two young Government backbenchers, Jackson and Kent, were unknown dullards. They both had dark hair, cheap suits, lifeless vowels. A select chairman is grateful for ciphers. They reduce the competition and if they dissent from a report's findings they will not gain much attention owing to their blandness. The fourth member of the committee was Levy, a polite old gent from Devon who had sent an apology for his absence. Mears did not foresee trouble from Levy. He was keen on his garden and kept a cruiser on the Dart estuary. There was talk of suntanned matelots.

Davies, the Welsh nationalist, would act as deputy chairman of the committee. Davies was hungry for a knighthood. 'He wants it for Mrs Davies,' said Bryce. To be Lady Davies would set her apart from countless other Davieses in their doom-teetering valley. She would be given priority at the hairdresser. Butchers, over shoals of shiny calf liver, would hail her as her ladyship. Davies would know that the honours committee trawled for 'views' before recommending knighthoods. Mears, as his committee chairman, would be consulted. 'Sir Elfyn' was duly placed on Mears's reliable list. Mears also put Netty Peake there, dotty though she could be. Netty was the 'half' in Mears's calculations simply because she could sometimes forget to turn up and even forget how she had been told to vote. She was not here today, for instance. Perhaps one of her fillings had fallen out or an afternoon television quiz show had reached a climax. He would detail one of the committee researchers to act as Netty's minder. One of the young men. Netty liked handsome young men. Maybe the same youth could attend to Levy.

Another committee member was Hamid Butt from the Government benches. He might not always vote the way Mears wanted but his devotion to the Father of the House, Sir Tudor Matthews, was that of a bearer to his Raja. Butt wanted to be liked. 'Hamid, I am happy to bow to your expertise,' said Mears in an exchange. The flattery worked visibly, his neck and shoulders stiffening. Butt would not be a problem. It was a pity he wore quite such a clagging aftershave. If you shook hands with him your paw smelled of patchouli for hours.

In almost every fine sky a distant cloud hovers. So it was for Mears. Hilda Hawke was, like him, a rejected frontbencher. She had briefly been Deputy Leader of the House. Hilda had once been spoken of as possible Cabinet material but her long-windedness had been her undoing. Even her husband had given up on her. There is pillow talk and there is pillow talk ad nauseam ad perpetuam ad divorce courts. Hilda could well be trouble but at least she would be bad at attracting support. Mears looked down the U-shaped committee table. She had chosen the end seat on the left side and was rummaging in her bag – so large it would not have been allowed on a budget airline.

'To business,' said Mears. 'Mr Kendrick. You have a proposal.'

'Thank you, Chair.'

★

WESTMINSTER central lobby has four long benches, placed near the walls. They are upholstered like London club land seats. Sit there for a few minutes and you will soon see ministers and their Whitehall ducklings waddle past. Members of the House of Lords queue at the lobby's Post Office to buy stamps and collect their pensions. Visitors admire the ornate ceiling. Often there is a television camera doing live interviews with MPs.

On one such bench sat our friend Pike of the *Dispatch*. He had sent a text and was awaiting a response. It came quickly – as did the person who sent it.

'You came fast.'

'You said it was urgent,' said Bryce. He had come himself rather than send intern Adrian. 'What is this "potentially awkward document"?'

Pike produced the sheet of vellum paper he had been sent anonymously. 'This arrived at my office.' Bryce read the short message.

'I didn't send it to you.'

'I never thought you did.'

'Why show it to me?'

'It touches on a friend of yours.'

'Dymock? Hardly a friend.'

'And that developer, Greenhill.'

'Well, I wouldn't know about it.'

'If there's nothing in it, I'm sure they have nothing to worry about and will not mind telling me these allegations are false. I've put in a call to Dymock. I'll have the note back, please.'

'I thought you were giving it to me.'

'I just wanted you to see it. Wanted to see your reaction.'

'My reaction?'

'I do believe you've gone quite red,' said Pike.

'Someone must be attempting blackmail.'

'If they have not done anything wrong, how can anyone blackmail them?'

Bryce remained silent for quite a long time before he looked at Pike and said: 'Quite.'

THAT weekend, Ross sat in Herefordshire, preparing his sermon for the next day's matins. Writing was not entirely easy because his right hand still ached from the fire and was still bound by a light bandage. Theresa was on the piano, Barney at her side, asleep. She had been a reasonable player in her day. Chopin's *Nocturne Op 9, No 2*, drifted into Ross's study.

The village was abuzz with talk about the surveyors who had turned up to measure the church with a view to development. Ross's assurances that there was no chance of it happening had been heard but not necessarily believed. He would use his sermon to reinforce his insistence that the church was going nowhere. Not that there would be many to hear him. They all loved the church building but did not come to services.

Theresa rose from her keyboard and walked down the corridor towards her husband's study. Not that Ross noticed, for the music continued, as it often would in that strange old house. She saw him sitting at his desk, his back to her, and she gently placed her arms round his neck and embraced him. He looked up without surprise. Just exhaustion. All the time Chopin's perfection filled the air and Barney the terrier snored happily while the keyboard did its ghostly work.

15

'How Important He Had Become'

THE Monday brought rain to London. Though Mears's office was in a new wing at Westminster, it already leaked. The minimalist design placed little premium on practicality, novelty trumping tradition. Jean sploshed to work. She stood at a pedestrian crossing, obediently awaiting the green signal, her shoes sponging the wet as bus tyres and drab vans hissed past her.

Her first duty on wet days was to mop the puddles around the windows and place a bucket under the leak. Each drip quivered before it fell, almost whistling in its descent before it landed and created ripples. Mears steamed in soon after ten o'clock. His gloved hand wrenched on the handle and he slammed the door without apology before removing his raincoat and hanging it on the stand in the outer office. He did not initially see Jean and was making *tsk tsk* noises as he sucked his gums in irritation at the wetness, at his slight lateness and at the cares of statesmanship. The morning newspapers, irritatingly, had enthused about events at the church of Alleluia Jesus! Bashirah's return was reported at length, colour writers gushing about her beauty, the solidarity of the congregation, the tolerance of the Church of England, the stirring hymns, the deft theatricality. Leader articles praised Anglicanism's neglected genius for traditional pomp and the way its openness was as one with the innkeeper at Bethlehem and the doctrine of love. The coverage really could scarcely have been more irritating. Yes, that was the word. Irritating.

When he spotted Jean he ceased his little gum clicks. No longer would he look at her, not even with his former pity. She felt him shun her, felt it deeply. She was no bigger than one of those drips of water. Mistaking his crossness, she wished she had never picked this trouble. Yet he would never – could never – sack her. She knew secrets and in politics secrets are armour.

As he passed her desk she handed him the morning post. He snatched it from her red, wrung hands and for the shortest second it seemed he might say something. One of the researchers chose that moment to arrive at work. Mears turned his shoulder. Jean had opened the external mail for him, filleting and stapling and collating, but she always left unopened the letters that came in the internal post. He liked to open those himself. He settled for a single, piggy grunt and disappeared into his lair.

A minute later Jean and the researcher heard a thump and a loud cry of 'Bugger!' This was followed by more thumping and more 'buggers'. Was Mears kicking his chair? Was he hitting his desk?

Had the chaplain already taken action?

The researcher shot Jean a look of concern but they said nothing until, after another thump, there came a louder crash and a cry of alarm. They rushed next door to find Mears on the floor. A bookcase had fallen on top of him. 'Help!' he said from under the bookcase.

'Gracious,' said Jean.

'How did that happen?' asked the researcher.

'I was kicking the wall and the bloody thing fell on me,' groaned Mears. In his hand he was still holding the letter that had sent him into such a rage. 'Bugger, bugger.'

'Are you all right?' asked Jean.

'Of course I'm not all right!' snapped Mears.

'If I lift the bookcase a little you can roll out,' said the researcher.

'Why do these people have to be so bloody difficult?' Mears complained as he slowly escaped. 'Why couldn't he just limp on as a non-attending member?'

'Who?' said the researcher.

'Levy. That old fool from Devon. He's resigning from my housing committee. Says it is not "fair" that he should occupy such a privileged position without giving the work his full attention. Fair! Since when was politics fair? Just means he wants to spend more time on his cruiser on the Dart estuary. Gin and tonics on the poop deck with a Captain Birdseye hat and some bare-chested catamite tugging on his anchor.'

Bryce arrived in the office as the bookshelf was being righted. 'Poltergeist trouble?' he enquired. 'I was rather hoping to talk to you about something but perhaps it is not a good time.' Bryce did not know about Levy's resignation. It was rare for Mears to be able to tell him something. He used a landline while Jean and the researcher tidied the books off the floor and restacked them.

'Well?' said Mears when Bryce had completed his call.

'I have spoken to the Usual Channels. One concerned professional to another. They learned of Levy's decision only this morning.'

'Surely they can just tell him to stay on the committee. Tell him to get back in his box.'

'Not the best turn of phrase, dear heart. Comrade Levy has discovered that he is terminally ill. He wants to spend his last mortal months enjoying the estuary breezes. You can hardly blame him for not wanting to spend them on your wretched committee listening to that leaden bore Kendrick.' He lowered his voice. 'By the way, what has Jean done to her hair? Has she been cutting it with nail scissors?'

'My committee's not wretched.'

'It will be when you hear who your Whips are putting up as a replacement for Levy.'

'Who?'

'That sleek streak of piss Branton-Day.'

'Bugger, bugger!'

'You can say that again. In fact you just did. You're not in the right mood for the other thing I need to tell you. I'll come back later. Goodbye.'

'Bugger, bugger, BUGGER!' cried Mears again after Bryce had left. The last one was accompanied by a kick at the wall – and the bookshelf again crashed to the floor. Jean, next door, looked at her colleague, pursed her lips, and returned to her typing with quiet satisfaction. No secretary is ever entirely distressed when the boss receives a setback. She and the researcher left it a few minutes before they responded to Mears's raging yelps for help.

PERHAPS Levy had not been able to face the curt satisfaction with which Mears ran his committee. 'Order! Order!' Yes, it felt better every time, at least for him. 'This is the first public hearing of our inquiry into rebalancing the public estates and we have a busy day, with a morning and afternoon session. Our day will be punctuated by Prime Minister's Questions and by lunch. I am sure we look forward to both.

'Without further ado I ask our distinguished witnesses to identify themselves for the record.' His tone left no doubt that their distinction was below that of himself.

'My name is George Leakey, Member of Parliament and Second Church Estates Commissioner.'

'Augustus Dymock, founder of the Thought Foundation.' Olga and Jo were sitting behind him. Mears had told Olga that morning that she must not wave at him.

'Thank you,' said Mears. 'I start by putting on record the

committee's thanks to the Hon Member for Devon South, Mr Levy, for his long service to the committee.'

'He's abandoned ship,' said Hilda Hawke.

'We wish him a speedy recovery. And we welcome Mr Branton-Day in his place.' There had been just the faintest pause before 'welcome'. Branton-Day, seated next to Hilda, bowed ostentatiously to the chairman. Mears felt his guts knot. 'Mr Jackson, you have the floor.'

Jackson, one of the nonentities from the Government side, opened by asking Leakey about his role. Leakey explained that the Second Church Estates Commissioner was the Church's point man in the Commons and the Commons' point man in the higher counsels of the Church. Heaviness soon infected the air. The blinds had been lowered, reducing any sense of sunshine. Leakey gave a history of the position, talked about the honour he felt to occupy it, spoke of the Church's programmes of outreach and modernisation and poverty reduction, its ability to be the 'eyes and ears' of the welfare system, its duties to the wider nation and its expertise in maintaining the fabric of the nation, both material and spiritual, this day and forward, for ever and ever, Amen.

'Shorter answers would be welcome,' said Mears.

Traffic noise from outside suggested a world where people were busy with their lives. Mears added: 'Your historical exposition is no doubt fascinating but might perhaps be submitted as an appendix to your written evidence. We seek informative brevity, not a sermon.' Leakey gave a ghostly smile. Mears invited Kendrick to take up the questioning.

Kendrick: 'Mr Leakey, how many churches do you have in England?'

'At the last census,' said Leakey, shuffling notes, 'thirty seven thousand and fifty one.'

'Thirty seven thousand and fifty one,' said Kendrick slowly. 'All full?'

'Full?' said Leakey.

'Full of hot air and fools' hopes,' said Dymock, to laughter.

'Full,' said Kendrick, 'of people? How many churches are packing them in? How many are empty?'

'It is no secret that patterns of worship are changing,' said Leakey. His fingertips trembled. 'Last Christmas we saw a rise in attendance. Baptisms are on the increase.'

'How many are going concerns?' said Kendrick.

'The Church is not interested in profits.'

'It depends how you spell prophet,' said Kendrick.

'And if I might say, the word "concern" has a second meaning,' said Leakey. 'Are we "concerned" if a congregation is small? Is it improper to have "concern" for an individual and not a crowd? Is the spiritual aspect of life to be ignored if, for some parishioners, it has slipped from fashion? Christians have little time for fashion. They try to serve the truth.'

'The Church has more members than our political parties,' said Hilda Hawke.

'Order!' said Mears. 'Mr Kendrick.'

'Thank you, Chair. I am simply trying to establish from the Second Church Estates Commissioner the support his organisation enjoys.'

'Perhaps I can help,' said Dymock.

'Mr Dymock,' said Mears.

'The committee will see from papers we supplied for today's meeting that churchgoing is down five per cent a year.'

'Not so,' said Leakey.

'Mr Leakey, you're still with us,' said Mears pleasantly.

Leakey said: 'Surveys show the church's presence is still valued, even by non-churchgoers. Christmas congregations were higher. Same on Remembrance Day.'

'If we can get back to bricks and mortar,' said Kendrick. 'Thirty seven thousand churches, I think you said. How many of them are needed?'

'All of them.'

'All, Mr Leakey?'

'Well, the Church would still survive without churches.' Some laughter. 'It would,' flared old Leakey. 'Of course it would. The early church, the church of Peter and Paul, the church of the first century AD . . .'

'He means Common Era,' said Dymock.

'No I do not. I mean AD, Anno Domini. The early Church had no buildings, no roofs to leak, no bricks to crumble. It survived. My God, it survived.'

'We do not mean to offend, Mr Leakey,' said Mears.

'I'm just trying to establish how many of our church buildings are – well, "essential" is not the word, perhaps, but how many you could do without. Ten per cent of them? More than that?'

'Our figures suggest at least half of them,' said Dymock.

'That's crap,' said Leakey. Crap! From the Second Church Estates Commissioner! The parliamentary sketchwriters, loafing at the press table, gurgled with pleasure.

'I don't know if the parliamentary record will permit that word, Chair,' said Kendrick, 'but we can at least note that the Second Church Estates Commissioner denies – with Old Testament vigour – that half his churches are unwanted. So what is the figure?'

'Go to the parishes,' said Leakey. 'Go to the communities. Ask them, "Do you want your church? Would your community be the same without a church? Would you mind if we chopped off the steeple? Would you mind if we turned your church into a disco or off-licence. Or mosque." See what they say.'

'This is not about nimbyism,' said Kendrick. 'It is a matter for the nation as a whole. We have a severe shortage of housing in this country. People are living in deprivation because they cannot find a decent home.'

'So runs the propaganda,' said Leakey. 'But it's put about by people with a financial interest: the house builders, the mortgage brokers. We've long heard talk of a crisis in housing but people still find homes.'

'You are surely not denying,' said Kendrick, 'that council tenants face long waits for housing. Families are cramped and the lack of space makes them unhappy. All this property exists, owned by the Church, and it is going to waste.'

'I doubt the housing shortage is as severe as you say,' said Leakey.

'Might I ask about property values in your constituency? Might I even ask about your own property portfolio?'

'What's that got to do with it?' said Branton-Day.

'Order,' said Mears. 'Mr Branton-Day, you do not have the floor.'

Kendrick continued: 'I saw a reference in a newspaper to our witness owning a three-million-pound mansion with stables for polo ponies. Would you care to comment?'

'I most certainly would not,' said Leakey. 'Mind you own business.'

'Far be it for me to interrupt a fight,' murmured Dymock, 'but I may again be able to help. In page xxix of our written evidence you will find statistics about the number of churches which could make do with a fraction of their current space. We estimate that redundant space in churches could house a hundred thousand hard-working people.'

'What if they are not "hard-working"?' asked Hilda.

'Order!' said Mears.

'Oopsie,' said Hilda, patting herself on one wrist.

COMMONS technicians had increased the amplification from the Speaker's Chair. It seemed wrong that from so noble a Chair, canopied Fount of Authority, very Seat of Democracy, there should emanate so anaemic a voice. Onlookers, beholding the Throne of Parliament, expected a *basso profundo*. They braced themselves for a rich roar, fruited as Dundee cake. Instead they had to cup their ears to catch Aldred's husky squeak. Great structures demand great occupants.

'Questions to the Prime Minister.' The quavery delivery was magnified through the Chamber like some love coo from Olympus.

The Leader of the Opposition opted for safety. Disestablishment had taken off as a topic in the blogosphere and the editorial pages but he had a dinner coming up at the Palace. There would already be enough trickiness given recent rows about the Civil List. Now was not the time for him to raise the Church's future; but Kendrick was listed on the Order Paper. 'Mr Kendrick,' whispered Aldred. He might have been a snooker commentator.

'Does the Prime Minister agree,' began Kendrick, tense, astringent, 'that an Established Church must obey the law of the land? Recently, not a mile from here, the Church of England sheltered a man suspected of a violent attack with racist undertones.' The word 'racist' was given a full twist of Celtic lemon. 'Will he condemn this behaviour and urge the Archbishop of Canterbury to get a grip on his turbulent priest, who as I understand it has gone undisciplined?' Get a grrrrip. Again came that wrist-flick of Valleys briskness.

The question drew a swell of interest. Heads turned to the despatch box. 'What I would say to my Hon Friend,' said the Prime Minister, and with this a little nod of acknowledgement which may also have been a plea for peace, 'is that the Established Church must never allow itself to be used as an excuse. Faith must not become a legal loophole. Churches are sacred places but many church buildings receive financial assistance from the state. This House is the proper place to change the law. Render unto Westminster what is Westminster's.'

JEAN had taken the day off, telling the office she felt sick. So much was racing through her head that she was indeed disorientated. The television in her little flat was tuned to the BBC parliamentary channel and she was watching the afternoon session of Mears's committee.

Netty Peake opened the questioning. 'Mr Calvert, you are the Church's official spokesman.'

'National Communications Dean,' said Calvert. 'I try to explain the Church's role and its position, on everything from the Resurrection to rent controls.'

'Our interest today is housing,' said Netty. 'What do you make of this debate about church landholdings?'

'Challenge is always stimulating.'

'You're not being challenged. You're under direct attack.'

'We are happy to be scrutinised.'

'They're trying to do you in.'

'They?'

'Atheists and property sharks.'

'We hope not.' Calvert gave Netty a smile that stretched slowly under his nose. 'I believe you have copies of a paper we commissioned for a forthcoming Synod. We have been aware for some time of a disconnect between our estate holdings and our ongoing ministry needs. This paper suggests a measure of controlled reduction of certain parishes could actually strengthen Christian outreach.'

'So you're ahead of the game?' said Mears.

'You accept you own far too many churches,' said Kendrick.

'We are still consulting,' said Calvert.

Branton-Day gave a hollow laugh. 'They've already caved in. Typical Church of England.'

'Order,' said Mears.

'Clearly,' said Calvert, 'the Church can do better. Our Lord did not own temples, as I believe the Second Church Estates Commissioner pointed out this morning. Church worship is but part of our ministry.'

'Run the white flag up the church tower!' said Branton-Day.

'Order!' snapped Mears.

Netty reclaimed the questioning. 'Is it true that vicars are being offered cash incentives, cruises, pension pots, by property developers?' she asked. 'That's one rumour.'

'Wild rumour is not unknown, even in the Church,' said Calvert.

'It would be illegal, wouldn't it?' said Branton-Day.

'It sounds – well, I don't quite know the word,' said Calvert.

'Corrupt,' said Netty.

'Bungs from property sharks? Never!' laughed Branton-Day. Mears kept quiet.

Calvert said: 'The Church frequently receives commercial propositions from a variety of sources. It would be irresponsible not to listen to proposals.'

Mears intervened to allow Butt some questions. 'Mr Butt,' he said.

'Thank you, chairman,' said Butt. 'Mr Calvert, you seem remarkably complacent.'

'Complacent?'

'You're smooth. I congratulate you on that. You speak the language. Our language. The political language. But I do not gain the impression you are fired by any great, indignant belief.'

'I am sorry you think that.'

'We are what we are. It's probably my fault – eye of the beholder and all that. But why don't you fight more for your Church?'

'Fight?'

'Why not get angry – tell us politicians to get lost?'

'I hardly think . . .'

'My lot would,' said Butt.

'Your lot?'

'I'm Muslim. When politicians try to interfere in mosques, the imams tell them to get lost. Believe me, I've been on the receiving end. It ain't pretty. But you Church of England people are so obliging.'

'They're polite, that's all,' said Branton-Day.

'I have the floor,' said Butt.

'Order,' said Mears. 'Mr Butt, we are not here to discuss Islam.'

Butt ignored Mears and said: 'Mr Calvert, there is a political push on here. Some people see a lot of pound signs. Prime acres might be coming on the market. Developers would love it for hundreds of churches to be sold. Bribes are no doubt being contemplated.'

'Order!' said Mears. 'Mr Butt, we must be careful with accusations.'

'Mr Chairman, I just want to ask our witness: does it not worry him that at a time when the Church is being urged to downsize, a rival faith, my faith, Islam, is building mosques. Is this good for the country? Are you being eclipsed, Mr Calvert? You're giving up the ghost. Muslims can't believe their luck. Isn't that what's going on, Mr Calvert? You're disarming while Islam is on the march. My constituents don't want this.'

Mears said: 'Mr Calvert, do you wish to respond to Mr Butt's wild scenario? No? Very well. We will move on.'

How commanding he was, thought Jean. How important he had become. And how unimportant she remained. It was hopeless, really. Now that the Russian harlot was in his flat – now that she had had her triumph at the ball and was toted almost daily by the gossip columns – what hope had Jean with her dreary bun and Hitchcock chin?

PETROC studied the Prayer Book Ross had given him. Its words might at first seem as pungent as old parsnips yet it was a handsome book with its gold-edged pages. Each collect's first letter was given gothic detail and a red-inked box. He could see the sense of ownership with this little book, the richness of its print hooking the aesthetic. It became one's secret indulgence, there in one's pocket, bumping along with every stride. Be thou my companion, my battle-shield. Bump, bump, bump. And how unyielding it was – harder on the individual than newer, meeker, more elastic prayers. Here there was no safety in numbers. There was no one to raise your hand in ecstatic acclaim during a worship song. It was Common because the prayers were designed for common usage with other men yet it was frequently singular in its commands, commendations, declarations. Prayer, here, was personal; but morality? When a man was killed? When potential police evidence was destroyed? And when temptation loomed? Could temptation remain a matter for one man and his God or was it more open to the parish's rebuke? See here, on these skinny yet fierce pages – the Commandments written at length, their language unaltered from the days when men burned, screaming, at the stake. How could he talk to Ross when it was Ross's professional ward – a woman Ross was to join in holy wedlock to another man – that he, Petroc the Priest, loved?

'WHAT we need is for your Mr Mears to produce a really fiery report.'

'Fiery?' said Olga. She had the duvet pulled up to her chin. Dymock was admiring himself in the mirror while he dressed. He pulled hard on his belt, fixing it in a tight notch which confirmed his suspicion that he had put on weight. It would need to be lost.

'I mean critical of the Church. He could make a name for himself, your friend. Could become Politician of the Year. They love public recognition. All he has to do is deliver the goods. Kick the Church where it hurts. He could even say the Commons should get rid of its chaplain. If this report is strong, I'm sure there will be all sorts of rewards for little Mears.'

'Rewards? For Les-uh-lee?'

'Yeah,' said Dymock. He took out a high-value banknote and left it on the bedside table. 'Here. I don't know what's been wrong with you recently but maybe a little retail therapy will wipe that pout off your face.' Olga looked hard at the money. Dymock continued. 'You're doing brilliantly with him. I know it can't be much fun. Such a ghastly little man, so prosaic and provincial. But string him on. Tell him the world will look up to him. The world will respect him as a visionary. If I were Mears, I'd go for it. This is his one chance.'

'I don't want your money,' she said. It was spoken quietly first, more loudly the second time, when she tore the banknote into several pieces.

Dymock shrugged. 'Fine. Have it your way. But look, I need you out of here pretty soon. A *Vanity Fair* photographer is coming at eleven thirty. You can take the rest of the day off and I'll see you at the gallery later.'

16

Death And An Opening

ONLOOKERS heard the policeman sing 'Speeeeee-kah!' and, as the procession neared, Mates's studded heels struck the flagstones to a slow beat. This was followed by a slithering, as though someone was wiping the floor. It was the best gait Speaker Aldred could manage.

The Serjeant at Arms and Doorkeeper Mates made their right turns, taking them towards the Members' lobby. Aldred was just starting to make the right wheel when he sank. Ross, behind him, initially thought the old man had stepped in a hole. It was a daft notion but no less daft that the Speaker should be collapsing before his eyes.

There was little instant drama. It was not so much a fall as a slow curtsey.

Nurse Harris was quicker than anyone else. She was kneeling beside him, one strong hand cradling Aldred's snowy head, before Mates and the Sergeant had even stopped marching. Ross heard her talk to the old man almost in a pigeon's call. 'We're here, beauty, right here and we're not going anywhere. Just you take it easy.'

Ross crouched, hissing: 'Is he OK?' Of course he wasn't OK. OK would have been walking into the Commons Chamber, which was what they should all have been doing instead of him lying on the floor. Dying.

Ross could hear Mates cotton on to what was happening. A couple of people were gasping. One of the duty policemen in the central lobby said: 'If you wouldn't mind, ladies and gents, thanks, just move back a little, just for a moment.'

'His pulse,' said Nurse Harris. 'It's barely there. We need to get him warmer. Blankets or something.'

'I could go back to the Robing Room,' said Ross.

'No time.'

'Need a coat? Here, Padre,' said Mates. He stripped off his tails and waistcoat.

Ross stared emptily. Then: 'Here, my cassock and surplice, too.' He threw his surplice on the ground and started to unbutton his cassock. Mates was already crouching beside Nurse Harris, arranging the tailcoat over the stricken Speaker. Mates was a powerfully built man, even in his sixties. Ross saw the back of his shirt was wet with sweat.

Aldred's lips parted in the silent cry of thrush chicks in a nest. His gaze, too, had something avian. He was alive, just. There was a stickiness at the edge of his mouth and the skin under his eyes had turned yellow. He was trying to say something. A word of pain? A confession?

'Take it easy, honey,' said Nurse Harris. With one hand she buttressed his head, with her other she smoothed the old man's wispy hair. She announced: 'I'll get the defibrillator bats.'

Mates stopped her. 'I don't think there's any point.'

'No, I'd better.'

'I don't think so. Look.' Aldred's eyes had lost their gleam. His grip was gone.

'Oh my . . .'

'Let him go, love,' said Mates.

Ross crossed himself. Nurse Harris urgently checked for a pulse and put her ear to his chest. With infinite tenderness she closed Aldred's eyes.

Mates twisted his neck. 'Padre?'

'What?' Ross had not even finished taking off his cassock.

'Padre!'

'What?'

'Say something. A prayer, I don't know. As he joins his fore-fathers.'

Normally death came so slowly, in a nursing home or hospital ward. Doctors made no demands and family members quietly accepted. The suddenness here, the glare of lights, the crowd – Ross swayed.

There was indeed a prayer, known by every proper priest – 'by the authority committed unto me by the Holy Ghost, I absolve you from all your sins in the name of the Father, Son and Holy Ghost' – but it had to be earned. It could be said only to those who had obeyed. Did Aldred qualify? Ross stared at the body below him. His head filled with white noise.

Mates coughed. A show had to be made.

Ross had his prayer book. He flicked to the pages for evensong and lifted his head like a competitive diver. Though he knew the *Nunc dimittis* by heart, the book would lend him authority. It would make a spectacle, a ceremony. 'Lord, now lettest thou thy servant depart in peace, according to thy word . . .'

Nurse Harris crossed herself and said 'Sweet Jesus'. One or two people started to kneel under the boss of that great ceiling. 'To be a light to lighten the Gentiles . . .' Ross's voice acquired an almost flamboyant strength. As he said the Gloria, about ten people murmured its words. Ross knelt on the flagstones. 'Unto your tender hands, O Lord, we commend the soul of your good and faithful servant. God have mercy on him and on us.'

The only prayer they would likely know was 'Our Father'. He began it and this time a few more voices joined. Arriving paramedics stilled, the only sound coming from their walkie-talkies. Mates was kneeling, his head was lowered. Nurse Harris sat on her haunches, hands over her face. Ross turned to Psalm 103. The further he got into the psalm, the more assertive he became. *As for man, his days are as grass: as a flower of the field, so he flourisheth.*

Silence was kept until Mates, dusting his knees, said quietly: 'OK, everyone, I think we should clear this area.' The crowd started to disperse. A policeman shook Ross's hand without saying a word.

In the Robing Room later, Ross said to Mates: 'I was useless. I froze.'

'Padre, the words spoke. They do, even when we fail. Go to Miss Harris, sir. She needs support. Peace, Padre. Mr Speaker is at peace and so should we be peaceful.'

ALDRED'S death dominated that evening's portrait unveiling at the British Portrait Gallery. Who would be the next Speaker? Should Aldred have been retired months ago? What would happen to his seat in the by-election? And had those last rites been his undoing? Last rites! What was this: London or Bujumbura, ancient spells mumbo-jumbo'd over a shrivelled corpse? Why had the medical experts not tried to revive the Speaker?

Pink cava was served in tall glasses filled halfway. Canapés – shaved porcini on bullets of Italian bread, rabbit-dropping minced lamb cradled in mini lettuce leaves – were circulated on easels by waiters dressed in smocks and berets. A flautist fluted. A harpist strummed.

'Evening, Bryce.'

'Leslie! And my dear! *Enchanté.*' Bryce took Olga's hand and brushed it so lightly against his lips they might never have touched it. Even so, he was assaulted by her scent: essence of bubble-gum. Her scarlet cocktail dress bared an expanse of wriggly back. The fingernails may still have been Moscow street tart yet there was undoubtedly something about her that even he could comprehend

– the daring heels, the lithe legs, the goose pimples at her sinuous neck. She sipped frequently from her glass, not quite knowing how quickly to drink. She threw her auburn hair sideways, smiling hard. Bryce soon managed to palm her off on another guest.

Mears said: 'Do you think they could have saved Aldred?'

'Mates and the nurse responded well but the chaplain was useless. Speaker died. Vicar dried. Do you suppose Aldred is hearing harps too right now?' Bryce, as he spoke, did not deign to look Mears in the eye, but slowly moved his head, copping the scene. 'I do hate harp music. Strum strum, pickety pick. Enough to quite put one off heaven.'

'But do you think the paramedics could have revived Aldred?' asked Mears.

'Does it matter?'

'It might. If the chaplain . . .' A waiter passed with globules of prawn froth on coins of cucumber. Bryce's catalpa-shaped digits quietly lifted one to his tongue, a lizard taking a fly.

Mears tried again. 'If the chaplain caused the Speaker's death by refusing to let the nurse fetch the defibrillator, it becomes a story. Prayer buggers up the emergency services. Priests should not obstruct medical personnel. You wonder how often this happens in hospitals. We need to get rid of this God-botherer.'

Bryce finally looked him in the eye. 'It almost sounds as though you have been talking to Dymock. I am impressed. But the priest may have helped you. How does "Speaker Mears" sound?'

'I'm serious. Should one make an issue out of it? A vicar so eager to push another punter through the pearly gates that he stops paramedics. I could call for an end to the Speaker's chaplaincy – discredit the interfering fool.'

'Tush, less odium, dear heart. War-game it for me.' As Bryce spoke he lifted his cava glass at a firebrand MP from the North Country, a man he hated with intensity. The MP returned a comradely smile. The wine could have been colder.

'There's no written rule saying a Speaker has to have a chaplain,' said Mears. 'It's only custom.'

'Getting rid of the chaplain would cause a stink,' said Bryce.

'If he frustrated medical efforts I reckon he's vulnerable. Secularist would-be Speaker's radical agenda signals end of medieval flummery. Exit chaplain in disgrace. Another tile falls off the old order.'

'Does the House really want a radical in the Chair? Ideas can be tiresome. They require thought.'

'The country would notice the new man in the Chair. Good for politics. Good for MPs. Anyway, the Church is in retreat. It is going to have to dispose of property assets.'

'You really do sound like Dymock!'

'The chaplain lives in a grace-and-favour parliamentary house with, I hear, a big garden. If he goes, an estate agent will have to sell that asset. Last time I looked, there was a discreet fee payable to people who find big houses for vending agents. Quite a tidy percentage. This house could be worth fifteen million.'

Bryce allowed a waitress to refresh his glass. Raising it to admire the bubbles, he said: 'Don't lead the campaign yourself. Let Kendrick do his man-of-principles routine. Or that hothead Mackie. The fatal seconds when a cassocked vulture prevented a brave black nurse from saving the Speaker. Yes, it has possibilities.' The speeches were starting.

'Laydees and Gentlemen!' Five hundred eyeballs lifted to the dais. Dymock stood there with the artist, a scruffy creature in t-shirt and tattoos. His hair was gelled and he sported in his nose the sort of brass ring favoured by bulls at country shows. Everyone clapped when the silk drape covering the painting was removed. The portrait showed Dymock at a window. Sunlight threw a halo around his white head. One arm pointed through the window, as to a promised land. Round his neck he wore a cross in the form of an X. This, the artist explained in nasal Estuarine, was a symbol of democracy.

'Friends, we are fortunate to have here tonight a man I am proud to be able to call my friend. Give it up for the Don of Doubt, Augustus Dymock.' Applause.

'Not quite the Mona Lisa, is it?' murmured Bryce to Mears, but Mears was busying himself with repairs to his tie, having been attacked by an exploding vegetarian ravioli packet. Olga was on the other side of the room, having her neck touched by an alternative therapist who had persuaded her she might be suffering tense nodules.

Dymock took the microphone with affected reluctance. He was holding a glass not of cava but of Campari. He liked its unrelenting, metallic taste. 'I know I normally speak about science,' he began. 'But what of art? This portrait gallery can be a chastening place. Dead eyes stare down at us. We may feel daunted by our predecessors' achievements, particularly in a country so irrationally nostalgic. We know we will not live long. We can feel chastened by the artistic ability of painters. Christians speak of artists having "god-given talents". What they mean is that a genetic process has left some with a certain eye – an ability to compute line and length and perspective. Art is the product of natural selection, species development. God-given? Hardly.' He took a swig of Campari. 'My good friend the artist . . .'

'He's forgotten his name,' murmured Bryce.

'. . . did not paint me with the help of any deity. He painted me with the help of skills he acquired during his training and genes he inherited from his father.'

'And his mother!' shouted a woman.

'OK,' said Dymock. His rare concession of a point of argument created mild amusement in the contingent from the Thought Foundation near the back of the room. Among their number was Zac, who was not alone. He had given an invitation to his boyfriend. The two of them had been knocking back the cava.

Dymock continued: 'Art is no more god-given than the

ability of a carpenter to hammer a nail in two blows. Art must explore the new because that is how a species develops. Embrace change. Chop our intellectual clay. Abandon yesterday. Tradition was innovation before it stagnated. Around us in this gallery are portraits of innovators long dead. Their eyes bore into us as a reprimand. Let us live for our own time, not to creeds of old. Progress is achieved by raucous challenge and reward, as I always tell my son Zac, who is, I think, here tonight.'

'He's here,' said someone, holding up a hand. Everyone turned. At that very second Zac was whispering to a boy next to him and kissing his ear.

Dymock said: 'Oh.' The two lads flirted until they noticed a silence had fallen. Zac, giggling, patted his blond hair into place, quite the coquette.

'Here's to art!' said the artist, breaking the awkwardness.

'Art!' everyone said, save Dymock, who was staring.

'And innovation!' said someone else.

'Innovation!' said the room, followed by applause and a buzz of conversation and, alas, some laughter.

'Is that the time already?' said Bryce. 'I must away. What an unfortunate little moment. Leslie, we will talk in the morning. If I were you, I'd go and make sure Olga is safe. Some man is thumbing her as though he were testing a Camembert.'

DYMOCK swept from the gallery and slammed shut the door of the waiting limousine. He was accompanied by Jo, his office manager, and a couple of paces behind by a sheepish Zac. Dymock sat in the front of the car. Drizzle had made the streets greasy and drivers were reluctant to give way.

'There were cameras there. Jesus!'

'You don't believe in Jesus,' shouted Zac.

'You know what I mean.'

'I'm gay, Dad. Get over it!'

201

'You're not gay. Not properly. No one is. You were drunk. Rebelling. That's a natural phenomenon. Young males seek to assert themselves. I can see that.'

'I like him,' sobbed Zac. Jo, who was sitting beside the boy in the back, reached out an arm to advise him not to bother arguing with his father. The limo was still struggling to get into the traffic. The windscreen wipers swabbed and squeaked.

'Did you hear the room laugh?' said Dymock.

'So?'

'They were mocking you. Mocking *me*. Normally they applaud. Tonight they laughed. All the papers were there.'

'Guys, leave it till tomorrow,' sighed Jo.

'I have a dodo for a son.'

'Guys . . .' said Jo.

'I wish I'd never been born, not into this stupid, ambitious world,' said poor Zac.

17

Operation Chaise

DEPUTY Speaker Tewk was asked to hold the fort while a period of mourning was observed for Aldred. This would allow the House to consider what it required in a new Speaker – and it gave Bryce's haricots time to type a memo entitled Operation Chaise. It was sent to Mears's email address.

A would-be Speaker must show himself devoted to the House. He attends the start of Questions every day and adjournment debate every evening. Statements, Urgent Questions, Opposition-day debates – all attract his presence. Even Westminster Hall.

A would-be Speaker has a safe seat and can therefore afford to be magnanimous in debate. By arguing against pork-barrel issues he will present himself a politician of principle and impress the weekly columnists who deplore low populism. Immigration is a worry in his seat? He makes a speech deploring racism. It will cost him a few thousand votes but he will impress Hon Members whose political views are so much more refined.

A would-be Speaker is rude to his own frontbenchers, yet not to backbenchers on both sides. He catches the eye of those who have just spoken and nods in agreement. He may even write these MPs notes of congratulation and have them taken immediately to the recipient by the doorkeepers. He extols the 'clarity and verve' of plodders. They will be pathetically grateful. He tells ranters that 'despite the false polarities of our parliamentary system and the silly convention that we should heckle one another, it must remain possible to hear a colleague on the other side of the House speak – "as you just did with such remarkable succinctness and courage" – and agree with every word that is uttered'. These letters may be composed in a florid hand, in a fountain pen.

A would-be Speaker will also defend any MP who has been attacked by the newspapers. He will disdain those who 'undermine the work we all do in this place'.

Mears followed Bryce's advice. Not everyone was suckered. The Father of the House, Sir Tudor Matthews, stopped him loudly outside the Smoking Room. 'Something I want to waise with you, Mears.' Sir Tudor had twouble with his Rs.

'Sir Tudor, always a pleasure.'

'Not for me. I have noticed you making eyes at colleagues.' Sir Tudor addressed him from a height, rocking on his heels and closing his eyes mid-sentence.

'Have I been neglecting you, Sir Tudor?'

'I know what you're up to and it stinks. We are not sent here to flatter and fawn. We are sent here to pass laws and do our best for our unfortunate constituents.'

'Indeed . . .'

'In the case of your constituency, the misfortune is only magnified.'

Mears did not need to take this from Sir Tudor, even if the old blunderbuss had been in Parliament since the Norman Conquest. He was about to protest but Sir Tudor said: 'To save you the twouble of soliciting my vote for the Speakership, let me assure you that I would sooner vote for cowwupt George Chance or even the appalling Bwanton-Day than for it to be handed to someone who has so shamelessly schemed for the job.' With that, Sir Tudor Matthews swept off, destined for a glass of champagne at the Athenaeum. Mears watched him depart with such fury that a nerve under his moustache twitched. He wanted to beat the Sir Tudors and Branton-Days. He ached to screw them all.

★

PIKE'S column, as ever, looked for the best in everyone.

WHO will inherit swanky Speaker's House – hot and cold running flunkeys and a fabuloso cellar? Speakers receive invitations to Buck House banquets and a to-die-for pension. Slippery George Chance has blown it. Mike Branton-Day has his fans – in the gentry. What about Les 'Mouldy' Mears, chairman of the housing committee? Oddball Mears has a Uriah Heepish manner and little more charisma than the Basingstoke bypass. That moustache: a russet brush but far from foxy. His Russian girlfriend could pout for the Kremlin. But falling out with his party's leader and Whips has made 'Mouldy' popular. Establishment sweats fear he could prove 'revoltingly independent-minded'. 'Whispers' is inclined to think 'Mouldy' is a seeping gumboil. Deputy Speaker George Tewk is dull but he claims admirably few expenses. Good man.

Bryce rang Mears to tell him the happy news.

'What do you mean, happy news? It's bloody offensive.'

'Don't take it personally,' said Bryce.

'How am I meant to take it?'

'As a boost. By your enemies are ye defined. Everyone hates Pike. The attack on Tewk is damaging.'

'Attack? It calls him a good man. And what's this Kremlin line about Olga?'

'Low stereotyping. The stuff on Tewk implies he is a martinet on expenses. That may impress the public but will horrify this electorate – the MPs. The last thing they want is some stove-hatted puritan. A Speaker who would irk the Whips, however: now you're talking.'

'You're a Whip.'

'I know. So I will never be suspected of planting this item. Perfect.'

18

The Night Of The Debate

ARRIVING for the Big Faith Debate, Ross was met by a tall publicity girl in a skirt short as an Aztec's temper. Bronzed legs, painted talons, teeth like a corn-on-the-cob champ. She greeted Ross almost as an old squeeze.

'Tom! Fab!' Kiss.

'How do you do?'

'I'm Phoebe. Everyone's in the Green Room. Love the collar. So cool.' Ross caught her scent, a hint of sugared grapefruit.

He was given – coaxed into, her fingertips encircling its stem – a glass of wine. White Gascony. Almost as if they had been told. It would reduce the pain in his right hand, which had again been throbbing.

'You must meet so many people! Bet it's a great life.' Any existence felt acceptable now, after what happened to Speaker Aldred. In Phoebe's orbit, Ross certainly felt alive. He felt the urge to impress her, show her what he was made of, lust in the old hound yet. The glass was large but who did schooners nowadays? The wine sloshed around the bulbous bottom. When he drank some he tooled a slug down his chin and shirt front. Damn.

'Top up, Tom?' She was there in an instant. 'Need a napkin?' Discreet mopping. Ruddy wine glass. They were shaped like this to accentuate the bouquet but all he could smell was sugared

grapefruit, freshness, sex. 'Hey, that's catchy. Top-up-Tom!' she said
'Yes.'

'Top-up-Tom! Drop more?' One for the road to dusty disgrace.
He took a swig to make room. As she leaned across, pouring, he
caught again that tangy scent.

Dymock had been escorted to a private area – a side chapel for
the cardinal. Ross met the other two panel members, one being
trade unionist Sheila Henderson, the other a Zen Buddhist. He
was in red robes and had brought his plastic begging bowl. He was
filling it with some of the crisps, peanuts and stodgy little vol-au-
vents provided by hospitality.

'I'm the token woman,' said Sheila, extending a hand. 'Sheila
Henderson. You're Thomas, right?'

'Tom Ross. I'm the token Christian. The tethered goat.'

'You've got a Buddhist to help you.'

'It looks like he's helping himself. Fancy a vol-au-vent before
he jobs the lot?' A fleck of puff pastry shot from Ross's lips and
landed on Sheila's shoulder. 'Sorry.' He tried to dab it off but it
was damp from his spit and smudged into the jacket Sheila was
wearing over her blouse.

'His name is Denzil,' said Sheila, unaware.

'Who?'

'The Buddhist.'

'I thought Denzil was a Welsh name.'

'I daresay it is possible to be Welsh and Buddhist.'

'Jones the Monk,' said Ross.

Magnus Bacton arrived with his hairdo. Bacton was chairing
the debate. He told them he was sure they would all be 'wonderful'
then left, coxcomb erect, to be beautified in make-up. Ross had
declined make-up.

'Aren't you having a drink?' he asked Sheila.

'Not before speaking,' she said. 'But don't let me stop you.'

Phoebe returned with the bottle. Slender body, decent nose,

delicious. The wine. 'So you two have met,' said Phoebe. 'No making friends, please. We want you to be at each other's throats in the debate! Only joking. Love your blouse, Sheila. Where did you get it? It really suits you. Tom, splosh more?' Ross had not noticed Sheila's blouse. It was a pale pink silk just visible under her jacket – the one with the pastry splodge on the shoulder.

By the time they were led towards the hall – 'Your moment has arrived, Tom,' growled Phoebe – Ross was cheery. He was surprised by the size of the hall. There must have been four hundred people and the panel table was on a raised, narrow stage. Ross felt no fear.

'The Don of Doubt draws a faithful throng,' said Sheila.

'Do you know him?'

'Does anyone?'

'Everyone's heard of Dymock.'

'That's not the same thing.'

At Dymock's entrance the crowd whooped. He found his seat and gave a half-raised hand of acknowledgement. White locks at his neck were starting to curl. He withdrew a slim propeller pencil from his inside pocket and, after adjusting it – a vet priming a deadly syringe – made a few notes. Sound checks ensued. Here was the gradual hymnody of secular performance, as familiar as stages of prayer to communion. Testing, testing, one two, one two. Kyrie eleison. Microphones were fixed. We do not presume to come to this thy table, trusting in our own voices but in thy manifold great mysteries of amplification.

Sheila, Ross and Buddhist Denzil told the floor manager, in headphones and whiffy shirt, what they had had for breakfast. Floor managers always asked this question. They could have asked for a few lines of favourite verse or the moment you fell in love. Instead they asked what you had for breakfast. 'Nothing', said the Buddhist. So short an answer was it that he was obliged to say it five times before the floor manager was satisfied.

'Fair-Trade muesli with blueberries,' said Sheila.

'Leftover kedgeree, cold,' boomed Ross, to a whine of feedback.

Dymock, when asked what he had had for breakfast, initially said 'sex'. Nervous laughter. 'Well, I am programmed to tell the truth.' He then went into a spiel — the hall was rapt — about how he actually wanted to say that this was the floor manager's birthday. 'Could everyone join a chorus of "Happy Birthday to You"?' They did, conducted by Dymock's propeller pencil.

'Perhaps someone will give him a less smelly shirt for his birthday,' muttered Ross. Sheila signalled to him to be quiet, reminding Ross that the floor manager, with his earphones and their mikes, would be able to hear anything they muttered.

'Thank you, everyone,' said Dymock after 'Happy Birthday'. 'There. A good communal sing-song. Shows we atheists can do it, too. All we need is a guitarist and some arm-waving and it could be Sunday service. Hope you enjoyed that, vicar.' Everything Dymock said delighted them. He could have read the self-assembly instructions to a garden wheelbarrow and they would have been thrilled. Here was the great star in their firmament, their prophet.

'Give 'em hell, Augustus!' shouted a shaven-headed supporter. Dymock held the propeller pencil to his lips as if to say 'Shush, we must not yet gloat'. Ross scoured the audience for friendly faces. Calvert was to one side of the stage on a small table equipped with two large clocks. Did Calvert count as a friendly face? Petroc had said he was going to come along but Ross could not see him. Phoebe had vanished.

'Is this being televised?' he asked Sheila, but she was fiddling with the microphone on her bosom and Ross averted his eyes. Denzil was mid-prayer, or maybe fighting off an attack of indigestion. The vol-au-vents had not been light. Halfway down one's gullet the pastry had acquired the consistency of builders' mortar. The floor manager was fiddling with a wire underneath the platform. Ross asked him Sheila's question. Was this event being televised?

'Bacton has brought a Channel Four documentary crew. It's only for background stuff.'

'Right,' said Ross.

'Just one thing,' said the floor manager. 'Don't move back too far in your seats, any of you. There's no lip on the dais.'

'Do you want a glass of water, Tom?' asked Sheila, pouring herself one from a carafe.

'I'm OK, thanks.'

Bacton started the debate without preamble. Ross realised that the wine he had spilt had left a mark down his shirt. Would the cameras spot that? Sheila had removed her splodged jacket but he could hardly remove his shirt. 'Welcome to the Big Faith debate,' said Bacton smoothly. 'What, why, where is Faith? Who believes in a god nowadays? How should society approach religion in what some call the post-Christian age? We're here to debate these matters. Earth is spinning on its axis and the clock is ticking. Let's start!'

Each of them had a two-minute opener and Bacton said that the timekeeper (Calvert) would be merciless in telling people to halt. An orange light in front of them signalled twenty seconds to go. When the red light shone, it was time to stop.

Sheila began with an admission of her own lack of belief but her respect for those who made the leap. The Labour Movement had roots in chapel worship. She suspected that the apostles would have been Labour voters. We now lived in a multi-faith Britain. While she had a fondness for Anglicanism, she suspected the Church would disappear within thirty years. It would be the task of trade unions to fill the gap. She completed her remarks with ten seconds to spare. Ross joined the applause for her, noticing that when he clapped with his elbows on the table, it wobbled.

Denzil began his two-minute slot with fifteen seconds of silence. Silence was a divine gift and we should have more of it, he announced. Just before the silence finished he pinged open his eyes dramatically and rang a little bell round his neck. The rest of his opening salvo was about harmony and inner calm and the joys of chanting, of which he gave a brief demonstration. This went down well with the audience, some of whom accepted his invitation to try their own chants. A certain amount of piss-taking was evident. 'The first two speakers have kept to time brilliantly,' said Bacton. 'Tom Ross, you're chaplain to the Speaker of the House of Commons. You have two minutes, starting NOW.'

Ross had prepared a text and he started to read but the lighting was bad. He could not focus. 'Think of faith as an oat,' he said. 'Oak. Faith has deep roots in our society and provides shelter, succour, sterility. Sorry, stability.' Sibilants splashed off his wet tongue, splotting and sploffing the microphone. He smiled wonkily at the audience. Silence. Not in a good way. Not in a Buddhist way. 'This oak has many branches. Sects. Sorry. Insects can derive nourishment from its roots while other creatures benefit from its bark and nest in its canopy.'

'Speed up!' shouted the shaven-haired man who had earlier cheered Dymock.

'Speak up, did you say?' said Ross. 'Sorry. Is this thing not working?' He tapped the microphone and leaned into it, shouting: 'Can you hear me?' The noise boomeranged off the back wall.

'It's fine,' hissed Bacton.

'I said "speed up",' repeated the heckler. 'Get on with it.'

'Oh, *speed* up. Sorry. Where was I?'

'You were telling us about your oak tree,' said Bacton. 'We'd reached the canopy.' Some laughter.

'Indeed. The oak . . .'

'It was an oat a minute ago,' shouted the heckler.

Ross, starting to hurry, said: 'The oak — it started as an acorn actually — the oak outlives us. We can plant it in our teens and by the time we die at four-score years and ten it will still not be fully grown. Faith is bigger than us. It dwarfs us. To have a faith is to admit that we are not the most important things here. But this life need not be the final say. I'm not saying we will all get a second chance.' The orange light was glowing. 'But there is a higher level, a higher form of being. Jesus showed us the way when he lived and died and lived again in Jerusalem two thousand years ago. Can we imagine a world in which there was no religion?'

'Time up!' shouted Calvert.

One or two people clapped. Calvert would not look at Ross. Ross spotted Petroc in the audience. He was sitting, Ross was pretty sure, with Nettle Greenhill. Petroc looked angry.

'Right, time for our fourth and best-known speaker,' said Bacton. 'Augustus Dymock needs no introduction. Two minutes.'

'Thank you. One minute fifty nine seconds coming up. Well, we have heard three opening sallies, at least two of them sober appraisals.' Laughter. 'I acknowledge that to those who choose to believe, faith means a lot – to them. But to the rest of society? This is la-la stuff. You might as well believe in the tooth fairy. Actually, don't get me started on the tooth fairy. Kids wrench out their teeth to win coins from this imagined being. They damage their gums. Fairy tales are absurd and we should ban them. We also overload our schools with history. Mathematics and science. These are the rational arts. These are the future. History congeals us. We swallow the Bible just because it has been there so long. Religion is a relic of primitivism. Need I mention all the wars fought in the name of some god? Need I mention the mutilations, executions, immolations, the lives blighted because science was held back by state-enforced witchcraft? Ye gods, indeed.

'My orange light has come on but I intend to ignore it because this debate is about violating unreasonable laws.' The crowd clapped violently. 'It is about freedom. It is about the liberation of Africa from machete violence conducted in the name of churches and mosques. Was a young woman in the days of the Roman

Empire really impregnated by a divinity before her carpenter boyfriend got a chance?'

'Time up!' shouted Calvert.

'Time is indeed up for religion,' said Dymock, to cheers and wolf whistles. 'Did angels appear at the young woman's side when she gave birth? Did that child turn water into wine, walk on a stormy sea and bring dead people back to life? I am open to scientific, material evidence. But please, don't wave ancient superstitions at me and say that they are too important to be questioned. Don't say oil acquires magic anointing powers just because a high priest has said abracadabra over it. Prayers said in Neasden will alleviate suffering in Nepal? Religion is no more factual than a homeopathic remedy for gangrene. These religious men are not holy. They are shamen. Shame on them, say I.'

'Time UP!' repeated Calvert.

'I'd finished,' said Dymock. 'Thanks, guys.' He lifted his water glass as in a toast. The hall burst into sustained applause.

'Well, that broke every rule in the book,' said Bacton. 'We will now have questions from the floor.'

The debate was expected to last an hour or so. The questions were a mixture of polite enquiry and hackneyed observation, generalised slander ('we all know the Roman Catholics are child molesters') and fey nonsense ('I just feel such a great karma when I listen to Augustus'). Ross was pressed on the Virgin Birth. 'I mean, do you really think it happened?' asked a woman next to the shaven-haired heckler.

'I believe that Christ was and is the son of God.'

'But the Virgin Birth?'

Dymock intervened. 'Do you think Mary became pregnant without human sperm?'

'Please,' said Ross. 'Can we not get too biological about this?'

'Not get too biological?' said Dymock. 'What, is science too truthful? Is science too difficult for theists? What I find odd is that

213

the very people who swallow the myth about Mary's pregnancy are the very same people who are so quick to condemn teenage mums. But in the case of Mary it's immaculate conception! No wonder the Church is dead.'

'It's not dead,' snarled Ross.

'It's run by hopeless sots who don't really believe what they preach and gargle back the communion wine,' snorted Dymock.

'That's not true,' said Ross.

'It's truer than the story about Mary being got up the duff by the hand of God. The hand!'

'Disgusting!' shouted a voice. Ross saw that it was Petroc. 'Leave him alone. And apologise for that slur. You should be ashamed! Blasphemy!'

'Well, well, what have we here?' said Dymock. 'The old blasphemy gambit. I wondered how long that would take.'

'Quiet, please,' said Bacton, who also recognised Petroc.

'It's not disgusting, it's valid scepticism,' said Dymock.

Petroc was standing and pointing and shouting – saying something about a 'corrupting influence' – but he was inaudible because Dymock's voice was amplified and his was not. 'This is a debate, isn't it? We're testing thesis with antithesis.'

'It's OK, Petroc, I can handle this,' said Ross.

'You know that guy?' asked Sheila.

'He's my flatmate.'

'He's a vicar,' said Bacton.

'He's a plant,' countered Dymock. 'The faith crowd can never rely on their own arguments. They have to pack the hall. Pathetic. Can't trust the truth so they bring along their boyfriends.' Security guards had arrived at the end of Petroc's row, telling him to be quiet.

'Can we have some calm, please?' said Bacton.

'Just so long as that man speaks with respect,' shouted Petroc, to which Dymock retorted that rational truth was the thing that most deserved respect.

Ross felt the moment was ripe. 'I know you're called the Dong of Doubt . . .' he began; he was going to say more but was interrupted by a burst of laughter from the crowd.

'I think you'll find it's Don of Doubt,' said Bacton.

'Hey, I can take Dong,' said Dymock. 'Even if Mary couldn't.' Again the crowd brayed.

'I'm sorry,' said Ross, realising what he had said.

'I forgive you, my child,' said Dymock. 'Have another drink.' He remembered Petroc's use of the word 'corrupting'. Hang on, was this the vicar who knew about his activities with Greenhill? Had Pike, or Jo, or all of them, got the wrong vicar? Was Petroc, not Ross, the one who knew? The thought soon faded.

Things settled down for a while. Someone asked the panel members if they believed in ghosts. 'Maybe,' said Denzil and Sheila.

'No,' said Dymock, 'unless you mean tricks of the subconscious, perhaps when someone is sedated. Apparitions as in *Hamlet*? No.'

'Tom Ross, do you believe in ghosts?' said Bacton.

'Of course.'

'Spirits, more like,' said Dymock.

Bacton flapped a hand at Dymock to hush him. 'You say "of course" you believe in ghosts, Tom? What are these? Troubled souls? Holy ghosts?'

'The Holy Ghost is a different concept.'

'But ghouls and ghosties – do they exist?' asked Bacton.

'You mean you know they don't?' said Ross. And for the first time he felt a stir of interest from the audience. 'Has no one ever walked over your grave? Have you never heard voices? Would you curse the newly dead or swear in an empty church at night? Would you hesitate before joining a séance? I bet a lot of people here would. Why? Because we sense that the frontier between life and death can be porous. Earth is not everything. The known universe is only that: known. How can our knowledge be complete? How can the universe itself, as we understand it, be the whole story?

If it were, that would mean it has limits – edges, like a coffin. What is beyond? What happens if you take the lid off the coffin? What is there? Light? A being? Another universe, another coffin? Our faith accepts that we do not know everything. We accept our insignificance. It is the sceptics and cynics who think they are so important. Yet they accuse theists of being power-crazed.'

'You said it, Noah,' said Dymock.

'There he goes again,' said Ross. 'Everything so flip and sneery. Please. Humanity is better than this. Who is really arrogant? The people who insist nothing beyond exists? Or those of us offering a code – a creed – by which frightened people can lead their lives? There are billions of us. We aren't all as sophisticated and ironic as Augustus Dymock. Darwinism's also-rans are poor and in need of comfort.'

'So you flog them a fraud?' said Dymock.

'We explain our faith in the greatest man who ever lived – Jesus. Why attack us for doing this? Priests don't do it for riches. Why are you so jaundiced and unhappy, Mr Dymock? You're the child on the beach who goes kicking others' sandcastles.'

'Is religion only a sandcastle?' asked Bacton.

Ross ignored him. 'We live in hope. We live to some of the greatest ideals ever formed. How can it be arrogant to try to lead a Christian life? What is arrogant about love and respect and peace and modest faith? The arrogance is in secularism which insists that nothing is possible. Nihilism is limiting, mean-spirited. It presses its thumb on your spine and tells you to stay in your place, little people. You opt for that if you want to, Mr Smart Guy, but I choose the possibilities and kindness of Christ any day. Ghosts? Sure. Why not?' And this time Ross won a round of applause, respectful rather than ecstatic but applause all the same.

Dymock was at it immediately. 'Where is the credible evidence? Decapitated kings walking round palaces with their heads tucked under their arms? This is bad fiction.' He made a woooo sound and threw high his arms. No one laughed.

'I don't mean ectoplasmic shades leaping from cupboards,' said Ross. 'But troubled spirits certainly exist. I have sensed calmer presences, too.'

'You've seen happy ghosts?' said Dymock.

'I have felt reassurance. Consolation.'

'Tricks of the mind.'

'I don't think so. Most priests have at some time or other been called to soothe turbulent spirits. I was asked if I believe in ghosts. My answer is yes.'

'Can you describe any ghosts you have seen?' pressed Bacton. 'Was there noise?'

'They have an energy which can cause noise,' said Ross. 'A door bangs, a plate falls. I have heard a voice, have turned round and seen no one there. One senses a presence. A stirring. A damp, rotting smell – of an opened grave. A smell of cigarettes. I have smelled garlic, as from the mouth of a medieval miller, in a country churchyard.' The hall was now silent. 'I have felt smoke where there has been none. I have shivered on the hottest days.'

'Next question, please,' said Bacton.

'I'd like to know about Buddhist meditation techniques and the role they can play in the path to faith,' said someone.

Ross leaned towards Sheila and whispered: 'Can you pass the water?'

'Denzil,' said Bacton. 'You've been fairly quiet. Tell us about meditation zones. You may be in one at the moment, for all we know.'

It was Sheila's fault. As she was saying 'sure' to Ross's request for the water jug she reached across with an arm and managed to snag her microphone wire. While untangling it she lost her grip on the neck of the carafe and it fell on her own glass, which spilled. Water gushed towards Ross and he, already worried about the mark down his front, shot back in his chair, forgetting the technician's advice to beware the edge of the dais. One chair leg found itself supported by nothing more than thin air. As the laws of physics dictate, it toppled.

All the audience knew was that one moment Ross was there, the next – with a muffled cry and two arms flung high – he was not. As he disappeared from view he flailed for anything to stop his fall and his right hand's fingertips, still clumsy from his burn, grabbed a side flap on Sheila's blouse. It ripped. One moment Sheila was there. The next, she, too, hurtled from general view, being yanked from her chair at such an angle that her sensibly shod hooves gave a strong kick to the underside of the panel table. Even at the start of the evening the table had not been the most solid construction. One good boot from Sheila was enough to make it collapse, with a shattering of carafe and glasses. Water fell on an electrical connection, which sparked and fused the sound system. Bang! Some in the audience mistook this for gunshot and in the confusion presumed that Ross or Sheila had been assassinated. Women screamed. Denzil continued with his answer about meditation. Bacton dived for cover. Dymock, fearing he was the target of the assassination attempt, said, 'Oh my God.' When Sheila stood up, her blouse was so badly torn that the whole world – and once the clip was placed on YouTube it pretty much was the whole world – saw her splendidly deep bosom, cupped in steel-reinforced lingerie.

AROUND the bridge's feet, water was eddying fast. The noise was incessant, as if a canal was whooshing through a lock gate. It was hypnotic, soporific, tempting. The drink had helped. Ross drained his hip flask.

What a sodding disaster. Despite the river's din he could still hear the crowd's laughter when he fell off the stage. Photographers had pounced, cackling as they clicked and snapped and flashed.

He had a memory of someone – Sheila Henderson? – hauling him off his bottom and pressing tissue-paper against a cut on his cheek. Poor Sheila. He should have apologised. We have left undone those things which we ought to have done. He should have prepared himself better for the debate. And we have done those things which we ought not to have done. Should not have drunk that wine and several snorts more afterwards at the Green Man. Should have rung Theresa to tell her he really had loved her. Should not have criticised Andrew. Should have surrendered his pass and the Robing Room keys to the Speaker's Office. It was better to leave things tidy.

The darkness, the lateness of the midnight hour, the spent nerves: each was enough to make a man drowsy. He wondered if pretty Phoebe had slipped him a Mickey Finn. They were like that in London. The ferryman's bench was hardly comfortable. He shivered. He heard pigeons like car horns. He caught a smell of shortbread, just as his mother used to bake; her touch as she curled the hair round his ear at bedtime; her wedding ring. Summery warmth started to replace the cold. He was hugging Theresa because their grandchild was going to be OK, rescued from the petri dish by the butcher's table – just before Augustus Dymock could throw it down the waste chute. One moment dead, the next reborn. Sheila Henderson advanced on him, naked. He himself was down to his baggy, grey underpants yet he had to give a sermon in five minutes. He was going to tell the congregation everything Jean had disclosed about Dymock and Greenhill and their bribing of Mears. Would they believe him? They never believed anything else he said.

Time passed and the river had risen. Ross came to with a slow sense of surprise. He was up to his thighs in water. The tide was licking at the ferryman's bench. The river roared as never before. Idiot! Which direction was the Commons terrace? He had to move – but as he rose he slipped. 'Tom!' Ross staggered to his feet. 'Tom!'

His face had struck the ferryman's seat. His right flank was soaked and his jaw ached. Was that blood he could taste? Perhaps he had lost a tooth. 'Tom!' Petroc had tried to reach Ross after the debate but had been prevented by security guards. They recognised him as the troublemaker and wanted him out of the building. He had stood outside but Ross left by another door. 'Tom!'

'Over here!' said Ross, but Petroc could not hear him. They might as well have been in the turbine room of a hydro-electric dam. Everything Ross tried to grasp was wet and clammy. The current pulled at his ankles.

Petroc spotted him as Ross lost his footing a second time. It was not that the cobbles were slippery from algae, which they were. It was the force of the water. Petroc rushed down the steps to the ferryman's platform. He, too, almost slipped.

'Hold the railing on the wall, sir!' said another voice. Mates.

'Tom!' shouted Petroc, mooring himself to the railing. 'Hold on to the seat!' Ross surfaced long enough to see Petroc. The edges of the stone seat were greasy. Ross managed a grip for a few seconds with his good hand but all the time he was being pulled towards the bridge by the river. It was sucking him slowly from his position – actually not an unpleasant sensation. Ross heard an oar. Its rhythm lulled him and now he was sure he could see a blade catch a glint of the bridge lights, the oar dipping into the water. A figure appeared amid the surging, rushing river. It was hooded, stooped like Aldred, and stood as though on the water, near the end of a shallow-bottomed ferry. Salvation was drifting towards him in the foaming flood. The figure did not say anything but as it came closer its hood slipped. This was not Aldred. This was a younger head, looking askance. It was working hard on the oar and its face showed the effort. It was resisting the force.

'Fight the tide, Tom! Fight the tide!' Petroc had made it to the bottom of the ferryman's steps and was waist deep in the water. With his right hand, he held the railing. With his left he stretched towards Ross. Mates had brought a boat pole with a net and hook but from the top of the steps he could barely control it. The pole swung.

'Fight the tide, Tom!' The hook was small and sharp. Mates feared it would cut Ross's hand if he grabbed it. 'You can do it!' cried Petroc.

The hooded ferryman floated just above the waters, assuming the professional nonchalance of a skipper waiting for passengers to board his vessel. Ross felt one leg being drawn completely off the platform. His other foot was slipping. 'Jump!' cried Petroc. 'My hand! Here!' The water's roar intensified. The boathook lurched round his head. Amid the blood he also drank dank, troutish water. The taste of death was enveloping him. The ferry must soon depart for the distant bank.

Ross leapt.

FISH, water, teeth, blood merged. There was a flurry of writhing flesh, a tugging and tearing. Then came stillness and the light fusion of cocktail jazz and conversation reimposed itself on the dining room.

The Thought Foundation team dinner at Bites in Maximilian's Hotel was not going entirely to plan. Dymock looked down the table and saw Zac sitting in a wet puddle of his own company. The useless boy was toying with a cola. Dymock felt a flash of anger, then pity. Pity! He hated himself for it. They had reached a truce after their row in the car but Zac plainly needed a kick or two. Perhaps an outdoor adventure camp would toughen him.

Maximilian's black-marbled restaurant had been designed when Russians were the spenders. Bling-and-blini oligarchs had long gone and Bites was fighting for survival. Maître d' Mahmoud had been beaten down in price by the Thought Foundation's Events buyer. Jo and her colleagues were upbeat, Jo in particular relieved that Ross had not come out with any allegations about the Greenhill money. Wine glasses in one hand, mobiles in the other, she and her workers busied themselves on social media. The internet already had footage of Ross toppling off the stage. Jo's underlings soon ensured that it was trending. If that could be sustained for a few hours, the credulous Peter Pans who ran the morning news broadcasts would follow it.

Amid his disciples, Dymock smilingly accepted their tributes. A strikingly sexy girl asked him to autograph her napkin.

'Who are you, then?'

'I'm Phoebe. I was working at the debate.'

'Hello, Phoebe.'

'Can you put a couple of kisses after your name?'

'Just a couple?'

'As many as you like!' Phoebe leaned over him. Dymock caught a breeze of grapefruit as she shook her hair and took a selfie of the two of them. Olga watched. 'Have you eaten well, beauty?' Dymock asked Olga. 'Who was that girl? Never seen her before.'

'Not hungry,' said Olga. She kicked her strapless, high-heeled shoe at an imagined object. Her pout could have collected rainwater.

'Caviar? We're celebrating.'

'This caviar is sheet.'

Banter filled the restaurant and from time to time one of the team would say 'Cheers, Augustus' and Dymock would raise his glass and toast the 'triumph' of the debate. He caught Phoebe looking at him. She smiled. He returned it, slyly. He did not swallow much alcohol. Jo had asked Mahmoud to bring a basket of bread for Zac. He was slowly spreading a chunk with butter from a levelled ramekin. Zac ignored the pretty girls but played with the timer buttons on his wristwatch. Dymock remembered being given a digital watch of his own, one of the early models, just after his own father died. He had used the stopwatch to test the drowning times of gerbils in the school science laboratory.

'I call minicab,' said Olga.

'Not yet, beauty.'

'I had enough.'

'Stay a little longer.' One of the young men from Design had gone to sit next to Zac. He showed Zac something on his mobile and Zac reached for his own and pulled up something on the screen. Dymock's neck bristled.

'We won the vote,' yelled Phoebe. The table cheered.

'What vote?' said Dymock.

'We were going to have a show of hands in the hall but the chaos prevented that. So we asked people as they were leaving the venue. Got them at the exits: is faith a good thing? By more than twenty per cent they came out saying "no".' She rose from her seat, showing off her slender frame, and came round to show him statistics on her mobile. 'See? Here.' Dymock did his best to concentrate. 'Just over twenty points ahead.'

'Is that what we expected, Jo?'

'Thereabouts,' said Jo. No, in other words. If a pissed vicar and a bonkers Buddhist had pushed to within twenty points of the secularist position in an audience of young metropolitans, that was a disappointment. Zac was still talking to the Design man and they were laughing. The man had his arm round the back of Zac's chair. The boy spotted his father's stare and pulled a face, as if to say 'Why are you looking at me?' Dymock, absurdly, felt indignant for Zac's other boyfriend – the one who had canoodled with him at the gallery.

'I should have done better,' said Dymock. 'Should have killed him. That vicar.'

'You did great,' said Phoebe. 'I thought, anyway.' She waggled back to her age group.

Olga said: 'You were cruel. You think others like that? Always you must destroy. How does that make people love you?'

'Love!' said Dymock.

'You think love is weak. But you need love. Without it – pffff. This is your problem. The church guy. He was nervous, got pissed, but he was kind. It was possible to love him.' Dymock shook his head but he sensed she was right. The drunken vicar had done better than Calvert had predicted. If it hadn't been for that accident at the end, would they be here celebrating? The old fool had fought. He had resisted. But he had wimped out of playing his ace. If he was the one. If Pike was right.

'Jo, I think we should stop the social media campaign revelling too much in his accident.'

'What do you mean, Augustus? It's hilarious. It'll go viral.'

'It's not fair.'

'He only had himself to blame.'

Maybe, thought Dymock. But what if he knows? What if he was keeping his powder dry? The fall had been lucky. Luck would let a wild cat escape once, maybe nine times, but it could never be a reliable saviour.

'Jo's right, you won that one tonight, Augustus,' said a young researcher whose name Dymock could not recall. So many of them looked the same: flat fringes, trouser suits, pale cheeks, tired eyes. Phoebe was different, though.

'You crucified him,' said Jo. 'You're not going soft, are you?'

'Course not! Your health.' Another pretend toast. Olga had her arms crossed and was concentrating on her mobile. All these bloody machines – and they called themselves humanists.

'This place,' said Olga. 'Why do you like it?'

A bell rang. 'You'll see,' said Dymock. At one end of the restaurant was a vast fish tank that contained three red-bellied piranha. A staff member approached the tank with a jug of water. 'Feeding time,' said Dymock.

The top of the fish tank was opened. Once the restaurant lights had been dimmed, the contents of the jug were emptied into the tank. A large crab descended towards the sand and a few sprigs of greenery. Before the crab reached the bottom, the piranhas struck, tearing at it.

'Did you place a bet, Augustus?' asked Jo.

'Fool's game,' said Dymock.

Other diners started to cheer their piranha of choice. The crab did not surrender easily. Its claws snapped and it scored the flank of one piranha. Within seconds the three fish had devoured the crab. As the bout ended, Mahmoud came greasing round the tables.

'Mr Dymock, you will take a digestif on the house?'

'I won't, Mahmoud, but I am sure my friends will have more wine.'

'Indeed, sir.' Mahmoud bowed. 'Ah,' he added, 'look. This is always good – you are lucky.' He gestured towards the tank, which was still thrown into relief by the lighting. 'Cannibalism.' The piranha wounded by the crab was trailing a thin line of pale-brown blood. It sensed it was in trouble for it was swimming near the surface of the water. The other two fish started to shadow their stricken collaborator. The attack came as fast as the flick of a knife. Mahmoud said: 'They do not attack a fellow fish unless there is a good chance they will win. It is the behaviour of the bully.'

'It is the behaviour of a rational mind,' said Dymock. 'It is the behaviour of the politician. I'm afraid you need to restock, Mahmoud.'

'An occupational hazard, Mr Dymock.'

When the lights came back up, Olga had gone.

BARNEY'S eyebrows crinkled as Theresa Ross played solitaire on the kitchen table. The only sound, apart from the dog's panting, was of the grandfather clock and a gusting wind outside. 'You're terribly noisy, Barney. Right old Puffing Billy. Now, what shall I do next? I'm stuck.'

Barney yapped, two, three, four times.

'Maybe.'

He barked again, a different tone, and leapt from his basket. The lights fizzled and the kitchen door swung. In that moment Theresa dropped a marble. 'Now look what you've made me do, you silly sausage. Shush. It's just the wind.' She bent to look for the marble. Maybe it had rolled towards the range, or near the fridge. 'Come on, Barney. Help me.'

Theresa was on all fours, looking for the solitaire ball, when she heard a plop of glass marble landing in wooden slot. She got back on her feet, saw what she had been looking for and resumed her game with a 'thank you'. Barney gave an enormous yawn and returned to his basket. Before falling asleep, the little dog licked his right paw. He did so assiduously, as if engaged in necessary, important repairs – as many as fifty times, finally examining the paw and finding it to be satisfactory.

AT that same hour in London, Ross sat at Base Camp, being fussed over by Nettle and Petroc. Nettle had been busy in the kitchen – had even cleaned it – and brought a tray into the drawing room.

'Tea,' said Petroc.

'It was a disaster,' groaned Ross. If he sounded a little absent-minded it was perhaps because he was examining his right hand with a certain puzzlement. 'Total disaster.'

'Not total,' said Petroc.

'Calvert said he had never been so embarrassed in his life.'

'He's had a sheltered life, that's all.' Petroc had no desire to discuss Calvert. The man had written, telling him disciplinary procedures were being instigated as a result of the televised service where Matt had been reunited with Bashirah. The diocesan authorities were in a fury that they had not been consulted. He would tell Ross, but not yet.

'I got pissed and fell off the stage,' said Ross. Nettle stirred three sugars into a mug of tea and placed it at Ross's side; a plate of toast and honey, too. 'I nearly drowned myself in the Thames. Thank

God for Mates.' Ross's prayer book was drying on a towel. The net of Mates's boathook had recovered it from the ferryman's seat. 'I felt this heave, as though someone was pushing me.'

'Probably the current,' said Nettle.

'No, the water was pulling. This was a push. The ferryman waved at me.'

'The ferryman?' said Nettle.

'What a mess,' said Ross.

'You loosened your tongue, Tom, that's all' said Petroc.

'I was pissed.'

'You spoke about the frontier of life and death,' said Petroc, 'and you stole the show from that blaspheming bastard Dymock.'

'Petroc!' said Nettle.

'Sorry, darling.'

'Darling?' said Ross.

'You're both my darlings,' said Nettle.

'You're going to be married soon,' said Ross.

Petroc said quickly: 'You stood up to the bully.'

'Bollocks. I fell off the stage, the table collapsed and I ripped off that woman's blouse.'

'And the blokes in the audience thought, "At last, the Church of England does me a favour". Did you see her bra? I've never copped one like that before.'

Ross, biting into his toast so that the butter dribbled, said: 'I should hope not. Anyway, what was all that stuff you were saying about Dymock being corrupt?'

'He corrupts our society. Our children.'

'Ah. I thought you meant something else.'

Ross again inspected his right hand. Perhaps the river water had been good for it. The pain from his burn had gone completely.

OLGA closed the flat's door and caught her breath. The taste of cheap caviar lingered on her tongue and she needed to clean her teeth. Mears's bedroom door was ajar. He woke at the sound of running water.

'You all right, Olga?' In slippers and dressing gown he waited until she came out of the bathroom. She stood in its doorway, holding her wash bag and towel. She had removed her make-up and was wearing a onesie with a childish design from the Sochi Winter Olympics. She started to convulse with sobs. 'What's up, girl? What's the matter?' Mears rushed to assist and had no alternative but to hold her. This only made her cry more until she was in full flood, howling. 'Shhhhh,' said Mears. His hands barely knew what to do.

In his arms she felt a permanence. She could smell his native scent under the carbolic soap and the wool of his dressing gown with its undertow of mothballs. The men she had known had tended to smell of drink and cigarettes or at very least of manipulative oils and leather.

Mears returned to his bedroom, saying 'Just a moment'. He reappeared with a small box. He knelt. She opened the box to find a ring. 'How about it? We could make a go of it, couldn't we?' The moustache, the brushed hair, the pyjama top buttoned to the end, the absurd contrast of his intense political ambitions. If she accepted, how could Dymock fail to react? She could use the leverage to get Mears to do the Thought Foundation favours, so she would become unsackable. But did she still mind what that selfish bastard Augustus felt? Would her friends in Moscow be impressed? But how important were they to her now? Her duty was to herself. Where would she be safest?

'Yeah?' asked Mears. His moustache twitched imploringly. 'Marry me?'

Olga sniffed, curled her fists inside the sleeves of her onesie and nodded. 'Da.'

19

A Speaker Is Elected

MATES'S wife struggled to swallow the communion wafer. A couple of days had passed since the tribulations of the tide. Mates had rung that morning to ask for a home visit. Ross said Holy Communion in her bedroom, she in a high-backed chair with an old antimacassar. Mates sat on the bed and rose at the relevant moments. The Gloria had been difficult. Normally it was spoken with confidence. Mrs Mates's lips had moved to the words but no sound had emerged. Ross and Mates whispered the lines. 'Have mercy upon us, have mercy upon us, have mercy upon us.'

'It's only a matter of time,' said Mates at the door.

'It's only a matter of time for all of us. Look, Walter, I want to thank you.'

'I'm the one who is thankful, sir.'

'I mean by the river the other night. You and Petroc saved me.'

'We were there at the right time, that's all.'

'I wasn't feeling quite right. I saw something.'

'The ferryman, sir?'

'You saw him?'

Mates waved his hand in a bored gesture. 'All this death. Makes you grateful for what you've had. I wasn't always good to her. We had spells apart. Cyprus mainly. I had a girl there. I think she guessed.' It was raining again. 'You got an umbrella?'

'She loves you, Walter. You are her familiar, her friend.'

'I won't keep this place.'

'It is your home.'

'When she's joins the platoon, it can't be mine alone. Houses are only camps, sir. They're for the mothers, really. We men can rest our heads anywhere. This place will be too full of – ghosts.'

'She will find Paradise, Walter.'

'She will, sir.' Ross shook his hand.

He took a taxi to the Commons. Cabbies often asked if he was an MP. 'Chaplain to the Speaker? What, like his personal vicar?'

'That's right,' said Ross.

'The old Speaker just passed away, didn't he?'

'He did, God rest his soul.'

'Where does that leave you?'

'They will elect a new Speaker and I suppose I will be his chaplain, unless he chooses another.'

'Do you want to be dropped here?'

'As it's raining, right inside, please.' Through the gates into New Palace Yard, a salute from the policeman.

'Fourteen quid, please. Want a receipt?'

'No thanks. Call it fifteen.'

'No receipt? The MPs always want one. I had one the other night. You should have seen the wad of notes. He pulled them out of a grip and broke the seal on a clip of twenties.'

'Been to the races, probably.'

'Don't think so. Wasn't dressed for that. Miserable bugger. Red moustache. Shut the window on me. Twenty-five-quid fare from St John's Wood. He wanted a receipt. No tip, though.' Ross was walking away when the driver called him back: 'Mears. That was his name. I saw his picture in the paper. Rolling in it, he was. Thanks, guv.'

MEARS, indeed so long a miserable bugger, strode through Westminster a man transformed. To one and all, even journalists, he radiated bonhomie, offering violet creams. His smile was beyond that of the gulled Malvolio. His vocabulary became modern. When walking down corridors, he clicked his fingers in a jaunty manner. He had stopped biting his nails.

Colleagues were stopped and enquiries made after their spouses – by name. Those with a birthday received a card. Those with a significant anniversary – a jubilee since first election – received good wishes. He remained there from before breakfast to the last sloshings of night, joshing with the Breakfast Club over bangers and beans, mulling on the fumes of brandy balloons in the Smoking Room with northern exiles after the Chamber adjourned. Hon Members who had not previously met Mears became a magnet for his fascination. He followed football scores to be able to give thumbs-up signs or looks of glum sympathy to devoted Gunners and Evertonians. He approached intellectually pretentious Members and beseeched their advice on knotty issues – perhaps they had recommendations for his reading list, for he respected their taste. He joined all-party groups from asthma to soft-fruit farming. His ardour for others' early-day motions became insatiable. Any Member with a letter in the national Press received a 'hear hear' text soon after dawn.

The announcement of his engagement was made on the Court pages and followed by diary paragraphs. Olga and he posed for photographs. 'From Russia with love,' said the headlines, with dreary inevitability. She showed off the ring. It sparkled, as did Mears's candidacy.

Promenading the parliamentary acres he was often accompanied by Kendrick, his campaign manager. Kendrick brought in the Celts, the itchy loners and the few working-class Members still inhabiting the Westminster swamp. Waverers without private money were sounded out, discreetly, to see if they might like to be considered for the Speaker's Panel, the list of MPs who chair debates in Westminster Hall. A useful few extra thousand pounds a year came with that. Former Cabinet ministers were asked if they had heard of Mears's proposal to hold a series of lectures, to be held at Speaker's House, and to be collated in a hardback volume. Mears was a great admirer and hoped the Rt Hon Member might consider making one of these groundbreaking lectures.

Bryce did not wish to be linked to his candidate. He made noises that were only lukewarm. 'Les and I go back a long way. Part of me would love him to get it, for old times' sake. Straight as an arrow, is Les. But it'll probably be Tewk.' In due course it was learned that Tewk would not be seeking the Speakership. His candidacy had failed to achieve traction, owing to a feeling that the Whips wanted him to have the job.

A profile of Mears in the *New Statesman* suggested that Mears and his Russian fiancée would 'turn Speaker's House into a lively salon, giving MPs greater access to the grace-and-favour mansion'. Olga's work at the Thought Foundation showed she was an intellectual, a woman with strong views, and the magazine happily suggested that she was already influencing Mears's political views. Pike's column in the *Dispatch* continued to be unenthusiastic about the Mears candidacy. Bryce was most grateful.

Dymock had barely reacted to the engagement. He had not forced her into bed since. The more he ignored her, the more liberated she felt.

'If I get this,' said Mears one breakfast, when she again had burned the toast, 'we'll have staff. You won't have to cook.' He tried to cuddle her. She said she respected him too much to give herself to him fully before they wed.

'I wish we could marry tomorrow,' he said.

'First you become Speaker.'

'If I get this, Olga, you'll go to embassies. You'll be invited to coronations. You'll meet all the visiting presidents and their wives.'

'Da?'

'The Kremlin would really love you then!'

She pushed his shoulder playfully and disappeared into the bathroom for a long soak.

MARRIAGE would always be their glue but Ross and Theresa spoke little these days. He had become even more subdued since a yellow notice had been placed in the church porch, seeking public views about local housing provision. Its provenance was uncertain but, this being England, no one doubted an official-looking notice on a public noticeboard.

At weekends they busied themselves with their own chores. She always laid a place for his lunch and supper – perhaps a stew from the bottom of the Rayburn, or cold meats from the fridge. She seldom laid one for herself.

One moon-strong night Ross went to Andrew's boyhood room. It was still decorated with football posters, a child's thesaurus, his autograph book. The single bed bore its faded coverlet. Ross had read him stories and they had said their prayers together. Though they still breathed, much had died. Ross hoped he might hear or see something – something that would show him a solution – but not a bat stirred. The other world did not dance to terrestrial whim, particularly the whim of a man who has not tried to help himself.

SIR Tudor Matthews rose to a House that was packed, yet quiet enough to hear Sir Tudor's waistcoat buttons sigh at their moorings. His leather brogues creaked, their upper casings dating to the Edwardian age. From his belly came molten bubblings and volcanic easings.

Sir Tudor was standing at the Table where the Clerk, Sir Roger Richards, normally sat. Behind shimmered the Chair, empty. The purpose of this afternoon was to elect its new occupant. 'As of this morning there were thwee candidates for the Speakership,' said Sir Tudor. One or two MPs chuckled. Sir Tudor looked up and repeated the word. 'Thwee.' He continued: 'However, shortly before I came to the Chamber today, one of the candidates withdwew.' This created a buzz. Who had ducked out – what had been the deal? 'The name of the Right Hon Member for Manchester South will not, therefore, be put to a vote.' Eyes swivelled towards Manchester South. George Chance sat like a cat in the sun. 'We should be grateful to the Hon Member,' said Sir Tudor. 'It will make pwoceedings today shorter. It becomes a contest between two candidates.'

Bryce sat on the front bench listening to the speculation. Had the tabloids nobbled Chance? Had he been bought? Had he won a plum job in exchange for his supporters switching allegiance to another candidate?

'The Member for Oakford and the Member for Long Valley will make speeches. The House will hear them without interventions. A vote will follow.'

'Point of Order!'

Sir Tudor saw Hamid Butt on his feet. 'Point of Order, Mr Butt.'

'On a point of order, Sir Tudor, can you give guidance to those of us who, finding it difficult to separate the two candidates, might wish to see another name before us. I refer, sir, to the Father of the House – your good self. How can we force you to become our Speaker?' The House laughed and gave an enormous 'Hear hear'.

'Too early in my career,' said Sir Tudor. 'I'm keepin' meself for next time.' More cheers.

'Point of Order!'

'Point of Order, Miss Peake.'

'I am sorry to delay the House,' said Netty Peake from under a mess of hair and spectacle cords, 'but is it in order for an election to be held with only male candidates? Where are the women?' Various female voices piped agreement. Others sighed.

'Any Member – male, female or undecided – could have stood. The Rt Hon Lady herself did not choose to enter the contest.'

'Don't encourage her!' shouted a Government backbencher.

Sir Tudor looked round the House. 'Any other points of order? Vewy well. The speeches will be made in alphabetical order. I call Mr Michael Bwanton-Day.'

Branton-Day fastened his Savile Row jacket and smiled sleekly. 'May I begin by thanking the Father of the House? There was widespread dismay when Sir Terry Wogan retired from presenting the Eurovision Song Contest. We now see who should have become his successor.' Hear hears.

Branton-Day began with the burdens of the Speakership. He touched on how many Speakers over the centuries had lost their heads, how they had been attacked by the Crown, how some had been ne'er-do-wells. 'One Speaker in living memory was so over-refreshed from the sherry decanter – he did not consider sherry to be strong drink – that he closed his eyes during a debate and slid to the floor,' said Branton-Day. 'It gave new meaning to "parliamentary session".' Groans.

As an after-dinner speech, it would have worked. Branton-Day was a confident orator. He wore a Guards tie and his face was craggy and tanned from sailing on the Solent. 'There is a custom that the new Speaker is dragged to the Chair,' he said. 'We should not be too hungry for this historic role.'

'Historic role' had looked good on paper. It had already been leaked to the Press as a hint of what Branton-Day might say. He had styled himself the candidate who would cherish the courtesies and gravity of the role. He intended to wear a full-bottomed wig and to be a remote, judicial figure.

'So why do I want to be Speaker?' he said.

'It's good money!' shouted a heckler.

'Order!' shouted Branton-Day supporters. The heckler, from the Opposition benches near Mears, was tutted.

'Money has nothing to do with it,' flashed Branton-Day. 'I am fortunate enough not to need it.' Oh dear. 'That's exactly what's wrong with this House. Too much cynicism. Too much selfishness.' The House, which had just heard itself insulted, fell to a sullen silence. 'If I am elected your Speaker, I will not take the extra salary which is offered. I will donate it to charity.' Around the country this might have been greeted as a noble gesture but in the Chamber it was felt to be a little pointed. It may be a fine thing for a Speaker to tell Members to be less mercantile – but only once he has been elected.

He spoke for another five minutes, promising to exercise impartiality and devote his spare hours to good causes. A lay onlooker might have applauded his fine sentiments; Hon Members felt a little got-at by so much piety from a rich man who could afford to disavow money. Tribute was paid to Speaker Aldred, mention of his name allowing Branton-Day to promise that new 'energy' would be brought to Speaker's House. He mentioned his grown-up children, his wife. He cleaved himself to Queen and country, Parliament and people. By the end it was a sound speech, even a fair speech, better than many had expected. When Branton-Day resumed his seat he received respectable support. Yet the speech had not glinted.

. 'I call Mr Leslie Mears,' said Sir Tudor.

The House rearranged its limbs and settled for the second part of the entertainment.

'I call him short,' bellowed a joker. Mears stood. 'Go on, stand up, then,' shouted another.

'I would certainly need stilts to stand shoulder-to-shoulder with our Father of the House,' began Mears. 'He is a man for whom the word "stature" could have been devised.' Hear hears, not least because it appeared to be extempore. Unless, of course, the heckles had come from Mears supporters who had teed up some prearranged repartee.

'We have just heard a fine speech from a fine parliamentarian,' said Mears. 'The reality today is that one candidate will win and one must fall. If, as seems likely, I come second, there will be no dishonour. The Hon Member for Long Valley has shown today that he has our historic interests at heart and that he operates from noble instincts that have long guided our squirearchy. To contest this election with him is, for me, an unanticipated privilege.

'I cannot claim a fine education, nor the physical attributes that would suit a full-bottomed wig and courtly tights. My ankles and calves are inelegant. For this reason if no other, the House will understand if I am less wedded to ancient customs of dress. I must confess, however, to wearing a moustache. It has been with me all my working life. You can tug it if you like. It is real, just as I am real.' Some laughter. The moustache issue had probably needed to be parked. The wise parliamentarian makes a comic asset of his absurdities.

'England has generally been happy in her rulers. We are lucky, alongside us, to still have several examples of that enlightened, landed class which for centuries has taken a benevolent hand in our public affairs. This is not an angry republic. It is a kingdom modulated by slow reform. It says everything about the progress of our society that I, a working-class boy from the Midlands, can stand before you today and speak about my dream of serving this living Legislature to my best abilities. Yet it must now evolve to the next stage of its essential life.

'I have already won prizes beyond anything my parents hoped for when they sent me walking off to my secondary modern. As for personal ambition, is it not the greatest privilege simply to represent, here at Westminster, our fellow citizens?

'We must serve them as never before. For that to happen, the House must operate in an efficient way. It must be modern. It must growl like the Maserati favoured by a certain Member from inner London.' This was a reference to the Member for Mayfair, who drove sports cars. He raised a hand to acknowledge the chuckles. 'It must be quick to respond and indignant when scorned. It must strive for respect and challenge those who slander and libel us – the sneering, negative elements who look for our every tiny failing and magnify them. Let them remember who is elected here and who is sent here by some press baron.'

'Hear hear!' Several MPs pointed at the press gallery.

'We must subject the Executive and officials of Government to the third degree. We must quibble and cavil and, where necessary, criticise our rulers. Tradition is not enough. We must surge with intention from all sides. This is what I, as Speaker, would encourage.

'I have served as a shadow minister. Briefly! To the Shadow Cabinet, not least to the Leader of the Opposition, allow me to make this blatant pitch for votes: if I am fortunate enough to be elected to the Chair, they need never endure me seeking to return to their high councils. A vote for me will be the best insurance against having Les Mears back on the front bench!' The Leader of the Opposition gave Mears a big thumbs-up.

Hon Members: 'Oh!'

'Nero raises his thumb!' said Mears. More laughter and delight. Nero! The Leader of the Opposition's many enemies loved it. 'I will not test the patience of the House,' said Mears. 'Let me conclude. The committees of this House see some of our best work. We should allow more time for their reports to be considered on the floor of the House and any consequent votes should be reflected in Whitehall policy. The Privy Council, currently freighted by scores of non-parliamentarians, should surely include both chairs and deputy chairs of our select committees. Let there be substantive votes, in Government time, on motions from the backbench business committee. Basically, I submit my name because I want the Commons to ride shotgun for our voters. This working-class titch wants the people to walk tall.'

PETROC was watching the Speakership election on the television in Base Camp's drawing room. That voice. Mears. The man with the moustache, there on the screen. The taste of Nettle's first kiss came back to him. Of course! Les Mears was 'Leslie'. Petroc gave his forehead such a slap, it left a mark on his brow. But telling Ross would mean explaining what they had been doing and why they had been hiding in the utility room. Now that he was likely to lose his incumbency at Alleluia Jesus!, Petroc did not much care what the Church authorities knew about him but he was not yet ready for Ross to know how he had abused his trust with Nettle. Meanwhile, the television screen transmitted the result of the Commons vote. Mears won with comfort. He was 'dragged' to the Chair by Kendrick and by Netty Peake, the three of them pantomiming the business amid cheers and general horseplay. The camera focused on Mears as he took his new seat as Speaker-elect and it caught, in his gleaming eyes and his pumped lips and slow nods of a swelling head, an expression of triumphant, sinister intent.

THE attack on the Press helped, as had the idea of making all committee deputy-chairmen 'Rt Hons', but initial comment focused on the transformation of 'Mouldy' Mears. Credit for his victory was given to his 'political activist' Russian love. It was Olga's moment as much as his. Photographers clamoured to take snapshots of her towering above him, beauty and the beast, bending over her fiancé so that his face was obscured by her embonpoint.

Immediately after his election, Mears was escorted to the Lords to be introduced to the Upper Chamber. A trip to the Palace was delayed. The Monarch was said to be taking supper (boiled eggs with soldiers) before an early start next day for Sandringham. It would have to wait until the Monday morning. If the Speakership had gone to Branton-Day, better still poor Tewk, Her Majesty would have discarded her boiled eggs for a celebratory glass of Dubonnet. Tewk knew about horses. Branton-Day was handsome gentry. Mears was – Mears.

Staff at Speaker's House lined up to greet their new master. Cooks, cleaners, train bearers, flunkeys – but no Mates – assembled down the grand staircase to clap as Mears and his moustache entered. He was accompanied by Olga, who kept being stopped for selfies. Sir Roger Richards effected introductions, guiding the new Speaker with a flat palm to his back. He did not like to touch Mears's coat too much. It appeared to contain nylon. 'We will go upstairs and have you measured, Mr Speaker,' said Sir Roger. 'I took the liberty of organising a house visit from the tailor we use in Savile Row.'

'I'm more a high-street man.'

'This is a bespoke matter, Mr Speaker.'

'So long as I'm not paying. Ah, here's my chaplain.'

'You know Tom Ross already?'

'I know of him.' Olga was still a few paces behind, talking to people.

'Congratulations on your election, Mr Speaker,' said Ross.

'Ta.'

'I suspect you have had a tiring day and would like us to disappear,' said Ross.

'Right on both counts,' said Mears. 'We want you to disappear altogether, Reverend. We're not religious.'

'We?'

'You surely have other things to do with your life.'

'I don't understand,' said Ross.

'It's not that hard. We don't want you any more,' said Mears. 'Do we, Olga?' He turned back to the Clerk and to Ross. 'My fiancée works for Augustus Dymock.'

'Sorry?' asked Olga. She had missed the exchange and Mears briefly explained.

'I know Dymock,' said Ross with a note of anger.

'Perhaps we can discuss these things in a day or so,' said Sir Roger. Olga had cottoned on to Ross's presence and stretched out her hand.

'You were very brave in the debate,' she said. 'The debate with Augustus. I admired you.'

'You were there?' said Ross.

'We won't change our mind,' Mears told Sir Roger. 'You'll soon learn that, you know. We don't float in the breeze. Not like the Church of England. No, we'll not have prayers in my House of Commons. Now, who else do we have to meet here? Come on, Mr Clerk. I haven't got all day.'

Sir Roger took Mears further down the line. Olga followed but as she moved off, she again shook Ross's hand. 'I am glad to meet you, Father.' As she left him she gave a small bob.

AT Base Camp's kitchen, over hot drinks, they gossiped about Mears, about his threat to sack Ross. And Olga. 'She wasn't what I was expecting,' said Ross. 'I got an impression she was a churchgoer, presumably Orthodox. I don't suppose she has as much power over Mears as people say. My chaplaincy was pretty much coming to an end, anyway.'

'It's so wrong,' said Nettle. 'How can they do it?'

'You're a priest for life,' said Petroc, 'unless you really err.'

Nettle had come round to drop off the Order of Service for the wedding and had found the two men in a gloom. She seemed more cross than the two of them combined. Flashes of her mother? Or was it pre-wedding nerves?

Ross reached into his pocket but for once it was not to produce his hip flask. It was a letter. 'Mates left this for me in the Robing Room today.' On lined paper a looping hand had written: *Dear Mr Ross, my Phyllis passed away last night. She was very weak but seemed to know I was there. You were good to her and made sense of this sad time. She will be waiting for me in a Better Place. So will the little one we lost years ago. I will not be on duty for the rest of this week. Thank you again, W. Mates.*

Petroc returned the letter to Ross. 'You made a difference

there, Tom. We can, you know. We can create light and peace and love.'

'Another believer gone. I dread the day, Petroc. I dread the day our Church is down to its final congregation.'

'It's not all death, Tom. I had an email today from that boy Matt. The one we gave sanctuary. He's going to marry Bashirah and they want to use the church. Isn't that wonderful?' Ross barely reacted. Petroc said: 'You're tired, Tom.'

'They're after our church at home, too.'

'What?'

'Theresa heard talk at the village pub and then we saw the notice. Surveyors have taken measurements. Augustus Dymock's lot. Now there is a buy-up bid and the diocese is taking views. I asked Calvert if he knew anything about it. He said it was happening all over the country. He seemed rather pro the idea.'

'Get some rest, Tom,' said Petroc. 'Nettle, you need to get home. And I have an early service in the morning. We can't do anything more tonight but we need to fight this. It's like the river, Tom. We must fight the tide.'

20

Wedding Day!

SPEAKER Mears did not waste time. On the dot of nine the next morning, a man with a clipboard knocked on Base Camp's door. 'Name of Ross?'

'Yes.'

'I'm from the Works Department. They want me to measure up.'

'Measure up to what?'

'Measure this house. Do a property audit. Preliminary step.'

'Preliminary to what?'

'Reallocation, s'pose. That's what they usually do. Most of the grace-and-favour places are going. I'm doing the Clerk's place on Whitehall this afternoon. Sir Roger's not going to like that. I can come in, yeah?'

'We can hardly refuse.'

'Sorry to be a nuisance.'

Ross told Petroc when he returned from his breakfast service. 'They're winning, Petroc. If the Speaker doesn't want a chaplain, he will not need a chaplain's house.'

'You're not just there for the Speaker. There's the whole Westminster village.'

'It's not a village though, is it? Villages have children and concerned neighbours. Westminster is a gamblers' cruise liner, pitching

243

in a high sea while the punters shake their dice. I'm the ship's padre. I say grace at the captain's table, get lashed on rum and despatch the occasional soul to a briny oblivion. Now the cruise line management reckon they can use my cabin more profitably.'

'The Commons should have a priest.'

'But this house is valuable and we'll never win the argument on utility. It's all very well saying "fight" but what can we do?'

Petroc was about to say something. He was about to show his hand. He checked himself. Ross may not have noticed.

The security cameras at the Greenhills' house would provide evidence. Nettle had been there, too. *Greedy bugger. Wanted five grand. I gave him three. But told him there was plenty more where that came from.* But the security cameras would also catch him and Nettle entering the house. They would have to explain. Calvert had been right. Petroc was out of his depth. They would not hesitate to blackmail him. He had been hiding under the stairs – without his trousers – with a pretty girl he was supposed to be preparing for her wedding. Calvert and the bishop would get their man. He would be out. He would lose not just his incumbency but his priesthood. Was Base Camp that important?

MRS Greenhill had not been sleeping well. Speaker Aldred's death had not helped. What a thoughtless old fool. Could he not have held on a couple more weeks? A business alliance worth millions was in the balance. There was the cost of the flowers and ice sculptures, the hotel bookings and first-class flights from Goa, the limousines, marquees. Waiters had been booked. God knows how many geese had been force-fed and slaughtered for the foie gras. At least three wine merchants had been dredged for their best vintages. Don't even mention the dress. But, no, the silly old fool had to up and die! So much had been thrown into doubt by an attention-seeking old man who upped and died.

It had been a relief when Gordon's little friend had become the new Speaker. That had been one worry out of the way, but there were plenty more. A woman's work was never done.

That mid-December Saturday, the sun rose reluctantly over London. Milk floats clinkingly completed their rounds. The streets were swept. Steam rose from the nostrils of the mounts at Horseguards. In a palatial residence not too far distant, Mrs Greenhill lay flat with two roundels of kiwi fruit on her eyes, a masseur at her feet, secretary at her side and her mobile telephone to hand as she barked orders. Had Mr Greenhill's shoes been polished? Had Nettle's corsage been watered? Was the chauffeur taking her to Parliament a safe driver? The rings: could the Indians be trusted to bring them? No doubt the men would all have hangovers. Why could they not have found Nettle a Muslim?

Owing to the kiwi-fruit roundels, Mrs Greenhill did not see her husband enter, in boxer shorts and shirt tails, and tiptoe to collect his spongebag trousers. He managed to keep his exit unde-tected, holding a finger to his lips to ensure that the secretary said nothing. All the while Mrs Greenhill jabbered of the day's arrangements, the guest list, the probability that the photographer would be scruffy – were photographers not always scruffy? It was something to do with living life through a lens. They looked but could never imagine being watched. The secretary started to agree but was promptly crushed by a fresh torrent of instructions.

Final preparations were completed for the noon nuptials. The crypt chapel had been decorated with an avenue of juvenile fig trees, flown in from South Africa to ensure they were in leaf. Jasmine and frangipani, warmed to awaken their blooms, filled the Undercroft with a scent of summer. A red carpet wound through a Westminster Hall whose flagstones had been strewn with petals. Statuary of cherubs and unicorns had been added. The wedding organiser slumped in exhaustion.

When Ross arrived, wedding programmes were being threaded with ribbons pink and green. The colours signified Britain and

India as well as the two companies whose interests in property and hotels would be joined in matrimony. The colours also represented the couple who would stand before God's altar: pink for Nettle Greenhill, green for Chundy, as-yet unseen by anyone on the distaff side.

From photographs on the programmes, Chundy looked presentable enough, if unlikely ever to play the role of the Mahatma Gandhi. It was a pity the snapshot was so blurred. Yet how romantic it was, this assignation with the unknown. Would he be tall? Serious? The sheer faith involved! For let it not be forgotten that Chundy, being unseen, was himself unseeing. He had not met Nettle.

Organist Mark was in place at the Undercroft's dandy little William Drake organ, practising voluntaries and Bollywood hits. He made the latter sound like Bach fugues. At eleven o'clock sniffer dogs checked the chapel for bombs. Indian ladies in gorgeous saris sucked their teeth as they reached the venue. By quarter to twelve the small chapel was full, the air thick with scents and unguents and betel breath and a hint of booze.

On the day of a wedding a priest has much to do. Ross had prepared the register and ensured that there were two fountain pens for the signing. He had brushed his hair. He had lit the candles and prepared an address to the precise length stipulated in Mrs Greenhill's order of battle. After a few swigs from his hip flask, he hummed to himself *Fight the Good Fight*, as he usually did before a wedding.

Nettle, beautiful Nettle, arrived in Westminster on time. Her heart thumped and in her mouth she could taste the ash of sacrifice. She trod as an actress to her opening scene, dread yielding to fatalism. She thought of Petroc, of her family duty and the thing she was about to do. She had often been told by her mother that she had been bred for this moment. Her father's will be done. Thou shalt do as thou is ruddy well told, saith mother.

Her body had been sewn into a dress of ivory silk. Its train swayed to the movement of her hips. Her curves, flowered tresses, petite shoes, a line of pearl buttons down the back of the dress accentuating her lovely shape; all was just so, her blonde ringlets carefully highlighted. She wore a silver choker and her honey-skinned shoulders were bare. Here was Nettle as a virginal asset, an innocent in a wicked world. She stepped from the bridal Rolls-Royce in New Palace Yard. The one thing she had not managed was her contact lenses. Petroc was the only person who had ever managed to sort them out. Petroc!

Greenhill took her arm and led her through the medieval hall, which had overnight been transformed into a scented bower. 'All right, love?' As he walked he silently cursed his wife for buying him new shoes. His penguin suit nibbled at his soft parts.

Nettle offered no answer.

'You look smashing, kid. Proud of you.'

No answer. Was that a tiny sniffle?

'You'll knock 'em out, just you see.'

Silence followed silence.

'It was your mother's idea.'

Nettle started to shake her head when the photographer and his assistant asked bride and father to pose at the steps leading to the chapel entrance. It occurred to Gordon Greenhill that business deals often went wrong at the final moment. Should he offload some stock? It was a Saturday. Bugger. The markets would be closed.

At the front of the pews on the groom's side sat Chundy's family. Ross, by the altar, clocked the parents, two shrivelled ancients. With them were various chaps in national dress. Ross, hoping to identify Chundy, discerned a couple of likely candidates. It was an odd wedding but who was he, the hired temple wallah, to question such rich clients?

The congregation stood at Nettle's entrance. Mark broke into

The Queen of Sheba. Ross watched the vision approach. She walked slowly, in dread of the sacrificial table. When she reached the top of the nave she did not look sideways to the groom through her veil. She stared at the Cross, which she was learning to adore.

'Dearly beloved, we are gathered here together in the sight of God . . .'

For Mrs Greenhill, in the front pew on the left, the climax approached. Across the nave she did not see saris and shiny suits. She saw only hotels on Goan beaches. She saw dark-skinned bellboys leaping to her every whim. She saw beach bars and paths through palm trees. Rupee heaven. She shuddered with satisfaction.

'. . . to join together this man and this woman in Holy Matrimony; which is an honourable estate.' Ross paused to let the interpreter catch up with him; sensing an indifference, he exaggerated the Anglican grandeur, addressing the congregants as though they were Ooty Club bearers taking an order for tiffin. The interpreter's tone did not alter.

Ross was the only person who could see Nettle's eyes, round as gobstoppers.

'. . . and therefore is not to be enterprised, nor taken in hand, unadvisedly, lightly, or wantonly, to satisfy men's carnal lusts . . .' He had not warned Mrs Greenhill that he would use the Prayer Book's full text. She heard the word 'carnal' and gave a jolt. Ross did not think the Indians would mind, given those carvings at Khajuraho.

Speaking the old words, barely needing the page, Ross sensed a bridegroom moving into position. He was about to inspect Chundy when he was distracted by a glint of something on Nettle's cheek. A tear? This dutiful daughter was being played as a business chip and he, God's minister, was collaborating in the grubby deal.

'Thirdly, it was ordained for the mutual society, help, and comfort, that the one ought to have of the other, both in prosperity and adversity.' Yes, a fat tear was edging down the left of her face and was being pursued by a second – jungle raindrops on a lily pad. Ross tugged himself away from Nettle's face and turned to Chundy, who was by now standing alongside her. The waxy normality of Ross's smile took a second or two to adjust. Standing in front of him was not some square-jawed youth, some caramel-cheeked modern maharajah. The vision Ross beheld was rotund as a buttered chicken. It wore lipstick, eyeliner, rouge. Teeth stood at angles from Stonehenge. The earlobes glistened with garnets and the eyebrows, long plucked, were a streak of henna pencil. He must have been well over fifty and was plainly as distraught as Nettle. His best man looked on the brink of emotional collapse.

The words stalled in Ross's mouth. He jump-started his spiel. 'Therefore, if any man can show any just cause why they may not lawfully be joined together, let him now speak, or else hereafter for ever hold his . . .'

'Objection!' Thank you, Jehovah. A voice rang from the back of the chapel. 'She doesn't love him!'

'. . . peace.'

'She doesn't love him and he doesn't know her. This isn't a wedding. It is a business deal!'

The interpreter started gobbling. Ross felt the same detachment as when Aldred died and as when he fell off the stage at the Big Faith debate. It was becoming a habit.

'Petroc!' said Nettle. She turned for the first time towards her intended husband, peered a little closer, and gasped. 'Oh my God! I mean, sorry.'

Nettle lifted her veil and, lacking her contacts, squinted down the nave. Petroc was at the back of the chapel, near the organ. He had been able to contain himself no more. The words of the Prayer Book had jolted him to action.

'This young woman is being sold against her wishes. Do not

proceed with the service!' he was shouting. Ross had never seen him so smart – or so wild.

'What's going on?' cried Mrs Greenhill. 'Get him out of here.' Two bouncers bore down on Petroc. They were about to remove him when Gordon Greenhill intervened.

'Leave him be one moment.' The Indian side of the chapel buzzed with confusion. Ross gawped. Mark the organist watched with interest. Petroc bloody Stone. The man got everywhere. If this went wrong for him, he might have to be removed to a very distant parish, or a loony bin.

Greenhill said: 'Nettle. Do you know this bloke?'

'Yes, Dad.'

'What, really know him?'

'Dad!'

'Do you love him?'

'Dad!'

'Well I love her, sir!' shouted Petroc, and he started to stride down the nave. 'Nettle Greenhill!' the name echoed. 'Will you be my wife?'

Some shouted 'Get him out of here', others clapped, and a few women in the congregation went eggy-eyed. Chundy turned to have a look and as he did so there came fresh gasps from the English side of the church as they had their first sight of him.

'Well?' said Petroc. He knelt by Nettle, took her hand. 'It's now or never, my love. Will you do me the most immense honour, here before God, of agreeing to grow old with me?'

Mrs Greenhill had produced a mobile telephone from her diamante clutch bag and was telephoning the emergency services. 'Police,' she was saying. 'I want officers here i-MEED-iately.'

'Well, girl, what are you going to do?' said Gordon Greenhill. He was risking his wife's wrath but he could no longer do this to his daughter. 'You can't just leave him there on his knees.'

'Say yes!' shouted a voice from the English side of the chapel.

'Give him a kiss!' said another.

'I'll have him if she says no,' added a (male) voice.

'No I am NOT joking,' barked Mrs Greenhill into her telephone. 'The Palace of Westminster. No, that is most certainly NOT a pub. Put me through to your supervisor.'

'Petroc,' said Nettle. 'I didn't think . . .'

'Well?' said Gordon Greenhill.

'Well?' said Petroc.

'Well?' said the congregation.

'Yes.' said Nettle, laughing and crying. 'Yes. Yes!'

From all sides came cheers. Chundy himself gave a little clap of his hands, danced on the spot and embraced his interpreter before collapsing into sobs. Nettle fell into the arms of her new intended and Petroc, priest in holy orders, gave her a long, deep kiss. Mark played *For He's a Jolly Good Fellow*. Ross retreated to the corner of the altar, turned his back on the celebrations and took a nip from his flask. Mrs Greenhill stared at her mobile. She was not accustomed to people hanging up on her.

'You might as well do it now,' said Mr Greenhill.

'Dad!'

'Get married. I mean, it's all laid on, isn't it? Paid for, too.'

'Proceed with the wedding?' said Petroc.

'I don't see why not,' said Greenhill.

Stares swivelled towards Ross. He was restoring the cap to his hip flask. 'I'm not sure that would be possible,' said Ross.

'Bollocks,' said Greenhill.

'Dad!'

'He might have a point,' said Petroc. 'There's all the legal palaver. The banns and all that.'

'Ridiculous,' said Greenhill.

'Rules are rules,' said Ross. 'It'll have to wait a few weeks.'

'One moment,' boomed another voice that will be familiar to those of you who have been following this long and tangled tale.

251

'The normal rules do not apply.' Sir Roger Richards, Clerk of the Commons, had been attending the wedding as a proxy for the Speaker.

'The wine's on sale or return,' offered Mrs Greenhill. The interpreter had given up and the Indian side of the chapel had sat down. Chundy and his best man were cooing to each other like two budgies.

'How do you mean, the normal rules don't apply, Roger?' said Ross.

'It's a Royal Peculiar,' said the Clerk.

After a good five seconds Ross uttered an elongated 'Oh yes.'

'It falls outwith any diocese, and therefore any requirement for banns,' added Sir Roger.

'A royal what?' said Greenhill.

'Technical term,' said Ross. 'It means that this chapel answers only to the Crown.'

The Clerk continued: 'In usual practice that authority lies in the hands of the Speaker but Mr Speaker disclaims any interest in matters ecclesiastical. I think it can safely be interpreted that the power of proxy passes to the next Royal appointee, the Clerk of the Commons.'

'Who's that?' everyone asked.

'That,' said Sir Roger, 'is me.'

'It all sounds a bit peculiar,' said Mrs Greenhill

'Indeed it is,' said the Clerk. 'Peculiar. In the old sense of the word. Particular.'

'What about a ring?' asked Petroc.

'You want a ring?' The best man who had not, in the end, been best man, delved into his trouser pocket and produced a ring.

'We couldn't possibly . . .' began Nettle.

'Please,' said the best-man-who-had-never-been. 'It is pleasure for me. Am so happy.' And he kissed Chundy's hands.

21

'Not Only With Our Lips But In Our Lives'

THERESA placed a Christmas wreath on the airman's grave. A sharp wind ruffled the ivy leaves. Barney had been touring his responsibilities, checking smells, trotting around proprietorially. When the little dog was in this mood Theresa would check the inside of the church and remove last week's hymn numbers, returning the bent, furry-edged cards to their wooden box. A pale afternoon light seeped through the windows and she lit a votive candle.

She left without closing the door. It took care of itself and the flame barely wavered when it shut, apparently of its own devices. The door's exterior carried a diocesan notice advertising the consultation about the buy-up proposal. A public meeting was to be held. Interested parties were invited to attend, whatever their creed (or none).

By the time they got back to the house, a long, silvery car – German, expensive – was parked on the paving slabs by the browning lady's mantle. When Theresa spotted it, she felt a stab of irritation that it had not used the parking area by the stream. Barney went nuts, sprinting ahead and barking.

'No, Barney!' Theresa stuck her fingers in her teeth and whistled hard. The Sealyham halted on a sixpence and stood, growling, ten yards from the executive gleamer. A chauffeur – tall, trousered, young – walked round the car to help her passenger alight. All Theresa saw at first was a helmet of white hair.

'You must be Mrs Ross.'

'Must I?'

'I'm so sorry to disturb you.' Barney barked at this man.

'We've been on a walk.'

'My name is Augustus Dymock. I have met your husband.'

'Shush, Barney!' Barney was yapping at Dymock's heels. Dymock froze. Theresa grabbed Barney and took him away to his kennel. 'Sorry about that,' she said when she returned. 'Come inside.'

Theresa, kicking off her muddy gumboots, allowed the Don of Doubt into the old house while Barney went bonkers in his kennel.

THE wedding reception proceeded as planned – everyone was curious to see inside Speaker's House and learn more about Nettle's unexpected husband. The reprieved Chundy proceeded to get plastered, kissing Petroc and pinching his beard saying 'hairy man!' Mrs Greenhill teetered round wearing the tightest of smiles. Her husband was on expansive form, ordering more champagne. 'We may not be related by marriage but we can still do business,' he told Chundy's cousins.

Ross became almost as relaxed as the ice sculpture in the over-heated room. Before leaving for the West Country he went in search of a lavatory. There was one he knew next to the Speaker's modern living quarters. Aldred had never minded him using it. Ross was finishing in there when he heard raised voices in the corridor, followed by the slamming of a door. A man and a woman were arguing.

'Let me in, Olga!' Mears was saying. Ross heard a door open and the voices became less distinct. He gingerly let himself out of the lavatory and was about to edge away when he heard the word 'church'. He lingered a little, moving towards the room where Mears and Olga were talking. They had not quite closed the door.

'A Russian church? I didn't even know there was one,' said Mears.

'Augustus does not understand. I do not tell him.'

'I'm not sure I like it. Everyone thinks you're this big atheist.'

'Of course not!'

'But you work for Dymock.'

'I work but I do not belong. Not now. Church is bigger than Dymock.'

'Maybe, but this is confusing, my love. This is not how politics works. I can't have you all god-squaddy.'

'I hate Dymock! I like church.'

'You don't understand what you're saying, love. Keep this quiet.'

'Why?' she shouted.

'Well, because the people who put me here – put us here – don't want to hear that sort of talk at all. You bloody well keep quiet, see, if you want to become Lady Mears one day.'

'Lady Mears?'

'Bound to get a title now, aren't I? Speaker, see? So you – we – need to leave out this church stuff, in public at least.'

A telephone rang in the room and the row came to an end. Ross slipped away to collect his coat. On the Tube he fell into a doze, missing the connection at Baker Street and ending up in Kilburn. By the time he reached Paddington he had missed his train and had to wait an hour. He found an unyielding metal bench near a Japanese food bar. Diners morosely watched dollops of raw fish pass them on a conveyor belt. Occasionally, joylessly, they took one.

'I missed the six-thirty,' he bawled into his mobile. He found these things damnably hard to hear and that made him tend to shout.

'Oh dear,' replied Theresa.

'Probably won't be home until ten o'clock.'

'Did the wedding go all right?'

'It took a rather marvellous turn. Will explain later.'

'I had that Dymock man here.'

'What?' Theresa could hear the station announcements in the background as Ross swore.

'He is down here for a couple of nights for the literary festival. Said he wanted to see you so he dropped by. Huge car chauffeured by a woman.'

'Bloody hell!' One of the customers at the Japanese food bar turned and, seeing Ross in his dog collar, frowned.

'It's all right. He was perfectly civil.'

'Bloody Dymock!'

'Darling, it's OK.'

'What did he want?'

'Something to do with making us an offer. He's coming back tomorrow on his way back to London. It might be to our benefit, he said. He even thinks he can help Andrew.'

'Andrew!'

Theresa had retired to bed by the time Ross made it home. He poured himself a Cognac and dealt with his week's post. Amid the charity advertisements there was a diocesan survey about rural congregations. After years of decline, numbers had risen. Ross saw the golden liquid leave a tidemark each time he swished it round the brandy balloon. Would he leave behind even as much as that? The small, leather-bound prayer book was beside him, its outer skin pocked by burn marks. It was propped against the bottle; as he was watching it, it fell back and opened, as of its own volition, to the General Thanksgiving. *We thine unworthy servants do give thee most humble and hearty thanks.* He indeed gave thanks for the way his right hand had so suddenly returned to normal. He turned to the book's inside front cover where his father, in childish hand, had written his name. The thanksgiving continued: *That we shew forth thy praise, not only with our lips, but in our lives.*

The dead could no longer contemplate choice. He almost envied them their rest – to have escaped the duty to act. For what was the point in carrying this prayer book unless one actually *did* something?

'All RIGHT!' said Ross. 'You have made your point.'

22

A Spirited Defence

'OH, hello again.'

'Theresa!' Dymock uncoiled himself from his car. 'Good to see you!'

'Mr Dymock.' She was holding a clump of blackened asters she had been pruning.

'Augustus, please.'

The jacket of his London suit hung in the rear passenger window. Theresa could see the fit frame of his physique inside his ironed shirt. He wore Italian slip-on shoes; no tie.

'You're safe – Barney's out with Tom. They've gone for a walk, up by the church. A box of candles needed taking there.'

'Did you tell him I would visit?'

'I did. He was not entirely pleased. He feels under attack.'

'I don't see why.'

'We both do. Try to see that.'

'Will it make me a better person?' Rooks were mobbing a sparrowhawk that had flown near their nests. It was all right for the rooks. They had the numbers.

'It might,' said Theresa.

'Being good will help us reach Heaven?'

'Only if we believe in Heaven, which I'm not always sure I do.'

'You're a vicar's wife.'

'You think vicars' wives don't have doubts?'

'How can you live a lie?'

'I don't think it is a lie but I cannot be entirely sure. What stark certainties you atheists demand. Let me put this into your language. Goodness can make you stronger. People will love you and protect you. If you must, think of it as a shield – the defence of your community, your church. Is that sufficiently utilitarian for you?' The rooks had seen off the sparrowhawk and were returning to the nests in the spinney, cawing, but she would not reward Dymock with anger. 'You'll find Tom at the church. Head up the hill, jink across a couple of crossroads and turn left down an unpromising track. There used to be a sign but the potato lorry flattened it in September. When you get there, Barney may bark. I have no idea how my Tom will respond.' My Tom, my impossible, tense, unhappy, angry Tom.

'Fine,' said Dymock. The wind rippled his shirt and white locks. 'On that other matter we discussed, my office made a booking with your son's company. My son has been booked in for next week. Perhaps your son can make a man out of him.' He slid back into his mobile lair. Wheels turned on the balding gravel and the car purred away, down the potholed drive, a trail of vapour from its exhaust pipes being all that remained after Charlie gunned the throttle and it accelerated up the hill in search of two crossroads and a left turn.

BARNEY was being a pain. In Bluebell Wood he kept disappearing into the ferns. Ross whistled and cursed. The dog eventually obeyed, the years having taught him to recognise the limits of his Master's patience. Near the disused cottage was an old badger sett. Here Ross lost sight and sound of Barney. He waited five minutes but the terrier did not emerge so Ross continued to the church. The light was fading. He needed to leave the new candles in the vestry and empty the collections box before locking up for the night. A tawny owl escorted him up the graveyard, a daub of white on its feathers. Ross was glad not to be a shrew.

The porch was littered with dry leaves. At his approach they were blown from his path, as if swept by some obliging broom. The alms box contained a pound. Assailed by weariness, Ross extracted two of the candles and lit them. They always needed an initial burn to glue them in place. He sat in his favourite pew and watched the flames.

Chauffeur Charlie took a wrong turn into a farmyard whose cobblestones were coated in wet muck. The tyres started to spin and Charlie sacrificed plenty of rubber as she pressed the accelerator. Dymock had to give the car a push. In the process he stepped in some dung, which applied itself to his Italian slip-ons. 'Use goddamn Google maps,' said Dymock.

'No signal,' despaired Charlie.

'Turn here. There's a sign for the village. Find a human being, if there are any, and ask directions.' The first building was the pub. The landlord obliged with directions, telling her 'it rattles with old chains, that graveyard.' Charlie, climbing back into the Mercedes, wrinkled her nose at the smell.

'He said it's the most haunted churchyard in England.'

'Is that why so few go to church?' said Dymock. 'Come on, let's find this blackmailing lunatic.' When the car drew up at the lych-gate, a star was already venturing into the sky. 'I'll have a quick look,' Dymock told Charlie. 'If he's not there, we'll head back to London. You could give the inside of this car a quick clean while I'm up there.'

Bats flittered out of the lych-gate eaves as Dymock alighted. Bats at this time of year! The church clock struck the hour. When the lych-gate banged behind him, Dymock jumped.

'Jesus!'

'You all right, Augustus?' called Charlie from the car.

'Yeah.' Something in the air made him duck. How come this

smell of garlic, too? He looked back with envy at the car, where he could see Charlie in the courtesy lights as she began to sweep the inside with a stiff brush. Was that the sound of its strokes on the car seat? It seemed closer, more like a whip thrashing in the air. He could hardly turn back. What? Scared of a few squeaks and bangs? Illogical. What could he fear from a graveyard?

Ross had just enough light from the candles to open his prayer book. He turned to the Litany – *Graciously hear us that those evils, which the craft and subtilty of the devil or man worketh against us, be brought to nought.* Brought to nought. The rhyme tied a knot. God's providence would disperse threats – *that we thy servants, being hurt by no persecutions, may evermore give thanks unto thee in thy holy Church.* The worst persecutions came from neglect of love. Had he neglected Theresa? And Andrew?

The Litany's opening medley of mumbles – *have mercy upon us miserable sinners* – did not find favour with the self-propelling age. God as a fount of potent judgement? God as the clement emperor? Only Albanian peasant women in the black weeds of widowhood stooped to such babbling obeisance. Modern man was too mighty for primeval humility, but Ross gave it a go. *Have mercy upon us, miserable sinners.* Kyrie, kyrie. Again he mouthed it. Twice. And more. Over the centuries these church stones had heard many a bundle of bones utter those words. What good had it done them? They had beseeched but had they been heard?

He heard leaves crunch in the porch.

A few hundred yards away, in the woods, some signal rang in the head of a small dog. Barney reversed from the badger's sett and sprinted.

The door creaked. Someone was standing in the church entrance. 'Ross?'

'Who is it?'

'Augustus Dymock. Are there any lights?'

'Your vision will adjust.' Dymock stepped into the church, relieved to be away from the bats. 'I was just saying the Litany.'

'The what?' said Dymock.

'A medieval supplication.'

Dymock sat at the end of the pew. Candlelight glinted off the altar cross and made shapes dance on the ceiling. Dymock's shadow bore little obvious relation to his bodily vessel.

Ross said: 'Your lot want to turn this place into weekend flats. Chichi get-aways. We've had surveyors poking around.'

'They want to build dreams for the aspiring classes.'

'We build dreams here as it is. More than dreams.'

'But you can't live in them. You can't make money out of them.'

'Money, no,' said Ross. He thought of the pound in the alms box. 'But we can pass them on to our sons and daughters.'

'Some sons may not be interested.' Ross glanced at Dymock. 'Your wife told me,' said Dymock. 'Don't worry. You're not the only one to have a difficult child. Look, Tom. I know you know.'

'About what?'

'The Greenhill business and certain MPs.'

'I'm sorry?'

'The money. We can sort this out, Tom. It needn't become a problem.'

Ross was shrewd enough not to let his face show surprise. He had never intended to expose the financial shenanigans Jean had told him about. He took the view 'render unto Caesar' and all that. His concern had been on a more personal level, the other matter raised by Jean. Tapping the Prayer Book he simply said: 'In this little book here there is a phrase about "the Church militant". The Church militant fights, Mr Dymock. Until I met Petroc, I would have caved in. I would have thought fighting a bit happy-clappy. But now I see the point of it and so I have today decided to do something.'

'You haven't already?' asked Dymock.

'I wasn't sure it was true. But now you have confirmed it. I will compose a letter to the Commissioner for Standards and will send it unless we have a stop to this nonsense.'

Dymock felt anger, sickness and a sense of stupidity in one.

Ross continued: 'This church is our inheritance and I want to preserve it for the next generation, not as some listed country cottage. We don't want that sort of conversion. We want a living Church.'

'We? I don't see many of you here.' He gave an acid laugh.

'*Fear not, little flock.* St Luke, Mr Dymock. He was a doctor, a doctor with faith. A rational man who believed. We may be small but we must not be timid. If we fear God, as we do, why ever fear God's enemies? To us that is – how do you say? – irrational. What sense can it make to quake before a loser like the Devil? The Devil can only tempt us. So long as we believe, he cannot terrify us.'

Bang! The church door shot open, so fast that it hit the adjacent wall and swung back with another bang. Ross, who knew what had happened, did not move an eyebrow. He had heard it too many times. But Dymock leapt so high his buttocks left the pew. 'Good God!' he screamed. By now Barney – who had long ago learned that he could open the church doors if he pushed against them with sufficient force from his front paws – had started barking. The little dog bared his teeth, his legs planted low and wide on the flagstones.

'Barney,' said Ross, 'Mr Dymock was just leaving.'

'I was?'

'You were.'

'You won't discuss this? You need to, Ross. I have the ear of the new Speaker. You want to stay on as chaplain, don't you?'

'At first I thought I did, yes. But not if it means caving in to you lot.'

'Don't be a fool.'

'A fool is exactly what I have been, too long. Barney will show you out.'

He did, too. Silhouettes on the church wall showed a round-shouldered figure scuttle towards the door, pursued by a leaping canine. As he hurried out of the porch, Dymock bumped into the metal scraper on which parishioners could remove the mud from their boots. This time it removed a layer of skin from Dymock's shin. Swearing, he limped towards the lych-gate down the path that was now black as a well. He stumbled off the path, treading in clumps of wet grass and being jabbed by thistles. As he passed the graves of the squire, the miller, the twins and the airman he was strafed again by the hooting owl, which peeled away like an RAF Spitfire. Barney snapped at his heels. Dymock tried to kick the terrier but in the act he fell over, grazing his face on the gravel and placing his hand in a drift of thorns.

As he fell he heard a disembodied voice laugh – or was it just the blood pumping round his head? Was that footsteps marching on gravel? The toll of a bell? He heard choirs chant and a rural voice call a platoon to arms. There came a screech of electric guitar, or saw blade on gravestone. Was it the ring of a concussive blow on the head? Or was it a rationalist mind being opened to the hidden dimension? 'Charlie!' he shouted, scrabbling to his feet.

Chauffeur Charlie, who had been trying (with odd lack of success) to tune the Mercedes radio, did not hear. She blipped open the locks only when she heard thumping on the window. Dymock's face was pressing against it, staring in desperation. She could see bats fluttering and – could it be? – a second, white face in the glass. She later supposed it was her reflection but it was the face a miller might wear after suffocating in flour.

'Let's go!' blurted Dymock, as he fell into the back seat, hand flapping to make sure the bats did not enter the car. Was that one inside the Mercedes? He screamed. Charlie screamed. 'No, it's OK, it's just part of my jacket, I think.' But no, it really was a bat.

'Open the door!' cried Dymock.

'A bat!' cried Charlie. She pressed her key-fob button which first locked, then unlocked all the doors and the boot popped up. Now the car's hazard lights sprang into life. Ruddy burglar alarm. Barney, seeing Dymock's door open, lunged forward, still barking. An almost military voice shouted 'Here' and Barney retreated a yard.

'The bat's gone!' gasped Dymock. 'Lock the doors again. I don't want that mad dog savaging me.' Charlie pressed the starter button. The engine did not respond. A second and third time she tried. Still no good. Dead. Dead. Dead.

'Oh for Chrissake!' shouted Dymock.

'Seems weird,' said Charlie. She fiddled with the key fob, checked the instruments, opened and shut her door. Double and triple blipped the security system.

Ross closed the church door, turned the key and whistled for Barney. 'Come on, boy.' Before he left the porch he took down the yellow notice about local housing needs.

Barney heard his master's summons and, like the best Christians, sprinted to its command. There came a roar from the Mercedes as its engine burst into life. Exhaust shot from its rear end. As the last, high hint of dusk illuminated a gap in the clouds above the proud old church, all that could be heard was the squeal of wheels as an expensive machine containing one quite illogically terrified atheist, shouting at his equally petrified driver, bunny-hopped and coughed and eventually sped away in search of the bright-lit citadel. Dymock's precious hair stood on end as though he had been next to a van de Graaff generator.

MORE than a hundred miles to the east, in London, Jean lay a-bed in her dress. The pills were white, too. She swallowed five at a time. She was not often a scotch drinker but it felt patriotic to wash them down with whisky. On the bedside table was a newspaper with a paean to Speaker Mears and his Russian doll. The pills took effect. Her drowsy mind filled with memories of a sunny afternoon years ago, when she gave herself to a boy she loved.

23

High Tide

HIGH on the Cambrian coastline a minibus disgorged six reluctant adventure cadets. The teenagers had hard hats, rucksacks, food packs and other paraphernalia for a thirty-six-hour exercise. The day would take in three headlands, ten miles of walking and some kayaking. Already the wind was up. There had been hail.

Andrew Ross said goodbye to Morwen, who was driving the minibus. She would head first to the beach to drop the life-jackets and then to the camp zone to dump tents and sleeping bags. Andrew called the youngsters into a circle. 'Guys, listen up. It looks like being a lively day weatherwise so we want to be at our destination early. I will set a brisk pace. Should at least keep us warm. You on for that?' The youngsters nodded. 'Burn the calories from that breakfast we just had, yeah?' More glum nodding. He did not like to lead the session on his own but Morwen was feeling unwell. One adult to six teenagers should suffice. It was not ideal but manageable. Money had been too tight to turn down the late extra recruit. 'By the end of this trek you will be a team and have some great blisters. Any questions? Billy.'

'What happens if one of us wants to stop?'

'We take a group view. Raz?'

'Will the minibus follow us?'

'No. We're on our own. Stick together. One for all and all for one. Zac, isn't it?'

'Why did we have to leave our iPhones?'

'Cold turkey time. I have one for emergencies but mobiles are a distraction we can do without. If you're texting, you're more likely to walk off a cliff. Now: keep close. I will lead. If anyone gets into difficulties, shout "man down" and we'll stop. Let's head towards Borth and Merlin's Dolmen. We'll have a brew there and crack open the biscuits, yeah?'

HEREFORD Cathedral was filling for Speaker Aldred's service. It was neither a funeral nor a memorial but a celebration of his service to county and kingdom. The organist was doing twiddly-diddly, something-to-find-your-seats-to things. The air was heady with candle wax and the chalky dryness of old masonry, plus maybe an undertow of morning amontillado. The bar of the Castle Hotel had seen early custom. Dean and Precentor scuttled across the green in cloaks, bent against a December wind that had whipped up unexpectedly from the west overnight. The Lord-Lieutenant made sure that all was ready for the eleven-thirty start.

Theresa dropped Ross at the East gate so he would not be soaked by the slanting rain. 'I'll see you afterwards, darling. Good luck.'

'Thanks. I love you.'

Theresa blinked in surprise. 'And I . . .' she said. 'And I love you, darling. Nothing is ever going to change that.'

Robed vergers stood in the porch, handing out orders of service. Ross was asked for his invitation. 'My wife has it.'

'It's all right, I can vouch for him.'

'Mates, hello. I didn't know you were coming.'

'Wouldn't have missed it, sir. He was all right, was Speaker Aldred.' Beside the door was the Gurney, a vast Edwardian gas heater, which roared. Ross envied its red-hot core.

A special train had run from Paddington. Some of the London lot had never been west of Oxford. As Ross hastened to the vestry, the organ parped into something more stirring, making him jump. Sir Roger Richards bustled in and the Dean and chapter were in gold-braided copes while the choristers, in ruffs, smelled of coal-tar soap rather than the usual fruit chews. Occasional draughts blew in from the Booth porch when someone forgot to shut the door.

'Everything under control, Tom?' asked Sir Roger.

'I'm not really the person to ask.'

'You're doing the sermon?'

'Yes. The PM's doing the first lesson. Tewk second lesson. Typical of bloody Mears to refuse to travel.'

'He said it would have been hypocritical to attend a church service when he does not believe.'

'If everyone took that attitude we'd never have a civic service.'

'The public secularist is the most orthodox of creatures, Tom. The Leader of the Opposition in the Lords is representing his party. There are three ambassadors, one duke, a deputy governor of the Bank of England, the Lord Chancellor, the Mayor of London.'

'Better keep him away from the Lord-Lieutenant.'

'He wouldn't dare.'

'He might. She has a pretty set of ankles. Have we got a full house?'

'Nearly. Stragglers are still arriving. We've got more than two hundred MPs here and as many peers. You'll need to speak up. Half of the congregation is deaf and the wind is whistling round the central tower. Good luck.'

MEARS'S constituency office in the Commons was less busy these days but Jean's absence was a nuisance. The researcher tried ringing her at home but the telephone was engaged. Same story one, two and three hours later. The operator said it was off the hook. By mid-morning, after going round to knock on the door, the researcher told the janitor and he used the master key.

There was still a pulse, just.

MERLIN'S Dolmen took longer than expected. On a fair day walkers had a view of the coast but the incoming front put paid to that. Andrew boiled water on a camp stove and gave the boys tea and chocolate biscuits. While they sat under the mossy stone he told them about the Lowland Hundred, the sunken lands of old repute, which stretched miles to the west before being taken by floods.

'What, like Noah?' asked the boy called Raz.

'Possibly.'

'My dad says that Noah story is a lie,' said Zac Dymock. The wind was wettening with every minute.

'It's an old story and old stories have their own values,' said Andrew. 'The story of the Lowland Hundred says a drunkard called Seithenyd left open the sluice gates and the waters stole in like marauders. Another version blames a water maid who forgot to empty the well. The water rose up, gurgling up the shaft, destroying all in its path. Do we believe that literally? Or is it a metaphor? In Borth bay you may see old trees poking their heads above the sand. They look like buried warriors, a battalion of sunken soldiers. We need to watch the tides, by the way, because they move fast. Everyone done? Tie your mugs to your rucksacks. Who fancies some kayaking?'

THE Commons Chamber, which had started its Friday sitting at half-past nine, was near empty. A third of the House was in Hereford for Aldred's service. Other MPs had jumped at the chance of a day off. Questions to the Minister for Equalities ran out of customers ten minutes before its allotted time. The weekly Business Question to the Leader of the House (his place filled by a deputy) lasted a mere thirty minutes as opposed to the normal hour. The Foreign Office, decently, had offered a Statement on the Middle East Crisis. There was always a crisis of some sort in the Middle East. That used another half-hour or so.

'There being no further questions or Government statements, we will move to the main business,' said Speaker Mears. The Chamber's clock read twenty past eleven. 'The clerk will now proceed to read the orders of the day.'

'Third Reading, Civic Regulations Bill, tenth day,' sang one of the deputy clerks.

'Third Reading, Civic Regulations Bill,' intoned Mears.

'Beg to move,' said the Minister of State, the only person from her team of Departmental ministers not to have travelled to Hereford.

'Thangyew,' said Mears, bowing to the minister, who had touched the top of the despatch box momentarily, as custom demanded. The minister bowed back. The clerks bowed to the minister. The minister bowed to the clerks. One of the assistant clerks took delivery of a bundle of documents in a ribboned file. From his sedentary position he bowed crisply to the deputy clerk who had given it to him – a manoeuvre less easy than it sounds. The deputy clerk bowed back, retreated a short distance from the Chair, bowed to the Chair with a click of his buckled shoes, and left the Chamber with his nose raised aloft, through the double doors that were held open by a spotty attendant.

'I propose,' said Mears in a conversational manner, 'to select the manuscript amendment in the name of Mr Kendrick. Mr Kendrick.'

'Thank you, Mr Speaker,' said Kendrick. There came a certain confusion on the front bench. The minister looked at the Chair with puzzlement. 'In this manuscript amendment,' continued Kendrick, 'I hope to add an important idea which I feel is in keeping with the thrust of the Bill . . .'

'Er, point of order, Mr Speaker.'

Mears indicated that Kendrick should cease. 'The minister wishes to make a point of order. Let us discover the reason. Minister?'

'We were under the impression the Third Reading was to proceed unimpeded, sir.'

'I can't think why. Mr Kendrick has submitted a manuscript amendment. That may be unusual at Third Reading but it is not unknown.'

'But we did not know, sir.'

'I cannot help it if the Hon Lady does not know the conventions of the House as laid down by Erskine May.'

'No, Mr Speaker, I mean we did not know that the manuscript amendment had been tabled. We do not appear to have been notified.'

'It was listed in the usual manner,' said Mears in a cordial enough manner.

The minister had an urgent discussion with her parliamentary private secretary and said: 'It would seem, Mr Speaker, that the parliamentary intranet was not working last night. It went down at nine o'clock and came back up only this morning. That is why we were not aware of this amendment.'

'I am not sure that is a matter for the Chair. The manuscript amendment was handed to the Clerk's office on time, was it not, Mr Kendrick?'

'It was delivered to the Clerk's office at half past six yesterday evening, sir,' said Kendrick. 'The House did not rise until later.'

'The Clerk himself had left for the West Country by then, I believe, Mr Speaker,' said the minister. 'I spoke to him myself because he telephoned my office to ensure that we were content with today's Order Paper. He had a train to catch.'

'The Clerk himself may well have left, sir,' said Kendrick, 'but his office was still open. The amendment was submitted. I wrote it by hand myself.'

'But,' said the minister.

'It does seem the procedures were observed,' said Mears. 'The minister can say "but" as often as she wishes but it does not alter the facts. Now it may be that the intranet' — he elongated each syllable and rolled the r — 'which is but one of several devices which publicise the daily agenda, was not fully operational. The reliability of electronic channels of information is not a prime absorption of the Chair. If we were to suspend debate every time somebody's computer developed a fault, we would not get much done. It might also be that the Clerk, in his haste to abandon his post, gave an erroneous impression to the minister. But the rules of the House are unflinching, immutable. We have a light programme of business. We have visitors in the Strangers' Gallery, some, I have no doubt, having journeyed far to watch democracy in action. Are we to cheat them of debate? Is the House simply to say it is closed for the day because some novice minister was not ready?'

'But,' said the minister.

'It should not be beyond the wit of the minister to seek instruction from her controllers while the amendment is being put. Let us hear from Mr Kendrick.'

'But Mr Speaker,' said the minister, 'the House is deserted.'

Anger bubbled inside Mears. He had already had to put up with Olga's nonsense about the Russian church. He had received word from Bryce and Dymock and Greenhill that there was now an urgency to get this legislation through the House. He was not in the mood to tolerate further cheek from this whippersnapper minister. 'We are quorate. Yes?' He made a show of checking with the assistant clerks in front of him. They assented. A vote had been taken at the start of the day to confirm that sufficient MPs were in Westminster. 'It is not for the Chair to take into account the non-availability of certain members of the payroll vote. It is not for the Chair to arrange business to the convenience of Right Hon Members who may wish to be absent from Westminster for a service of the Christian religion to which, I believe, a minority of this House now adheres. It is my duty to ensure that Bills are debated in an orderly fashion. I call Mr Kendrick.'

'Point of Order!' came a booming voice.

Mears sighed. 'A point of order from the Father of the House, Sir Tudor Matthews. Sir Tudor, you are not in Hereford.'

'Mr Speaker,' said Sir Tudor. 'Far be it for me to suggest that something slippewy has gone on. And no, I am not in Heweford. I would have liked to pay my respects to the last Speaker of this House – a man who occupied his office with proper dignity – but I long ago learned not to abandon my post. Might I ask if the Usual Channels were aware of this manuscript amendment?'

'I thank the Father of the House for that point of order, if indeed it was a point of order,' said Mears. 'It might more accurately have been termed a request for background information. I see that the deputy patronage secretary has entered the Chamber. Perhaps he could shed light on any subterranean arrangements which would assure the House that proceedings are in order. Mr Bryce.'

Bryce rose elegantly to the despatch box, placing his fingers on the old box. 'Mr Speaker, it is not the custom for Whips to speak.'

'We will take it that the Usual Channels have no objection to democratic debate, even if they do not support the amendment. Mr Kendrick, the moment can be postponed no longer. You may speak.' Mears reached into his pocket and withdrew a violet cream. Perfect.

The deputy clerk discreetly left the Chamber and sent a text message to Sir Roger Richards, seeking urgent advice.

TO the churning chords of *The God of Abraham Praise*, the cathedral choir entered in procession. Ross, near the back of the procession, thrilled at the swell of the hymn's Hebrew melody and the sway of the cross. Between each verse, the click of the chapter members' footsteps could be heard, marching to the beat. Sir

Roger Richards, at one end of the third row of pews, was singing 'Jehovah, Father, great I AM' when he felt his mobile vibrate in his trouser pocket. There were two verses left and the Dean and chapter were taking their places in the choir stalls. The processional cross was being moored and the final crescendo was beginning. Sir Roger discreetly read the text from Westminster. 'Hail! Abraham's God, and mine!' Sir Roger tucked his reading glasses into the top pocket of his morning coat and disengaged himself from his pew. He slipped into a side chapel, closed the door, and telephoned his office to find out what the Devil was going on.

TEACHING Zac to wear his kayak helmet the right way and tie his lifejacket had taken a while. The jacket was an adult size and had been intended for Andrew. The other teenagers laughed at the Dymock boy. Zac had been slow on the walk, complaining of sore feet. He showed no more aptitude on the water. Billy and Raz and the others squirted across the bay, laughing in the quickening rain. Zac found it hard to make the boat move in anything but a circle. Andrew needed to show the leaders the way across the bay. 'Look out for the currents – the tide is on the turn,' he shouted. 'Billy! Stop mucking about!'

'Yeah, Billy. Stop mucking about.'

'OK, Raz, we can do without you joining in.'

'Yeah, Raz,' said Billy.

'Come on, Zac,' said Andrew. 'Let's get across this bay. The weather is turning foul.' The boys in front must have caught a current, they were moving so fast. Andrew exerted himself to catch them and point them in the right direction. Rain whipped into his eyes.

'Hey, sir! Billy's gone over. Capsized.'

'OK, Raz. Just coming.' He was there in twenty seconds and Billy was flailing in the sea. Andrew put him right. The wind was whipping water off the top of white horses, into his eyes.

Spray stung the cheeks. In a short space of time a mini gale had established itself.

'You all right, Billy?' The bravado had gone out of the boy and he announced that he wanted to return to dry land. 'I think we've all had enough, yeah? OK, guys, follow me. Quick as you can now.'

'AND it is for those reasons, Mr Speaker, that I feel confident in presenting this amendment. We solve a problem of housing need. We relieve the Church of a burden. We preserve old architecture. We regenerate our urban spaces. This is an amendment that is good for families, good for struggling faith communities, good for business, good for Britain.' Kendrick sat down to silence.

Mears was about to call the minister. He was prevented by the Father of the House. Sir Tudor Matthews did not wait to be called. He just stood and started talking.

'It is regwettable that this amendment has been pressed at such a time on such a Bill with such a speech, which was better matched to a Second Reading debate. It is also notable that a similar amendment was floated at an earlier stage but was withdrawn. I mean no diswespect to the Chair when I say that.' The hands of the Commons clock showed it was not quite noon. Beside Sir Tudor sat his faithful batman Butt. Kendrick lurked beyond the gangway. The minister and her PPS were in their places, as was Bryce, duty Whip. On the other side of the House there were ten backbenchers from the main Opposition party, two Celtic Nationalists, an Opposition Whip and an Opposition spokesman with his bag carrier behind him. The Members were outnumbered by the doorkeepers, a deputy Serjeant at Arms, two deputy clerks, the Speaker's deputy Secretary and, in the Strangers' Gallery, a few tourists.

'The Second Church Estates Commissioner is not in his place,' said Sir Tudor. 'He feels strongly about this matter and would have been here if he had known it was to be debated.' Butt nodded.

A doorkeeper slipped a message down the empty bench towards Butt. 'Parliament deserves to hear more than one side of an argument,' said Sir Tudor. 'And yes, this is the High Court of Parliament. It is the elected part of our law-making assembly. It is a serious place, not a parlour for games. It is not a Chamber where you should try to force law on to the statute books by twicks, holding a debate when others are many miles away, paying solemn twibute to a much-liked Speaker. I see no honour in feints and wuses. Wuse is the word. This amendment is a wuse! A dirty, disweputable wuse. The Member should be ashamed of it. I am dismayed it has reached the floor of the House.

'Now I intend to speak at some length, if the Chair permits, because there is much to discuss. As you have noted, Mr Speaker, we are not short of time. There will therefore be no need for me to curtail my speech out of wespect for the west of the day's business.'

Mears rose and Sir Tudor yielded him the floor. 'The Father of the House is right to say that we have plenty of time on our hands. But that is not to say that speeches should not be in order. I trust he will not stray outside the confines of the amendment and its proposals.'

'I hope I am never out of order, Mr Speaker,' said Sir Tudor. 'And if I look to be in danger of overstepping the margins of this scurvy amendment I am sure you will tell me.' Mears nodded with elaborate courtesy, so repeatedly that it almost acquired a menace. 'Good,' said Sir Tudor. 'I know where he stands. And he knows where I stand, which is on my two old feet on the floor of a House of Commons I have belonged to since before he and the amendment's proposer were even twinkles in their mothers' eyes.'

Butt had by now scribbled a response to the note he had been sent and returned it to the badge messenger, who hurried from the Chamber towards the clerks' office.

'Now where was I?' said Sir Tudor. 'Ah yes. Let us begin,

perhaps, with a little histowy. Are you sitting comfortably? Then I shall begin.'

HEREFORD'S choristers were building to a high note. The Fauré anthem filled the cathedral's highest glories. Sir Roger Richards had returned to his seat and was in whispered discussion with the Leader of the Commons. 'Sir Tudor is going to filibuster but he only has Butt for cover.'

'Don't we have the usual reserve?' It was usual for at least thirty Government backbenchers to remain in Westminster, in case of emergencies.

'Most are at lunch. That includes your Whips.'

'Who is on duty in the Chamber?'

'Bryce.'

'Oh.'

AS they stepped out of their kayaks, Andrew did a count. Where was Zac? The Dymock boy was missing. Another count. Five boys. Man down. 'Anyone see what happened to Zac?'

'He was at the back,' said Billy. 'He's such a loser.'

'Did no one keep tags on him?'

'It was hard to see,' said Billy.

'Jesus, Billy!'

'I presumed he was with us.'

'WHICH brings us to the twelfth centuwy,' said Sir Tudor Matthews. 'It is, I feel, important that we look in some depth at the histowy of Church land ownership in this country and the owigins of the pawish system before we leap into any ill-guided attempt to legislate on these matters . . .'

THE Prime Minister, having read the first lesson, was led back to his seat by a sidesman holding a wand. The organ struck up *Praise to the Lord, the Almighty, the King of Creation.* The Prime Minister noticed that a few people were consulting their telephones. Had something happened? Normally he would have asked his Chief of Staff but he was a few pews back.

Ross, who was sitting in the choir, was aware of Sir Roger at his side only when he felt a nudge. It was the third verse and Ross always enjoyed the line 'ponder anew what the Almighty can do' – more like a crossword clue than a line in a hymn. Sir Roger tugged Ross's arm. Ross resisted. It was not yet time for his sermon. That would not come until after the second lesson and the choir's *Te Deum*. He shook his head but the Clerk was insistent and summoned him into the side chapel.

'We have a problem.'

'Roger, I have to preach.'

'First you have to make an announcement.'

'What?'

'Mears has pulled a fast one. The Commons is debating the seizure and disposal of Church lands. It is happening now, as we worship. Can you read this screen?' He gave him his telephone.

'Just about.'

'I don't have pen and paper so I am going to write a brief announcement on this screen. I want you to explain that something urgent is happening at Westminster and that events have overtaken us.'

'It's hardly the time.'

'It is exactly the time. OK, if you don't do this, the country will not notice. If you do do this – and it will kill you with Mears but I think that's already happened – you will become a hero.'

'I've got the whole Establishment out there.'

'Exactly.'

'What are you going to write on your phone?'

'Basic instructions to MPs to hurry back to London. I am

arranging for the special train to leave early. Back we go to our seats. They're about to start the *Te Deum*.'

BACK into the kayak, back down the bay, paddling fast. 'Zac! Zac!' Damn, he should have telephoned Morwen and got her to alert the coastguard. 'Zac!' How could it be so gloomy in the middle of the day? 'Zac!'

BUTT made a point of order. 'Would it be permitted, Mr Speaker, for me to borrow the water carafe from the Table and provide the Father of the House with a drink? And would it be in order for him to continue his speech from a sedentary position?'

Sir Tudor had been talking almost an hour. His lips were dry. Butt could see that the Father of the House's leg was beginning to shake. A couple of other supporters had doughnutted round him. Word had gone out that a filibuster was under way. These two MPs not having been present at the start of the debate, they would not be allowed to speak, but they had started to make points of order and interventions to assist Sir Tudor. Every intervention used another minute or so. But the Tudorites were outnumbered still by Kendrick's crew. Butt noticed two adherents of the all-party Humanist group entering the Chamber. Kendrick gave them a knowing nod. Another arrived via the door to the left of the Speaker's Chair. Kendrick had plotted well but had he prepared for a filibuster? If only Sir Tudor were stronger.

Mears coldly said that Sir Tudor should stand. It was the custom.

SIR Roger, crouching, handed Ross his mobile as the choir changed gear for the final time in the canticle. *Vouchsafe, O Lord, to keep us this day without sin.* Ross squinted at the words Sir Roger had written on the screen. In his hand he held the paper text for his sermon. Hours of work had gone into it. Seconds had gone into the telephone message. But his Church was in pressing peril. God was not just present. God was breaking news.

Ross raised his eyes to the vaulted ceiling, the stained glass of the East end, the golden corona. The masons who had built this place would not have stood on ceremony if the great buildings of Anglicanism were about to be turned into flats.

SIR Tudor was listing. Had he been an ocean liner, the lifeboats to starboard would have been inoperable. Almost time to abandon ship. Sir Tudor churned on, rasping out sentences ever more slowly.

'By the Victowian age,' he said, each word occupying a second of its own, 'churches were going thwough a wenaissance and we see new life in the church building – its use by ladies' gwoups and empire associations, a bwoadening of function which was now enriching the idea of pawish, community, town, village, hamlet, somewhere the wich and poor, landed squire and his tenant farmer, or more particularly their wives and children and nannies and servants and other appurtenances, plus welations and welatives, fwiends who might be staying for the weekend, sisters and cousins and aunts, to quote from Gilbert and Sullivan, could assemble and pass the time of day, or night, or afternoon, or morning, in whatever week or month or season they found themselves – a place for communal kinship . . .'

'Point of Order, Mr Speaker!'

'Point of Order, Mr Kendrick.'

'Much as we admire the Father of the House, sir, and much as we can appreciate that he is following parliamentary tradition in making this filibustering speech . . .'

'Order! Filibusters are, as the Hon Gentleman knows, out of order. So far I have not heard the Father of the House stray out of order, though there may have been times when he has gone close. Sir Tudor.' During the point of order, Sir Tudor was tended to by Butt, who sponged down the old boy like a corner man repairing his prizefighter. Sir Tudor's suntanned brow was damp. Butt mopped it with his handkerchief. He offered the veteran a glass of water. Sir Tudor took it with gratitude.

'Are we expecting any more reinforcements?' he asked.

'Word has gone to Hereford, Sir Tudor,' whispered Butt.

'Sir Tudor,' said Mears. 'You have the floor. Unless you have completed your speech.'

'Completed it?' said Sir Tudor, who took a good ten seconds to rise from his bench. 'Good gracious, no. I am just concluding my intwoduction, Mr Speaker. Now where were we? Which century?'

'We are inhabiting the twenty-first century, though you wouldn't think it,' shouted Kendrick.

ROSS bowed to the sidesman and mounted the pulpit steps. The last echo of the choir faded. Heads were raised towards the priest. In the front row Ross could see the Prime Minister and the Aldred family. 'In the name of the Father, Son and Holy Ghost.'

'Amen,' murmured several hundred voices.

'Ladies and gentlemen, this is a solemn occasion, a family event but also a political event. I hope you will forgive me making a parliamentary announcement.' Ross could see Sir Roger standing in an aisle, flicking his tails. 'We have many MPs here. They have made the journey to honour our departed Speaker. I am sorry to have to tell them that their absence has been abused by elements in Westminster.' Ross squinted at Sir Roger's telephone and read: 'While we have been worshipping here, an attempt has begun in the Commons to appropriate a Bill which had been agreed by the main parties. The proposal being discussed – at this very moment – could do the Church of England grave damage, resulting in the seizure of Church lands by local authorities.' He scrolled down the screen. 'Urgent action is needed. Members of the Commons are advised that a train to London leaves Hereford railway station in fifteen minutes. It will travel directly and get there, we hope, in time for a vote on this unexpected measure. Will all MPs who wish to vote please leave this service now. I repeat: will all MPs please make for the railway station immediately? The rest of us will wait while our legislators leave the cathedral.' Already, MPs were making for the door amid confused chatter. Sir Roger was directing them. The hubbub in the cathedral was that of a market place – a public gathering place, a parliament of souls.

Sir Roger grabbed the Second Church Estates Commissioner and held on to him for half a minute. When he saw the Prime Minister and his entourage making for the exit, Sir Roger interceded. 'Prime Minister, I need to brief you.'

'Roger, what in God's name is going on?'

'I am afraid the new Speaker has gone mad. Sir Tudor Matthews is holding the fort with a filibuster but he may not be able to keep going much longer.'

'Is there anyone else?'

'Butt and a couple of also-rans. Do you have room in your helicopter for the Second Church Estates Commissioner? You will be in London before the rest of them.'

'We were meant to be flying to Battersea.'

'This is an emergency, Prime Minister. Land in Parliament Square. Take the Second Church Estates Commissioner with you. He will assist Sir Tudor.'

ZAC was drifting in the wrong direction when Andrew found him. 'You're heading out to sea!' he shouted at the boy. 'Go back! That way!' At first he presumed that Zac could not hear him, so fierce was the squall. Yet even when he was up close, the boy did not respond. The current was strengthening.

Andrew saw he was too tired to paddle. He could barely move his upper body in that big lifejacket. Andrew took a gamble on the depth of the estuary. If he could stand in the water, he could push the boy towards land. Without rope there was no other way to grapple the kayak. If he could not stand, he would have to try to push it with his swimming strokes. He manoeuvred himself out of his own kayak and found – damn – that the water was too deep for him to stand. It could not be much further than a hundred yards and he was a strong swimmer. He just had to hold on to the side of this slippery kayak. There must be a current somewhere that would sweep them back to the shore. The right choice would lead to safety.

Zac sat motionless, paralysed by – what? Fear? Cold? His eyes were open. Andrew shouted encouraging words at him but the boy did not respond.

He was in much the same state when the other children found him at the shore half an hour later. By then he was alone.

FINALLY Sir Tudor ran dry. He sagged to his bench saying that he could speak no more. Butt leapt to his own feet and began speaking. Kendrick tried to move proceedings to a vote but Mears was too slow on the uptake and Butt was launched, after a fashion. In his devotion to Sir Tudor, Butt could not be faulted. In oratory and parliamentary protocol he was less proficient. He spoke for a few minutes about the churches in his constituency and their value to the community. He delivered a pretty if short detour on the pride the Islamic community in his area took in their town's historic churches. He recalled his childhood in Pakistan, his belief in assimilation, his sorrow over immigrants who attacked the culture and practices of their new country. Mears ruled him out of order.

'I say to the Hon Gentleman, who is less experienced than his Rt Hon Friend, that he must stick to the amendment. Otherwise we will move to a vote.'

'But Mr Speaker . . .'

'No buts, Mr Butt.'

'If the Hon Gentleman will permit,' croaked Sir Tudor.

'I think we have heard quite enough from the Father of the House,' said Mears.

'It is up to the Hon Gentleman whether or not he takes an intervention,' said Sir Tudor from his seat.

'I do not need to be schooled in the procedures of the House,' said Mears.

'I happily give way to my Rt Hon Friend,' said Butt.

'Mr Butt, I rule you out of order. I rule your speech out of order. I rule that you do now resume your seat. Your speech has ended.'

'And another will begin!' cried a voice from the far end of the Chamber. And through the double doors there came striding – running – the Second Church Estates Commissioner, Leakey. No sooner was he beyond the bar of the House, he started making a speech, even while still walking to his place.

'Order!' shouted Mears. 'Only Members who have been present since the start of the debate may speak.'

'Point of Order!' shouted the Prime Minister, who had entered the Chamber a pace or two behind the Second Church Estates Commissioner. 'Point! Of! Order!'

'Prime Minister,' said Mears. 'What are you doing here?'

'The point of order, Mr Speaker, is this: since when did it become acceptable for a Speaker and his co-conspirators – a Speaker with co-conspirators! – to conspire to slip through legislation on the sly?'

'That,' said Mears, 'is not a point of order, and the Prime Minister knows it.'

'I know exactly what it was,' said the Prime Minister. 'And I know exactly what has been going on. I suggest an immediate suspension of this House until some two hundred parliamentarians travelling from Hereford have reached this place and can vote on what has been going on here, as is their democratic right, without let or hindrance – or any seedy sedition.'

A MAN'S body was washed up near Borth later that day. It bore no marks. But for the pallor, he could have been asleep. A windowless ambulance was summoned and a windbreaker erected on the beach while police officers attended. They had little difficulty concluding he had drowned. The currents could conquer the strongest swimmer and he had worn no lifejacket. At Aberystwyth hospital they did not immediately tell Zac, waiting for his father to arrive from London by private aeroplane. Only on landing had he been told Zac was definitely safe.

Had Dymock prayed on the journey? Prayer is a private matter, but when he reached the hospital and saw his son he buried his face in the boy's hair and sobbed: 'Thank God.'

WE will not intrude long on the scene that evening in the Ross household following Morwen's telephone call. Theresa's eyes were red-rimmed. Ross himself had not yet found tears. He felt too much anger – at himself for not having made his peace with Andrew; at Dymock, for spawning the child who had caused the crisis; at God, wherever God was.

Theresa extracted one of Andrew's old jumpers from his bedroom – a present from her one Christmas long ago – and clutched it. She could smell her boy in the wool. She feared that each time she sniffed it, the smell would diminish.

Barney yapped. 'It's all right,' said Theresa, 'good boy.' But Barney yapped again and rose in his basket. 'There must be someone there, Tom. I'll go and look.'

Ross felt unable to move from his seat by the Rayburn. A mug of tea had gone cold at his side. The kitchen clutter of family photographs taunted him. Would any of them ever learn to smile again? In the hallway, Barney yapped some more and Ross heard the door open and a man talk to Theresa, and now another woman. Barney was making friends with the visitors. Ross could hear the Sealyham squeak with excitement. The woman's voice said 'Aren't you a lovely boy, then?'

'Tom,' said Theresa. 'Look who's come all the way from London.' Ross slowly rose.

'May God in Heaven have mercy on his soul, Tom. And may He have mercy on us all.' Petroc stepped across the kitchen and gave his friend an engulfing hug. Nettle was behind him. Petroc's grip on Ross was almost violent. He put his mouth close to Ross's ear and, so defiant it was practically a growl, he said: 'May His light reach us wherever we are. May your pain be mine. In your suffering we will march with you every step. We are Church. We are one. We are God's.'

Ross's shoulders started to shake. Soon his whole upper body heaved with dry chokes. His mouth fell agape and the tears finally flowed. All this while Petroc held him, squeezing him, almost lifting the breath from him with his brotherly embrace.

24

They Shall Know

PETROC offered to go but Ross would not hear of it. The trip to the hospital in London would do him good.

'Hello, Jean.' She was hooked to a drip and wearing a mask, yet she opened her eyes. 'Don't stir yourself,' said Ross. 'I came to tell you off and it's easier to do that if you don't reply.' She gave a tiny cough of amusement. 'God doesn't like people trying to queue-barge, Jean. It's against the rules.' The monitor blipped a regular beat and nurses bustled past the door of this side room. Self-harmers were kept out of the wards. They were bad for morale.

Her arms could move little but she gestured that she wanted to speak. Ross removed her oxygen mask.

'In my handbag,' she said. He found what she was referring to and replaced the bag just as a nurse entered.

'Hello,' she said. 'Jean was hoping you would turn up. She's doing well, aren't you, dear? Soon have her right as rain.' The nurse made a couple of checks, straightened the sheet and had barely left the room when two other figures entered, one taller than the other, talking loudly and dressed in bullet-proof tartan.

'I expect she is in here – ah, yes, there you are, Jean. Oh, you've got company.'

'It's all right,' said Ross. 'I'm just leaving.'

'We mustn't force you out.'

'It's fine.' Ross politely made his excuses. 'Goodbye, Jean. See you soon.'

As he wandered down the hospital corridor he heard church-warden Georgina Brack administer Christian outreach as only she could. 'Right, dear, look what we've brought: a fruit cake from Fortnum's. How about that? We've got all the time in the world and we want your advice about the Christmas Week services. Because, Jean dear, you are needed. And loved. So there. No getting out of it. Right, Antonia. Plates, napkins, and where are those glasses? We've brought a half-bottle of Moet to toast your close-shave. But we must not have a repetition of this foolishness. You'll have us all doing it otherwise. Now, let's have some fizz.' As Beetle struggled to open the champagne, the Widow Brack told her to blazing well get a move on because she was as dry as an Egyptian.

MR Speaker Mears's conduct on the day of the Hereford service was a source of intense controversy for a few days. After that, other events took precedence in the bulletins. The Thought Foundation propped up the Speaker, calling a press conference to assert he had done his constitutional duty in allowing the Commons to hold a 'long overdue debate' on the Established Church. Aldred's widow declined to exacerbate the matter. The Prime Minister understood that the more he agitated for Mears to go, the more likely Mears would survive. He knew that Mears was wounded and that was good enough. Besides, Olga had been such a media sensation. There was talk of her being asked to appear on a reality-television show. Amid such excitements, the police quietly announced that no charges would be pursued in the death of the protestor outside Petroc's church. Bacton's film crew had handed over their footage to the police and some of the un-broadcast material clearly showed the dead man holding the knife in his own hand, advancing on Petroc. Before he could do any mischief, he was pushed over by unintentional pressure from the crowd. The knifeman fell awkwardly – on to his own blade. As for the case of young Matt, Westminster magistrates found that it would be adequate for him to pay a small fine and be relieved of his driving licence for a year. The airline whose office he had attacked had decided not to pursue the matter further and offered Matt and his fiancée, the blushing Bashirah, hearty congratulations. Perhaps Bacton had advised his contacts in Islamabad that it was time to repair the airline's corporate reputation.

Three days later, half an hour before the daily procession, Mears was finishing his lunch in the empty State Room at Speaker's House when the door opened.

'Ross? I thought I explained we no longer need you.' Mears had a small plastic tray on his lap. It bore the final portions of a cold sardine sandwich and a cup of tea. A silvery fleck of sardine skin was lodged in his moustache.

'This is my colleague Petroc Stone.'

'Was I expecting you?'

'We had no appointment.'

'In that case . . .'

'It need not take long,' said Ross.

'What is your business?' asked Mears.

Petroc was about to let rip but Ross silenced him. 'Our business is private but it will not remain so unless you do your duty, Mr Speaker. We know about you and Greenhill. We know about a visit you made to the Greenhills' house before your election and we have two witnesses.'

'What's wrong with visiting a businessman?'

'You accepted large sums from Greenhill,' continued Ross.

'Cash,' said Petroc.

'Cash that has not been declared in the register of interests,' said Ross.

'Cash that will need to be declared to the Revenue,' said Petroc.

'The deadline for returns has not yet passed,' said Mears with an almost demure innocence.

'There is another thing,' said Ross. He reached into his pocket and withdrew, first, his hip flask. 'It's in here somewhere,' he said.

'Is this some joke?' said Mears. 'Olga? Are you there?' A Russian voice sounded from the adjacent room. 'Can you call some help? I need these two men thrown out and taken to the ...'

'Here we are,' said Ross, just as Olga was entering the room. 'These are photocopies. The originals are a little crumpled but safe.' He handed two photocopies to Mears.

'What are they?' asked Olga. She tried to take them but Mears snatched them, looked at them, uttered an unreportable oath and tore them into pieces that fell to the floor.

'Well?' said Ross. 'Do you want to make a confession?'

'Confession?' said Olga.

'Not in front of you, though,' said Ross. 'The Speaker of the Commons wishes to be alone with his chaplain. His new chaplain.'

He escorted Olga from the room, leaving Petroc and Mears to come to an arrangement, while the torn photograph of Mears and Jean all those years ago at Gretna Green, along with the copy of their wedding certificate, remained on the thick carpet.

LIFE is a brief insurgency. We have our flesh on hire. When Theresa Ross sat alone long in the little country church, she understood this. Tranquillity would return, as grass covers soil on a grave. Lifelessness returns.

Mud sits heavy on a gravedigger's spade. He hurls it over his shoulder and it lands in a puddle; there dissolves. There is soon little to show that it existed, let alone that it nurtured worms. Theresa occupied the pew where once she had sat with Andrew. Unlike some boys he had never scratched his name on the wood. Yet he had carved himself in her heart.

A lake diver plunges into tendrilled depths. It is the same at birth. All is disturbed and bubbled as our limbs writhe. Slowly the water settles. The diver, if quiet, can float at the surface and imagine a world without end. When a door opens in a country church, dust dances at a newcomer's advance. After time the disturbance abates.

As daylight faded, the single votive candle acquired greater focus. The day thou gavest, Lord, was ending. Tom's pulpit stood just out of sight and beyond the flickering flame she caught a gleam from the golden cross. All else was gloaming. All else was black.

Small, breakable man, bagger of baubles, rots, erodes, is borne away. Then what?

THE funeral of Andrew Thomas Hugh Ross was held on a fine afternoon before Christmas. Holly danced under the yew as his coffin was lifted from the hearse. A single, tolling bell had been muffled. High in its yew an owl watched.

The coffin was met at the lych-gate by Petroc in his robes. He bowed. As he bared the nape of his neck to God he prayed for strength or to be severed headless. The words would be familiar to many yet to him they were intoxicatingly, dauntingly new. *I am the resurrection and the life, saith the Lord.* The Sentences – the sealing, triumphant peak of Cranmer's creation – were written to be shouted. They acquire a declamatory impetus, defiance in grief. The pallbearers started the long climb up the churchyard.

He that believeth in me, though he were dead, yet shall he live. Let the people hear the words. Let English Protestants strive for their own settlement with God. Gravel crunched underfoot. A sprig of flowers on the coffin swayed. *And whosoever liveth and believeth in me shall never die.*

Ross was inside the church beside Theresa. As the coffin drew near they could hear the first catches of Petroc's voice. Theresa gripped Ross's hand. *And though after my skin worms destroy this body, yet in my flesh shall I see God*. Ross barely felt her grasp. His eye was fixed on one of the altar candles. If he could concentrate enough on its heat – on the centre of the flame, its hottest point, where martyrs plunged their wrists – he might briefly forget the iciness of his son's brow.

The pallbearers paused at the grave of the airman. In Petroc's hands was the prayer book he had been given by Ross. Wind rippled the pages. Petroc had tried to memorise the service for the Burial of the Dead and had noticed how worn were its pages. Generations had gone. Generations would follow. At a drop of the senior undertaker's ebony stave, the convoy continued. *We brought nothing into this world and it is certain that we carry nothing out. The Lord gave and the Lord hath taken away*. Another pause at the west door of the church allowed the junior undertaker to rearrange the flowers. The pallbearers sweated. The bell ceased. Barney sat below them in the outer porch, his eyebrows creased.

As the organ signalled *The Lord's My Shepherd*, the congregation began to sing. Barney followed as Andrew's coffin was taken towards the altar. As the doors closed, the Sealyham hopped upstairs and watched from the old gallery.

What Barney saw was a church packed to the limit. Theresa could hear the singing behind her. The Clerk of the Commons was the most important guest, if funerals have guests. Barney heard, and surely felt, the phrases as polished as Tudor flagstones. The little dog's eyes glinted. Petroc intoned *De Profundis*. Order and rhythm were asserting command. All would end but it should end well. Sir Roger Richards stepped to the lectern and spoke from Revelation about the multitude that no man could number, standing before the throne. He spoke firmly. Doubt's devilry was not offered an opening.

Psalm 103 fell to Ross. *Like as a father pitieth his own children: even so is the Lord merciful to them that fear him*. Returning towards his pew he stopped at the coffin. He squeezed his eyes to form a dam.

When he reopened them he saw, in a pew at the back, two figures, one with a head of utterly white hair.

Ross made a hand gesture that said, 'Come to me'. He repeated it. Augustus Dymock gave Zac a small nudge. The boy was dressed in a black suit too long for him in arm and leg. Zac walked up the nave and placed a flower on the coffin. Ross saw that the youngster had a shoelace undone. His hair was awkwardly parted. His eyes were blotched and his chin was covered with down. The boy was weeping. Ross embraced him and kissed his head.

Nettle sheltered under the brim of a chic, black hat. At the back of the church, Mates stood to attention, Nurse Harris slipping a hand through his arm. At the front, in the place of privilege accorded to widows, sat Morwen, almost motionless. Theresa looked at her daughter-in-law and extended a hand to the small bump under her dress. Morwen had told her that morning. Andrew had gone but his line would live – Abraham and his seed forever.

DEAD from most ancient of days, we breathe, we breed, will weep, must die, recruits to the dread battalion. Rust-inked ledgers list losses from earliest times. Nothing is new. Bookish Bede salted his broth with tears. Boudicca battled and flinched and fell. Doom tames us, claims us, the bony beckoning, Harold at Hastings hooked, Henry Tudor swift unzipped. Our scene is brief and Heaven with her clipboard shrugs. We shrink, postpone, delay, defer, yet death can never be dodged. In sweeps each surf of men, so swank, so sure. So what?

We stand as a harvest. Soon we will join their swaying ranks, fall in step with skulls and bones, the fleshless throng, the gaping platoon. Five rows to the fore: the child who died young. Near them, lost siblings raise a fist of acclaim. Here comes the stir of a parent much loved. They stretch ahead, skinless feet swirling dust of the dead. Staves strike a rhythm and we march to the bark of familiar command, comrades all, quick and the dead.

They shall know how we did. They shall know how we do. They shall know and shall judge, they can guide and inspire. Their memory should haunt us. Let them shame us to good. Let us serve, let us shine.

The service reached its final hymn, *Jesus, Lover of My Soul*. The tune was Parry – *Aberystwyth*, chosen for the place Andrew died. *While the nearer waters roll, while the tempest still is high.* Mark, on the organ, took it slowly enough for the pallbearers to step in time. The door of the little church was opened wide for the coffin's removal. The western sky stretched golden yet cold. High up, a skein of geese went flapping, their honks receding. Snow was coming and the pallbearers' breath formed little clouds in the air.

Ross felt old as the oaks. On his hands he saw veins on autumn leaves. Our humdrum country priest was shrivelled, his tread heavy. Soon he would taste the clay at his throat, yet God was not quite finished with him. There was earth to sprinkle at the grinning grave. There was grief to be gnawed. Ross gripped Zac's shoulders and turned the guilt-stricken boy so that he faced the winter's sunlight. 'Come, son, the world is watching.' He took his hand. 'Let a coffin lead the way. There's life to be lived.'

Acknowledgements

I am grateful to the following for their advice, inspiration and the occasional kick up the rump: my wife Lois, my brilliant mother, my late Father whose voice I still hear when I read the Prayer Book; the Rev Paul Barlow, the Rev George Bush, Andreas Campomar, Father Gillean Craig, the late and Rt Rev Thomas Cranmer, Father Peter Mullen, Maggie Pearlstine, Tunku Varadarajan.